THE WEIGHT OF LOSS

ALSO BY CHARLES VAN EMAN

On The Way To Pomona

The Weight of Loss

To Mary,
much love and best wishes !
Peace,
Charles Van Eman

CHARLES VAN EMAN

MUD PUDDLE DANCE

Book design by 52 Novels

Cover design and illustration by Sandy Farrier

ISBN 978-0-9856458-4-7
ISBN (kindle) 978-0-9856458-6-1
ISBN (ePub) 978-0-9856458-5-4

mudpuddledance@gmail.com

For my sisters, Debi and Tracey
and my mother, Patricia Van Eman

Outside among your fellows, among strangers, you must preserve appearances, a hundred things you cannot do, but inside, the terrible freedom!

Ralph Waldo Emerson

1

From water in darkness to jewels in the light then back to watery shadows, the raindrops passed through the headlight's beam looking to Gil Linnetti like a shower of incandescent opals. Why, he wondered watching the torrent of gems cascade in front of the Oldsmobile, had he never noticed the phenomenon before.

The Oldsmobile's horn honked twice. The passenger side window went down. A woman quickly waved then pulled her arm back inside. The window closed, and with tires hissing, the car accelerated up Hargrove Avenue. Gil solemnly watched the red halo of tail-lights fade into the rainy darkness. Fewer people were coming by now that the television crews had finally given up on his story.

Thunder boomed. Drumming rain on the patio umbrella over his head grew louder. Shifting in the beach chair to keep his legs dry, Gil pulled a white garbage bag of dirty clothes onto his lap and moved a Tupperware container of Cheerios to higher ground.

Across the street, the lofty silhouette of an oak tree was barely visible through the downpour. Gil focused on where the upper-most branches reached for the sky. His gaze softened. Rain droned on the umbrella. Thunder rumbled in the distance. Gil's eyes remained on the tree.

• • • • •

Madison was running. Breath escaped and returned in a rhythm elevated along the steady baseline of her heartbeat. Shoes pounded the dirt path taking the up-tempo lead as she accelerated over a rise and down to the creek. Cool air filled her lungs. A chorus of birdcalls rang out. The creek's rushing water added urgency to the orchestration of sound. She breathed deeply taking in the rich loamy smell of damp earth. Above her, through the canopy of green, the sun splintered through an overcast morning sky. When she glanced back to the trail, he was there.

Running in front of her, golden hair flowing back over tanned shoulders, his feet seemed barely to touch the ground; calf muscles, hamstrings, and gluts powerfully flexing and releasing, gracefully propelling him forward. Certain things in the world are meant to be, she thought. His body in the act of running is one of those things. Madison pushed herself to go faster. Her arms pumped, her legs rushed her down the wooded trail. She knew it was impossible to catch him, but she always tried.

As they emerged from the woods into a sun-streaked meadow, a red-tailed hawk suddenly took flight. She felt the impulse to call to him, to point to the hawk rising majestically up and over the pine trees, but she knew he couldn't hear her. She reminded herself, once again, that it was enough just to be running with him.

As Madison began her descent down the hill, through the trees she could see the plank rectangle of the community center. Built twelve years earlier, it was the first construction work she had ever done. That summer, her skill with a hammer and her willingness to climb high into the apex of the roof had earned her the respect of most of the men at Fair Haven. Despite what some of the women thought, she hadn't done it to impress anyone. The weight of the hammer, the quick motion of swinging it, and the violent collision with the nail, had exhilarated her. She'd discovered that she not only enjoyed doing it, she absolutely needed to do it. During those hot, exhausting construction days in July and August, no one at Fair Haven realized that she was doing more than pounding nails. She was bashing a face. The face of someone she was working hard to forget.

Back on her heels, calves and quads burning, she slowed her descent down the steep, rutted trail. In front of her, he was running with his hands chest high, palms forward. Madison smiled then checked her watch. Forty-five minutes. There would barely be enough time for a quick shower and an apple for breakfast. She didn't want to be late. The kids would be raring to go for the last day of school. She leaned forward onto the balls of her feet and let out her stride. He did too. They hit the bottom of the hill running hard.

At the vegetable garden the trail curved right. A rabbit bolted across the path. Madison watched it disappear into a rhododendron thicket then picked up her pace for the final stretch to the house sheltered in a grove of fir trees sixty yards ahead. She had inherited the cozy A-frame five years earlier after its builder and only other occupant, Sky, died of a massive heart attack while hiking in the hills above Fair Haven. One of its original founders, Sky came to Oregon in 1967 full of poetry, peace and anti-war sentiment. With a group of like-minded individuals he helped purchase the land and establish the Fair Haven commune. Originally inspired by B.F. Skinner's novel, *Walden Two*, Fair Haven had evolved over the years into an eco-community promoting a lifestyle of nonviolence, appropriate land use, and energy conservation. Shakti, also one of the founders, was the last person to see Sky on the morning of his death. When she asked him where he was going, he'd lifted his warm brown eyes up to the forested hills and said, "I don't know. Somewhere I've never been before." In the far northwest corner of the 1200 acres that make up Fair Haven, Sky's Grateful Dead loving heart had quit the band. It took three days for rescue dogs to find him in the cave he was exploring, and another day to get his hefty bulk out of the bat-infested darkness.

In front of the house, Madison eased her pace and began walking. As her breathing gradually slowed, she reached back and lifted her hair off the back of her neck. The air felt cool against her damp skin. This is always the hard part, she thought. Running four miles is not difficult. Seeing him leave is another story. How many years had she been doing this? Too many, she heard from somewhere deep in her rational mind.

Putting her hands on her hips, she watched her running companion move toward the trees. God, he is beautiful, she thought. *Still* beautiful, was the internal response. At the corner of the field he slowed down. His head turned and — he was looking at her. A shiver tingled up from her belly. She stared into his suntanned face. His eyes — clear, certain, and with the hint of a smile, gazed back at her. Helpless to stop the giddy grin spreading across her face, she marveled that after all these years he was still able to make her feel so much, so intensely. He nodded to her then was gone — his lean sixteen-year-old body fading into the stand of fir trees, and back into her memory.

• • • • •

Through the kitchen window Marjorie Davenport could see that something was wrong. She dropped the red oven mitt on the counter and walked to the open French doors.

"Dominic," she called across the flagstone patio.

She stepped outside. A morning breeze blowing south all the way from Lake Erie lifted the hem of her skirt. She didn't push it down. Proud of the physique she'd diligently worked to maintain since her competitive swimming days at Duke University, Marjorie Davenport was well aware that she had good legs.

"Dominic!" She called again, her voice straining against her emotions. She hurried to the flagstone steps leading down to the lawn. Her eyes swept the immaculately manicured back yard. For a moment it appeared empty, then movement behind the forsythia caught her eye.

"Dominic!" she shouted, her anger now in full bloom.

A head of wispy, white hair poked out from behind the bush. Deeply lined and with eyebrows like rows of cotton, Dominic Angelo had a face that had seen many a midday sun. He stepped out from behind the forsythia and with a crisp snap of his elbow raised his pruning shears and saluted Mrs. Davenport.

"Yes, Madam."

Marjorie's fingernails dug into her palms. Not only was he absent-minded, now she had to put up with this ridiculous saluting. She almost fired him three years ago, but he was absolutely, hands down, the best gardener in Pittsburgh. If he wanted to, he could make roses bloom in the middle of the Allegheny River.

"Dominic," she said, trying to control the tone of her voice. "I asked you to put the impatiens on the left side of the bird bath and the marigolds on the right."

"Yes, madam," he said, and again saluted.

This time she didn't watch her tone. "Please switch them before you finish today," she snapped. "And I told you, I want that forsythia taken out. It's grown too," she paused, her eyes shifting from Dominic to the snarled branches of the bush, "wild."

"Yes, Madam," he said, this time without the salute.

Twenty years of dealing with that man, she thought, turning back to the house. Green thumb or not, he'd become the most impudent person she'd ever met.

Inside the house she breezed from room to room checking the flower arrangements: white tulips in the dining room, irises in the front hallway, and calla lilies in the den. She always tried to have them in the house when Steven returned from business trips. It was her welcome home present to him. She went to the CD player. *The Marriage of Figaro* was already in the carousal. She checked her watch. Five minutes before eleven. He would be home any minute. She pressed the play button. Thirty-one years and he still appreciated her loving touches.

She went to the powder room and turned on the light. The brightly painted mirror frame above the sink had been a source of irritation since the day, three years earlier, when Steven brought it home from a business trip to Asia. When she explained to him that it didn't fit the contemporary style of the house, he'd said, "Come on, art is art. It'll be a conversation piece." When she refused to put it up, Steven did what he had been doing since she'd been his statistics tutor at Duke. He seduced her. His slow, steady touch had brought her around to his way of thinking. The next day she tried to plead temporary insanity, but he wouldn't listen. In the end, it hung there, a mirror frame that looked like it had been finger-painted by a child.

Marjorie checked her makeup and hair in the mirror. Lipstick was fine. Eyes were bright. The skin at her throat had, in the last few years, noticeably begun to yield to the laws of gravity. Nothing you can do about that darling, she told herself, except go under the knife, and you certainly aren't ready for that. She fluffed her shoulder-length hair then paused, staring into the mirror. She reached up and with an irritated grimace plucked a gray hair from the top of her head. For a moment she stood there, the hair pinched in her fingers. Not in the wastebasket, she reminded herself. Steven might see it. She lifted the lid of the toilet, dropped it in, and flushed. Turning back to the mirror she once again scrutinized herself. She shrugged her shoulders and tugged down her blouse, revealing more cleavage. Marjorie fluffed her hair one more time then headed for the kitchen, reminding herself to speak with Klaus about the new girl who had done her color the week before.

In the kitchen she pulled a metal baking pan of cinnamon rolls out of the oven and put it on the stove to cool. The sugary smell filling the kitchen made it tempting, but Marjorie willed herself not to indulge. Watch the carbs, watch carbs, she repeated to herself as she searched through the cupboard next to the stove. She found the last of her large rectangle Tupperware containers and put it on the counter. I must remind Steven to collect the others that he'd left at the campsite on Hargrove Avenue, she thought. That poor man, Mr. Linnetti, would be finished with them by now. Well, maybe not the Cheerios.

2

Autumn held up a picture cut from a magazine. It was a black and white photograph of a seventy-eight year old women in Atlanta, Georgia.

"Mrs. Fleming doesn't care whether they have good grades," Autumn said, "She gives the prize to the student in the graduating class who does the most for the community."

Madison watched her class of fifteen students react. Even though most of them had been given this assignment before, they still responded in unpredictable and touching ways to the uplifting news items. From ages six to sixteen, they were a rag-tag group of tie-dyed, dread-locked, fun-loving kids. They were bright and intuitive, and to Madison, who had known many of them all of their lives, they had become almost like her own.

"That's pretty cool that she doesn't care about grades," said Trinity, a sixteen year-old lanky blond and the best math student Madison had ever taught. "That means that if Dylan actually did anything around here he would have a chance at winning."

The rest of the class laughed, some of them turning to look at shaggy-haired Dylan. Not Madison's most ambitious student, or the most productive member of Fair Haven, Dylan lifted his head off the desk and rolled his eyes at Trinity. She gave him her best big-sister-know-it-all grin. The class, sensing a fight, immediately began rooting on the combative siblings.

Madison sighed. It was true that they were a great bunch of kids, but on last day before summer they were also easily distracted.

"Autumn," she said, over the din of hecklers. "Tell us more about Mrs. Fleming."

Autumn tucked an errant strand of dark hair behind her ear and looked down at the magazine article in her hand. As she absent-mindedly played with one of her twelve earrings, the class grew quiet again.

"She's been giving the prize for thirty years," Autumn said. "One student a year, every year."

"That's thirty thousand dollars," Hawk blurted out.

"And she washes people's clothes." Autumn said. "That's how she makes a living."

Sage, Fair Haven's highly skilled bee keeper, scratched her blond crew-cut and said, "She's a maid? My aunt does housework and she doesn't make enough to give anybody anything."

Autumn held up the picture of Mrs. Fleming. "She says here that saving money is easy if you're doing it for the right reasons." Autumn grinned. "Cool lady, huh?"

The class gave a spontaneous round of applause.

"Good, Autumn," Madison said, looking around the circle. "Who's next?"

Lumina reluctantly stood up. "I'll go."

The only daughter of Madison's close friend Hannah, Lumina was pencil-thin with big blue eyes and thick dark eyebrows like her father. Madison watched her pull a copy of a newspaper clipping out of a blue, three-ring binder. Thirteen years ago, on the night Lumina was born, a storm knocked an elm tree through the wall of the old meeting house. Thirteen years, Madison thought, how is it possible?

"Okay," Lumina said forcefully. "When Madison told us that we had to bring in a happy-news story, I remembered a thing my Dad told me a few months ago." She held up the newspaper clipping. "I went to the library in Eugene and I found it. Yay, extra- effort points for me."

The class gave her a good-natured booing.

Lumina blushed and hung her head. Always desperately shy, she had just begun to emerge out of her cocoon of self-consciousness. Helping students like Lumina was one of the reasons why Madison had taken over the teaching duties at Fair Haven. World history had its place — grammar, math, science, and creative writing also contributed in developing the mind of a child — but it was self-esteem and self-confidence which Madison believed formed the foundation of having a spontaneous, productive life. She knew from her own arduous psychological journey what it felt like not to be in touch with a positive self image. Consequently, she was vigilant in her role as a teacher in providing opportunities for her students to bolster and hone these essential attributes. Even if they weren't brilliant math students or writers, she wanted them to be able to walk with their heads up and their hearts open.

In front of the class Lumina still struggled to get comfortable. You're beautiful and brilliant, Madison thought, sending support out to Lumina. You can do this and so many more great things in your life. Trust yourself. You're worthy of being seen.

Lumina peeked up at Madison, her eyes seeking encouragement. Madison smiled and winked. A shy grin flicked across Lumina's face. She took a breath and shifted her gaze to the rest of the class.

"It's a story about a mentally handicapped man who does flowers for people. This man," Lumina said, her voice growing stronger, "Gary Thurlow, plants flowers all over the town where he lives." She glanced at the article. "Chester, Delaware — that's where it is – and he does it for free." She gave a quick shrug of her shoulders and started to sit down.

"Why do you think he does it?" Madison asked, purposely giving her more time in front of the class.

Lumina tensed, unsure of how to respond.

Come on, hang in there kiddo, Madison thought, watching Lumina struggle not to lower her head and hide. Lumina's eyes darted around the room then settled on her best friend Kiki.

"He likes flowers," Lumina said. Kiki flashed a grin. Lumina straightened her shoulders, shifted her eyes off Kiki, and boldly took in the rest of her classmates. "He likes flowers," she repeated more confidently, "and he wants other people to enjoy them too."

"That's great," Madison said proud of Lumina's little victory. "He sounds like a nice guy, doesn't he?"

Lumina nodded and sat down, pleased with her accomplishment and relieved to no longer be the sole focus of the class.

"Okay, now one of the boys," Madison said. "Who wants to go?"

The newest addition to the commune school, fourteen year-old Cassidy, opened his laptop computer. "I got something," he said.

Three months at the commune from the hustle-bustle of New York City, Cassidy was proud that he had one of the few laptops at Fair Haven.

He began pointing his cursor and clicking as the other students crowded around him.

"It's from a few months ago," he said, "but it's, I don't know, cool and sad and stuff." He leaned back. "Check it out."

A television news broadcast began to play on the computer screen. A woman reporter was standing next to a tree.

"Four months ago," the reporter said solemnly, "there was an accident here." She turned and looked to her left. The camera followed her gaze to an intersection. Across the street a wooded area was visible.

"On December eighth two vehicles met at this intersection."

The camera panned across the street to where the other road ended at a stop sign.

"The violent collision not only shattered a family, it resulted in the birth of a mystery, in fact, several mysteries."

The camera panned across the street toward the trees. As it moved to the right, a faded blue patio umbrella could be seen poking above the goldenrod.

"The police investigation into this accident discovered that it started with a car-jacking and ended in the tragic death of a woman and her two children."

The camera zoomed closer. A gray sweatshirt and a pair of blue jeans hung from a line strung between two maple trees. A brown two-man tent was staked out next to several opaque plastic storage boxes and a red ice chest.

"On March 24th, the husband and father of those killed came back to the scene of the accident."

Sitting on a beach chair, his beard scruffy and his hair unkempt, the camera revealed Gil Linnetti.

"For nearly three months he has been here," the voice of the reporter went on. "Supported by food, clothing and camping gear donated by friends and neighbors, 34 year-old, Gil Linnetti stands vigil over the site where he lost his wife Bonnie, his seven-year old son Drake, and his four year-old daughter Lindsey."

Cutting back to the reporter, the camera moved with her as she stepped into the road. Brushing a strand of hair-sprayed blond out of her face, she continued her report.

"Why is he here? How long does he plan to stay? What is he hoping to accomplish? These are questions for which we have no answers. Who was the driver of the stolen SUV? We don't know that either. What we do know is that three people are dead."

A tight close-up of the man in the beach chair suddenly filled the screen. His intensely weary blue eyes stare back at the camera.

"Help Gil Linnetti find out who was responsible for destroying his family. If anyone has any information about the car-jacking and the subsequent hit and run accident, please contact the Pittsburgh Police. For Channel 2 News, this is Celia Davis reporting."

The video clip ended. For a moment no one in the classroom said anything. Finally Trinity broke the silence.

"Jeez, that's not happy news."

Cassidy opened his hands palms upward. "Whadaya mean? That Gil guy is there, man. He let it all go, his life, his job, everything, to be at the place where they got killed. That's a cool thing to do. It's a celebration, man."

"He's showing his commitment to them," Kiki said excitedly. "He's letting them know that he still loves them."

Franny snorted and shook her long red braids. "Nah uh. It's a protest, you dummies. A Gandhi thing. Civil disobedience. He's doing it to remind the cops that they haven't solved the crime yet."

Lumina spoke up. "I think he's hoping that someone will see him and come forward to tell what happened."

Several students nodded in agreement.

"What do you think, Madison," Lumina asked. "Why do you think he's doing it?"

The class turned to their teacher. Immediately they fell silent.

Madison was staring at the computer screen, her eyes filled with tears. She didn't look at the class or blink or say a word. She was focused on where the image of Gil Linnetti had once been.

After a moment or two Madison was able to pull herself together. She explained to the class that the man's tragedy had overwhelmed her. She couldn't imagine how devastating it would be to lose a single child, let alone your entire family. When she dismissed the class, Trinity, Lumina and several of the older girls insisted on walking her home. Forced to talk with them about their summer projects, the boys they had crushes on, and their vacation plans with their families, it was all Madison could do to keep from screaming.

At the house, the cushions of her sofa felt like heaven as she settled back and pulled her knees to her chest. With the look of a sailor anxiously gazing at a hurricane bearing down upon him, Madison stared out the front window. Outside, a Black-chinned humming bird hovered at the feeder. Another soon joined it. This pleasant distraction from her feelings dissolved a moment later when both birds darted away. Madison sank deeper into the couch. It was as if a bubble had been pierced as she watched the news broadcast on Cassidy's computer. During the rest of school and on the walk home, all of her energy had been seeping out. Now, alone on her couch, she barely had the strength to lay her head down. Tears welled in her eyes and ran down her cheeks. She didn't want to cry but she could do nothing to stop herself. It had been a shock to see him again.

She drew up into the fetal position and closed her eyes. Memories swam to the surface, uncoiling through her body. Her muscles clenched and trembled. She fought the memories back, driving them over the wall she had constructed in her mind years earlier. I will not allow them to get me, she thought. Not now, not after so long. Suddenly sick to her stomach and with her chest feeling like someone was sitting on it, she dragged herself to the bathroom and dry-heaved into the toilet. She didn't want to think or feel. She wanted to let it all slide away into the darkness of sleep. Laying face down on the cool tile of the bathroom floor, Madison closed her eyes. "Noooo," she immediately cried out as a disturbing memory from the past flashed in her mind. She staggered to her feet bumping her shoulder against the towel rack. Leaning on the sink for support, she glimpsed an unfamiliar reflection in the mirror. The tormented flitting eyes and frightened down-turned mouth couldn't be her. But sadly, it was. Lurching across the room and stumbling into her bed, Madison nestled into the safety of her comforter.

Remembering Sky and his warm, calming presence, she asked, *Sky, what do I do? How can I make this better?"* She focused on an image of him from one of their foraging trips to the mountains. Leaning against a tree, a band of sunlight emblazoned across his chest, Sky had grinned back at her. They had been close. With no children of his own, Sky had treated her like his daughter. From her first day at Fair Haven he had extended to her his respect and a gentle, loving kindness that touched her deeply. Undoubtedly he had his theories about what had brought her there, but he never asked. Instead he gave her the time and space to adjust to her new surroundings. Three months after she arrived he came to the house where she was living with Jasmine, Kona, and their two boys, Marley and Jack. With Jasmine at her side, Sky led Madison into the yard and quietly said, "I'd like to tell you about the work I do." From that day until his death he taught her the ins and outs of his beloved mushroom collecting business. He showed her that instead of cutting chanterelles, she should use a twisting motion to free them. He told her that unlike what many people believed, he found more mushrooms in years of above average temperatures rather than above average rainfall. He educated her on prices and buyers, and he warned her who would be fair and who might try to rip her off. Foraging together for chanterelles and morels among the towering Douglas firs, Madison learned, by way of hidden and circuitous routes, of his early-season stashes; places high on the mountain ridges where mid-summer rains were caught and the mushroom spore flourished. Together over the years they built the business into an important source of revenue for the commune. Those afternoons in the forest enjoying only their thoughts, occasional bird calls, and the shifting wind in the trees, were healing for her. Sky's sturdy, protective presence infused Madison with the confidence she needed to make a life for herself at Fair Haven. When he died, Madison was once again thrown into the clinging anguish of being abandoned by someone she loved. Coming ten years after her initial jarring separation, the ominous sensation of being cast adrift, although familiar, wasn't any less painful to endure. Eventually her teaching, the mushroom business, and running the trails provided her with the focus and distraction to move beyond the grief of Sky's passing.

Pulling the comforter over her head and burrowing deeper into the bed, Madison knew that fond memories of her life with Sky would not be enough to make it all go away. She had seen Gil Linnetti on the computer screen. There was no denying it.

In the safe cocoon of her bed, Madison agonized over what to do.

3

Gil Linnetti's eyes snapped open. He had to pick up Drake at soccer practice. He stumbled to his feet and took two hurried steps before the tent, Tupperware containers, and Coleman stove registered in his mind. Completing this harsh reentry into consciousness was the noisy rumble of a diesel engine. Gil turned just as a Dodge pickup pulled away from the stop sign. In a daze he watched the trunk accelerate up the road. Then, with shoulders sagging, he sank back down into his beach chair.

Above him the midday sun poked through low clouds. The air, polished clean from the rain, had begun to warm up. He pressed the heel of his work boot into the wet ground. Water seeped into the imprint. "The world is different when it rains," Bonnie used to say. "Everything opens up." She was the only person he ever knew who would intentionally go for a walk in the rain. When Drake was old enough he would go with her – the two of them bundled in yellow slickers and hats.

Gil rubbed his face feeling the spiky stubble of his beard. Quickly thrusting aside the memory of his wife and son he stood up and walked to where his supplies were stored. Raising the tarp, he pushed past several empty Tupperware containers and pulled out a soggy bag of M&Ms. He turned back around and his daughter Lindsey was standing by the patio umbrella.

Dressed in her favorite blue jean overalls, she was looking at him sweetly. In her right hand was the stuffed toy monkey Gil's sister, Jackie, gave Lindsey for her third birthday. Christened Dobo by her brother, Lindsey had taken it with her everywhere she went. The last time Gil saw it was in the wreckage.

Lindsey sat on the ground and lifted Dobo for him to see. She smiled and gestured for him to come and play with her. Gil took a step toward her, but then stopped. As comforting as it was to see them, when his family began appearing at the campsite he knew that to interact with them was to cross a psychological line that, even in his vulnerable state, he knew was dangerous. So he looked from his adorable daughter to the low, blotchy gray clouds in the sky. I love you sweetie, he thought, thanks for coming to say hi. He lowered his gaze and turned back to her. Lindsey was gone.

This time he couldn't restrain himself. Wiping tears from his eyes with the back of his hand, he fondly remembered the righteous anger that engulfed him at the time of the accident. He didn't sit around crying back then. He took action. He badgered the cops about finding the driver of the stolen SUV. He campaigned against General Motors, calling their offices in Detroit, yelling at anyone he could get on the telephone about the dangers of large sport-utility vehicles. After that he turned his rage against county and city officials. "There should have been a traffic light at this intersection years ago!" He ranted at them over the telephone. "My family's blood is on your hands!"

Giving him momentum and purpose, his anger fueled his waking hours with energy and discipline. It also allowed him to avoid his feelings of loss. But when he moved to his campsite at Hargrove Avenue things changed. At the intersection there was no one to yell at and no one to blame for the tragedy. He was alone with his memories and his pain. At first he suffered terribly, waking at night to the sound of smashing steel and rushing flames. In his mind, he saw his children's mangled bodies and heard the running footsteps of their killer escaping into the woods. He grieved, beseeching God to bring down upon that cowardly maniac a death equal in brutality to that which had taken his family. After weeks of anguished torment, the confusing glare of news cameras and lights, and also the kindness of well-wishers, he began to sense a shift. The devastating dreams ceased to dominate his nights. A tangible presence emerged. He began to sense a connection to his family. Just as Lindsey had appeared to him, Bonnie and Drake would suddenly show up at the camp site. Some times he would see them and other times it would only be a sensation of them being nearby. While it often made him weep, their presence also provided reassurance. They weren't really gone. They were just out of reach. And so he began to write to them in his journal and to talk to them when he was alone. It provided him with much needed light at the bottom of the dark chasm of grief into which he had tumbled. Their illumination also brought with it questions of purpose: why was he remaining at the camp?

He got his answer one night after a hard downpour. Sitting outside the tent with his shirt off, his mind on nothing other than enjoying the cool, night air, he suddenly sensed Bonnie next to him.

"Hi Bon," he said. "Nice rain, huh. You and Drake taking a walk?"

Sitting quietly, feeling the presence of his wife next to him, it slowly bloomed in his mind. His vigil was no longer only about *his* personal pain and loss. Thousands of people had felt the impact of his family tragedy. He had an opportunity to be of service to others. What that might be or how it would play out, he had no idea. So that night with Bonnie by his side, he devoted his austere existence at the intersection to something larger and possibly of even greater impact than solving the death of his family.

Gil paused in mid-chew. Healing himself certainly didn't include wolfing down handfuls of M&Ms. He could almost hear Bonnie scolding him, "Please don't eat that junk. You're killing yourself." He reluctantly put the bag down. She had become a culinary snob after taking a series of gourmet cooking classes. As life-long junk-food junkies her conversion to fresh chopped herbs and basil tomato butter caused a dramatic shift in their lives. Outlawing Red Vines, Hostess HoHos and Gil's all-time favorite, Cracker Jacks, Bonnie pursued the art of fine dining with the fervent zeal of a reformed cigarette smoker. Eventually Gil was lured away from his hamburger, French fries, and Milky Way diet by Bonnie's more creative cuisine: seared tuna and asparagus, sea bass in cornhusks with lime cilantro butter, Tandoori game hens with crispy rice pilaf, and his new favorite dessert, fresh peach crepes with cajeta sauce.

Gil ate another handful of M&Ms. Even with his mind window-shopping back over Bonnie's culinary delicacies he still thoughtfully chewed each and every morsel, savoring the candy as if it was a cloud of meringue smothered in organic raspberries. Hunger, Gil learned since arriving at Hargrove Avenue, had a way of leveling the preferences of a refined palate.

Gravel crunched as a gleaming black BMW pulled off the road in front of Gil's campsite. The trunk of the sedan popped open and a deeply tanned man graying at the temples stepped out of the car. With a taut, athletic build, he looked like an aging country club tennis pro.

"Put the water on, Gil," Steven Davenport called. "Let's have a cup of tea."

Since the second week of Gil's vigil, Steven Davenport had been bringing food to the campsite. Originally his wife Marjorie's idea, Steven had resisted getting involved. But after several awkward deliveries he was surprised to find himself looking forward to his visits. Hearing the tremble in Gil's voice as he talked about his children, seeing Gil's eyes blink back tears and his fingers flex and clench, grasping for something that was no longer there, was heartbreaking. At the same time it was extraordinarily compelling. The storm of sadness, helplessness, and fear that whipped through Gil stripped him of the masks behind which most people hide. In those moments Steven saw truth in Gil's gaunt, weary face; a rare and beautiful truth. Being in the presence of such raw, uncompromising realism made Steven feel more alive.

"It's good. Don't you think?" Steven raised his cup of tea.

Gil nodded.

"Raming is a tea company in Thailand. I bring home boxes of their stuff every year." He took a bite of cinnamon roll and followed it with a sip of tea. "Marjorie did a good job on the rolls too."

Again Gil nodded.

"Any news from the police since I've been gone?"

Gil shook his head. "I'm surprised they'll even speak to me after the way I got in their faces."

"You were distraught. Your wife and children had been killed."

Gil bowed his head as a stream of grisly snapshots flashed in his mind: Lindsey's flattened cheekbones, her nose torn away. Drake, sitting at the point of impact, nearly unrecognizable, his skull split and partially severed. Bonnie's face with only a small, crescent shaped cut above her left eyebrow but the rest of her body totally crushed. A hand on Gil's shoulder brought him back from the photo album of horrors.

"It's okay." Steven squeezed his shoulder. "You're going to be all right."

"Thank you," Gil choked. "For everything you've done. Thanks."

Steven could feel the heat coming through Gil's shirt. He knew intense emotion did that to a person. It's strange, Steven thought, how the body reacts under different conditions. Once when he was a boy he got so nervous his hands felt like blocks of ice. His feet were the same way, giant blocks of ice.

"I miss them," Gil said, his voice ragged.

"I know." Steven focused on the tremor at the corner of Gil's upper lip. He's fighting the pain, Steven observed. Moving his gaze up, he stared at the deeply furrowed crease between Gil's eyes. Curved slightly to the left, the intensity of that muscular contraction fascinated Steven. His pain is a living thing, he thought. It is shaping his skin and muscle. It travels out through his pores, stirring the chemistry of the air, touching me with that same horrible truth that cleaves at him. Steven gently patted Gil's shoulder, searching for the right words. Then he knew.

"Tell me again about your daughter's last dance recital."

The tremor in Gil's lip stopped, the furrow released, and he began to sob. Steven, anticipating the reaction, already had his arm around Gil's shoulders. He held him close, like he would a son. This is the pain, Steven thought, this is the heat and this is the loss, this is the pain, this is the heat, this is the loss, this is the pain, this is the heat, this is the loss, this is the pain, this is the heat, this is the loss.

· · · · ·

"Does this have to do with what happened at school?" Shatki's dark eyes were leveled at Madison.

Madison gave her a cheery smile. "No. I want to travel and see some things. I've hardly ever left Fair Haven. I'll probably be gone a month or so."

Shatki didn't return the smile. She leaned the hoe she was holding against the wire fence and stepped out through the log-pole gate of the garden. Her long, gray hair shifted in the breeze.

Madison took a breath and tried to relax. At fifteen, when she first came to the commune, she had been frightened of Shatki. With her no-nonsense demeanor, Shatki had helped steer the original vagabond troop of hippies into a productive, working community. The same characteristics that allowed her to be an effective leader did not, however, make her the easiest person to be around. She constantly scrutinized everyone, probing for strengths and weaknesses. She viewed the members of Fair Haven as assets who, if given the right motivation, could turn the group's dreams of a utopia into a reality. Madison also felt that Shatki had been jealous of her friendship with Sky. It was common knowledge that Sky and Shatki had once been lovers and that he had broken it off. When he took an interest and began teaching Madison his mushroom business, Shatki had put up a wall. It wasn't until after Sky's death that the two women became friends.

Shatki reached for Madison's hand. Madison could feel the woman's sinewy strength from her years of gardening, building, and yoga.

"I never asked you about what brought you to Fair Haven," Shatki said. "I know it wasn't good. That was obvious." She squeezed Madison's hand. "Sky believed a person's past should never interfere with who they could become at Fair Haven. So we never questioned you." Shatki turned and gazed toward the hills. With tenderness Madison had never heard from her before, Shatki said, "Life isn't without its sorrows." She patted Madison softly on the back of the hand. "Go do what you have to do. This is your home. We'll be here for you."

"Thank you."

"And remember," Shatki added, flinty-edged determination back in her voice, "don't take any shit from anyone."

• • • • •

"Train to Portland, now boarding," a man's voice announced over the PA system. For a moment Madison didn't move. It was as if the man's words had welded her feet to the floor. Finally, and with what felt like great effort, she bent down and swung her backpack to her shoulders. With a determined shrug she repositioned the load and started toward the train.

As the neighborhoods of Eugene gave way to a less populated rural landscape, Madison gazed out the window gripping her journal in both hands. For fifteen years she'd lived within the safe confines of Fair Haven. Was going back east the right thing to do? She closed her eyes and offered up a silent prayer for courage.

Sky preached to her for years about forgiveness. Every time they foraged for mushrooms or worked in the garden he would quote Krishnamurti or Ram Dass or Jesus Christ. For ten years she listened to him and for ten years she deceived him. Oh, she read the books he suggested and told him over and over how much she appreciated what he was sharing with her. But instead of a literal acceptance of Sky's philosophy, she accepted it symbolically as a gesture of his kindness. His deep rumbling voice, his grand manic gestures, and his jovial enthusiasm were all part of a healing light directed at her. To Madison the specific words didn't matter. His focus and concern were on her. And for that she was enormously grateful. So she nodded her head as if agreeing with him about the importance of forgiveness, but she never really believed it.

The McKenzie River came into view. As the train crossed the bridge, Madison leaned her forehead against the sun-warmed window. Two people in bright yellow kayaks were moving slowly upstream. A man and a black lab stood on the bank. The sun gleamed on the surface of the water, jangling in brilliant white shards. Startled, Madison jerked back from the window. A childhood memory had surged over the wall into her awareness: the Good Ship Lollipop, her eighth birthday, the old paddlewheel churning past Point State Park, the fountain throwing water high into the air, sunlight dancing through the misting spray.

Madison stared at the journal in her hands. It had been years since she'd thought of her childhood. Training her mind to ignore who she had been and where she had come from had not been easy. The concentration required for Tai Chi and meditation, both taught to her by Sky, Shatki, and other members of Fair Haven, had helped. Working at night while she lay in bed, Madison had mentally constructed a shield between herself and her past. Built of three metals found on a dark planet orbiting somewhere in her teenage imagination, Madison welded together, piece by piece, her great wall of forgetting. The boy was the single memory permitted to cross over before the wall was completed. He was her prized possession, her mental totem of courage.

Madison opened her journal to a blank page. Returning to Pittsburgh wasn't going to be easy. But if she ignored what she had seen on Cassidy's computer, she would never be able to live with herself. What about the rest of it, she asked herself. What about that? She distracted herself by looking out the window. In Portland she would get on the eastbound train. Chicago would be interesting, she mused. The Sears tower, Lake Michigan — she had seen pictures — but what about the rest of it? She looked down and distracted herself by doodling in in her journal. First she drew a daisy and then a snapdragon.

The rest of it...

4

Flesh slices open, hot blood running, a garbled scream, body thrashes, the tree branch groans. Hanging upside down, the body shifts, squirming to escape. He calmly switches the straight razor to his left hand, clenches his right hand into a fist and pounds the bloody gore in front of him. The body moans. The razor changes hands. The new cut is deeper. Back muscle separates. Shoulder blade white shows through the wash of red. Feces and urine gurgle from the grisly form. Disgust and triumph register at the same time. He fights the urge to abandon control and batter the thing into oblivion with his fists and boots. The steel is working, he reminds himself. The blade is finding its way, don't shorten the process with brutish impulses. Teach this thing a greater understanding of itself. Bring balance where there is inequality. The body twitches and shivers.

"I won't ever forget you," he says to it. "And you better not forget them." The blade, carving gracefully like a figure skater, slices across the lower back and into the right buttock. Justice is not a simple concept, he thinks. But it feels simple. The blade, like a brush in his hand, turns and draws blood directly up the spine to the base of the skull. "I am an artist," he says, staring proudly at what he's done. "Upon you and with your own blood my grief is etched." The puckered flesh quivers. A low moan comes from the body. "I am righteous in my revenge," he says, sinking the razor in just below the clavicle. "God is on my side."

Gil Linnetti's eyes snap open. The recurring dream fades. On the roof of his tent, rain softly patters.

• • • • •

Marjorie lifted her hair off the back of her neck and brushed it from underneath. The brush gave a slight pull on the follicles, stimulating her scalp. She watched herself carefully in the vanity mirror as she continued brushing her hair. The new conditioner Klaus recommended was making a difference. Her hair seemed thicker, with more body. She lifted it, piling it on top of her head. Should I wear it up? She wondered.

"Come on doll face," Steven said, walking into the bedroom. "We have to be there by eight."

Fresh from the shower and his usual brisk towel rubbing, his wet hair stuck up in all directions. She eyed his reflection in the mirror. His abdominal muscles, no longer perfectly defined, were still wonderfully taut, as was the muscular definition of his shoulders and arms. Her eyes moved lower. Yes, and what about that? She felt a tingle in her belly, remembering their morning lovemaking. Steven disappeared into the walk-in closet. Even more fastidious about his workouts than she was, his butt still looked good for a man his age.

"How about going to the Blankenship's on Sunday?" Marjorie asked. "Suzy called this morning. For brunch?" She knew Steven was not likely to agree to the invitation. Roland Blankenship was a pompous, ultra-conservative who enjoyed baiting people into political discussions. He was not a favorite of Steven's. So she was not surprised when Steven came out of the closet carrying his underwear and socks with a frown firmly planted on his face.

"Blankenship is a blow-hard and a bully. I'd rather eat glass than waste my Sunday morning with him."

"Shall I take that as a no?"

Steven looked at his wife. Perched on the edge of her vanity seat, her delicate hands and slender neck gave her a bird-like appearance. She wasn't frail by any means. All that swimming had given her a substantial set of shoulders. Still, there was a delicate quality about her.

Marjorie resumed brushing her hair. "I'll tell her we're busy." Yes, she thought, looking at her hair in the mirror, I'll wear it up tonight. The black strapless Armani, the new Manolo Blahnik pumps and my Kate Spade purse — perfect.

Steven pulled on a pair of white boxers. "That kid of theirs isn't much better. What an odd ball. Course what do you expect coming out of a household like that?"

Marjorie's hand stopped. Her fingers tightened on the handle of the brush.

"Eric is fine," she said. "He's very bright. He made the dean's list last year."

"Yeah, but does he have any friends?" Steven sat down on the bed to pull on his socks. "That kid is strange with a capital S."

Marjorie's brush hit the vanity harder than she intended. Steven's head jerked up.

"He's their only son," Marjorie said, her voice taut. "He adores his mother. He respects his father, and he's kind to both of them. What more could you want from a child?"

Steven's eyes met hers in the mirror. For a moment neither of their reflections spoke.

"You're right. I'm sorry," Steven said. He bowed his head and went back to putting on his socks.

Marjorie slowly let out a breath. Immediately she felt a pang of regret. She didn't enjoy speaking to her husband that way. But Steven's comments could be terribly harsh and insensitive. Most of the time she let it slide, but when it came to children she didn't have much patience with him. Her mother would have given her a scolding if she'd heard her reaction to Steven. Her mother's devotion to her father had been absolute. Throughout her childhood there had never been any bickering in the house. She had been taught to respect her father's brilliance and dedication to his career. His home was to be a sanctuary from the demands of his work. He needed understanding from his wife and obedience from his children. Barbara, Marjorie's mother, encouraged that philosophy every opportunity she could. She drilled it in to their minds that as Dean of the business college at Duke University, Marjorie's father was a highly respected member of the community. His children's behavior reflected upon him and the way he would be able to do his job. If they wanted to have food on the table and clothes on their backs they should think twice before they talked-back or misbehaved. The indoctrination worked. All four children graduated from high school at the top of their classes and all four attended Duke, each graduating with honors.

Marjorie stood up from the vanity and went into her closet to get dressed. Her little outburst at Steven was anomaly. Over the years she had seldom expressed her pain in front of him. She was usually much more secretive about it. At Christmas time and on birthdays while shopping for her nieces and nephews she would occasionally get emotionally over whelmed. Her eyes would fill with tears and her heart would begin to race. In those moments she would quickly walk to her car, drive to a deserted corner of the parking lot, and have a good cry. It wasn't a frequent occurrence, she refused to live in the past, but on the rare occasion when a particular dress or sweater would set her off, she would allow herself fifteen minutes of tears. It was always something pretty that caused these breakdowns. Something Elizabeth would have liked.

· · · · ·

Steven thought the man to his left looked familiar. The man's young wife certainly did.

As he searched his memory for their names, Marjorie leaned to him.

"Stan and Cheryl McCormick," she whispered. Steven glanced across the ballroom of the Hilton Hotel pretending that Marjorie had pointed something out to him. Then, as if noticing the other couple for the first time, he extended his hand.

"Stan, how are you? Good to see you." Stan McCormick shook hands with a grip that felt to Steven like he'd been caught in a car door. Why do that? Why the macho posturing? Why the incessant competing to be the dominant male? Steven shifted his eyes over to Cheryl McCormick.

Cheryl was looking up at him, smiling. "Nice to see you again, Steven."

"Hello, Cheryl." He put his hand behind his back, flexing loose her husband's over-zealous grip.

"We missed you at the auction."

"I was out of the country on business."

"We made $230,000 dollars for the kids."

"Lotsa fun too," Stan said. "Danced my hind-end off. We were really cuttin' a rug that night weren't we?"

Cheryl nodded. "The band was wonderful."

Marjorie reached for Cheryl's arm. Her hand stopped just short of touching her. "Wasn't it the same swing band from the New Years Eve party?"

"Right you are," Stan said.

"Yes," Cheryl said, enthusiastically. "That saxophone player, the one with the tiny dark glasses, he was – oh my, I've never heard anyone play like that."

"Remember," Marjorie said, "at midnight, the laser show they put on?"

"And the balloons," Stan added.

"Yes," Cheryl said excitedly, "all those balloons. I thought we might drown in them."

Stan stepped closer to the women and said something in a hushed, conspiratorial tone. Steven didn't hear it. He had turned away and was raising his glass of vodka. As he took a sip, the other three erupted in laughter. Drinking, Steven had learned long ago, was the only way to get through one of these society charity events. Showing what you had by giving away more than your neighbors, was, to Steven, an extraordinarily boring way to spend an evening. He attended the parties out of obligation to Marjorie, and also for his business. She had grown up in this social circle and was compelled by a sense of nostalgia to continue. He, on the other hand, was not of the gilded spoon. He was from the wooden spoon side of life. The row house in Akron, Ohio where he was raised was smack in the middle of a turbulent, blue-collar neighborhood. Philanthropy was a word no one knew the definition of let alone actually practiced. Instead of swing bands on Saturday nights his block resonated with the sound of drunken fathers and screaming mothers. His own father's crimes against the family would send a priest scuttling out of the confessional muttering Hail Marys and frantically crossing himself. Surviving his childhood had taught him many things. Negotiation and compromise, both important aspects of packaging deals, had been Steven's bread and butter when it came to dealing with his father. Steven could read people at a glance and bluff like a world champion poker player. He knew when to push for more and when to let it go and do the best with what was presented. Knowing how to keep his head down and protect his investments when things got unpredictable was the trait his clients most respected about him. "You won't get burned with Davenport," his clients would tell their friends. "Steven knows the game." What they didn't know was the rulebook from which he had been forced to learn.

Out on the dance floor Esther and Marty Braverman were holding each other awkwardly and moving in shuffling steps. Marty had been a client of Steven's since the beginning. On the surface, Marty was a kind-hearted elderly gentleman who adored his eight grandchildren. In business, Marty was a rabid dog. In the name of profit he had put eighteen companies out of business, destroyed four marriages, helped nudge one executive over the edge to suicide, and destroyed the low income housing of five hundred families in El Paso and Houston, Texas. Rude, blunt, obsessively focused on the bottom line, and cruel to the point of maliciousness, Marty never hesitated to go out of his way to destroy a perceived competitor. In his years of doing business with Steven, Marty had become a wealthy man. From the first day Steven met Marty he tried to figure out what had turned Marty into such a single-minded brute. Marty's small stature, the way his hands frequently raised up in front of him, and his overly aggressive attitude, indicated to Steven that Marty may have endured some kind of physical abuse. But every time Steven steered the conversation that way, Marty deftly redirected it back to business. After two years of gentle probing, Marty finally talked, but it wasn't to Steven.

At a dinner party Marjorie and Steven threw in celebration of Marty's acquisition of Tremont, the largest industrial foundry on the east coast, Steven, having just opened a bottle of vintage port, had gone upstairs looking for Marty to offer him a glass. At the top of the stairs he heard voices coming from Elizabeth's room. As he got closer to the open door he heard Marty say, "No, I was a little younger than you. They were all three or four years—"

"But girls aren't supposed to be that way."

Elizabeth's voice was higher than normal. Steven could tell she was upset.

"Uncle Marty, I never did anything to them!"

"Either did I honey." Marty was trying to sooth her agitation.

"But why Uncle Marty? I didn't do anything!"

"Sometimes you don't have to." Now his voice had a bit of smile in it. "And girls can be as bad as boys, let me tell you."

"Really?"

"Oh yes, they really can. Girls are toughies when they want to be."

"Jeeze."

Steven knew why Elizabeth was upset: the week before she had come to Marjorie complaining about a group of girls at school who had been bullying her. The five girls called her names and tried to knock her down in the hallway. Marjorie told her to ignore them. If they persisted, Marjorie promised, she would contact their parents.

"What did you do to those boys who beat you up?" Elizabeth asked. "You must have hated them."

"They caught me many more times. The last time I was hurt pretty bad and had to go to the hospital. Two of the boys went to a reformatory and the other two got thrown out of school."

"Can I get Carrie Linder thrown out of school?"

Marty chuckled. "No. But what you can do is study really hard, get really smart, and create a wonderful life for yourself. Success is the best revenge."

Later, after everyone had gone, Steven bribed Elizabeth with chocolate ice cream and got her to tell him the rest of Marty's story.

They were called the Seventh Street Gang and they liked to beat up on younger kids. Marty was small and wore glasses and was a prime target for the bullies. They beat him up the first time just outside the schoolyard. After that it became a game. Marty would try to sneak home by different serpentine routes and the gang would try to find him and beat him up. Sometimes he would make it and other times they would jump him.

Steven used this new knowledge of Marty's childhood to inspire the man's loutish deal-making. And even though it was sometimes unpleasant to witness the carnage, Steven enjoyed rooting for the old timer. He likened it to the divergent emotions experienced while watching a bullfight. Even if you deplored the violence done to the bull, you still had to admire the courage of the matador. To stand in front of thousands of people, cape in hand, facing down 1,700 pounds of angry bull, took something not many people had. Trying to convince Marty to be less intimidating and more genial would be like attempting to train a giraffe to stand on its head. The infrastructure was incapable of supporting the desired result. Over the years the bullies of Seventh Avenue had been right-crossed, round-housed, and kicked in the teeth during the course of Marty's many business negotiations. Steven gladly participated in Marty's psychological revenge. The enormous commissions he earned and the prestige of dealing with one of the most powerful men in the city had made Steven wealthy and respected. Many deserving charities also profited handsomely. The newly renovated cancer wing of Children's Hospital was the result of Marty's philanthropic generosity. Steven's position in the community and the community itself had benefited dramatically because of those grade-school hooligans in the Seventh Street Gang.

"Dance with me," Marjorie said, as the band launched into a new number. Taking her hand and leading Marjorie to the dance floor, Steven reminded himself that he had clients in the room. Crushing his wife's toes in front of millions of dollars of investment capital was not good business. She swung easily into his arms. It had never been a secret between them that he didn't like to dance. What she didn't know was the pressure he put on himself to make it look good for his clients. Marjorie knew little about the specifics of his business life. He had instituted a don't ask, don't tell policy early on in his career. She was not to question him about the deals he was working on or where he was investing other people's money. It was a matter of privacy and strategy. If she inadvertently mentioned something to someone who knew a third party, a deal could be corrupted. So instead of business they talked about her friends, the house, movies, politics, working out, or sports. She took excellent care of him, the house, and their social activities. They had a good life and he didn't want to disrupt it. His flippant comment earlier in the evening about Blankenship's son had been imprudent. He had disregarded his own simple set of rules: give Marjorie what she wants, when she wants it, and never create a situation that brings up the past.

He held Marjorie tighter and moved with the music. In and around the mellow jazzy arrangement he was able to recognize "Goin' Out of My Head," by Little Anthony and the Imperials. Marjorie squeezed his hand, appreciating his efforts. She seems fine, Steven thought, maybe a little quiet. But she's a good sport. She's never burdened me with too much guilt over what happened. When he brought up drugs, she hadn't argued with him.

"Drugs?" she'd said, "Could have been. I saw her come back from running one day and her eyes were glassy."

"Maybe she wasn't really running," he'd said. "Maybe she was smoking crack or something." He'd brought up Lindy Jenkins, who had been caught at school with marijuana. Marjorie knew that Lindy was one of Elizabeth's closest friends, so it all fit together. It had been a tough time back then, but Marjorie came through. Their marriage was strong, he assured himself. She loved him. And if he watched his mouth she would continue loving him.

5

Madison was startled to see the man staring at her. When she'd fallen asleep, the seat across the aisle of the train had been empty. Wearing a faded black T-shirt and blue jeans, the man was thick through the chest with close-cropped blond whiskers sticking out on his chin. His dark, wrap-around sunglasses were aimed directly at her. Madison's stomach gave a twist. Like the headlights of an on-coming truck, the dark glasses bore down on her. Before she realized it, the smile was on her face. Sweet, girlish and submissive, it was meant to tell him: I mean you no harm. Please don't hurt me. You are large and I'm not. Even as she felt the smile blooming like a cheery sunflower upon on her face, she loathed herself for it. I'm strong, she thought. I run four miles a day. I use power tools. I teach children for God's sake. Why am I reacting like an idiot? But the smile was still there — frozen on her face like a mask from another time and place.

The man across the aisle didn't react. He continued staring, his thin lips slightly parted in what looked like a grin. Madison's hands went clammy. The nauseous feeling intensified. She commanded herself to stand up and get away from him but she couldn't move. Stepping into the aisle would put her too close. She pressed herself back against the window of the train. The dark glasses stayed on her. His lips pursed and opened. Please don't come near me, she silently pleaded. Please don't! His right arm flexed. Madison's skin crawled, electric with adrenaline. Pressing back into her seat, she drew her knees to her chest and closed her eyes. Please don't come near me. Please don't come near me. Please don't come near me. Suddenly she jerked upright, her eyes going wide. It was him! In her mind she had seen his face again! She buried her head in her arms. Please don't, please don't, please don't, please don't. She raced the words faster and faster until they blurred into one long dissonant sound like a growl deep in the back of her throat. Hearing it both surprised and saddened her. It had been left years earlier on the other side of her protective wall. But now it was back, droning in her head, building a fire of panic in her heart, and a pasty sick feeling in her stomach. And there was something else. Another sound was blending with her snarl. It was softer but with a deeper resonance. Madison raised her head from her hands.

Across the aisle the man in the sunglasses was still staring at her. His lips had opened wider and his upper body was turned toward her. His chest filled and then relaxed. A groan of air released. His chest filled again and let go. Out came another rumbling snore. It took a moment to sink in, and then she realized — he was sleeping. Behind those dark glasses the man was sound asleep. A cool wave of relief immediately washed over her spiky levels of adrenaline. Her body went slack. She turned to the window and covered her face with her hands. It wasn't the intensity of her fear, and it wasn't the joy of knowing that she was safe that made her cry. It was acknowledging that the great wall of forgetting, the architectural wonder of her youth, was breaking down. Like snapshots from a photo album, memories of her old life began flashing through her mind: the sweat on the back of her legs and the tingling sensation of the breeze cooling it as she rode her bike to the top of Squaw Valley Road. Looking down the long, steep hill at the houses below — their lawns green, flowerbeds choking with early summer blooms — she was triumphant. Not only had she made it to the top of the hill, she had done so in direct defiance of her parent's command to never leave the neighborhood. Her childhood fantasies of long distance running were the next memories to force themselves through to the present. With warm air streaming by her face, and throbbing power in her skinny legs, she was Joan Benoit winning gold in Los Angeles. She was Julie Moss battling the stifling heat of the lava fields in Hawaii, pushing herself to the extreme, collapsing then crawling across the finish line in the Iron Man triathlon. Fierce and wily, her imaginary competitors respected her. The medals platforms, the crowds going wild, tears streaming down her face, the cover of Sports Illustrated, the Wheaties box, hero to thousands of women athletes, and the wind in her hair.

And there was also the boy.

The first time she saw him he was standing still. He seemed surprised to see someone else running, as if the trail in the woods was his private domain. His shoulders, not nearly as muscled at they were soon to become, still gave him a squared off look below his neck. She passed him, feeling his gaze upon her. An older boy, she thought, a cute older boy. A moment later she heard him coming. He ran up fast behind her then slowed down and stayed there. Nervous at first, she eventually relaxed and let out her stride. They plunged down Rawlings Trail and rattled over the plank bridge. Six feet behind her, she could hear his breathing, rhythmic and steady. It made her relax. She let out her stride some more. Her arms and legs moved as if they were a part of the air, no resistance, no effort. Her body was running and she was along for the ride. Going left at the split in the trail, they were almost to the picnic tables when he came around to pass her.

"Good form," he said. "Try and stay with me." She followed him, running like she never had before. She was able to breathe more slowly and with greater control. Her legs felt stronger. For the next two miles they flew over the trails. At Jones Creek he looked back, gave a quick tip of his chin and was gone, running down the trail toward the lake. She slowed her pace watching him run, his long hair flowing, his arms and legs graceful in their movement. It made her feel something that she'd never felt before. She'd had crushes on boys in school but this was different. This was something she didn't understand.

Running the trails became a regular part of her life. Her parents told her to stay on the path around the lake but it was in the woods that she would find him. Sometimes she would hide along the trail waiting to see him. Days would pass and he wouldn't show. Then suddenly he would be coming up behind her on the path. "Hey," he would say. "Hey," she would say, and then off they would go blurring the green.

She didn't know his name and he didn't know hers. Once at a football game she thought she saw him with some other boys. It looked like his hair, long and sort of messed up, but she couldn't see his face in the fast moving crowd.

They ran the trails together for most of that year. In the spring, after not seeing him all winter, her heart did backflips at the sight of him. He was coming across Townsend Field. He seemed bigger. His shoulders and arms looked strong. His neck was thicker too. When he got closer he smiled. "Hey," he said. "Hey," she said. And that was it. He went past, she fell in behind him, and off they ran together.

Did he notice, she wondered. Did he see them? He didn't seem to. But they were there all right. Boys at school had been looking at her differently. She hoped they wouldn't get too big. Running wouldn't be very much fun if they got as big as Monica Leven's breasts.

Madison shifted in her seat. Outside the train the sun was just starting to poke up over the edge of Montana. A new day, she thought. And two states closer to her destination. She grabbed her backpack and got up. Her legs were stiff and she needed to go to the bathroom. Looking down the aisle she could see that no one else was moving around.

She went toward the rear of the car and down the stairs. Sleeping for another two nights on the train wasn't going to be easy. Even though the seats reclined and there was a leg rest it still was difficult to get comfortable. She should have flown but that would have presented a different set of challenges. She'd been on an airplane once and it had been a harrowing experience. On a flight from Portland to Boulder, Colorado the jet hit an air pocket and dropped five hundred feet. Her boyfriend at the time, a dulcimer player and carpenter she'd met at the commune, didn't have his seat belt on. Micky flew up, gashed his head on the overhead compartment, and bled on her new turtleneck sweater. Madison had white-knuckled the rest of the flight.

Downstairs she walked toward the women's bathroom. Just as she was about to open the door she stopped. From inside she heard a woman quietly sobbing. As Madison lifted her hand to knock and ask if the woman needed help, the sound changed. Lower and more breathy it became a pant not a cry. A husky moan of pleasure was followed by a gasp.

"Yeah, baby, yeah," the woman urgently pleaded. A man's voice said something that Madison didn't understand.

Madison glanced over her shoulder. No one else was nearby. She leaned closer to the door. The couple's breathing got louder. Madison knew she should walk away but it had been three years since Micky. Three years since she'd had a man's hands on her body. The woman inside moaned and the man moaned with her. Madison saw Micky's lean face and smelled the fresh cut lumber from his day's work. She felt the roughness of his hands. It hadn't been easy for her to get comfortable with him. She'd only had one other lover at Fair Haven before Micky. That relationship hadn't gone well. She wasn't able to open up sexually. But Micky was patient and sweet. He gave her time and allowed her to pull away when she needed to. Having that control made all the difference. As kind as he was, the relationship with Micky still never felt real to her. Something kept her from truly connecting with him. He could feel her distance and although she knew it wasn't entirely fair to him, her aching need to be loved demanded his affections.

The woman's breath was dancing faster now, held up by the man's hushed but steady moans. Madison remembered the last time she made love with Micky. On top of him when she came, her orgasm had made her thighs tremble. The next day Micky left Fair Haven for a remodeling job in Portland. She got a letter from him a month later. He said he'd met someone. She was an eighth grade music teacher, and they had already moved in together.

"Oh God, baby!" The woman's voice clawed at Madison through the bathroom door.

"Yeah, yeah," the man urgently whispered. An image of the boy flew into her head. His arms were around her, comforting her. She could smell the musky scent of his T-shirt and feel the hard, smooth muscles of his chest. She was safe with him. No one could get to her. He had saved her. From inside the bathroom the woman cried, "Oh God!" A second later the man made a growling strangled sound.

For a moment there was silence. Then the man said, "All aboard Amtrak." He laughed. The woman giggled.

Madison quietly walked away.

6

The silver Ford Escort had cruised by Gil Linnetti's campsite slowly the first time. Thirty minutes later it was back. This time it pulled over across the street and stopped. Gil raised his hand over his eyes to shield the afternoon sun. It looked as if there was one person in the car. A baseball cap and sunglasses were all he could make out.

Gil dipped an aluminum pot into the plastic tub of dishwater. The green scrubber his parents sent him cut through the film of lentil soup congealed on the sides and bottom of the pan. He sloshed the pot around in the suds a few more times then gave it a quick dip in the tub of rinse water. Behind him, a squirrel chattered in the woods. Further up the hill came the dull thumping of a woodpecker. Gil smiled. The neighbors are restless today.

Over the months since coming to the campsite, he had become aware of the subtle way in which his mind had changed. No longer fraught with schedules, paying bills, and the responsibilities of work, Gil's awareness of his environment intensified. He saw and heard things differently now: golden particles of dust drifting in shafts of sunlight, the organized efficiency of a colony of ants, rain drops cascading like gems through the beam of a headlight, and the oak tree majestically silhouetted by the moon. In these moments when the doorway to rational thought remained closed, he experienced something he'd felt only twice before in his life. At the birth of both of his children, the presence of something greater than himself had been palpable. Now, at his campsite, that same potent force, disorienting at first, gradually had become a comforting part of his existence. Its power left him feeling encouraged and invited in on a secret. But at other times he would feel weak and unmanly because he wanted his family's killer caught and severely punished. Exacting justice only in his dreams wasn't getting that job done.

Across the street a car door slammed. The driver of the Escort was walking toward the oak tree. Medium height and on the slim side, she was wearing blue jeans, athletic shoes and a black and gold sweatshirt. The hair sticking out of the back of the baseball cap was dark. In her arms she held a bouquet of flowers. She knelt down and leaned the flowers against the trunk of the oak. She crouched there for a moment then straightened up and looked directly at him. He raised his hand and waved. She didn't move. They looked at each other a moment longer then she hurried back to the car. Gil couldn't see what she was doing, but it looked like she was resting her head on the steering wheel. He started walking toward the car to see if she was all right. Suddenly her head came up. As soon as she saw him, the Escort's engine roared to life. Gil stopped walking. For a moment the two of them stared at each other across Hargrove Avenue. Gil raised his hand and waved again. She didn't react.

He turned and started back toward his camp. He'd taken three steps when the Escort once again fell silent. Gil hesitated but didn't look back. If she didn't want to talk to him that was her business.

He picked up the red spiral notebook he was using as a journal and sat down in his beach chair. Some days he wrote letters to Lindsey and Drake reminiscing about things they had done together or telling them stories he'd never gotten around to telling. Other times he simply listed the day's activities:

1. *Got up. Ate a banana and some grapes.*
2. *Saw a squirrel get hit by a white Mustang.*
3. *Ate peanut butter and jelly for lunch.*
4. *Guy in a cement truck stopped by and gave me a box of oranges.*
5. *Thought I saw Drake in his soccer uniform standing by the tent.*
6. *Heard an owl hooting just before going to sleep.*

Today, he decided to write to the kids and tell them about his tenth birthday. Gil settled back in the chair and began writing:

My father had been promising to take me to a Pirate game all summer. Finally, on my birthday Dad and I loaded into

the station wagon and headed for Three Rivers Stadium.
Halfway between the parking lot and the stadium, Dad
leaned over and told me that because I was such a big kid
now, I was going to be able to have a grown up birthday. I
nodded, not exactly understanding what he meant. When
we got to the entrance gate we met a man who shook hands
with my father and then with me. I didn't know the man
but my father seemed to. I followed behind them as they
made their way all the way down to the first row behind the
Pirate dugout. "Okay," my father told me. "This is as far as
I go. You're on your own now." I didn't understand. I looked
at my father, then at the other man. Both of them were grin-
ning. "Keep that mitt ready," the other man said, "Foul balls
can come at you pretty fast in the dugout." In a daze I was
led around to the —

A gunshot rang out. Gil's head snapped up. The woman in the car was slumped forward on the steering wheel.

Jumping to his feet, Gil ran toward the Escort. He wanted to go faster but his legs felt like bags of concrete. In the middle of Hargrove Avenue he heard himself yelling, "What have you done? What have you done?"

Her head jerked up at the sound of his voice. The sunglasses were off. Her small, pale face was contorted. She was crying.

"Are you hurt?" he called to her. She straightened up in the seat, raising her arm as she did. Gil saw the revolver she was holding and stopped running. She looked from Gil to the pistol then back to Gil. He was immediately struck by how young she was.

"Put the gun down."

She stared at him, her eyes wide with confusion. "I missed." She began laughing and crying at the same time.

The sound of a car coming up Hargrove caused Gil to turn away. In that instant of distraction the Escort's engine revved to life. Tires spun in loose dirt. The Escort shot forward onto the asphalt and sped down the street.

• • • • •

"Marjorie."

She knew the voice before she turned around to see the face.

"Hi there," Linda McKelvey said cheerfully, coming around the rack of blouses. "Here we are shopping again." She flashed Marjorie a manic grin. "Summer sale madness!"

Marjorie laughed.

"I saw Steven's name in the paper last week. A merger of some kind. The man doesn't slow down."

"He loves the challenge. How's Tom?"

"Good. We just got back from Tahiti. Sarah and Marko met us there. Emily and Dave wanted to come but their two boys would have been an unholy terror on a flight that long."

Marjorie smiled. Out of all her women friends, Linda was the one person who never hesitated to talk about her children. Other people would avoid the subject all together, or upon being asked, give quick perfunctory responses then steer the conversation to another subject. Fifteen years after the fact and people were still being careful. Did she give the impression of being that fragile? Did everyone think that she would fall apart if they told her that their children were doing well, getting married, or having babies? She knew they were trying to be kind. But every hesitation, every grandchild not joyously celebrated out of deference to her was like a punch in the gut.

"Sarah brought up the story," Linda said, starting to grin, "the girls and the jelly."

"Oh, yes, the infamous grape jelly incident."

"Marko had never heard it before."

"We never did figure out how they got it on *top* of the refrigerator," Marjorie said, enjoying the memory.

"I know, I know. And the look on Tom's face when he saw that mess in the morning," Linda started to laugh. "Oh, it was classic. He was speechless. He came back into the bedroom and said—"

"Honey," Marjorie said, knowing the story by heart. "Would you like a little jelly with your dishwasher?"

Linda laughed.

Marjorie wiped her eyes. "Our girls were too much. Five years old and into everything,"

"Marko thought it was a hilarious. The thought of his sweet, dainty wife spreading grape jelly all over the kitchen—it really tickled him."

"He didn't have to clean it up."

"And the dish towels."

"At least they wiped off their hands before going back to bed."

"The little darlings."

Marjorie reached over and rested her hand on Linda's arm. "We had fun with them, didn't we?"

"That's for sure."

"Please tell the girls I said hello. And give those two bruisers a big hug next time you see them."

"They're getting big. Sean is already wearing Tyler's clothes."

"Two strapping boys."

Linda squeezed her hand. "It's great to see you. You always look fantastic."

Marjorie's smile broadened. "Thanks sweetie."

"I feel like little miss frumpy next to you."

Marjorie gave her a playful push. "You're beautiful."

"In a round kinda way."

"Stop it."

"Alright, alright, enough about my not-so-skinny self. There's shopping to be done."

"Give my best to, Tom."

"I will. And mine to, Steven."

Linda McKelvey watched Marjorie walk away. She's a tough one, Linda thought. No one could say she isn't. Sure the years have been kind to her. She looks great with her long legs and slender figure. But inside she must be a hundred and four years old. What she's been through… Linda turned and started toward the escalator. For three years Marjorie had a private investigator searching for Elizabeth. He never found her. There was the initial letter when Elizabeth first disappeared and then another three months later — something about finding a home and being happy and not to worry about her. A knife in the heart, Linda thought, to never see her only child again. And why had Elizabeth been compelled to leave? She'd been a little on the precocious side when she was younger. But as an only child that wasn't so unusual. As she got older, Elizabeth became quite the daredevil. Emily and Sarah would come home breathless with admiration for her. The bicycle journeys out of the neighborhood, the time she raced through the O'Dells' back yard just to see if she could out run their Doberman, Reggie. The girl had nerve. But why run away from home?

Linda stepped off the escalator and walked toward a stacked display of pots and pans. How Marjorie and Steven's marriage survived that kind of strain was remarkable. Steven had always impressed her as a man who could handle just about anything. Marjorie was no pushover either. She'd been a college athlete. You have to be mentally tough to perform at that competitive level. Linda picked up a pale-green salad spinner from the display. They must truly love each other, she thought. How else could they have survived? Linda cradled the contraption under her arm and pressed the black plunger on top. Inside the basket spun.

7

Madison had two hours in Chicago before the Capital Limited left for Pittsburgh. Other than the trip to Colorado with Micky, she hadn't been in a city other than Eugene since she'd left Pittsburgh fifteen years earlier. She stashed her backpack and sleeping bag in a locker in the train station and walked outside to see the sights. Along Jackson Boulevard commuters hustled for trains, rush hour traffic blared, and exhaust fumes swirled.

Women in business suits coming from the city, some busy on cell phones, others steely-eyed and focused on getting where they needed to be, strode past her with a sophisticated, determined attitude. The isolation and tranquility of the commune was a paradise many steps removed from this clamoring reach of American technology and culture. Madison was both drawn to and repelled by what she saw.

If things had been different, she wondered, could I have ended up a business woman in a big city somewhere with a closet full of designer suits and a generous expense account? What had I wanted to be back then? Had I even thought about a career? I was so young. I had only just begun to think that boys weren't complete knuckleheads.

Half way across the bridge she stopped. Looking up at the daunting concentration of skyscrapers on the other side of the Chicago River she imagined going to theaters, movies, and restaurants — everyone bustling here and there, going, going, going. Maybe if I had come here, she thought, I wouldn't have had to work so hard constructing my great wall of forgetting. Maybe I could have become so busy with city life that all thoughts of the past would have been over-run by the daily hustle. She gazed up at the cloud-jabbing pinnacle of the Sears Tower. The important thing, she reminded herself, was that I did get away. If that hadn't happened, I might have become a drug addict, a crazy person, a whiny insecure neurotic, or maybe even a murderer.

It was from Chicago that her last letter to her mother had been sent. Sky came to the city for the funeral of his younger brother who had been killed in a boating accident. She decided that mailing the letter from Chicago would be safe. She wrote it quickly before she could stop herself. She wanted her mother to know that she was safe and that she had found a home. She refused to write about the rest of it. They would find each other one day, she remembered thinking, and they would work it out together. But that never happened. For fifteen years she was unwilling to put herself in a position to once again experience what she had gone through.

Madison walked back along Jackson Boulevard to the train station. In a crowded shop she bought a bottle of spring water and a hot pretzel and made her way through the maze of stores to the original section of Union Station. Upon entering the Great Hall, she felt her spirits lift. The vaulted skylight above the marble floor cast soft, calming light. The tall columns and bronze floor torches made it feel as if she had entered into another time and place. She sat down on one of the long wooden benches and looked up at the ceiling high above her. It's like a cathedral, she thought, The Church of the Holy Traveler. She closed her eyes.

In twelve hours the Capital Limited would deliver her to Pittsburgh. Once there she feared it would be impossible to keep her great wall of forgetting in place. Memories feed on familiarity. Hers would grow strong again. They would rise up, crush the wall, and reveal the grim fairytale of her youth. She quickly slid her mind away from this disturbing possibility to a brighter place — running in the park with the boy, tree branches sweeping high over the trail like the green curl of a wave, the wind in her face, her body strong and sure, her young heart fearless.

• • • • •

The cell phone in Gil Linnetti's pocket rang as he was about to step into the Porta-John. Only his parents and Jackie had the number. He checked the screen. It was his sister.

"Hi," he said, holding the phone to his ear. On the other end of the line electric saws whined and hammers pounded.

"Hey, Gil, how are you sweetie? Everything okay with you today? Sorry for the noise. The director just changed his mind. We have to redo the cave. Three days he gives us. Mr. Academy Award is about as decisive as—hold on a minute."

Even with her hand partially over the mouthpiece Gil could hear Jackie barking orders at someone. Gil smiled. When they were growing up she had been interminably quiet and shy. A bookworm and a secret sketch artist, it wasn't until Jackie was in her second year of college that she finally emerged from her shell. When she came home from Penn after her fall semester it was as if another person had taken over her body. Not only was she now strongly opinionated, she was cracking jokes and telling racy stories about her roommates. His parents immediately suspected that she was on drugs. She assured them that she wasn't. After watching *Bridge Over the River Kwai*, a film she'd never seen before, she realized that life was short and she had no intention of having anything less than a full throttle experience. Five years of going head to head with producers and directors as a set designer in Hollywood hadn't slowed her down one bit.

"Hey, I'm back, sorry. This movie is a mess," she said, her words tumbling out fast and furious. "A guy on my crew — his wife is about to give birth, two other guys want off this weekend because the Dodgers are playing, whoever, I don't know, someone good. You believe that. We have three days! 'Smoky Mountains,' Academy Award boy screams at me. 'Give me Smoky Mountains.' It's a dark fucking cave for chrissakes!" Jackie laughed. "Am I amped or what? Sorry. So is that outhouse thing working for you?"

Gil looked at the plastic exterior of the Porta-John. "Yeah. The cops gave me some grief, but then they let it go."

"Good. Can't have those TV reporters catching you with your wiener hanging out."

"I appreciate that."

"What else can I do?"

"I'm okay."

"You wouldn't be living in a tent on Hargrove Avenue if you were okay."

"Jackie."

"I know, I know, I'm sorry. It's just— Mom and Dad and I were talking yesterday. They're really worried about —" Her voice cracked and there was a pause. "I can't let these dingdongs see me cry," she whispered into the phone. "I wish you would come out here and let me take care of you."

"I'm okay."

"You have to try and move on. It's eating you up."

"Goodbye, Jackie."

"Gil, no! Come on. Go back to work. Re-do the house. Change the landscaping. Go on a trip. Do something. Pull yourself out of this…this…whatever it is that has you living where they—" There was an abrupt silence on the other end of the phone. Gil could hear her trying to muffle her sobs. "Fuck," she muttered.

"Jackie," Gil said quietly into the phone.

"I'm sorry." Her voice was stronger, more in control. "I know you don't need to hear this now. Mom and Dad don't know what to do."

"I'm okay. I'm here for a reason."

"Oh, Gil, I know you think you should be there. And don't get me wrong, I want you to do what feels right, but…when will it end? When are you going to come back and join us in the real world?"

"Which real world is that? The one that I was living in before December eighth? That world doesn't exist anymore."

"I know sweetie. But you can create something new for yourself."

"That's what I'm doing."

"Come on, Gil.

"Trust me, Jackie, something is going to happen."

"Like what? You get pneumonia and have to go to the hospital?"

Gil looked across his ragtag camp at the oak tree on the other side of Hargrove.

"In stillness can be heard the thunder of all things," he said.

"What's that supposed to mean?"

"It means I'm staying here."

On the wooded rise behind Gil Linnetti's camp leaves crunched. A hand — fingernails with chipped gray nail polish — moved into the open pocket of a nylon backpack. The blue steel barrel of a .357 revolver stuck out. The hand reached deeper. It emerged from the backpack with a bite size Milky Way bar. Eyes staring out from under the visor of her faded black baseball cap, Darla Seelbach, the sixteen-year-old driver of the Ford Escort, quietly unwrapped the candy bar and raised it to her mouth. Two nearly faded pimples on her chin, a small mole on the right side of her forehead, and dark circles under her eyes were the only islands of color on her pale, drawn face.

Lifting her hand to the fallen tree she was hiding behind, Darla moved up into a crouch. Once he went into the outhouse she wouldn't have much time. A mosquito buzzed in front of her face. She didn't move. Above her, a rustle in the trees told her that the squirrel was back. He'd been keeping an eye on her since she'd arrived. Just don't start yapping at me again, Darla thought. Not now. Holding perfectly still she imagined that she was a part of the decaying oak tree. Her arms were branches, her hair a cluster of dead leaves. Darla's mind soothed to the muted colors and stillness of the woods. Animals can sense you, her father had taught her. But if you don't stand out or draw attention to yourself they can't see you. He got a deer every season so he knew what he was talking about. After five years of being his official thermos carrier, last season she was the one who did the shooting. He had presented her with his old Winchester .30.30 two months before opening day of deer season. He'd taken her to the shooting range and gotten her familiar with the feel of the rifle. She shot all right but not great. When she suggested that a scope might help, her father shook his head.

"No one in my family ever hunted with glass," he told her. "If you can't make the shot with just your eyes and your brains you don't deserve the kill."

On the second day of hunting she got her deer. A six-point buck bounded up from the creek, the Winchester went to her shoulder, and she squeezed off the shot before her father ever saw the deer. That night at Mike's Tavern, through a haze of cigarette smoke, he boasted to all the guys. "No pussy-footing around with Darla. No praying over the shot. She pulled that Winchester up – boom! That deer went *down*."

It had been great to see his face lit up like that. She didn't even like hunting. The walking in the woods part was fine but the rest of it, shooting, disemboweling, and skinning — no thanks. It was being with her father, that's why she did it. Her younger sisters weren't interested and he didn't have any sons. So she went with him. He seemed to enjoy having her along. He told her stories about hunting with Grandpa Freddy.

"Your Grandad could shoot the center out of a nickel at 100 yards," he told her. "And that's not using glass, that's straight up shootin'."

One time Grandpa had been out for six days on a hunt with her Uncle Brady. They were starting up a hill and a 10-point buck bolted. It ran down a draw away from them, hit the bottom, and was running full out through the trees along the creek. Uncle Brady saw Grandpa pull up his Remington .270. Brady didn't know what Grandpa was thinking, the buck was all brushed in. But 150 yards away there was an eight-foot break in the trees. When the buck hit that opening, and he was running full speed, Grandpa Freddy squeezed off his shot and dropped him. Uncle Brady about swallowed his chew of Redman.

Her father's deep voice, his breath billowing in foggy clouds as he whispered to her in the stillness of the woods, was one of her favorite things about going hunting. "Keep your eyes open, Darla, we're going to get one today. I can feel it in the heart of my bottom." He said that every day, every year they went out. She'd giggle and hunker down. He would do the same. A few minutes later he'd shift around and dip some Skoal. It was tradition, their tradition.

What would my dad say, Darla wondered, if he'd seen me put the gun to my head? The bullet had torn a groove in the molding around the driver's side window. I have to protect him from my darkness, she had thought as she pounded out the groove with a wrench so he wouldn't know what caused it.

Darla quickly brought her focus back to the campsite. She watched Gil Linnetti click off his cell phone and shove it in the front pocket of his jeans. He opened the door of the Porta-John and stepped inside.

Darla grabbed her backpack and was moving before the door closed all the way. She came quickly down the hillside, leaping over branches and ducking through the trees. Circling away from the outhouse, so as not to alarm him, she crept to the edge of Gil's camp.

It's now or never, Darla told herself. With her heart pounding double time she quickly glanced around. The road was clear. The other side of the street was empty. She pushed up from where she was crouching and sprinted into Gil Linnetti's camp. At the beach chair she dropped to one knee. Now her heart was going triple time. Her hands trembled as she thrust them into her backpack. Suddenly, she heard a car was coming down Hargrove Avenue. She quickly pulled a paper bag out of her backpack and placed it on the beach chair. The sound of the approaching car grew louder. She snatched up the shoulder straps of her backpack and after a quick look to the outhouse, ran toward the woods. It was only twenty-five feet, but it seemed to take forever. The trees finally closed around her just as a black BMW pulled to the side of the road. She ducked behind a tree. The door to the outhouse creaked open and then banged shut. Gil Linnetti walked back toward his camp.

8

Steven Davenport, wearing a golf hat and sunglasses, got out of the BMW and waved to Gil. "How are you?"

Gil nodded to him.

Steven hefted two plastic jugs of water out of the back seat of the car. "Give me a hand. I've got four more for you."

Darla peered around the tree. She could see the shiny hood and door of the BMW. She glanced over her shoulder. If she cut straight up the hill she could make it back to her car. She slipped the backpack on, ready to run.

Steven and Gil walked into the camp and put the water jugs on the ground next to the coolers.

"So, how's it going?" Steven asked. "Whataya' think? You almost finished here?" Behind his sunglasses, Steven watched for Gil's reaction. The flush of emotions was right on cue. Gil's eyes welled up and his cheeks went rosy. Steven threw his arm around Gil's shoulders. "Maybe you need a little more time."

Gil nodded, wiping the tears from his eyes. "Yeah."

"I'm here for you," Steven took off his sunglasses. "You know that. Whatever you need."

Gil turned away and looked toward the woods. "Did you hear that?"

"What?" Steven turned and looked in the direction Gil was facing.

"I thought I heard someone." Gil searched the tree line on the north side of his camp.

Steven looked around. "I don't see anyone."

Gil took a couple steps in the direction of Darla's hiding place. He stopped and again searched the trees.

Darla's hand clamped tighter over her mouth. Her eyes were wide. Struggling to muffle her sobs, she pressed herself closer to the tree. Blend in, don't move and keep your eyes open, blend in, don't move and keep your eyes open, blend in, don't move and keep your eyes open — her father's words spilled through her mind. She pressed her cheek against the rough bark of the tree hoping the pain would stop her from crying. It's wrong, she told herself. It's really, really wrong. He shouldn't be helping. It was for her to do, not him.

Steven Davenport shrugged. "Probably just a squirrel."

"I had a problem with some drunk kids yelling at me from the road a few weeks ago."

"People should be more respectful."

"Not everyone is like you."

Steven put on his sunglasses. "Let me know if you need anything." He started toward his car.

"Hey," Gil picked up two Tupperware bowls.

Darla watched Gil walk over to Steven and hand him the bowls. Steven went to the car. The door slammed. The BMW started up and slowly pulled away heading down Hargrove Avenue.

Darla wiped her tears with a weary hand. She was tired of feeling lousy. She wanted the pain to stop. The voice of guilt reared up in her head. *You're the one who wanted to go places. You wanted to be somebody. Well, look at you now.* Darla squeezed her eyes shut. Her father's hunting advice was the next thing she heard — blend in and be alert. But she hadn't done that. She'd dreamed of living a life like the girls in her magazines and TV shows. She wanted experiences more interesting than what Everton, Pennsylvania had to offer.

Darla absentmindedly plucked at the split-ends of her hair. She longed for the days when she would happily burrow into her bed and snuggle herself around the long feather pillow Grandma Annabel had given her. She went to bed now knowing that she would just lie there, praying for sleep to come. Two hours a night, maybe three, that was all she got. Her mother thought she was sick. Teresa, her youngest sister, was convinced that Darla had become a vampire. As a joke she put a crucifix on Darla's dresser and hung cloves of garlic in her closet. Her father, thinking that a boy had broken her heart, told her, "There's a lot of fish in the sea, honey." The way he looked at her when he said it was sweet. He wanted to make it all better. But he couldn't. And she wasn't going to tell him the truth. It would kill him.

Darla peered around the tree. Gil was loading trash into a black garbage bag. He looks a little like my father, she thought. The color of his hair was nearly the same and they both had blue eyes. He's not quite as big across the chest and shoulders, but there's something — a gentleness they both have. They could be good friends. They could go hunting together. I'll bake them my special triple chocolate brownies and they'll drink coffee and swap stories.

A robin swooped low across the campsite. Gil, sensing it flying past, turned and watched it land on a branch behind the tent. He could be a hunter, Darla thought. He's paying attention. Her eyes moved to the brown paper bag she'd left on his chair. Well, maybe not to everything. *That won't make up for what you did to them,* came the unrelenting voice of guilt in her head. Darla squeezed her eyes shut. Her mind, desperate to see anything but the images of that night, performed a high-speed search of her memory. Yes! Her mother's fingers in her hair — Yes! The memory came on stronger — White Rain shampoo, aloe vera bubble bath, the soothing sensation of her mother's hands gently rubbing her head. Darla concentrated on feeling the warm water running down her neck. She didn't want to see the other thing. Not the blood in the road, not the bodies. Her mother was washing her hair and softly humming. The gore spun back. Her mother was washing her hair and she was safe. The calming vision made her sleepy. She stretched out on the ground and laid her head on her arm. I'll lay here for a minute, she told herself. I just need to close my eyes.

She woke up in the dark with no idea where she was. Dead leaves clung in her hair. Mosquito bites on her arms and neck pulsed and itched. Her left arm, dead asleep, felt stiff as a slab of wood. As Darla rubbed it, trying to bring it back to life, she heard a voice.

In the bubble of light from a Coleman lantern she saw Gil sitting in his chair. The grocery bag she brought was open on the ground next to him and he was eating one of the mini Milky Way bars. He crumpled up the wrapper and arced a shot toward an open garbage bag ten feet away. "Two," he called out as the wrapper dropped into the bag. "The fans go wild." He unwrapped another Milky Way. "This is number six, honey," he said. "Forgive me, I have no control." He shoved the candy bar into his mouth.

Darla smiled. He's enjoying it, she thought. That's good. That's really good. She remembered the day three years earlier when she walked into the funeral home and saw Grandma Annabel lying in the casket. The woman looked strange, like she had been frozen. Her cheeks had never been that rosy when she was alive and her hands looked fatter. After the service Darla's father didn't talk all the way home in the car. When they got to the house, Mrs. Childress, Connie Messina, and Debbie Rapp were preparing food and handing out drinks. Her father, ignoring every-one, went into the den by himself. An hour later, Darla screwed up her courage and peeked in. He was sitting on the couch staring at the wall across the room. She wondered what he was looking at but she was afraid to say anything. He was so still. It was like he was some place else. That's when she saw the mound of wrappers sitting on the coffee table. He was eating Milky Way bars. Later, when she went into the den after he'd left, she found fourteen wrappers. That's a lot of Milky Ways. But he did seem better. He was in the kitchen talking to people and he didn't look so sad.

A sense of optimism swept over her. If Milky Way bars brought a smile to Mr. Linnetti's face what else could she do for him? I could make him happy again, she thought. He would never have to know. I'll be his secret guardian angel. The voice of guilt rose up taunting her, *Candy bars or cookies or a hammock or anything else you try and slip into his camp won't make him forget what happened. You let down your guard. You stopped being a hunter and let yourself be the prey.*

Darla, her optimism now deflating, stared blankly into the glow of Gil's lantern. For the first few weeks after the accident she had been numb. But as the shock of what happened wore off, her thoughts became more and more frayed. That's when the guilt-voice got closer. In her ex-hausted and weakened state, she no longer had the strength to push it away or ignore it. It was there all the time, nagging her and bullying her into doing something to redeem herself. It frightened her, but it was also company in her isolated existence. The voice was the only one who knew her secret. Except for Robert — that's what he'd called himself, Robert Kelman. Later, she'd read in the newspaper that his real name was Steven Davenport.

He had been charming in his e-mails and on the telephone. When she finally met him he was handsome and well dressed. He told her he owned a chain of stationary stores. He said that he wanted to expose her to the finer things in life, open her mind so she could become like the girls she watched on TV. He was going to take her to New York City. "Would you like that Darla?" he asked. "Have you ever been to the Metropolitan Opera? I'd love to take you."

It had all been lies.

Darla quietly rose to her feet, anger sparking in her chest. It wasn't right for him to spread his lies onto Mr. Linnetti. It wasn't right for him to be at the campsite. She shifted the backpack on her shoulders, feeling the weight of the .357. He had to be stopped. And she had to stop him. Darla turned and stepped deeper into the shadowy gloom of the woods. Quietly moving away from the camp, she felt herself begin to brighten. For the first time in months she had a purpose.

9

Madison settled behind the wheel of her blue Toyota rental car. She adjusted the seat and opened the driver's side window. On the train ride from Chicago someone had thrown up and the sour smell of vomit hung in the air. The entire way she squirmed and tossed in her seat unable get to sleep. Finally she'd drifted off. When she awoke the train was pulling into Cleveland. For the rest of the trip to Pittsburgh she stared out the window into the flitting darkness, struggling against her escalating feelings of dread.

Madison turned the key in the ignition. The tinny four-cylinder engine whined. Not quite the same as Bruno, she thought. Named by Sky after a pet bulldog he had as a child, the '79 Ford pickup belonging to the commune had a gutsy-V8-rusted-exhaust kind of sound. Bruno was a tank. On their journeys into the high country for mushrooms, Madison and Sky had driven the truck into places no ordinary vehicle would go. It had a dog's name, Sky used to say, but the heart of a mountain goat.

Madison switched on the radio. She wondered if WDVE was still on the air. The third button she pressed brought up the familiar call numbers, 102.5. The Rolling Stones, "Let It Bleed" played dimly from the speakers. She moved the console shift to drive and pulled out of the parking space.

With the green hills of western Pennsylvania rolling before her, Madison reassured herself that everything was going to be all right. Like the women she saw in Chicago, she had business to attend to. She wouldn't let herself fret about the past or dwell on what she was feeling. She had one goal. Nothing else mattered. She pressed the accelerator hoping that more speed and the rush of wind would distract her. But the smell of the air, the sight of the hills, and slate-gray sky were already stirring memories. Gaping holes were being punched in her great wall of forgetting. She tightened her grip on the steering wheel trying hard not to remember.

• • • • •

Dominic Angelo downshifted and eased his pickup truck to a stop at the bottom of Gorham Road. He looked at the oak tree off to his right. A bouquet of flowers leaned against the trunk. He quickly turned away. He didn't like to think about what happened to the young man's family. The children were especially hard for him. It made him think of Michael.

Across Hargrove Avenue, early morning light slanted through the trees behind the campsite. The young man must not be up yet, Dominic thought. He was usually sitting in his chair or doing chores. Dominic glanced up and down Hargrove Avenue. He slipped the gearshift into first, and pulled through the stop sign. Turning left, the whine of the power steering reminded him that it was leaking. He would have to replace it soon. He silently said a prayer for the young man's family, another for Michael, and a last blessing for Irene, his wife of 47 years. Since the day of the car accident he had offered up prayers every time he crossed through the intersection of Hargrove and Gorham. Several mornings he'd considered bringing the young man something: a bag of apples or tomatoes from the garden. But he never did. He didn't want to look in his face and see what he knew he would see. He couldn't bear to feel the pain of his own horrible loss all over again. It was better this way. He said prayers and thought good thoughts. That was enough.

Dominic pressed the accelerator. The old truck hesitated, and then began to pick up speed. He hated to pour more money into it but he couldn't bear the thought of giving it up. The Ford was one of the few reminders he had of his past. Most of his friends were dead. Irene and Michael were gone. And for several years now his memory was in the habit of abandoning him.

Dominic abruptly pushed those thoughts out of his mind. The Davenports, he thought, moving to a brighter subject, had been kind to the young man after the accident. Not exactly the warmest people, it pleased him to see the couple extend themselves to someone in need. They knew loss. Their little girl had gone away. Only six years old when he first came to work for them, she used to follow him around the yard digging in the flowerbeds and picking up twigs and dead leaves. He taught her the names of flowers and shrubs. She used to draw pictures of them in a green cloth-covered book. And she had allowed him, through her playfulness and innocence, to talk about Michael.

"How old are your kids?" That was how it started, the little girl standing next to him as he knelt in the flowerbed. With her question came the suffocating blankness. It washed over him, dulling his thoughts and burying his emotions under its stifling weight. It was the same feeling he used to get when Irene tried to talk about Michael. His marriage suffered every time he shut down and verbally and emotionally pushed his wife away. Irene eventually stopped trying, the gulf of Michael's death too deep and treacherous for her to cross. But with the little girl it was different.

Her hand lightly touched his shoulder. "I bet your kids know the names of all the flowers, huh?" She was smiling, a petunia bloom cradled in her hand. In that moment he saw Michael, young and curious, following him through back yards, asking a million questions, hauling shovels and pruning shears far too heavy for a boy his age. As he looked into the girl's dainty, smiling face, much to his surprise the blankness lifted.

"My son Michael," he said. "He knew the names of a lot of flowers."

After that he talked with her often about Michael. He told her about the day Michael played third base in his first little league game and the afternoon the two of them dug up an old tin can with 100 dollars worth of coins inside. When she asked about Michael, and she always did, he would make up stories about what he was doing in his life. He told her that Michael had three children, a boy and two girls. They lived on a farm in Vermont. Michael was a park ranger and spent his days walking in the woods taking care of the trees and animals. Elizabeth seemed to enjoy his Michael stories. He did too. His son was still alive in those conversations. Michael was doing what he loved to do. He was playing with his children and calling home to his mother and father on the weekends. One day after it rained Elizabeth's mother scolded her: "Young ladies do not play in the mud." After that Elizabeth had to stay in the house when he was working. The following week when he was in their back yard he found three pieces of white ribbon tied to the bushes. When he looked to the house, Elizabeth was in the upstairs window waving at him. After that it became their secret code. The ribbons were her way of saying hello.

A blue car turned off of Westfield road and came toward him down Hargrove Avenue. Dominic glanced at his watch. He had better hurry if he wanted to get his coffee and donuts before starting work at the McKim's house. No, he thought, correcting himself. Not the McKim's. He was there two days ago. For a minute he couldn't remember where he was supposed to be. These moments, mildly irritating when they first started, now with their increasing regularity, ignited panic. The white brick house on Sutton Court, he suddenly and triumphantly remembered. He couldn't come up with the family's name but that didn't matter. With a surge of confidence he knew that after the white brick house he would go to the Tuberts and the Rogers and then watch the Pirate game on his back porch with a pitcher of iced tea. The team was on a five game winning streak and the Dodgers were in town. As the blue car sped past his truck, Dominic remembered a double play the Pirates turned in the bottom of the eighth in a game many years earlier. Shortstop Tim Foli going to his left scooped up a ground ball, tagged second base, leapt into the air to avoid the sliding runner then rifled the ball to Willie Stargell at first. That was a team back then, Dominic thought. Those boys could do just about anything.

The bright blue car passed the old pickup and slowed down as it approached the intersection of Gorham Road and Hargrove Avenue. Madison's nervousness increased as the campsite came into view. She made a U-turn and parked in front of the camp. Fifteen years, Madison thought. She opened the car door.

Half asleep, Gil heard the car pull off the road. When the engine went quiet he rolled onto his side and peered out the flaps of the tent. He expected to see Steven Davenport walk up the embankment. Instead, a woman's face came into view.

Madison looked around the camp. It reminded her of pictures she'd seen of hobo jungles along railroad tracks. Clothes were drying on a line stretched between two trees. Boxes and bags were neatly stacked. She spotted a Porta-John nestled in the trees. Well, that's a luxury, she thought.

"Can I help you?"

Madison turned. Ten feet away, arms hanging loose by his sides, Gil was unshaven and wearing a T-shirt that looked as if it had been slept in for a week. His hair, no longer long and blond, was now brown and unkempt. Bigger than the sixteen-year-old boy she remembered, he was thicker in the body and fuller in the face. His arms still looked strong, and his hands — she had always loved his hands. From the back seat she had watched, mile after mile, his long fingers bending and straightening, adjusting the rear view mirror, pulling his hair back, tapping to music on the radio. They seemed to her to be kind hands, hands that did good things, hands she could trust. Later, when he'd held her, she knew she'd been right. Now, standing before him, that familiar nervous thrill shooting up from her belly, Madison looked into his eyes.

"Hello, Gil."

"Hi." He looked at her curiously. "Ummm."

It took a moment for her to realize that he didn't recognize her. She quickly reminded herself that it had been fifteen years.

"We met a long time ago."

"Oh. In school?"

"No. The park."

He peered at her, a puzzled expression on his face. Finally a look of recognition popped into his eyes. His chin tilted up. The wonderful sparkle she'd held in her heart for fifteen years lit up in his eyes.

"Hey," he said.

"Hey."

For a long moment neither of them spoke. Madison waited for him to embrace her. In her dreams and fantasies that was always what happened. He'd throw his arms around her and hold her to his chest. She would nestle into his body, her arms around his waist, breathing in the smell of him, feeling safe and protected. But that's not what he did. He stood there looking awkward as if he didn't know what to do. It's me, she wanted to say, remember how you held me? Remember how you comforted me when I was crying? Don't pretend you don't know who we are.

"It's good to see you, Madison," he said. "I always wondered how you made out."

"I'm okay." She forced herself to sound upbeat. "Thanks to you. You saved my life."

"I just drove the car."

"You kept my secret."

Gil shrugged. Another moment of silence passed.

"I'm still at the commune."

"Really?"

"I teach. All the kids."

Gil nodded, but didn't say anything.

Madison gave him a smile. "You still running?"

"No."

"I do four miles a day."

Gil nodded again.

"I'm so sorry," Madison said, "about your family."

Gil glanced down. "Thanks."

A nearly overwhelming urge rose in her. She wanted to throw her arms around him and say that everything was going to be all right. She was there to help him. He could be happy again. Life would go on. But she didn't do it. Instead, she glanced toward the rental car at the side of the road.

"I brought groceries."

Madison made Swiss cheese and tomato omelets with whole-wheat bread toasted on the Coleman stove. Gil sliced up the watermelon and mango she'd brought. With cups of Ginseng tea and their paper plates on their knees, they sat in Gil's beach chairs to eat breakfast.

At first the silence bothered Madison. She wanted to rouse him out of his isolation, to remind him of who he was and how he could step back into his life. Then she remembered their four days driving across country. He'd tried to get her to talk but she refused. She didn't want to accidentally reveal something that might jeopardize her secret. She was disappearing and no one, absolutely no one, was going to find her. She stayed in the back seat keeping an eye on Gil's hands and watching the corn and wheat fields of the Midwest roll past. In Wyoming she saw antelope bounding along the interstate. In Idaho Gil pointed out an eagle perched on a fence post. At night the stars were amazing.

"What ever happened to your cousin, Kona?" Madison asked, finally breaking the silence. "He and Jasmine and the boys left Fair Haven — what's it been, nine years ago at least. Last I heard they were in Taos, New Mexico."

"They moved to Bali." Gil chewed a piece of toast. "Jasmine started a clothing line with a woman she knew from Berkeley. Kona, he's actually going by his real name again, Stan, he handles the distribution.

"What about Marley and Jack?"

"University of Washington."

"Both of them?"

Gil nodded.

"I can't believe they're already in college."

"Yeah."

Madison looked thoughtfully down at her plate. "They were wonderful to me. Jasmine especially. She was like a big sister and mom rolled into one."

"Stan cut off his dread locks."

"You're kidding. They were sacred to him."

"What about you? What are you doing here?" Gil forked a slice of mango and raised it to his mouth. "I thought you were never going to set foot in this city again."

"I came back because of you."

Her direct gaze unsettled him. He looked away. "Why?"

"Because," Madison said, struggling to keep her composure. "You're a hero to me. And you have been for 15 years. I'm here to help you any way I can."

"But I don't need any help."

"Then I'll just sit and we can talk. How would that be?"

Gil thought for a moment. "I'm not a hero. I was just as scared as you that day."

"You were amazing."

"I've often wondered if I did the right thing. I always hoped you were having a happy life, but I didn't know."

"Yes, you did the right thing. You saved me that day. You really did."

"Okay. Then I'm glad."

They looked into each others eyes acknowledging the extraordinary bond that's shared between survivors of hard fought battles.

"That was a bad day," Madison said quietly.

"Yes, it was." Gil's mind reeled back through the years. It was the week after his seventeenth birthday. He was running his usual route along Rawlings Creek. Twenty feet before the plank bridge, she'd stepped out onto the trail in front of him. She was shaking and her face was streaked with tears.

"Take me away. I need to get out of here."

He sat her down on the side of the trail. That's when he saw the dried blood on her leg below the edge of her running shorts.

"Are you hurt? What's wrong?"

"He raped me."

He stared at her, uncertain what to say or do. "I'll take you home."

Her eyes widened. "I won't go back there."

"Who did this to you?" Anger pinched his voice. "Tell me."

She put her face in her hands and sobbed.

"Who was it?"

"I told him to stop. But he wouldn't."

"I promise I'll help you. Who did this to you?"

She lifted her head, and in a voice still hollow with shock, said, "My father."

For a second he was stunned, unsure of what to do.

She looked down at the ground. "Why would he do that to me?"

"I'm going to call the police."

"No! It will be terrible for my mother."

"Your mother will want to know what happened."

"Please, I can't tell her what he did to me. I can't. I can't."

"But you have to do something?"

"I don't want to tell anyone." She began sobbing again.

"He needs to be punished for hurting you."

"Just take me somewhere safe. Some place where I can be new."

His cousin Stan flashed in his mind. He and Jasmine had been at Fair Haven for three years. Stan wrote to him saying that the commune was a place where everyone was free to be who they wanted to be.

Gil had pulled his Pontiac over at a wooded bend in the road. After checking for other cars and joggers, he opened the back door and signaled to her. She sprinted from the trees and jumped into the backseat of the car. That afternoon, after buying her food and water, he had left her under a blanket in the trunk. With his best upbeat attitude, he persuaded his parents to let him drive to Ocean City, Maryland to visit Chuck and Robbie, two friends who were working that summer at Phillips Crab House. He told his parents he would stay at the beach for a week or so and then come home and paint the trim of the house, a job he knew they wanted done. His negotiations had worked. His father gave him some money for gas and told him he had to call home every night. He threw some clothes into a duffle bag, withdrew money from his savings account, disconnected the odometer, and they were on the road to Oregon by six o'clock that night. Before they left town he persuaded Madison to write a letter to her mother. If she was a runaway rather than a girl who simply disappeared, the police, he reasoned, might not look as hard for her. She wrote the letter, explaining to her mother that she was okay. She wanted to be on her own and live somewhere else. She wouldn't be coming back to them ever again. When she dropped the letter in the mailbox on Route 8, he thought for sure she would cry. But she didn't. Instead she turned to him with that steady look in her eyes and said, "Let's go."

They were halfway across Ohio before he realized that he didn't even know her name. When he asked, she refused to tell him. It wasn't until late the next day that she finally told him her name was Madison.

10

Steven Davenport stood naked in front of the bathroom mirror. Other than the eleven o'clock conference call with a group of surgeons from Upper St. Clair, he had an easy morning ahead of him. The surgeons, referred to him by a friend of Marty Braverman, represented a considerable pool of investment capital. To get them onboard would immediately elevate his negotiating position with Craig Gillian, a real estate developer in Arkansas. The world didn't need another shopping mall but the deal Craig structured was well leveraged. The developer was willing to carry a second mortgage and guarantee rental income for the first year. Steven wanted in and he wanted in big.

Looking at his reflection, he pinched the slightly bulging love handles above his hips and thought of the desserts he'd have to skip to get rid of them. His eyes moved up his body. On his chest, just above his right nipple was a lumpy cord of scar tissue. No stitches that time, he remembered. His father used a piece of undershirt and strips of electrical tape to bandage it. He was supposed to have been outside playing, but he saw the look in his sister's eyes and he wanted to do something to make her feel better. His father and Kelly were on the bed when he walked into her room. Kelly's naked breasts and the hair between her legs so startled him that instead of running he had stood there staring at her. His father grabbed him, dragged him out of the room, and threw him down the hall. He hit the closet door and landed on his back. That's when his father swung the belt. Standing naked in the doorway of her bedroom, Kelly watched him get beaten. She no longer looked like herself. She looked blank. Like some part of her had gone away. Before he lost consciousness he told himself that he would find a way to help her. But he was never able to do it. Eighteen months later, at the age of fifteen, she was dead of a Dilaudid overdose.

"Honey breakfast is ready," Marjorie called from the other side of the door.

"Be right out." He began getting dressed.

Marjorie didn't know. He'd told her that the scars on his body had been from rugby injuries and a car accident when he was a teenager. He told her that an elderly couple adopted him when he was a baby. When they died after his freshman year at Duke he was on his own. That was part of what hooked Marjorie, he remembered. She liked the idea of him being an orphan. It made her feel like a necessary and important part of his life. And she was.

"I ran into Linda McKelvey," Marjorie said, passing him the salt as he sat down at the breakfast table.

"How is she?"

"Fine. They just got back from Tahiti. Sarah and Marko went with them. They had a wonderful time. Emily's two boys are getting big."

Steven shook salt onto his scrambled eggs. "Emily's husband — Dave, right?

"Yes."

"He's a tall guy. They'll probably be over six feet."

"I think you're right."

"She was always a pretty girl, Emily."

"Yes. She was. I think Elizabeth liked her a little more than Sarah."

Steven nodded and picked up his fork.

"Elizabeth led those girls around," Marjorie said. "She was the captain of that bunch."

Steven nodded again but didn't say anything.

"The house wasn't so quiet back then."

"No, it certainly wasn't." Steven raised a forkful of eggs. "Honey, these eggs are excellent. You amaze me."

Marjorie looked across the table at him. His smile, the one she loved, the one that could be charming and boyish and seductive was plastered on his face. A winning smile, that's what people said about him. This morning it looked to her like a billboard, and she knew what he was selling. He wanted to change the subject. His smile hung there telling her that he loved her and that she was a great cook and wouldn't she rather hear him talk about that that than drag up old memories of their vanished daughter. Marjorie wanted to wipe that smile off his face with the back of her hand. She didn't bring up Elizabeth very often. The least he could do was indulge her in a few minutes of conversation. But no, he wasn't willing to do that. Whenever she brought up Elizabeth he would unfurl his dazzling smile, do his charming soft-shoe routine, and carefully dance around the subject. Did he think she was stupid? Did he think she couldn't see what he was doing?

As Steven chewed a piece of toast he thought of Emily. She had indeed been a pretty girl. She wasn't as self-conscious as Sarah. She was sweeter and more open. He had seen her naked once. It was during one of Elizabeth's sleep-over parties. He accidentally walked into the upstairs bathroom while Emily was in the middle of changing her clothes. He didn't turn away. She was lovely. Her dark hair hung straight to the middle of her back. She had olive toned skin like her mother. Her breasts, just beginning to emerge, were pert, the nipples small and pink. She smiled and said, "Oops," then pulled her nightgown over her head. He often thought back on that moment. He wondered what Emily would have done if he had touched her. Would she have let him? He thought, yes, she would have. Emily was a curious girl. She would have allowed him to reach over and put his hand on her back. Then he would slide it down. Yes, he was sure of it. Emily would have allowed that to happen.

"More juice?" Marjorie asked, pulling him back to the present.

"No, thank you."

"Oh, I forgot the turnovers in the oven." She got out of her chair and walked to the stove. "I made cherry turnovers."

"Lovely."

Outside a breeze fought against the humid summer air. In the Davenport's driveway, under the protective shade of a maple tree, a handwritten note fluttered on the windshield of Steven's black BMW.

· · · · ·

Shooting the .357 made Darla's hand tremble. But she didn't mind. She lifted the revolver and sighted in the round target 25 feet away. She was feeling better than she had in months. The sleeplessness, sullen attitude, and distracted, haunted look in her eyes were gone. She was cheerful again. Her parents had immediately noticed the change.

"Joanne," Jim Seelbach had whispered to his wife as they were walking into church, "Darla is feeling better don't you think."

"Yes. But it sure seems like a sudden change."

"Kids are like that. They get over something and they're on to what's next."

"I guess," Joanne said, still uncertain. But her doubts had lessened when, upon arriving home from church, Darla asked her father to take her to the shooting range. Initiating an opportunity for the two of them to be together was a wonderful sign, Joanne had thought. It was a lift for the entire family.

"Squeeze the trigger easy," Jim told his daughter. "Let out a breath and then squeeze it off nice and slow."

Darla peered down the sight of the revolver. As had been happening since they'd arrived at the firing range, Steven Davenport materialized in her line of fire. Hello asshole, she thought to herself, and slowly squeezed the trigger. The .357 bucked in her hand, jolting her wrist and elbow. Davenport's body crumpled to the ground.

"Nice shooting, kiddo." Her father squinted at the target. "Heck that might be a bulls-eye."

Darla was giddy. It was like a video game amplified a thousand times. Davenport would appear and she would blast him down.

"Thanks Dad for bringing me out today. This rocks."

"Honey, I'm so darn happy that you're feeling good again. Boy o' boy I was worried there for a while."

She slid him a smile. "It's okay. I'm fine. Girl stuff, ya know."

Her father draped a beefy arm around her shoulders. "Don't keep it to yourself next time. Talk to your mother."

"Okay, Daddyo. Come on, let's see how I did."

They walked out to the target. Her father whistled low. "Two bulls-eyes and four just outside." He nodded approvingly. "You're shooting real good honey."

Energy pulsed through her body. Yes, Darla thought, the power of revenge.

"Okay, Dad. Your turn."

Her father laughed. "I might not be able to match that."

"Yeah, right."

As they walked back, she wondered what Davenport's reaction would be. She wished she could be there when he read the note. He thought he could get away with it. Not over your dead body, she thought to herself. Without breaking stride, she stepped over the corpse of Steven Davenport — bloody in the dirt, six bullet holes neatly clustered in the center of his chest.

• • • • •

Madison scrubbed melted cheese off of her plate and dipped it in the tub of soapy water. Fifteen years of living in memories and fantasies of Gil as a young boy made relating to him as an adult extremely confusing. She wanted him to like her. He hadn't even thanked her for traveling all the way across the country to see him.

A car on Hargrove Avenue was slowing down. From under the floppy sun hat shading her face Madison saw a black BMW came to a stop across the street.

Gil waved at the car.

"You know that person," Madison asked.

"Yeah. He brings me stuff. Food his wife makes."

The BMW suddenly pulled out on to Hargrove Avenue and sped down the street.

"That's weird." Gil said.

Madison picked up the plastic tub of dishwater. "Where does this get dumped?"

Gil pointed toward the trees. "Over there somewhere."

"I'm glad you use biodegradable detergent." She walked toward the edge of the trees.

"He usually stops and talks. That guy in the BMW. He's a good guy."

"Maybe he had to go somewhere." She dumped the dishwater onto the ground.

The trees alongside Hargrove Avenue blurred Steven's peripheral vision into a green haze. The double yellow lines running down the center of the road dipped and curved as the speedometer hit 70 miles an hour. Steven yanked his foot off the accelerator. The BMW's headlong rush slowed. He let out a breath, loosening his grip on the steering wheel. Tapping the brakes, he slowed the car to just over the speed limit. Everything is fine, he chided himself. The woman with Gil didn't write the note. He settled back in the leather seat struggling to regain his composure.

Weathering the police investigation and scrutiny from the press hadn't been easy, but he had done it with focus and restraint. But now — he glanced at the note on the front seat. Crazy girl, he thought. What if Marjorie had found it? What was Darla thinking? She knew that they would lock her up. He picked up the slip of paper. The lettering was in bold red marker.

ARE YOU IN PAIN? YOU'RE GOING TO BE IF YOU DON'T STAY AWAY FROM MR. LINNETTI.

It had to be her, Steven thought. After seeing it in the newspaper, she must have figured out his real name. He dropped the note on the seat. She was watching him at the campsite. That had to be it. Steven chewed his lower lip. A sweet, sensible girl when they'd met, he'd enjoyed getting to know Darla through emails and talks on the telephone. Everything had been going fine. She was enjoying his attention. She had liked it when he kissed her. He could tell by the softness of her lips.

He studied the road considering his options. She might go away like the others. He'd always been lucky that way. He pressed a button on the CD player. Wagner's opera, *Tristan and Isolde* began playing. He turned up the volume. Darla was a bright girl, he reassured himself. She didn't want to be arrested. She would let it go and everything would be as it should be. That's what made the most sense. He checked the clock on the dashboard. The conference call with the surgeons was at eleven. He needed to get to the office and prepare.

• • • • •

It is kind of confusing, her being here.

Gil looked up from writing in his journal. Madison was searching through her backpack. He began writing again:

I like it in one way. Just hearing her walk around and eat is comforting. I'm not alone anymore. And that makes me feel better. I know it was a big sacrifice for her to come. I'm sure it's not easy after what she went through. But at the same time I'm feeling all these nice things, I'm also feeling like I should push her away. I don't want to upset you Bonnie, or the kids. It might be confusing for them to see me living like this with another woman. No, she shouldn't be here. This is our place. I need to—

"Gil," Madison said, interrupting him. "Excuse me, but do you want to go for a run? Nothing big. Just a jog down the road."

"No. That's okay."

"Might be good to get the blood going."

"I'm—I'm doing this."

"You sure?"

"Yeah."

Gil settled back in the beach chair. Propping his feet up on the cooler, he looked down at his journal. He could feel her eyes on him.

"I was thinking," Madison said quietly. "Remember when we pulled over to sleep at the rest stop in Wyoming? The lady in the RV with the dog?"

"The poodle?"

"Yes. Remember how I was shaking? I couldn't stop."

Gil nodded.

"And that woman asked if we needed anything."

"Uh huh."

"She had a big smile on her face. She knew something was wrong, but she was smiling to put us at ease." Madison leaned closer to him. "That's kinda' how I feel. I want to help you. But I'm not sure what to do."

Gil glanced down at his journal then back up to Madison. He shrugged.

Madison felt her face grow warm. "What does that mean?"

Gil looked across Hargrove Avenue. After a moment he gestured toward the oak tree. "Some days I want to get a chain saw and cut it down. Other days I'm happy watching the leaves shift in the wind, and the birds come and go." He turned to her. "You can't possibly know how to help me."

⋅ ⋅ ⋅ ⋅ ⋅

Confronted in the street by Sparafucile, Rigoletto listened as the assassin confided his methods. Darla reached for her cell phone as the performers' voices lifted around her.

Steven Davenport's knowledge and appreciation of opera was the only positive thing he contributed to her life. Prior to meeting him she had never heard an opera. After Steven purchased several CDs, leaving them at the counter of Barnes and Noble under her name, she was soon swept up in the music and pageantry. Curling up on her bed, she would eagerly read the libretto while the performance filled her bedroom. It made her feel grown up and sophisticated. *Tosca* and *Rigoletto* were her favorites.

As Darla dialed Steven's cell phone number she knew it was a foolish thing to do. But another part of herself, the bolder Darla, was unwavering in her commitment to Gil Linnetti. The phone rang once, and then it rang again.

"Hello," she heard Davenport say.

The sound of his voice made her cringe. She held up her cell phone.

Steven immediately recognized the opera. It was the famous Monologo Pari siamo soliloquy from *Rigoletto*. He listened, waiting for her to say something. The line went dead. He looked at the screen on his cell phone, punched a couple keys, and leaned back in his desk chair. This was going to stop immediately, he told himself. She wasn't going to continue to torment him.

Darla jumped when the cell phone rang. She picked it up from her nightstand. Davenport's number showed in the display window. A smile brightened her face. She was getting to him. She clicked the phone on.

"Stay away from Mr. Linnetti or you're dead." She hung up. Giddy from her boldness, Darla tossed the phone on her bed and danced over to the stereo. She turned up the volume. Rigoletto and Gilda were singing their duet. It was her favorite part.

Steven stood up from behind his desk. It was a game neither of them could afford to play and he was going to put a stop to it. He folded the slip of paper with Darla's address and put it in his pocket. The night of the accident Darla showed him that she was a fighter. But it would be different in Everton. Her family lived there. She'd want to protect them.

11

Madison smelled him before his face appeared. Grey Flannel, the cologne she'd given him for Christmas. Her eyes snapped open.

In the darkness of the tent her body was rigid, her hands tightly balled into fists. She curled onto her side in the sleeping bag and tried to slow her breathing. She was happy now that Gil had insisted on her sleeping in the tent. The small enclosure made her feel protected.

Pressing her knees together to still her trembling legs, she tried to force back the memory. It wouldn't go away. Her father's face stared down at her. His teeth were clenched, his lips moved forming words and sounds she didn't want to hear. Grey Flannel mixed with the sweet stench of bourbon penetrated her senses. The rest came in a rush — the sound of her bed creaking, his hands on her stomach, his voice blurry with booze, and the cotton-mouth taste of her rising panic. "You're so pretty," her father slurred, his hands crawling over her breasts. She felt the rough scrape of his whiskers against her cheek and the first probe of fingers between her legs.

Madison kicked off her sleeping bag and crawled out of the tent into the embrace of the humid night air. She stepped away from the tent trying to put as much distance as possible between herself and the memories of her father. Then she saw Gil.

Wearing only white boxers, he was facing away from her looking across Hargrove Avenue. His back was fleshier but still had the sexy V shape she remembered. His muscles, the ones she loved to watch while running, weren't as visible but the closer she looked, the more she could see them, and the more she could see them, the clearer she saw the boy. The recognition went through her body in a comforting rush. It drove away the awful image of her father and ignited a familiar heat in her belly. Before she could stop herself Madison was beside him, her hand pressed against the taut muscles at the small of his back. Gil turned to her. Without saying a word he pulled her into his arms.

It was the way she'd always dreamed it would be. Nestling into his neck, pressing herself against him, she felt light-headed. After fifteen long years she was back in his arms. Her fingers dug into his shoulders. His lips went to her neck. She let her head rock back surrendering her throat to him. His hands gripped her tighter. His mouth moved to hers. They kissed deeply. His hands moved under her T-shirt, his fingers tracing up her back.

"I missed you," he breathed in her ear.

"Oh, God. You have no idea."

She found his mouth again. His arms tightened around her. She held him, knowing in that instant that it had all been worth it — the train ride, facing her memories, all of it, to be close with him again.

"Don't ever leave me, Bonnie," Gil said his voice husky with emotion.

Madison went cold inside.

"I can't make it without you," Gil went on. "Life isn't the same."

Madison leaned away from him. "I'm not Bonnie."

As if startled from a wonderful dream, Gil suddenly looked confused. He stepped back. "What the hell are you doing?"

It felt like he'd slapped her.

"Leave! He pointed toward the road. "Get out of here!"

The angry look on his face frightened her. It was the last thing she wanted or expected. She loved him. She had always loved him.

"I had a bad dream. When I came out of the tent you were standing here."

Gil paced several steps then whirled back around. "You're messing things up."

"That's not — "

"I didn't ask you to come."

"You kissed me."

"I thought you were, Bonnie!"

"How could I be, Bonnie?"

Gil glared at her. Then his entire body seemed to sag under a tremendous weight.

"I don't know," he mumbled weakly, the fight leaving him. "I don't know." He buried his face in his hands.

Madison watched him, feeling oddly detached. Where is my hero, she wondered? Where is the golden boy who saved me? She stepped toward him.

"Come on. You need to sleep."

Leading him under the shelter of the blue tarp, she stood over him as he crawled into his sleeping bag.

"I'll leave tomorrow," she said. "I didn't come here to make things more difficult."

"I miss her."

The longing in his voice made it impossible for Madison to continue ignoring the truth. While she'd spent years secretly pining for the boy, he'd moved on in his life. To him she was nothing but a distant memory. She knelt down next to him. His confusion and sadness made him look younger, closer to the age of the boy.

"It's okay." She brushed a lock of hair from his forehead. "I think we were both kissing ghosts."

· · · · ·

The next morning Madison crawled out of the tent to find Gil standing over the Coleman stove. He was wearing a faded black and gold Pittsburgh Steelers jersey.

"Oatmeal and bananas!" He pointed to a pan on the stove. "And there's hot water for tea."

She had spent half the night mourning the loss of her fantasy and preparing for an awkward next day. Gil's happy greeting surprised her.

"There's a shower over there." He pointed into the trees. "I warmed up the water for you."

Madison looked where he pointed. She couldn't see anything.

"It's hanging on a tree," Gil said. "It's not a lot of water, so you have to be fast."

"A shower would be wonderful."

"Enjoy."

Madison ducked into the tent and grabbed clean clothes, a bar of soap, her razor, and a towel. As she walked toward the edge of camp, she wondered about the shift in Gil's attitude. Maybe he felt bad about what had happened. Or maybe he – no, she wouldn't do that to herself. And besides, she hadn't traveled all the way across the country to get into a relationship. She was there to help him with his life.

The shower was a gray, five-gallon plastic sack with a hose leading to a spray nozzle. It was hanging from a maple tree twenty yards into the woods. Gil had rigged a shower curtain of blankets between several saplings. She quickly glanced around for any unwanted spectators. Golden beams of sunlight shot through the trees. Above her and a little way off a squirrel began barking orders. Madison stepped behind the blankets. She slid out of her shorts and pulled off her T-shirt. She reached for the nozzle and pressed the release valve. Warm water splashed against her breasts. She lifted the nozzle over her head. The water ran down her shoulders and back. After bathing in the sink on the train the make-shift shower felt luxurious. She soaked herself then lathered up.

It's for the best, Madison asserted as she began shaving her legs. Getting the "boy fantasy" out of the way would allow her to accomplish what she had come to do. It would be less confusing. But even as she pledged herself to it, she was full of doubt. She had lived too long with the dream.

Gil was standing by his chair holding a cup of tea when she walked back into camp. He didn't move or speak to her. He was staring at something across Hargrove Avenue. Madison followed his gaze. On the other side of the street all was quiet. She turned back and looked at Gil. His eyes were fixed on one spot. She looked across the street again. It looked like he was staring at the oak tree. Madison quietly moved to the tent.

The air inside the tent was heating up. Putting her dirty clothes in a plastic bag, Madison remembered the night before when she found Gil staring across the street. It was as if he was in a trance.

"Oatmeal is served," Gil said when she crawled out of the tent.

"That shower felt fantastic. Thanks."

Gil handed her a bowl of oatmeal with banana slices on top. As they sat and began eating, Madison wondered if she should bring up the previous night's events. She didn't want to upset him, but she didn't want to pretend that it hadn't happened either.

"What were you looking at before?" She tilted her head toward Hargrove. "Across the street?"

Gil didn't stop eating or look over at her. "What do you mean?"

"When I came back from my shower you were looking over there," she pointed her spoon toward the street. "I looked but I couldn't see anything."

"Oh."

"It seemed pretty interesting. I mean you were really looking."

Madison ate a spoonful of oatmeal and waited. She didn't want to push it. She didn't want him to shut her out.

"I just…" Then Gil went quiet. Madison took another bite of oatmeal. Come on, she thought, don't clam up on me.

"The tree over there," Gil pointed to the oak. "That's where it happened…the wreck."

Madison looked across the street at the massive oak. "I know it was —"

Gil cut her off. "I'm sorry I upset you last night. I didn't mean for that to happen."

Madison turned to him. Nervous tension pulled at the corners of Gil's mouth.

"It's okay. You're a good kisser. Bonnie was a lucky woman."

For a moment Gil was uncertain how to respond. Then he blushed and the tension left his face. "She was the light of my life."

Madison ignored the sting of his words. "How is her family doing?"

"Her mother's a strong lady. She came and helped at first. But now I don't hear much from her. Too many memories get stirred up, I guess."

"I can understand that."

They shared a knowing look. Madison glanced down at the bowl in her hands. "What about her father?"

"He died just before I met Bonnie. Her brother, Danny came in for the funeral. But he lives in Japan so he hasn't been around either."

Madison gestured to her bowl of oatmeal. "This is good. Thanks."

"Sure." Gil's gaze had drifted back across the street.

"Was your family able to help you?"

For a moment Gil didn't say anything. He remained focused on the oak tree. When he turned back, she was looking at him, expectant and eager to help. Why, he wondered, why is she really here? And then he felt it, the same subtle breath of openness in the center of his chest that he felt when sensing the presence his wife and children. Without saying a word, Gil put down his bowl and reached for Madison's hand. He started talking. He told her everything.

12

The day after the accident Gil's parent's had flown in from their retirement home in Hilton Head, South Carolina. Frank Linnetti, barrel-chested, forearms like cast iron, and salt and pepper hair combed straight back, looked like the ex-middle linebacker that he was. At the University of Pittsburgh he had been a standout both on the field and in the classroom. He had taken that success with him into business, creating Linnetti Insurance. A trusted provider for nearly forty years, the company enabled Frank and his family to live a comfortable, privileged life. But none of those achievements made it any easier to face his grief-stricken son.

"When my father died," Frank said, "It was terrible. I tried to understand why he had been taken so young but I —" His throat caught as his emotions surged. For a moment he couldn't go on. "My good friend Dave," he said, changing his story. "Dave Bartlett, he was in Korea and never made it home, boy that was a tough one too. I tried to —-" Again he was overwhelmed with emotions. This time he didn't try to continue. He and Gil hugged each other and then stood awkwardly for a minute getting their emotions under control.

"Let's get out of here," Frank finally managed to say. "Go get a beer."

Six beers later, Frank was plotting with Gil on how they could track down the driver of the SUV and get to him before the police.

Gil's mother, Rose, dealt with her grief by laboring over the New York Times crossword puzzle, meticulously straightening up Gil's house, and cooking huge meals for everyone. She made Gil's favorites, linguini and clams, lasagna, a 25lb turkey with all the fixings, and a salmon as long as her arm. She baked ten dozen chocolate chip cookies and three different kinds of cakes. Every time Gil got quiet or looked sad she would thrust a plate of food into his hands and order him to eat. The pace she kept up never allowed her to grieve too deeply. Closets needed to be dealt with. Clothes and shoes had to be sorted through. Repainting the bedrooms was next on the list. Then there were the kids' toys. Around his mother Gil never felt like he was getting enough air. Her constant motion kept him gulping for breath.

The day after his parents arrived, Gil's sister, Jackie, flew in from Los Angeles. In between making phone calls to Paramount Studios, Jackie had cried non-stop. Bonnie had been the older sister Jackie never had. The two of them spent hours on the telephone gossiping about Jackie's movie star and director friends. Bonnie sent her recipes and helped Jackie plan dinner parties. Bonnie vicariously lived the high life through Jackie and Jackie experienced a quieter domesticity through Bonnie. Without any kids of her own, Jackie doted on Drake and Lindsey. They were her grounding rods in the make-believe world of Hollywood.

On a day when the wind chill factor was five below, four hundred people showed up at St. Alexis church for the memorial service. In front of the altar, white tulips surrounded a wooden easel holding a single poster-sized photograph. Gil had taken the picture three months earlier. Bonnie, Drake and Lindsey were in the back yard playing touch foot-ball. The photograph came after Lindsey scored her second touchdown. Bonnie and Drake had tackled her and the three of them were in a tangle of arms and legs on the ground. As they started to get up Gil had taken the picture. Bonnie's eyes were wide and she was grinning. Leaves hung in her hair. Lindsey, clutching the football in both arms, had a little-girl cocky expression on her face. Drake was laughing with his head tilted back. You could see the gap where he'd lost his front tooth the week before.

Gil had sat in the front pew between Jackie and his father. His moth-er, who had organized the service, sat next to his father twisting a white tissue into a tight coil. Gil tried to give his attention to Father Pat and the family members and friends who spoke, but he was only half-listening. He was staring at the photograph of his family while moments of his life flashed before his eyes: Oberlin College — his chin heavily bandaged from a spill on his mountain bike — jogging down the street on a cool, fall day, legs moving, lungs working, Nikes pounding the pavement. A pretty girl in a blue sweatshirt smiles at him as he goes by. He turns back to get another look at her and runs into a parking meter. Now, sitting on his butt in the gutter, the pretty girl in the blue sweatshirt is asking him if he's alright. There is real concern but she's also smiling. He nods, unable to speak because the air in his lungs was violently expelled upon impact with the parking meter. He doesn't want her to think him a bigger idiot than he's already shown himself to be, so he attempts to strike a cool pose. Contorted in pain and with a dopey grin plastered on his face, he realizes that rather than appearing cool he probably looks ridiculous. But still, she continues gazing at him. Her eyes wander down to the bandage on his chin. She's waiting, he realizes. She's giving me a chance. He attempts to take in some air which results in muffled gagging. Finally, her eyebrows rise up and she exhales softly. Then she's gone, walking away. Everything in his body and mind screams: stop her! Don't let her get away! You want to get to know this woman. You want to sit with her and listen to her form long, rambling sentences. You want to see her eyes get sleepy and sweet. You want to hear her laugh and tell you the story about the time she got drunk and told her father that bears in the woods know nothing about the Pope being Catholic. The air still won't come. He stumbles to his feet, gulping and gagging. I will chase her down, he declares to himself. I will physically stop her. Suddenly air rushes into his lungs. In a voice loud enough to turn the heads of everyone on the busy sidewalk he bellows, "PIZZA, TONIGHT?" Bonnie stops walking and turns around. Three years later they're married. Long dark hair against the white wedding dress, eyes glistening with held back tears. Uncle Bob loudly sneezing just after Bonnie's, "I do." Without missing a beat Bonnie turns, spots his trade-mark blue plaid sport-coat and says, "God bless you, Bob." Laughter echoes in the church. After eleven hours of labor, Drake's writhing baby body. Bonnie's face lit up like he's never seen it before. Engagement, honeymoon, nothing has transformed her like becoming a mother. He feels the shift, a powerful connection flowing from Bonnie to himself to his new son. They are a family. Bonnie's anguished face. Miscarriage number two has shaken her. Five months she'd carried the baby girl. Drake is quiet. He seems to know his mother's pain. He won't leave her side. It is as if they were in this together, the two of them. Gil feels strangely on the outside. Swimming in the deep blue eyes of Heather. Running in the park, her stride is strong. She is a Pirate fan. Heather's touch on his shoulder moves him in a way he hasn't felt in a long time. This isn't real he tells himself. Still, he meets her at a pub in Shadyside to watch the Pirates play Cincinnati. She is different than Bonnie, less self-assured, more at odds with life. His wedding ring seems to weigh 80 pounds. Coffee, lunches — she makes him feel like he's sparking on all cylinders. One night he comes home and Bonnie knows.

"I was grieving the loss of our child," Bonnie said.

"So was I. But you cut me off."

"I was upset."

"And I wasn't?"

"Obviously not. You went off and screwed some other woman."

"I didn't have sex with her."

"I don't care!"

There is she-lion intensity in her eyes that he has never seen before. It both intimidates and captivates him. He begins to talk to her. He tells her his feelings about the miscarriage and not being connected to her. He explains to her about meeting Heather while running in the park. Heather let him in. He needed that. He never slept with her. He never even kissed her. Bonnie hears it all stoically. Then she breaks down and reaches for him. That night they make love. Lindsey is conceived. Looking like she stepped out of a Gerber Baby Food commercial, Lindsey is perfect. She is beautiful and she is a rascal. Born on Gil's birthday, Lindsey is bolder than Drake and more to the point. Unlike her brother she is not particularly patient. Gil cannot spend enough time with Lindsey. Tucked into the jogging stroller, she is his favorite companion on his daily run in the park.

Gil glances away from the photograph on the easel and puts an end to his montage of memories. Eric Clapton's, "Tears in Heaven" is playing. Around him tissues flutter. Eyes are dabbed. His mother quietly blows her nose. Gil sees Mitch Bernstein, Drake's best friend since nursery school, sobbing into his father's shoulder. Gil clenches his fists. He didn't want the children to come. They don't need to suffer any more from the accident. Most of all he doesn't want them to be touched by his rage. He knows how children can feel things that adults have become desensitized to. He experienced it with his own children. Drake knew his mood the minute he saw him. Even when Bonnie didn't know, Drake knew. He was smart that way. There was no hiding from him.

Gil looks back to the photograph of Bonnie and the kids. He tries to open his heart and feel the love that must be there, but it doesn't work. The rage blacks everything out. He wants to kill. He wants justice. He tries to contain the darkness. Don't let the children feel this, he commands himself. Don't let the children feel this, don't let the children feel this, don't let the children feel this.

By the time his parents returned to Hilton Head at the end of January, Gil had buried his wife and children, donated their belongings to charity, gained twenty pounds, and he was back to work. He also found something constructive to do with his rage. Instead of quietly dreaming of murder, he launched himself into campaigns against General Motors, the county, and the police department. For the next several months his every waking hour was occupied with punishing someone for what had happened to his family. At work he was all over the place. At first his fellow employees were patient with him. Gil had known many of his co-workers since he was a boy. He went to their children's birthday parties and celebrated their promotions. Since joining Linnetti Insurance full time after college he had become good cop to his father's bad cop. When Frank retired and turned the company over to him, the entire staff threw Gil a party. But after the accident their patience lasted two months. Gil's inability to focus, and his brutally sharp tongue turned the office into a war zone. A once healthy cadre of employees suddenly began calling in sick. Lunches stretched to three hours. Meetings became opportunities to vent. Productivity lagged. Finally Fritz Timmerman, the second in command behind Gil, was forced to call Frank. Frank ordered Gil to step down and find a grief counselor. Gil didn't argue. His father was right. The company shouldn't be subjected to his suffering. On a rainy night five days after leaving the company, Gil drove away from his house. The chaotic jumble in his mind was calmed by the steady thump, thump, thump of the windshield wipers going back and forth. The act of steering the car gave him focus and a feeling of control. His neighborhood was quiet, the houses beaming soft yellow light through the misting rain. As he passed a large, two-story brick contemporary, he noticed the drapes in the front room were open. Gil slowed down, peering in the window. No one was there. Mike and Rose were probably upstairs helping Tommy and Cydney with their homework. Two houses down, the vintage mustang in front of Bob Marshall's house had a new dent in the right rear fender. Joncie, Bob's oldest daughter, had just started driving. The rain came down harder. Gil drove on. Terry and Kim's house on the corner had only one light on. Maybe they were out to dinner. Their son, Terry Jr., played soccer with Drake. Across the street, Mark and Sue Fudoli had twins a year older than Lindsey. Their big two-story house looked down on the road in a blaze of light. Gil turned away, averting his eyes. It was too much. He had barbequed with all of these people. Their kids played together. He shuttled their children home from soccer practice and school and camp. He made them lunches and read them stories during sleepovers. They were a tribe, a community. Now they still had their families and he was alone.

Gil had arrived at Hargrove Avenue without consciously realizing where he was headed. He parked the car leaving the headlights shining on the oak tree. The exposed wood pulp at the point of impact had darkened. Healing already, Gil thought bitterly, how dare you. He snapped off the headlights. The intersection was reduced to blacks and grays. The rain drumming against the roof of the car got louder. Gil unfastened his seat belt and leaned back against the headrest.

There were no skid marks from either vehicle, the police said. The impact zone was in the middle of the intersection. Gil closed his eyes. For the thousandth time he tried to see how the accident happened. Bonnie is at the stop sign on Gorham. The Suburban is coming south down Hargrove Avenue. Bonnie pulls out onto Hargrove. The Suburban hits the Honda broadside. The police said the Suburban was traveling in excess of sixty miles an hour. Pieces of the Honda were found fifty yards away. The Suburban plows the Honda twenty yards, slamming it into the oak tree, then the Suburban careens off, rolls thirty yards down Hargrove, and begins to burn.

Why would Bonnie pull out? That's what he couldn't understand. How could she not see it? Yes, Steven Davenport told the police that the Suburban's headlights were off, but it's a huge vehicle. How could Bonnie not have seen it? She'd never had an accident in her life. Why then, with Drake and Lindsey in the car? Why couldn't it have been in the parking lot of the grocery store? Why not a fender bender on one of the streets in the neighborhood? Why at that moment? Had she done it on purpose? Was she punishing him for something?

He knew that blaming Bonnie wasn't the answer. Intentionally killing her children and herself was not a possibility. His mind was desperate to attach some kind of reason for their random deaths. His guilt bludgeoned him for months. Why had he sat at home reading the newspaper while Bonnie went to pick up the kids? Alone in my own juices, he cheerfully thought as Bonnie had left the house that night. Twenty minutes of delicious quiet. And he had enjoyed himself. The ticking of the clock on the mantel was the only sound he heard as he read the sports section. Drake wasn't thundering up and down the stairs. Lindsey wasn't crying about being teased. He was a man alone, and it was quiet. But what if he had been driving? Could he have avoided the accident? What if he had taken his Land Rover? It was a much bigger car than the Honda. Would his family have survived? Would they be alive if he hadn't coveted a few minutes of quiet?

Rain was falling in sweeping curtains across Hargrove Avenue. Gil jerked open the car door and got out. Reluctant to cross the killing ground, he had hesitated before stepping away from the car and walking to the tree. He was soaked by the time he got there. Running his fingers through his sopping hair, he pushed it back from his face. The smell of wet leaves and earth was pungent under the oak. Reaching out, Gil pressed his fist against the tree's exposed wound. He ground his knuckles against the rough wood. If you hadn't been here, he thought, maybe they would have lived. As if in response he was suddenly aware of the sound of moving water. In the gully behind the oak tree, he could see the rain-swollen creek. A fifteen-foot drop, he thought. They may not have survived that either.

Gil looked back at the intersection. What kind of sick human being would run away from an accident like that? Carjacker or not, how does a man leave a woman and children trapped and helpless. The carjacker didn't know if they were dead? There was gas all over the road. The fire in the Suburban could have spread to the Honda. A small man, Davenport had told the police, with brown hair. That was all he saw when the man jumped in the Suburban and took off. Davenport, on his way home from working at his office, had stopped along the road to call his wife. He didn't like driving and talking on the phone, he told police. He'd heard about too many accidents happening that way. As he pulled out his cell phone to dial, the carjacker jerked the door open, yanked Steven from behind the wheel, jumped in and drove off. It happened so quickly that Steven barely saw the man. Any forensic evidence had been destroyed because of the fire that engulfed the Suburban. The police had no clues.

Gil leaned back against the trunk of the tree. The rain was beating steadily down on him. He was tired of raging at the world. And he was tired of missing his family. As a car came north up Hargrove Avenue the headlights struck him and then the car rushed by with its tires hissing water. Rain drummed on the roof of the car. The creek burbled contentedly in the gully. It isn't such a bad place, Gil thought. At least I don't feel so alone.

He never left Hargrove Avenue.

13

Steven Davenport pressed the accelerator and swung into the passing lane. The traffic on Interstate 79 was light. He would be in Everton in no time. He hoped to take care of his business with Darla and be home before dinner. He turned up the volume on the CD player. Wagner's *The Valkyrie* was playing. Siegmund had just pulled the sword from the tree and he and Sieglinde were escaping into the woods. Steven smiled fondly. It was his favorite opera. That it was completed in 1856 but not performed until 1870 mystified him. He believed it held some of the most powerful music ever written.

Steven considered what his approach should be with Darla. He didn't want to be too threatening. That might backfire on him. It was a matter of reminding her of the responsibility she carried for what happened to Mrs. Linnetti and her children. Shame, he had found, was a powerful tool in keeping young girls quiet.

At a dinner party years earlier he'd experienced one of those impulsive moments that completely overwhelmed and surprised him. He could have easily been caught had he not reacted quickly and decisively. He had left Marjorie and the rest of the party to go alone into his client's study to see the oak paneling and floor to ceiling bookshelves that had recently been installed. As he was admiring the workmanship he heard a noise from under the large mahogany desk near the windows. Steven walked around behind it. The eight-year-old daughter of his client was sitting cross-legged under the desk. She looked up at him with wide-set green eyes and a grumpy frown.

Steven grinned. "Have you ever put ketchup on pancakes?"

The girl's frown disappeared. She began to giggle. To Steven it was a cool splash of water on a hot August afternoon. The next thing he knew he had both arms tightly wrapped around her and was rocking her in his lap. The girl's tears didn't faze him at first. He was in over-drive — that blind surge of blood, which sometimes when he wasn't vigilant, swept him up and allowed him to do things that he wouldn't ordinarily do. Her fist hitting him on the thigh brought him out of it. The girl opened her mouth to scream and he clamped his hand over it. She glared at him with a fierceness that surprised him. Uh oh, he thought, I need to do something quickly or this is going to be a problem. He glanced to the door of the study. No one was there. He put his mouth to the little girl's ear, "I'm going to tell your Mom and Dad that you've been very, very bad if you don't stop crying right now." Immediately she shut up. "Good girl," he said. "I promise I won't tell anyone about how bad you are unless you make me do it. And if I do tell them, you will be in so much trouble. Do you understand? Now go upstairs to your room and go to sleep, right now." She nodded her head, wiped her tears, and walked out of the room. Returning to the party, Steven calmly drank a vodka and soda while chit-chatting with an architect Marjorie had met. At any moment he half-expected his client to storm into the room and confront him. But after twenty minutes nothing happened. There was no inconsolable crying and most importantly, no pointed fingers. That night, he took Marjorie home and made love to her more tenderly than he had in a long time. After Marjorie had drifted off, he lay awake remembering the fierce look in the little girl's eyes. She was brave, Steven thought, very brave.

• • • • •

Darla scooped mint chocolate chip ice cream onto a cone and vanilla strawberry swirl into a cup and handed them across the glass counter to a bushy-bearded, grinning man.

"Thanks Darla." He bobbed his black eyebrows up and down. He handed the vanilla strawberry swirl to the petite brunette standing next to him.

"Diet, shmyit." The woman dug her spoon into the ice cream. "This looks yummy."

Darla grinned and took the ten-dollar bill the man handed her. Mr. Lersch was a mathematics professor at Grove City College. Every weekend he and his wife came to Harmony Orchards to buy produce and ice cream. During the year that Darla had worked the counter, she noticed that most of her customers had favorite flavors and ordered them each time they came in. Not the Lerschs. Every week they tried something new. Mr. Soergel, the manager of Harmony Orchards, told her that the Lerschs were genuine ice cream enthusiasts. "They've been coming here for years," he said, "every Sunday, snow or rain. They buy peaches in the summer, apples in fall, and ice cream all year round."

Mrs. Lersch, a wise-cracking ex-beauty queen from New Mexico, once told Darla that the way to a woman's heart was through consistent exposure to chocolate fudge ice cream.

"My, my, my," Mrs. Lersch said. "I'm about boots up in heaven. This is sooo goood."

Darla handed Mr. Lersch his change. "Have a good rest of the weekend."

"We'll do." He licked a smear of mint chocolate chip from the corner of his mouth. "You have yourself a fine one, Darla."

"Thanks, sweetie." Mrs. Lersch gave her a wave.

They picked up their bags of groceries and walked toward the door. Across the store, Darla spotted Tracy Rockwell and Jimmy Vita coming toward the ice cream counter. Hippies Smell Nice was boldly printed across the front of Jimmy's T-shirt. He shot her the peace sign.

"Hey you guys."

Tracy stretched a green piece of chewing gum out of her mouth, wound it around her finger, stuck her finger in her mouth and pulled the gum off. Darla grimaced. Ever since the three of them were in first grade, Tracy had been doing that with her gum. In Darla's opinion it was childish and uncouth. When she encouraged Tracy to stop, Tracy said, "Better than plucking split-ends like you."

As they approached the counter Tracy caught Darla's frown. "Don't even say anything."

"Gum puller."

"Hair picker."

"You two are wacked," Jimmy said.

Both of the girls turned to him. "Dick grabber," they said in unison.

Jimmy blushed. "It's a guy thing."

"So is standing up to pee," Tracy said. "But you don't do that in public, do you?"

"Bite me."

Tracy made an exaggerated chewing gesture then laughed. Darla picked up her scoop.

"Do you guys want a cone? I'll give you my discount."

Out came the gum, the finger twirl, and the return. "Nah," Tracy said. "Not for me."

Jimmy shook his head. "No thanks. But hey, you're done soon, right?"

"Forty-five minutes." Darla glanced at the clock hanging over the dried fruit aisle.

"Cool," Jimmy said. "You wanna go to the outlet stores, hang out?"

Tracy nodded enthusiastically. "I think Crystal and Danny will be there."

Darla shrugged. "Thanks you guys but I have stuff to do at home."

"Oh." Jimmy shot a glance at Tracy.

Tracy leaned against the counter. "Okay, what's the deal with you? We've tried not to bug you. I mean you've been weird for months. Is there something, or maybe *someone* you need to tell us about?"

"Opera Man." Jimmy grinned.

Tiny prickles raced across Darla's scalp. She'd never told them about opera or Steven Davenport.

"Who?" Darla tried to look innocent.

Tracy and Jimmy exchanged a look.

"You know when your Mom came and talked to me," Tracy said, "when she was all worried about you and stuff."

"Yeah."

Tracy pulled her gum out and gave it a half twirl. "The thing I didn't mention to you was that she told me that you've been listening to opera music. Okay, that's kinda' wacked right there. I've known you since before you could spell opera. And I *know*, as good as I know that Jimmy will grab his dick at least three times in third period study hall that you wouldn't just decide, hey, opera music is cool, think I'll download some. I know you, hair-picker. Some guy turned you on to it, didn't he? I know it. And I've been trying to figure out who it is. Other than the time you said Kevin McDonaugh had a cute butt you haven't given anybody in school a second look. And I know Kevin didn't tell you about opera." Tracy pulled her gum out, did a double twirl, and plopped it back in her mouth. "Sooooo, are you going to tell us about opera man?"

Darla looked from Tracy to Jimmy and then back to Tracy. Slowly she began to shake her head. "You guys are really nuts. It was in a magazine at the library, that's where I read about opera. And like I told you before, the reason I was being weird was because I was going through a hormone thing. You know, mood swings and all that stuff."

Jimmy and Tracy eyed her intently. Darla knew they were searching for the tell-tale hint of a lie: a downward glance, a nervous smile, or a catch in her throat. She held her body motionless and kept her gaze steady. They can't find out about this, she told herself. No one can.

Jimmy was the first to look away. "Okay, whatever. It's just that we don't see you anymore."

Tracy pouted her lower lip. "I miss you."

A woman in a wide-brimmed sun hat with two young children walked up behind them. The tow-headed little boy holding the woman's right hand looked up at her with a wide grin and said, "Peach sherbet for me Mom. Please." The girl, taller and wearing red-framed sunglasses, said confidently, "Mocha mint, double scoop, please."

Tracy turned to leave. "Call me." Jimmy shot Darla the peace sign and fell in behind Tracy.

Darla watched them walk away feeling more alone than ever. How could she tell them about Steven Davenport? Why should they be burdened with the knowledge that her carefree life as a teenager was over? She didn't want to drag them into the same hole into which she'd thrown herself. And anyway, she was battling forces far more important than the fun to be had drinking mocha lattes at Starbucks or root beers at Pete's Pretzels. She was fighting to protect Gil Linnetti.

"May I have a peach sherbet in a small cup and a mocha mint on a sugar cone?" It was the woman in the hat.

"Double scoop, please," the little girl said.

The woman sighed. "Double scoop of the mocha mint."

The woman lifted her brown leather backpack purse to the counter and pulled out a wallet. Darla picked up a clean scoop and dug into the tub of peach sherbet. She raised the full scoop and then abruptly stopped. She looked at the woman.

"Can you hold on a minute?" She put down the scoop. "I'll be right back." She hurried around from behind the counter, and ran toward the door.

In the parking lot, Jimmy and Tracy were getting into Jimmy's Chevy pickup.

"Hey!"

They turned to see Darla standing outside the front door.

"I'll meet you there at three o'clock." Darla pointed at them. "Starbucks, okay?"

Tracy gave her a big smile and a wave. Jimmy let out a whoop, reached into the truck, and honked the horn twice.

· · · · ·

Everton's quaint tree-lined streets surrounding an open central square reminded Steven of communities he had seen in New England. He and Marjorie made two trips to the northeast. Once in college to ski at Stowe, Vermont, and the other, a ten-day fall color tour a year after Elizabeth disappeared. At the time they had briefly considered moving there. Marjorie thought a quiet place in the country would help her get over Elizabeth's absence. After a day of discussion, she'd reconsidered. She was afraid that if they moved, Elizabeth would not be able to locate them when she returned home. "I want to make it easy for her to find us," Marjorie had said, and he agreed. Moving would upset the balance they had found in Pittsburgh. He had access to a large pool of corporate wealth and Marjorie had all the social amenities she had grown to appreciate. "That private investigator is going to find her, I know it," Marjorie said. "He's the best, right?" "Yes," he'd told her, "with an outrageous weekly retainer to prove it." But what Marjorie didn't know was that he had fired the investigator two days after hiring him. "A family friend stepped in to help us," Steven had explained to him, handing him a full week's retainer in cash. For the next three years Steven micro-managed the private investigator contact info, and passed on completely fabricated oral reports to Marjorie.

Before entering the shady, residential streets of Everton, Steven passed through miles of cornfields. Buffering the town in its protective expanse, Everton corn was highly sought after. People came from all over the tri-state area to buy it. There was something in the soil, they said, or special seeds handed down through generations that made the corn sweet and tender.

Steven braked suddenly as a basketball shot across the road twenty feet in front of his car. A lanky, crew-cut teenager in baggy shorts and a sweat-soaked T-shirt stopped at the curb. Steven waved him across. The boy sprang from the curb and went after the ball. Steven waited until he picked it up and jogged safely back to the driveway. The teenager glanced over his shoulder and nodded to Steven. Steven raised his fingers from the steering wheel in a half-wave and accelerated down the street. A fine corn-fed lad, he absently thought.

At the end of the block, Steven looked up at the street sign — Ferguson Drive. The navigation in his car told him to turn left. A few more blocks and he'd turn right on Quimby Street. After a mile or so he'd take a left. Darla lived at 1406 Falcon Drive. He was almost there.

• • • • •

The Ford Escort was making a sound Darla never heard before. Somewhere between a thump and a gurgle, it had started just after she pulled out of the Harmony Orchards parking lot.

"Come on Essie girl," Darla urged the ten year old car, "get me home."

Purchased at a public auction in New Castle, the rear quarter panel of the Escort was dented and the trunk rusted through in two places. Darla didn't mind. When Uncle Brady and her father had given it to her three months before her sixteenth birthday she immediately loved the car like a new found sister. Essie, as she quickly named it, wasn't pretty but the car would get her where she wanted to go.

Darla checked the dashboard again. No red lights were on. The noise didn't seem to be getting worse but it wasn't going away.

She patted the dashboard. "You can do it."

If she could make it home, she would borrow her mother's car to drive to the outlet stores. Hopefully her mother would be home. Ever since she'd been let go from the bank and was doing full-time tutoring, her mom was all over the place. Sometimes she drove an hour to work with a student. On other days, kids came to the house. The summer hadn't slowed down her schedule much.

Darla knew that calling Tracy and Jimmy and telling them she couldn't come would be a disaster. They'd think she was blowing them off on purpose. And besides, she wanted to go. It would be fun. Like the old days. Time with them might be just the thing she needed. With a sigh of relief Darla turned right on Falcon Street. She was almost home.

The white two-story with green shutters was across the street and down one house. Steven immediately noticed the discolored siding and the missing bricks in the crown of the chimney. Fresh pulp marks up the trunk of the pin oak at the corner of the house told him that it had recently been pruned. The dirt-streaked Ford Taurus parked in the driveway had definitely seen better days.

Steven shut off the ignition. The other cars parked along the street were mostly older American models. His new BMW stood out like a shiny dime in a pile of corroded pennies. He hoped Darla wouldn't notice it right away. He wanted to have a chance to surprise her.

Steven looked down the street. It wasn't such a bad place, he thought. In her emails Darla described it as run-down and boring. It was a working-class neighborhood not much different from where he had grown up in Akron. Steven leaned his head back, remembering the sooty brick row houses along Crafton Road. Backed up against a steep hill there were no back yards to speak of so he was always out playing in the street. Paul Schmitt, his best friend, lived next door on the corner. The Nierling girls, and Joe and Roy Brewer lived at the other end of the block. In the summer they played kickball and Frisbee tag in the street. Kelly played too. She was better than most of the boys. Then the Schmitts moved to Delaware and his mother died of stomach cancer.

A car was coming. Steven blinked away the memories of his childhood and swung his eyes straight down Falcon Street.

"Yes," Darla exclaimed, seeing her mother's car in the driveway. She quickly parked in front of the house. The Escort chugged and wheezed when she shut off the ignition. That's not a good sign, Darla thought. Dad will have to take a look at it when he gets home from work. She grabbed her backpack, jumped out of the car, and ran to the front door.

She's grown, Steven thought, watching her cross the yard. She's even prettier. Darla reached the front door and opened it. Unlocked, he thought. That's good to know. Darla disappeared inside the house. Steven reached for his cell phone. He would simply call her and tell her to look out the window. He hesitated before dialing. The trouble with using his cell phone was that he wouldn't be able to look into her eyes. He wanted to know how committed Darla was to the game she was playing. He wouldn't be able to get a good read over the telephone. If he wanted to know what he was up against, he would have to get her alone.

A door slammed. Steven looked up. Darla was running across the lawn. She had changed her shirt and instead of athletic shoes she was wearing sandals. She ran to the Taurus, opened the driver-side door, and got in. The car started. Steven smiled. Yes, he thought. This is going to work out fine.

14

Darla ran the brush through her hair one more time then checked for split ends. The Taurus drifted to the right. She glanced up. Cornfields lined both sides of the road. She nudged the wheel to the left and went back to her inspection. Why, she agonized, after trying eight different kinds of conditioner couldn't she find one that helped. Was she going to be plagued with frizzy ends for the rest of her life? It wasn't like she didn't take care of her hair. She pulled a pink clip out of her purse, gathered her hair on top of her head and clipped it. There, she thought, out of sight out of mind.

She put both hands back on the steering wheel and pressed her foot on the accelerator. The car surged forward. She loved driving the Taurus. It was much faster than Essie. She turned up the volume on her phone. Natasha Bedingfeld boomed through her ear buds. She let herself go with the music, bobbing her head as she sang along. Out of the corner of her left eye she saw movement. A car was passing her. She glanced down at the speedometer. She was going 55 miles an hour. The speed limit was 50. Somebody's in a hurry, she thought. She kept both hands on the wheel like her father had taught her and concentrated on staying in her lane. The car paused as it came abreast of her. Come on, Darla thought, pass me don't just sit there. A horn honked. Startled, Darla turned and looked at the driver of other car. Steven Davenport grinned back at her.

The Taurus veered sharply to the right sending up a rooster tail of dirt from the side of the road. Darla screamed as the car careened half on and half off the road. A sign for Interstate 79 loomed directly in front of her. She swung back onto the road just missing the sign but sending the Taurus fishtailing across both lanes. An eighteen-wheeler bearing down on her from the other direction blew its air horn. Darla yanked the wheel to the right fighting to get back on her side of the road. The Taurus shot across the double yellow line, hit the berm and sent dirt flying. The truck roared past blaring its horn. Darla slammed on the brakes. The car skidded sideways and came to a stop in a cloud of dust on the side of the road.

Her knuckles bone white on the steering wheel and with a taste like blood in her mouth, Darla stared out the windshield at the empty road. "Shit," she muttered. "*Shit*."

She turned in her seat and looked back. The truck was disappearing in the distance. No other cars were on the road. She twisted around and faced the windshield. Had she imagined it? Was her mind messing with her? She leaned her forehead on the steering wheel.

She thought of the day when she parked by Mr. Linnetti's campsite and put the gun to her head. With the snout, as her father called the muzzle, pressed against the side of her head, she was able to imagine escaping into a serene blank void free of feelings and turmoil and self-doubt. Peace – she wanted peace. And no more crying. No more bad thoughts about herself and what she'd done. With her finger tensing on the trigger, Darla had closed her eyes, let out a final sigh, and surrendered to the sweet freedom. But before the final muscle contraction that would have forever delivered her from her pain, Darla was startled by the image of a little girl – Gil Linnetti's daughter. Darla's eyes had flown open and she jerked back in the seat. The gun went off, ripping a groove in the molding around her door instead of sending the bullet through her brain.

In his rear-view mirror Steven had watched as the truck nearly hit Darla's car. He made a quick, screeching right turn onto a narrow dirt road and parked the BMW between rows of corn. He merely wanted her to pull over so they could talk, but if the truck had hit her, hey, that wouldn't be such a bad thing. Her foolish note writing and phone calling games would be over. He jumped out of the car and began jogging through the corn toward the Taurus parked next to the highway.

Darla lifted her head from the steering wheel. Her brain wasn't spinning any longer. Everything had finally slowed down. Looking at herself in the rear view mirror, Darla rolled her eyes at the sight of her mascara all over her cheeks. She reached into her pack for her makeup. Her hand brushed the walnut grip of the .357. She reached around the revolver for the pouch containing her cosmetics. She pulled it out, unzipped it and — the passenger door swung open and Steven Davenport dropped into the seat. Before she could react, he reached over, turned off the car, and pulled the keys out of the ignition.

"Darla, we need to talk."

She stared at him, uncertain if he was real. She had just convinced herself that seeing him had been a guilt vision stirred up because she trying to be a normal teenager and hang out with her friends.

"This can't go on." Davenport leaned closer. "Leaving notes and calling me isn't safe."

Darla rubbed the pad of her thumb on the stubbly surface of her makeup pouch. Her mother had given it to her last year for her birthday. Made out of silk and beads it was from a country that Darla couldn't remember.

"I know you were frightened," Davenport said. "I saw the bodies too. It was awful, especially the little boy."

The scenes of that night, like her own private horror film, flashed in her mind. She saw herself fighting away from the airbag and climbing out of the Suburban. Flames lapped up the sides of the fender. Running toward the wreckage of the other car, she heard singing. It was strangely familiar. When she got to the Honda the boy was the first one she saw. The sight of his injuries sent her reeling back. In that moment of extreme horror she recognized the music coming from the car. It was from *The Big Blue Dog,* her favorite TV show when she was a kid. *...and the big blue dog barks woof, woof, woof and he wags his tail and* — Someone shouted and she looked up the street. Steven Davenport was running toward her. Headlights were coming the other way up Hargrove. The next thing she knew she was scrambling up a hill. With her purse in one hand and her shoes clutched in the other, she tore through the woods. Her feet were freezing by the time she made it to her car.

So much had changed since earlier that evening when she'd parked on the quiet side street. She had been full of anticipation. She was meeting a man, the man who had given her opera. He would hold her. His eyes would be gentle and kind. "You're beautiful," he would say. "I'm a lucky man." Then he would kiss her and her world would blur and bend and lift and it would be amazing. Just like on TV.

But that wasn't what happened. Parking her car a block from where she was to meet him, Darla had primped in the mirror for ten minutes before getting out of the car. Finally satisfied that everything looked just right, she walked the short distance with a giddy bounce in her step. Underneath her mother's overcoat she wore a new black dress. "You look hot in that," the sales woman had said when Darla tried it on. It took a big chunk out of her savings but it was worth it. She felt sexy and grown up.

Standing by the bus stop bench where he'd told her to meet him, Darla worried about her ability to continue walking in the black pumps. Taken from her mother's closet, they were a half size too small and her toes were already starting to go numb.

"Darla?" he'd said through the open window when he pulled up next to her. Gray at the temples, blue eyes smiling warmly, he was older than she thought but very handsome. She got in the car. His hand was cold when she took it. "Are you hungry?" he asked. It took 45 minutes to drive to the restaurant. She should have known then that he was trying to get away from anyone who might recognize him. In a high-backed corner booth, the low lighting giving them privacy from the rest of the diners, he smiled at her and suggested that they order appetizers. In the warm yellow candlelight Darla tried to focus as she scanned the menu. Other than her mashed toes she felt as if she were in a dream. Dressed in a classy gray suit and black turtleneck, he was handsome and obviously successful. The Suburban he was driving was brand new with leather seats. And the sound system was incredible. *Tosca* had never sounded so good to her. When she looked up from the menu to tell him that she would like the buffalo mozzarella with tomatoes and basil, he was staring at her. The intensity of his look immediately made her uncomfortable. She quickly glanced back down at the menu. When she looked up again he was buttering a roll. "Would you like one," he'd asked politely. Then everything seemed fine — for a while.

"I'm sorry for what happened." Behind Davenport corn stalks rustled in the breeze. Darla didn't want to look at him. She didn't want to believe that he was actually in the car with her.

"I never should have reacted like that." Davenport rubbed his hand on his thigh. "It's just that — you looked so beautiful and I'm really attracted to you, I just…" His voice trailed off. Darla shifted her eyes to him. He was slowly shaking his head. "I couldn't stop myself. You were too sexy. I was too turned on."

Darla felt it. She couldn't deny it. To be wanted so badly was exhilarating. It startled her to know that Davenport could still have that effect on her. How screwed up am I, she thought? He was looking at her now. It was the same unsettling stare he had given her at dinner. This time she didn't look away. A power that had been percolating just beneath the surface of her young awareness reared its seductive head. It moved Darla past her fear, filling her with a sense of control that she had not yet realized was hers to possess.

"I made a mistake." Davenport fiddled with her keys. "And it led to a horrible tragedy. I'm sorry that I put you in that position. I truly am. But nothing we can do will bring back that mother or her children." He flipped her house key with his thumb. "Like we talked about after the accident, if I came forward," he pointed the key at her face, "if I took responsibility for what happened, I couldn't do anything to protect you. You were driving too fast. You didn't turn on the headlights and you ran away from the scene. *You* killed them, not me." He let his words sink in. "You'll go to jail or some juvenile detention center. Those places are not safe for a young, beautiful girl like you." He grimaced dramatically. "It would be awful. Just *awful*."

Darla reached up and took the pink clip from her hair. She shook her head like she'd seen girls do in the movies. Her hair settled softly on her shoulders. He was looking at her now, curious about what she was doing. Yes, she thought, look at me. She reached for the top button of her shirt and slowly unbuttoned it. She watched Steven's eyes follow her fingers. After the second button his face went from curious to something else. It was similar to the look on his face when he pinned her against the side of the car and forced his fingers inside of her. Hungry, Darla thought. He looks hungry. She undid the third button and opened her shirt. It was her nice bra, the sheer pink one she'd gotten for Christmas. His eyes roamed over her breasts. Yes, she thought, don't take your eyes off of them. She reached for the front clasp of her bra then hesitated. A look of challenge came into her eyes.

"Lean back. I want you to watch."

His eyes remained on her but he didn't move. Darla felt a drop of sweat roll down her side. Halfway to her hip it stopped. She remained perfectly still and let him look at her with those hungry eyes. She remembered the sound he made grinding up against her as she struggled to get away. Not groans of pleasure, it had a desperate edge to it, like a ravenous dog devouring a steak.

Darla moved her hands submissively to her sides. "It's okay. Relax."

Davenport moved then, slowly easing back against the passenger side door.

A warm rush of heat radiated from the center of Darla's body. He was doing what she wanted. She had the power. She was in control. She reached up and slipped her shirt off of her left shoulder. His eyes shifted to take in this newly revealed portion of her skin. She let him linger a moment then she slipped the shirt off her other shoulder. In the instant of the shift, when his eyes moved from her left to her right shoulder, Darla reached into her bag and pulled out the .357. In a quick, smooth motion she pulled back the hammer, raised the gun, and pointed it at his chest.

Davenport reacted, moving back and up, bumping his head first on the window then the roof of the Taurus. Darla watched, detached and oddly calm. He opened his mouth to speak. Darla raised the gun and pointed it at his face. He quickly closed his mouth.

That's right, Darla thought, remembering her protests muffled against the palm of his hand while his other hand roamed her body, touching her in ways that made her feel sick and angry.

"Don't you want to take it all back?" Her voice surprised her with its strength. "Don't you wish you never went to that chat site, or told me about opera, or raped me?" Her hand began to tremble. She tightened her grip on .357. "You took something from me, and I won't let you pretend you didn't. *You* killed that family. You killed them with me. I was the bullet, but you pulled the trigger." The trembling in her hand got worse. "What made you think you could do that to me? I wasn't there for sex. I wanted — to see a bigger part of the world. Was that so wrong?" She wiped tears from her cheek with her other hand. Davenport started to say something. "No! No talking!"

He lowered his eyes submissively. He focused on the pink hair clip perched on the seat.

"If you thought you could come here and scare me," Darla said, "and get me to leave you alone, that's not going to happen." She steadied her hand. The .357 was pointed at the center of Davenport's chest. End it now, she thought. It will be just like at the shooting range. He's here and then he's gone. No more worries. She studied the place on his chest where the gun was pointed. Between the second and third button, that would do it. She imagined the roar of the gun and the jolt in her hands. The bullet would leave a small hole going in and a larger hole coming out. There would be blood, lots of it. There would be pieces of him on the inside of her mother's car. She wouldn't have to worry about him any more. But her parents would know.

"How many other girls have you done this to?"

Davenport cleared his throat. "It was a mistake. I'm sorry. I got carried away."

"Answer my question!"

"No one else. You were… I couldn't stop myself."

"Shut up!"

"No really, it was you. You were too much for me to resist."

"Fuck you."

Darla pulled the trigger. The loud click of the hammer jerked Davenport back as his face clenched and contorted. Darla shot him a vicious smile.

"I left an empty chamber. It was too much for me to resist."

His expression darkened and she thought he was going to try and hit her. It was like the look on his face when she'd gotten away from him after the rape. He had moved his hand from her mouth and nose to reach down and pull up his pants. As he started to get up she kicked him as hard as she could in the groin. Rolling away from him and jumping into the Suburban, she had roared down Hargrove Avenue frantically trying to find the switch for the headlights. Then the Honda pulled out in front of her.

"Put the keys on the floor," Darla said.

Steven slowly laid them at his feet.

"Now get out of the car. If you don't want to get shot I'd stay away from me and Mr. Linnetti."

15

Thrilled that he had opened up to her, Madison listened intently as Gil told her his story. The part when he met Bonnie and the birth of his children filled in spaces in her mind that for years had been painfully blank. It was strangely comforting to finally know the truth about his life. She no longer had to waste her energy holding him in place. He wasn't a sixteen-year-old running in the park. His long blond hair wasn't long or blond now. She could let her image of him go. It's a step, Madison thought.

But, when Gil started talking about the details of the accident, it was as if she was a lamp that someone suddenly unplugged. She was still there, but the light was gone. Steven Davenport, Gil told her, had reported to the police that the headlights of the Suburban were not on. Steven Davenport said that the carjacker was a small, brown-haired man. Steven Davenport had stopped to call his wife on his cell phone. *Steven Davenport!*

"I'm almost out of Cheerios," Gil shook the Tupperware container sending the remaining cereal ricocheting around inside.

Madison looked up from where she was sitting. "Gil, this Steven Davenport, what else did the police find out about him?"

"He's a financial guy. Deal maker, big shot in town."

"Do the police suspect him?"

Gil turned from where he was rummaging in his food supplies. "Steven? No. He's a good man. A woman in another car saw him running down Hargrove toward the accident." Gil went back to inventorying the food. "He brings me most of my supplies. His wife, Marjorie, she sends cookies and all kinds of stuff. That was him yesterday in the black BMW."

Madison's stomach clenched. In her mind she saw the car pulling away and speeding down Hargrove Avenue.

Gil opened one of the coolers and looked inside. "I hope he comes by soon."

Madison watched him but her mind was far away. Memories were stirring. Her first reaction was to fight, to shove them aside and keep herself safe. But then she stopped. Slowly, and with a great sense of purpose, she let out a long tired breath. Let it come, she thought, allowing herself to relax. Her days of standing guard on the great wall of forgetting were over. She was moving forward in her life. The trip from Oregon to Pittsburgh had shown her that. Talking with Gil about his life had reinforced it. The world was becoming a bigger place, but she couldn't go anywhere with Steven Davenport blocking her way.

Like a wild animal silently stalking her, the memory crept closer. Cautiously making its way through the rubble of her once protective wall, the scent of his cologne was the first to come. Madison's body went rigid. I can't do this, she thought. It will kill me. At the same time she knew she didn't have a choice. She had to move through it. Forcing herself to relax, the next thing to come was the sound of her bed creaking as he lay down next to her — his face — his hands. Madison's heart rate quickened. She told herself that Gil was nearby and that she was safe. But the panic came anyway, languidly coiling around her heart and lungs making it difficult to breathe. The images and sensations, held captive for so long, now lit up bright and threatening inside of her: his fingers caressing the arms and legs of the girl she had once been. Brushing over her stomach then probing lower — "You're so pretty," his voice echoed from a deep, hollow place. Wave upon nauseating wave rolled through her. Her voice stuck in her throat, unsaid words choking her, mouth and tongue working desperately to free themselves. Finally, "Please don't, please don't, please don't, *Dad please don't!*" His hand clamping hard over her mouth as she struggled, wanting desperately to escape her young body, tears flooding her eyes, his naked body rising up, pressing down into her, screaming into his hand as pain ripped her inside. His grunting, jerky motions followed by the sickly gush on her belly — warm blood on her thighs, his slurring voice high above her whispering, "Our secret baby, our secret."

Madison lurched to her feet. Out of the corner of her eye she saw Gil turn and look at her. Embarrassed but unable to stop, she ran to the edge of the trees and threw up. Heaving uncontrollably, her eyes watering and her legs shaking, Madison was horrified at Gil seeing her in such a state. But at the same time, and in a much grander way, she was experiencing a towering sense of victory. Her lonely years atop the wall of forgetting, guarding herself from the memory of her father, were over. She had re-lived her darkest secret and survived.

"Madison, are you okay?"

With her back still to him she called over her shoulder, "My name is Elizabeth."

• • • • •

Marjorie's arms sliced through the water. She turned her head and took a breath. She had the lane to herself and was swimming full out. She ducked into a flip turn. Pushing off the wall she rolled over and switched to backstroke. She imagined a crowd cheering. She pulled hard, enjoying the strain in her shoulders. The ceiling tiles moved past. She wanted to hit her turn just right. She had once lost a race in the conference quarter-finals when she blew her last turn. Stephanie Burgess won that race, a girl she had previously beaten three times. Marjorie stretched for the wall then flipped. Her feet hit and she pushed – perfect. She ended every workout with a backstroke turn. It was a reminder to always stay sharp. She swam a leisurely freestyle to the other end of the pool.

She spotted him when she was half-way up the ladder. As he walked toward her, his stocky, powerful body moved gracefully. He was older than her by several years, but he was in terrific shape. His goggles hung loosely in the fingers of his left hand. He smiled, the skin crinkling around his eyes.

"Hello. How was it today?" His dark eyes swept over her face.

There it is, Marjorie thought — the caress. She didn't know the man's name, she only saw him a couple times a month at the pool, but she appreciated the way he looked at her. He took her in, all of her. It wasn't that she didn't enjoy how Steven made her feel. But sometimes in her marriage she had a sense of having lost how she was perceived as a woman. Not simply as Steven's wife or Elizabeth's mother, but as a woman.

She smiled at him. "It was good. I felt strong."

"Yes." He nodded.

Marjorie started walking away. "Have a good one."

He would turn to watch her, Marjorie knew, so she took her time. She felt the eyes of the men in the Jacuzzi and the others sitting on benches outside the sauna. Fifty-something and I can still get their attention, she thought proudly. When she got to the wall Marjorie lifted her towel off the hook. Wiping her face, she casually turned around. He was standing there looking at her. Again she felt the embrace of his gaze. Men, she thought, such wonderful creatures.

• • • • •

Steven Davenport's second meeting with the surgeons went better than the first. This time he succinctly presented the Arkansas shopping mall deal. Ten of the twelve surgeons liked the idea. The two doubters, both younger than the rest, wanted the group to invest in a new film that George Romero, director of *Night of the Living Dead* was producing. They had met him at a cocktail party and he pitched them on his latest script. The two young surgeons went on and on about budgets and distribution and the famous actors George would cast in the movie. Having read a copy of the script, they delighted in turning everyone's stomachs with the gory details of the blood-drenched climax.

Steven waited. He had maneuvered his way through too many deals to be impatient. The young ones always wanted to initiate their ideas. You had to give them their stage. Let them feel the power of being heard. When they were done, Steven would glance at the older, cooler heads as if to say, jeeze that's idiotic, you smart guys wouldn't go for that, would you? The direct challenge to their business savvy would invariably compel them to rein in their youthful colleagues. Then, with Steven's help, the entire group would come herd-like to the consensus that the best place to invest their capital was with Steven.

The delicate nuance required in making a deal never ceased to intrigue him. Discovering how best to subtly press the right buttons at the right times was to him a delightful journey into the human psyche. From bold declarative statements meant to engage their ego and pride, to one-of-the-boys cajoling, Steven knew the ins and outs of ushering potential investors to sign on to the deal.

It was this much appreciated sense of control that was missing in his encounter with Darla. Yes, she had a gun. A large gun, and it seemed to get bigger the longer it was pointed at him. But still, she was a girl, and a frightened girl at that. He had never backed down before. He always had the courage to take action when it was needed. But his willingness to be bold was buffered by the same instinct that successfully informed him in business. And that highly refined intuitive sense warned him that it was best not to test her. She would have shot him. He knew it in his gut. If he had given her a reason she would have pulled the trigger, and not on an empty chamber. No, Steven told himself, he wouldn't put himself in that girl's sights again. She was dangerous and unpredictable. He didn't get the feeling that she would go to the police, but she wasn't to be fooled with. He imagined her lurking in the woods like a feral cat watching over Gil Linnetti's campsite. It wasn't worth the risk, he concluded. The girl was crazy. As far as Steven was concerned, Gil Linnetti was now on his own.

That night at the house, Marjorie and Steven sat down to a dinner of lemon roasted chicken, French cut green beans, and mushroom risotto. They opened a bottle of California Chardonnay and had fresh blueberries for dessert. Marjorie lit candles and played Chet Baker on the stereo. She wanted Steven to relax and have a good meal. For several days he had been distracted. She suspected it was the Arkansas venture, but she couldn't be sure. Steven had always kept his feelings to himself. And he didn't appreciate prodding attempts to get him to talk about what was bothering him. If he wanted to discuss something he would bring it up.

"Marjorie," Steven said with a warm smile. "That was wonderful. The chicken was done to a turn."

"And the night is just beginning." Marjorie smiled seductively and then dabbed the corners of her mouth with her napkin. She always felt shy after making overt sexual overtures. She loved doing it, and she knew Steven liked it too, but it still made her feel self-conscious. Across the table, Steven grinned. "What do you have in mind, Mrs. Davenport?"

Marjorie stood up and walked over to him. She ran her fingers up the back of his neck. "That's for you to find out my love." She picked up his empty plate. "Take your wine into the other room and relax. I'm going to clean up the dishes." She walked toward the kitchen. "I made some extra for Mr. Linnetti. You can take it to him tomorrow."

Steven frowned. No, he wouldn't be taking it to him tomorrow or any other day. The charity train had come to the end of the line. Steven stood up.

"Don't worry about Linnetti. He doesn't want me coming around any more."

"What?" Marjorie came back into the dining room with a look of surprise on her face. "What happened?"

"Nothing. I think it probably became too difficult for him. Seeing me all the time reminds him of what happened."

"He's living across the street from where they died. Why would you be any more of a reminder?"

Steven looked at her blankly then shrugged. "I don't know, Marjorie. He doesn't want us there. That's all I can tell you." Steven picked up his wine glass and walked out of the dining room.

Marjorie stared at the remaining dishes on the table. She was irritated and she wasn't sure why. She had enjoyed providing for Gil Linnetti. Doing so helped mitigate her feelings of responsibility. If their car hadn't been involved, Mr. Linnetti's family might still be alive. But, she admitted, if he didn't want any more of their help that was his business. So why was she irritated? Maybe it was the way Steven told her. It was just like him to bring up a sensitive subject in his usual matter-of-fact way. Sometimes it didn't bother her, but other times it did. The night of the accident for example, they were on the phone for three hours. He called as the police were arriving. She could hear the wail of sirens. He told her about the car-jacker and reported the details of the accident. He gave her a play by play of the firemen's efforts to extinguish the burning Suburban. In greater, more ghastly, detail, he described the condition of the bodies in the Honda. As if he was reading from a book rather than actually seeing the carnage, his comments were concise and factual, but there was no emotion in his voice. Steven had never been an emotional man, but she thought that witnessing a tragedy of that magnitude would elicit some kind of a response. When she picked him up later he was dry-eyed and calm.

His ability to tolerate stress and unpleasant circumstances had been honed to a fine edge during his childhood. He told her that his adopted parents struggled through many years of poverty. Working a variety of part-time jobs he had grown up contributing his earnings to the family coffer. Marjorie could understand how that kind of upbringing might create a level of stoicism. But at some point doesn't your guard have to come down? Not Steven. When Elizabeth ran away he never cried. He was extremely attentive, consoling Marjorie for months, giving her everything she needed to get through the ordeal, but he never broke down.

• • • • •

"We were somewhere in the Midwest," Elizabeth said to Gil, "I saw a road sign — Madison 350 miles. Later that night I told you that was my name – Madison."

Elizabeth nibbled on another cracker and took a sip of water. Her stomach was feeling better. After she threw up, Gil had dug through his supplies and found her some saltines. They were a little stale but the salt tasted good. He had gently sat her down in the beach chair and when he brought her a cup of water the kindness in his eyes made Elizabeth want to reach for him.

"It was like play acting," she said. "I was able to be a brand new girl."

"I always wondered about that. I never thought Madison was your real name."

"Oh, yeah?"

"I didn't say anything. You obviously weren't going to tell me the truth. So I went along with it."

"I was pretty messed up."

"Yeah."

Gil scuffed the heel of his boot in the dirt. "Did you ever contact your parents?"

Elizabeth shook her head. "I sent another letter a few months after arriving at Fair Haven. A friend mailed it from Chicago. I wanted my mother to know I had found a home and was happy."

"That would be tough. As a parent, I mean, for them to not know where you were or what you were doing."

"I had to protect myself."

"Oh, I'm not saying you should have talked to them. It's just that after having kids —" he paused, and then quickly pushed forward with the rest of his thought. "I can understand what your parents might have gone through."

"And what about me? What I went through?"

"Yeah, you're right."

"I was lucky. You brought me to the perfect place. At Fair Haven I was educated and nurtured in ways my parents never could have done. I was given responsibility and autonomy. It really worked out for the best."

Gil looked across the street at the oak tree. For a moment he didn't say anything.

He's gone into the stare, Elizabeth thought. I've lost him again.

Finally he turned and looked at her. "We've both been through a lot. But people have stepped up. What the commune did for you, Steve Davenport and his wife have done for me. They've really kept me going. Not sure what I would have done without them."

The pilot light of rage burning in Elizabeth since the night her father came into her room momentarily flickered. Her parents had cared for Gil. They brought him nourishment and companionship. They had protected him from further suffering. She was grateful that they had reacted to the tragedy in such a loving way. At the same time she couldn't help feeling a stab of jealousy. Why would her mother extend herself to a stranger but not her own daughter? She knew her father wouldn't want to find her, but why hadn't her mother tracked her down? How could the woman simply let her only child disappear? Because she knew what happened, Elizabeth reminded herself.

"What's your last name?" Gil was looking at her. "Now that you're finally giving up your ghosts."

Elizabeth's first instinct was to say, 'Davenport, and that nice couple helping you aren't so wonderful. Your buddy Steve raped me.' But Elizabeth didn't say that. Something stopped her. 'Why continue the pain?' That was what Sky always said in his talks about forgiveness. At the time Elizabeth didn't agree with him, but she now saw the truth of what it meant. It would be cruel to shatter Gil's image of her parents. He liked them and had come to depend on their kindness. To snatch that away would be wrong.

"My last name is Sandin."

It wasn't a complete lie. Sandin was Sky's last name — Robert Leonard Sandin. He had been like an adopted father to her.

"Elizabeth Sandin." Gil stuck out his hand. "Nice to meet you."

16

The blood fell gently at first. Hot against Darla's skin, it splattered and spread, covering her nakedness. Above her, floating like crimson storm clouds, three human bodies rained blood. The deluge increased until it became a stinging curtain of red battering down on her. She choked and gasped, struggling to breathe in the midst of the downpour. Rising warm and thick against her arms and legs it covered the bottom of the gleaming white room where she lay. It lapped at her ears, quickly covering them, sending Darla into an eerie silence. Under the surface of the blood she could hear her breath, rapid and panicky. Then Davenport's voice began droning in her head: "You were too much for me to resist, too much for me to resist, too much for me to resist." She tried to move but an invisible force was pinning her down. As she opened her mouth to scream, blood poured in gagging her into silence.

Darla woke up coughing and sputtering. She lay in the dark, her heartbeat slowly returning to normal. The dreams had haunted her since the accident: the bodies hovering above her, the horrible rain of blood, and the powerless immobility. To Darla the accident was a living thing inside of her. At night, when her thoughts stilled and her defenses relaxed, that's when it would communicate with her. The dreams were its language. I'm still here, it was saying — in all of my hideous glory.

Darla swung out of bed. Fumbling in the darkness, she pulled on a pair of sweats and her favorite Tori Amos T-shirt. It was time to end the nightmares. It was time to be proactive in her healing. She tiptoed quietly toward her bedroom door. Allowing Steven Davenport to roam free was not acceptable. She was the only one who knew what he'd done. He might try to kill her or attack some other innocent girl. She couldn't allow that to happen.

Down stairs in the kitchen she grabbed a strawberry Pop Tart, a can of diet soda, and the keys to Essie. Her father had replaced the thermostat and declared the car good as new. Easing open the back door, Darla quietly slipped out. The yard was dimly lit from the neighbor's patio spotlight. Wind brushed through the leaves of the pin oaks. Darla moved quickly down the driveway toward the car. It wouldn't take long. She could drive to his house and be back before her parents finished breakfast.

· · · · ·

Dominic Angelo fished around in the glove compartment for a stick of Juicy Fruit gum. He found a pack underneath his dirt-smudged sunglass case. Only two sticks left. He unwrapped one and folded it into his mouth. It was part of his morning ritual — black coffee, two doughnuts, and a stick of Juicy Fruit. He had been chewing the gum for over sixty years. In the hyper-fast world of cell phones, computers, and the internet, a world he felt less and less a part of, the sugary sweet taste was a comforting reminder of less complicated times.

He pulled out of the Blanchard's Donuts parking lot and headed north on Route 19. The sky was just beginning to brighten. Dominic clicked on his headlights.

"Better to be seen than surprised," he said out loud. He smiled. Irene used to kid him about that. "Surprise *me*," she would say, "Remember to take out the garbage."

He turned to the seat next to him. She would be there sometimes. Her long white hair pulled back, her eyes soft and blue. He would talk to her about the Pirates and the weather. Occasionally they would talk about Michael. "Remember the time he was in fourth grade and he brought home the drawing of the unicorn," she once reminded him. "And he told you it was a magic horse that would take him to a secret place under the North Park swimming pool." Dominic had cried when she reminded him of that story. She could do nothing to comfort him. She had watched him with that all-knowing look in her eyes that made him so angry. Just because she was dead didn't mean she had to be so calm and collected about everything. Michael was their son. His body had been blown into fourteen pieces.

"I have a different perspective now," she'd told him. "Michael is fine."

"Easy for you to be so gosh darned okay about it."

"That's one of the privileges of being dead."

Thinking about Irene only made him miss her. He turned up the country station playing on the radio. Willy Nelson's voice filled the cab of the truck.

Growing old isn't for the faint of heart, Dominic thought, but doing it alone was extra painful. Because of the fact that he hadn't been all that kind to Irene during the last half of their marriage, he felt an even greater loss when she passed. A month after her funeral, he had apologized to Irene for not being able to talk about Michael or his death. He had promised to discuss it with her if she would listen. So he did. It seemed to help.

He put on his signal and made a left turn on Asher Road. The Davenport's forsythia needed to be dug up. He'd get that done while the grass was drying then he'd drive to the Newman's house. It shouldn't take too long. He might even be able to squeeze in a nap before the Pirate game. They were playing the Astros. The new kid was pitching; the one who had been arrested for drunken driving. Making two million dollars a year and he couldn't call a cab. Dominic shook his head. Not the sharpest tool in the shed, but when you can throw a 98 mile-an-hour fastball some things are forgiven. Dinner tonight would be leftover meatloaf and green beans. No, he remembered, he'd finished that three nights ago. Maybe just a chipped-ham sandwich and some iced tea.

$$\bullet \ \bullet \ \bullet \ \bullet \ \bullet$$

Marjorie wasn't about to get up. The alarm clock hadn't gone off yet. She had twenty minutes to drift in the gauzy haze of half-sleep. She ran her hand down between her legs. She was sore. Steven had been rough with her last night. She rolled on to her side and pulled her knees up. It happened sometimes. They would be making love and he would get a look on his face and a kind of stare in his eyes and then he would go at her hard and fast. It would go on and on. Sometimes she could let go and get into it. The whole power thing could be a turn on if she was in the right mood, but most of the time it frightened her. It was the look on his face. He stared right through her like she wasn't there. And when he finally finished, he wouldn't say a word to her. It was as if someone had thrown a switch. She asked him about it once and he told her that he got like that because she turned him on so much. "And sometimes," he whispered with a conspiratorial grin, "guys just want to fuck. None of the nice-nice sweetheart stuff, just good, hard fucking." Marjorie didn't like that word and she seldom heard Steven use it. But she got his point. She didn't want to disappoint him or be a prude, so she never brought it up again.

• • • • •

The forsythia was taking over the corner of the back yard. Dominic hated destroying perfectly good shrubbery but Mrs. Davenport wanted something smaller put in its place. An azalea, she'd suggested. Every week she would look at him, look at the forsythia, and then shake her head. She was a woman, Dominic thought, who although quite attractive, could use a good talking to. "She thinks people owe her something," Irene had told him when he first started working for the Davenports. After Elizabeth ran away Dominic tried to be less critical. Uppity attitude or not, Mrs. Davenport had lost her little girl and that loss had to be respected.

The blade of the shovel sliced into the ground. The recent rains would make the job easier. He tossed the dirt onto a blue plastic tarp. It won't be long now, Dominic thought. The blood will be humming and I won't feel so God-blessed tired. It was taking him longer and longer to get moving in the mornings. He used to spring out of bed ready for the day's work. Now it was nothing but effort. And the coffee and doughnuts didn't inspire him much anymore. Irene used to get up and eat breakfast with him every day. She would pack his lunch and fill his dented green thermos with coffee. She always made sure that he had a piece of fruit for later in the afternoon. Sometimes they would talk, other times they wouldn't. Every day before he went out the door Irene would – Dominic abruptly reared back and drove the shovel hard into the ground. The force of the impact stung his hands. "Enough," he scolded himself. "There's work to be done."

• • • • •

Darla crept through the trees and underbrush at the rear of the property. Dew soaked her sweatpants and sneakers. She moved from tree to tree, her eyes sharply scanning in front of her until she was at the edge of the lawn. The house was quiet. A light in the kitchen was all that was on. She looked at the sprawling lawn. There would be no place to hide once she started across the grass. If anyone looked out a window they would be able to see her. She unzipped her backpack and took out the .357. Leaving the safety on, she slipped the backpack over her shoulders and got ready to sprint across the yard. No one would see her, she reassured herself. She would be moving too fast. Suddenly she froze. She tilted her head, listening carefully. A dull thump came from nearby. Darla slowly turned her head to the right. In the gray half-light she couldn't make out any movement. But there it was again, the thud. She gripped the revolver tighter in her hand. Maybe Steven Davenport was an early riser. Carefully watching where she stepped, Darla moved toward the sound.

• • • • •

Marjorie slipped out of bed and went into the bathroom. Without turning on the light she hiked up her nightgown and sat on the toilet. The seat was cool on her skin. She leaned forward, elbows on her knees and urinated. Spooling off a length of toilet paper she carefully wiped that still tender part of herself. She stood up and lowered the toilet seat. She didn't want to flush and wake Steven. From a stainless steel hook on the back of the bathroom door she slipped on the green silk robe Steven had brought her from Thailand. She tied the belt at her waist and walked out of the bathroom. A cup of tea would be nice, she thought as she walked past her sleeping husband, and then a visit to the garden.

• • • • •

Dominic paused to wipe the sweat from his brow. The root ball of the forsythia was partially exposed but still holding firm. He returned the red bandanna to the back pocket of his work pants then bent over and picked up a long iron bar. He raised it, like Ahab ready to harpoon the great white whale, and with all the strength in his wiry back and shoulders plunged the heavy pointed bar under the root ball. The point struck with a loud thud and buried itself deep. Dominic grasped the bar with both hands and leaned all of his weight on it. The root ball didn't budge. He pressed down with both hands in front of his chest. His work boots lifted off the ground. The forsythia didn't move. Damn, Dominic thought, and let go of the bar. He walked around the stubble of branches that remained of the forsythia looking for a vulnerable spot. He would have to go deeper with the shovel. He grasped the bar and gave it a strong pull. It didn't give. He braced his feet and leaned his back into it. The bar slowly slid out of the root ball. He dropped it to the ground and picked up the shovel. This was going to be harder than he thought.

Darla relaxed her grip on the .357. It wasn't Davenport. Through the bushes she watched the old man drive the shovel into the ground and then stomp down on it with his boot. He dumped the shovel full of dirt onto a blue plastic tarp. Darla turned toward the house. From where he was working he would be able to see her when she went into the house. There were a few small trees and shrubs in between, but if he looked, he would definitely be able to spot her. The last thing she wanted was a witness.

Marjorie finished stirring honey into her mug of tea. She rinsed the spoon in the sink and picked the mug up off the counter. She was looking forward to her time alone in the garden. She hoped to see some humming birds. And there was that other bird. She had seen it twice, the one with the red marks on its wings. She walked to the French doors and unlocked them. She slipped on her clogs then quietly opened the door and stepped out on the patio.

The air was thick and humid. It's going to be a hot one, Marjorie thought. She walked across the patio to the steps and down into the yard. A cardinal glided to the maple tree. She watched it hop from branch to branch. Why does Steven enjoy making love to me so hard that he hurts me? The thought flashed through her mind, startling her. She raised the mug to her lips, attempting to push the thought away. She sipped her tea. When she lowered the mug, the thought was still there. Tears welled in her eyes. Quickly marshaling her highly refined powers of self-control, Marjorie suppressed the on-coming emotional outburst. What was it that her father used to say, "Gardens are a place for thinking but don't let your mind get the best of you." She walked purposefully toward the back of the property. She wanted to sit on her bench by the birdbath and enjoy the stillness of the morning. Nothing was going to spoil that.

Marjorie noticed the blue tarp first. The next thing she saw was the forsythia. Hacked to stubs, there was now a shallow hole dug around it. Walking closer she saw the shovel and the long iron bar on the ground. Huh, Marjorie thought, Dominic is here early. She circled around the hole. Probably went to his truck, she thought. She turned and followed the path into the trees. As she came into the clearing, a robin perched on the edge of the bench flew into the trees. Marjorie walked over and sat down. During their trip to New England after Elizabeth disappeared, Marjorie bought the bench at an estate sale in Newburyport, Massachusetts. An old church pew that had been shortened, the seven foot oak bench had dutifully weathered the last fourteen years of blizzards, thunderstorms, and summer heat. Blending seamlessly with the low stonewall behind it and the still waters of the slate birdbath in front, the bench had grown to be part of the natural setting of the Zen Pod as Steven referred to this area of their property. Marjorie created it as a place to relax, look at the stars, or have a quiet talk. Although she and Steven never actually had a quiet talk on the bench or looked at the stars together, it was a tranquil spot she enjoyed just the same. When they returned from New England, Marjorie had come to the bench nearly every day. It was comforting to have a private place to express her feelings.

A twig snapped. Marjorie turned, expecting to see Dominic. She was surprised to see a young girl run out of the trees.

It was like calling turkeys. Darla had been with her father and Uncle Brady plenty of times when they lured in big toms. She'd made crying sounds to get the old man's attention. When he put down his shovel and came through the trees, she'd quietly slipped away. He would search for her and when he was unable to locate the distraught child he thought he'd heard then he would slowly walk back to the hole scratching his head wondering what was wrong with him. But by then she would be inside the house.

"Can I help you?"

Darla jerked back in surprise, instinctively raising the gun. As the .357 came level, she saw that it was pointed at a woman in a silky green robe sitting on a wooden bench. The woman's eyes widened. Her mouth opened. Her hand released its grasp on a white ceramic cup. The cup toppled over spilling its contents down the front of the bench.

A roar of discordant sound rushed in Darla's ears. Like a train amplified over and over, feedback shredding it into fragments no longer connected to anything recognizable, the sound was a thing inside of her. With nothing else to hang on to for stability, her grip tightened on the revolver. Then, from a decidedly calmer part of her brain, came the thought, *Davenport's wife*.

Marjorie went numb. A nauseous chill stabbed her mid-section frantically provoking her to run. But she didn't move. Her limbs were leaden and useless. She stared past the gaping muzzle of the gun into the girl's troubled eyes. She saw fear and anger. Who are you, Marjorie wanted to cry out. Why do you want to kill me?

Then, from deep within her, came the sound of a bed creaking and a desperate muffled cry, "No Dad! No!"

—122—

17

Being called Elizabeth was disorienting. It felt similar to the first time she lied and told Gil that her name was Madison. The initial sense of freedom in her new identity was clouded by a feeling of loss over no longer being Elizabeth. Now it was the other way around. Madison had been a refuge, granting her peace and renewal. The name Elizabeth carried a weight she was still uncertain she could bear.

After Gil's inventory of the supplies it had been clear that a grocery run was in order. He insisted that Steven Davenport would come by soon with more food, but she had told him she wanted to get a few things anyway. Since the day his BMW sped off there had been no further sign of her father. For this she was immensely grateful. Yet even as Elizabeth was appreciating Steven Davenport's absence from the campsite, she was turning left on Remley Street.

Linda McKelvey lifted the foam pad she had been kneeling on and moved it several feet to her left. It had been weeks since she'd worked in her flowerbeds. Tom's idea of yard work was cutting the grass. The rest was hers to do. She didn't mind once she got outside and was actually doing it. It was the initial getting out of the house effort that was the hard part. She leaned over the flowers and plucked several dead petunia blooms then reached for a clump of weeds. Emily had always been a big help. She was a green thumb girl. That's what they used to call each other, green thumb girls. All through college Emily hauled her collection of houseplants back and forth from Penn State. Now the spare bedroom in her townhouse was filled with bonsai trees, lilies, and orchids. Dave called it the jungle room. Sarah was more like Tom. Asking her to go outside and pull weeds was like asking her to play with spiders. She'd whine and complain until you got so sick of it you'd send her in to the house just to have some peace and quiet. A bit of a princess, that was Sarah. Marko had his hands full with her.

Getting up early to beat the heat had been a smart move, Linda thought. The cool stillness of the morning and the smell of freshly turned earth was a perfect way to start the day. Tom kidded her that her love of gardening came from her pot smoking days when she and her friends would go camping and spend hours staring at a tree trying to see it breathe. Linda smiled. Elizabeth Davenport once asked her if she had been a hippie. Elizabeth was a bright little girl and always knew when you were being straight with her. So Linda told her yes, she was a hippie. Elizabeth didn't laugh or ask a lot of questions. She just shrugged her shoulders and said, "I wish my Mom had been a hippie." The thought of Marjorie Davenport in Birkenstock sandals, faded bellbottoms and a tie-dyed peasant blouse made Linda smile even wider. Designer jeans were as casual as Marjorie ever got.

Behind her on the street, Linda heard a passing car slow down. She looked over her shoulder. A blue compact was going by the house. The car suddenly accelerated. In front of the next house, the brake lights flared and the car stopped. For a moment it sat there. Linda wondered what the driver was up to. Then the brake lights darkened and the car quickly proceeded down the street. Linda wiped the sweat from her forehead with the back of her hand and turned her attention to a row of geraniums.

Elizabeth gripped the steering wheel with both hands. Mrs. McKelvey…it had been so long since she'd seen her. Sarah and Emily — all of it was so long ago. She looked in the rear view mirror. Mrs. McKelvey was still kneeling in front of the flowerbed. Elizabeth brought her eyes back to the road. Of all of her friends' parents, Mrs Mckelvey was the coolest Mom. During sleep-overs she would tell them stories about going to rock concerts and war protests. She would dance with them to old Beatles, Rolling Stones, and Grateful Dead records. Sometimes Mr. McKelvey would dance too. This would send the girls into hysterics. He would shake his rear-end and hop around sending his glasses tilting up at odd angles. Sarah and Emily would act as if they were horrified, but Elizabeth could tell that secretly they were pleased. Their parents knew how to let their hair down. They knew how to have fun.

Elizabeth wondered what Sarah and Emily had done with their lives. Did they have careers? Were they married? Did they have children? Emily was probably married, but Sarah might still be single. She was always pretty picky about everything. The only job either of them ever talked about was when Sarah once said that being a travel writer might be an interesting career. She liked the idea of going to Spain or Tahiti and being catered to in fancy hotels and spas. Elizabeth tried to visualize how Sarah and Emily might look but their faces kept washing in and out of focus.

At the end of Remley Street Elizabeth braked for a stop sign. What about her own mother? What did she look like? Elizabeth stared at the house across the intersection. A boy was playing in the driveway with a re-mote control car. The yellow racer zipped down the asphalt then abruptly swerved into the bushes along the side of the garage. The vengeful side of Elizabeth wanted to believe that her mother, long suffering because of Elizabeth's departure, had become haggard and overweight. Elizabeth tried to imagine her with a dowdy middle-aged girth, hair hanging dull and gray, fleshy pouches beneath red-rimmed eyes, finger nails ragged and discolored. But Elizabeth knew, in the wiser part of herself, that this was highly unlikely. Her mother's vanity was an indestructible aspect of her personality. Probably still swimming, her long legs undoubtedly firm and lean, she was most likely being facilitated by her manicurist and hair stylist on a biweekly basis. She was taking good care of herself, Elizabeth decided, as she always had.

A horn blared. In the rear view mirror a teenage girl in a red Mustang raised her hands as if to say, *do something*. Elizabeth swung the wheel left and stepped on the accelerator. The little Toyota shot across the street. Elizabeth realized after making the turn that she was heading toward her parent's house.

Steven Davenport had been awakened by a scream. Disoriented and still half-asleep, it took him a moment to realize that the high-pitched sound was coming from outside the house. Seeing the empty bed beside him, he ran to the open bedroom window and looked down into the back yard. The sound suddenly stopped.

"Marjorie!"

There was no answer from inside the house or from the yard. He ran downstairs and was out on the flagstone patio before he realized he was only wearing boxer shorts. His eyes quickly took in the yard.

"Marjorie!"

He listened, but heard nothing.

An image of Darla wielding the gun flashed in his mind. He went down the steps and across the wet grass, his eyes searching the trees and shrubbery.

"Marjorie."

He took the path that led to the bench. Perhaps it was a snake that frightened her? Or maybe it wasn't even her. The scream might have come from the neighbor's yard. He stopped. Someone was moving through the woods. He lowered his body into a crouch. His heart rate kicked up. The sound of twigs snapping came closer. Steven's eyes swept the ground for a weapon. He found a branch as thick as his wrist and picked it up. Out of the corner of his eye came movement — Dominic Angelo.

Davenport stood up. "Where's Marjorie?"

"I don't know." Dominic struggled to catch his breath. "I heard someone scream."

Davenport ran down the path. His mind continued to convince him of her safety — she was probably out getting coffee or running an errand or — he burst into the clearing.

Marjorie was sitting on the bench. Her hands were folded in her lap and she was staring straight ahead. Steven took two steps toward her then stopped. His eyes flicked in the direction she was looking. In the trees and shrubs he searched for the shadowy outline of Darla.

"Marjorie." His eyes still probed the trees. "Are you all right?"

She didn't respond. Not seeing any sign of Darla, Steven turned back to his wife.

"Honey."

Marjorie continued staring and didn't speak.

Davenport took a step toward her. "I heard a scream. What happened?"

She didn't react.

He walked over and sat next to her. She didn't move or look at him. Her hands were tightly clenched into fists.

"Sweetie, what's going on?" He dropped the branch on the ground then gently rested his hand on her arm.

Marjorie turned to him. The look in her eyes was hard and deliberate. "My tea is cold."

He glanced at the cup next to her on the bench. It was empty. But before he could say anything, he noticed the blood on her hands.

As Elizabeth slowly drove down the street toward her parents' house, an onslaught of childhood memories charged at her from around trees, houses, and driveways — kickball games with the Garcia kids, bicycle races, refusing to be beaten by Cheryl Moulton even though she was a year older, sitting on the living room couch with her father listening to *Aïda,* trick or treating on Halloween dressed up as a princess, her father's car coming down the street and the double toot of his horn when he spotted her in the front yard, the night the Tubert's aunt had a heart attack and the screeching chaos of the fire engines and the ambulance, sitting cross-legged on the kitchen counter painting Easter eggs with her mother, laying on her back in the cool shade of the maple tree dreaming of having a sister or brother to play with.

Elizabeth gripped the steering wheel with both hands as the house came into view. The first thing she noticed was that the shutters, no longer forest green were now a deep blue. There was a rose bed on the left side of the yard where an elm tree had once stood. The trees in the yard were bigger, but other than that everything seemed the same. She slowed down as she approached the house. The night she left, slipping quietly out the front door, she had run across the lawn and never looked back.

Parked in front of the house was a pickup truck that caught Elizabeth's eye. ANGELO GARDENING in faded white letters was printed on the tailgate. Mr. Angelo — she smiled as she drove past the truck. She hadn't thought of him in years.

At the stop sign at the end of the block, Elizabeth sat for a moment as a shiny red Audi drove by. She felt strangely giddy and at the same time she was on the verge of tears. Having avoided memories of her childhood for so long, it was as if the current onslaught streaming through her mind had overwhelmed her ability to process in an appropriate manner. Intoxicated on the past, she was experiencing both warmth and gratitude, and also the pervasive sour nausea of sadness and rage. Her father's body and what he had done was a bitter shadow on the sunny feeling of once again being near her childhood home.

Elizabeth glanced in the rear view mirror as a thought suddenly came to her: her parents might not live there anymore. They could have sold the house years ago. They might have moved into a condo, maybe up on Mount Washington. Her mother always liked the views from there. Elizabeth looked in both directions then did a U-turn. She pulled over and parked across the street. Shutting off the car, she settled back in her seat. It won't take long, she assured herself. Someone will either walk out of the house or a neighbor will come by and I'll ask them.

Dominic watched Mrs. Davenport walk down the path. She had stood up from the bench, a coffee mug in her right hand, and without saying anything walked away from her husband. She moved slowly but deliberately as if she knew exactly where she was going but wasn't interested in getting there any time soon.

"What happened?" Steven was watching Marjorie walk away.

"I don't know."

Davenport swung his eyes over to Dominic. "*Something* happened."

"A girl was crying." Dominic's mind raced back over the events of the morning. "I was digging up the forsythia and I went to see what was wrong. I couldn't find anyone. I searched all the way to the back of the property."

"But who screamed?"

Dominic shrugged. "I don't know. I think it was Mrs. Davenport. I heard it and came as fast as I could."

"You didn't see anyone?"

"No. I just heard the girl crying."

"But you never saw her?"

Dominic shook his head. "I followed the sound but never found her."

Davenport put his hands on his hips. "How do you know it was a girl?"

"The voice, it was young."

"Not my wife?"

"I don't think so."

"Are you certain about this girl crying? I mean where did she go?"

Dominic was silent for a moment trying to remember the sequence of events. He had been hearing his dead wife talk to him for years. Maybe he hadn't really heard a girl crying. His mind may have played tricks on him again.

Davenport saw his hesitation and threw his hands in the air. "Did you hear it or not?"

Self-doubt and confusion sloshed through Dominic's mind. The girl's voice had sounded so real. But maybe—

"Great." Davenport shook his head at Dominic's escalating uncertainty. "Forget it. I'll figure it out."

Relieved to be off the hook, Dominic started back toward the forsythia. After three steps he stopped and turned around.

"Mr. Davenport!" He fished in the front pocket of his pants, remembering what he'd found. "I picked this up back there. Maybe it belongs to the girl I heard." The last part he said with a rush of confidence.

Davenport walked over and looked at the object resting in the worn creases of Dominic's hand. It was a pink hair clip. That it was Darla's, Davenport had no doubt. While sitting in her car he had stared long and hard at it while her pistol was pointed at his chest.

Dominic pushed his hand toward Davenport. "Do you want it?"

Steven raised his eyes and flashed him a forgiving smile. "Thanks." He plucked the hair clip from Dominic's hand. "I'll take it. It probably belongs to one of the kids in the neighborhood."

"Awful early for a youngster to be out prowling around." Dominic felt like he was back on solid mental ground.

"You're right. I'll check with the neighbors." Davenport gave Dominic a friendly clap on the shoulder. "Thanks. I'll see you later."

Marjorie was in the shower when she saw Steven's outline through the fogged glass. She turned back to the hot, streaming water. The places where she'd dug her nails into the palms of her hands tingled in the soothing flow of water. She raised her face letting the water drown out sounds she didn't want to hear and thoughts she didn't want to think. There were groceries to buy; she sternly reminded herself, and her sister's birthday card to mail. Maybe she should pick up fresh basil at the farmer's market, and tomatoes. She'd found the juiciest tomatoes there last week. After that she would go to the gym for a good long swim. Her left hamstring had been feeling tight. Maybe a workout and some stretching would loosen it up. And there was the man on Hargrove Avenue. She needed to drop off a care package for him. Yes, she thought, I have a lot to do. It's going to be a busy day.

Downstairs, Steven paced back and forth across the kitchen floor. Had Darla been in the back yard that morning? Had she found Marjorie on the bench and said something to her? And if Darla had told her the story, would Marjorie be compelled to call the police? He walked across the kitchen to the bottom of the stairs. He could hear the shower still running in their bathroom. I can fix this, he reassured himself. I've done it before. I'll put a spin on whatever happened with Marjorie, get her calmed down, and then I'll deal with Darla. I'll definitely deal with Darla.

Elizabeth watched the sky over her old house brighten. Streaks of morning gray were being shot through with bolts of light. Her memory flashed to a family vacation in Washington, D.C. The first day in the city she and her parents went to the Lincoln Memorial. As they were approaching, the clouds shifted and the sun struck the Memorial in such a way that the entire building seemed to glow. Her father saw it too. He'd stopped walking and stared. "That's something," he'd said. Her mother squeezed her hand and they stood there together until the light shifted and everything returned to normal.

Elizabeth fidgeted uncomfortably in her seat. Positive memories of her father only served to confuse her. He was sick and evil. The rest was a little girl still wanting to have a daddy to love. A loud bang caused her to look across the street. Dominic Angelo was loading a shovel into the back of his pickup truck.

Elizabeth slid down in her seat trying to make herself invisible. She watched Dominic shift though some tools in the back of his truck. He was thinner now and had less hair. How was his son doing? The grandchildren would be out of high school by now. She glanced at the house then at her watch. She didn't want to leave Gil waiting too long. Her eyes went back to Dominic. Fifteen years was a long time. No way could he recognize her.

She started the car. Dominic's head came up. He looked at her momentarily then went back to what he was doing. Elizabeth adjusted her sunglasses and pulled across the street next to his truck.

"Excuse me. I was wondering if you could tell me who lives here. I was admiring the house."

Dominic leaned forward on the tailgate of the truck.

"What's that?"

"Is the owner interesting in selling?" She gestured toward the house.

Dominic turned to the house then looked back at Elizabeth.

"Not that I know of."

"Oh."

He was about to go back to his tools but something stopped him. He looked at her again. Elizabeth raised her hand, trying to cover as much of her face as possible. Dominic walked around the corner of the truck and stood in front of her window.

"Who lives there?" Elizabeth's friendly tone was now gone. She wanted to get the information and drive away.

Dominic didn't respond. His eyes swept over her face. "I thought of you when I heard the girl crying. Was it you?"

Elizabeth's throat constricted. She had to swallow twice to get the words out.

"What are you talking about?"

"All these years. How have you been?"

"Who lives in the house?" Elizabeth no longer cared about being polite.

"Your parents. Was it you crying in the back yard?"

Elizabeth slammed the car into drive and sped down the street.

18

Gil was restless. Elizabeth had only been gone a couple hours but he was already missing her. He looked across the street at the oak tree. "It's comforting, honey," he said out loud, "that's all." Bonnie understands, he told himself. She knew the long days he'd spent alone. He walked over to his beach chair and sat down. Picking up his journal he began a new entry:

> *Love is not a simple thing.*
> *I don't want you to go. I don't know how to say goodbye.*

Gil stopped writing and looked up. A car was coming down the street. He waited to see the little blue compact appear, but it was a green Chevy. He looked down at what he'd written then lifted the pen and continued:

> *Sometimes I sit here and I can't help wondering what you're thinking. Are you and the kids laughing at me, or are you proud, or do they think I'm crazy? Sometimes when I feel you near me it makes me really angry. And that makes me feel bad. Because I think, how can I ever move forward if I know that you're always there? And at the same time, I want to know that you are always going to be there.*
> *I'm really screwed up.*
> *I want to still love you and the kids, but how can I continue to do that and go forward and have a life?*

Gil lifted his head. Across the street the leaves of the oak tree fluttered in a breeze that he couldn't feel. Again he began to write:

The person who killed you must be having terrible dreams. He has to be tormented. How can he sleep at night? Is he some kind of junkie? Does he even remember what he did? Maybe you speak to him? Or Drake? What would my sweet boy say to the man who ran you down? Would he punish him? Forgive him?

A yellow butterfly landed by the left toe of Gil's boot. Gil watched the delicate wings move slowly up and down. He felt both the impulse to crush and to gently take it into the palm of his hand and let it crawl on him.

I'm still falling between the darkness and the light... When will this end?

Another car was coming down Hargrove. Gil looked up. Elizabeth's blue rental came into view. Gil put his journal away and stood up. Her car slowed, did a U-turn, and pulled off the road in front of the campsite. He started walking down the slope to meet her.

"Hi." Elizabeth waved to him over the roof of the car. "Sorry it took me so long."

"It's okay."

She began pulling grocery bags out of the trunk.

Gil saw what was in the trunk. "You bought a lot of stuff."

"I don't like shopping. I wanted to get enough to hold us for a while."

"Thank you. I won't forget this."

She smiled. "Let's go fill the pantry."

They had everything nearly put away when they heard a vehicle pull off the road. Gil turned from where he was pouring ice in to one of the coolers to see a white TV news van come to stop in front of the campsite.

"Not these guys again."

Elizabeth watched two men unload a video camera from the rear door. The blonde reporter, Celia Davis, who Elizabeth recognized from the news report on Cassidy's computer, checked her makeup in the side mirror of the van. Elizabeth felt a rush of panic. She didn't want her parents seeing her on the six o'clock news. She put on her sunglasses.

"I'm gonna'—go. This is your thing."

Gil glanced over at her, but she was already heading for the woods.

"Hey," a voice called from the street.

"Get a shot of her!" Celia Davis charged up the slope toward the campsite.

Gil turned to see Elizabeth disappearing into the woods. Suddenly there was a microphone in his face.

"Who is your new camping partner Mr. Linnetti?" Davis' voice was rich with insinuation. The camera lens, a threatening Cyclops eye, loomed in front of him.

"I—she's a…"

"She's a what, Mr. Linnetti?"

"She is an old friend who came to help me."

"Why did she run into the woods when we pulled up?"

Gil glanced toward the trees and then back to Davis. "She's a private person."

"I see. What's her name?"

Gil frowned. "Like I said, she wants her privacy."

For a moment the reporter's eyes softened and the grim set of her mouth lifted. "I know this isn't easy to talk about. And I understand how difficult it must be, but our viewers are interested in what happens to you. If you have a new girlfriend they want to know about it. So come on, let us in a little." She flashed him a friendly smile.

Gil turned and walked away. He stopped by the coolers and pointed to the empty grocery bags on the ground. "She brought me food. She's not my girlfriend."

The camera panned off of Gil's face to the wooded hillside.

"Somewhere in those trees is a good Samaritan," Celia Davis said, "and we would like to know who she is."

"You've been respectful up to now." Gil closed the distance between himself and the reporter. "Why the sudden change."

Davis lowered the microphone and shrugged. "Sex sells. What can I say?" She gestured toward the woods. "She can't stay hidden forever."

The cameraman's cell phone rang. He exchanged a few words then hung up.

"Guy just got hit in a crosswalk on the south side. We gotta' go."

Davis turned to Gil. "See if you can get her to talk to us. We'll be back."

Gil watched as they loaded their equipment and then sped down Hargrove Avenue. Only after the van disappeared from view did he notice the white Volvo parked in the shade of a tree a short distance up the road. As Gil squinted to try and see the driver, the Volvo pulled out and came toward him. It stopped and waited while an over-loaded stake-bed truck labored up the hill. When the truck passed the Volvo did a U-turn and parked behind Elizabeth's car.

Marjorie Davenport got out. She offered a quick wave to Gil then ducked back inside the car and emerged with two plastic grocery bags. She walked up the embankment toward him.

"Mr. Linnetti, I'm so glad to see you. I'm Mrs. Davenport. You know my husband, Steven."

Elizabeth watched from behind an oak tree, mesmerized at the sight of her mother. She looks beautiful, Elizabeth thought. Dressed in pressed jeans and a white blouse, Marjorie's hair was pulled back in a ponytail. She looked healthy and tan. Gil took the bags and gestured for her to sit down, but Marjorie shook her head.

"Thank you, but I can't stay. I wanted to make sure you're all right." She looked at the grocery bags. "I see you have plenty of food."

"A friend brought it by. She went… for a walk."

"Good. I'm glad you're well taken care of."

"Thank you for everything you've sent. You and your husband have kept me going."

"You're so welcome. It's been my pleasure. I'm sorry for what you've gone through."

"Thanks."

"I hope my coming by hasn't upset you."

"Why would it upset me?"

"Oh, well… My husband mentioned that you'd prefer he not visit anymore."

"I never said that. I enjoy his visits. And not just the food you send. We talk – it's good."

"Oh. He must have been confused."

"I hope I didn't say something that upset him."

"No, no. I think he was concerned about your feelings."

"I was wondering why I hadn't seen him lately."

"He was trying to be respectful."

"Tell him to come by and say hello."

"I will. I'll do that." She gestured toward the road. "Those news people bothering you?"

"Yeah, well, what can you do?"

"I didn't want to get in the middle of things. That's why I waited until they left."

"You're smart."

Marjorie smiled at the compliment and said something that Elizabeth couldn't hear. Marjorie stepped toward Gil. Her face was serious as she took his hand in both of hers.

"I have great respect for what you've done. Paying tribute to your family this way is remarkable. But what's next? How can I help you move on?"

Gil smiled warmly back at her. "Mrs. Davenport, you and Steven have already done enough. Providing for me like this has been huge. There's nothing more you need to do."

Marjorie patted his hand. It looked like she was going to cry. "Well, tell your friend thanks for me. I'm glad she's taking good care of you."

"I'll do that. Give my best to Steven."

Marjorie raised her hand and waved. "See you soon."

Elizabeth felt tears on her cheeks as she watched her mother walk down to the Volvo. This is crazy, she thought, the woman had to know what happened to me and did nothing about it, why am I crying? She heard the car start and watched it drive up Hargrove. Elizabeth wiped her eyes and tilted her head back. Above, through the dark tangle of branches, she could make out patches of vivid blue sky. *Why am I doing this to myself? Why did I come back here?* She stared into the void a moment longer as if waiting to receive an answer, and then taking a few quick breaths to try and get composed, she pasted a smile on her face and walked out of the woods.

"Did you see that lady who was just here?" Gil was folding grocery bags. "That's Marjorie Davenport. She brought more food."

"I heard. Now you know why he hasn't been to see you."

"Yeah. That's weird. I never said anything like that to Steve. Why would he think I didn't want him coming by?"

"Don't know. Maybe he's not exactly who he seems to be."

"What's that supposed to mean?"

"Guilt drives a person to do things that they may not ordinarily want to do. You of all people should understand that."

Gil straightened up and put his hands on his hips. "You don't know what you're talking about."

"You don't think that's true?"

"Yeah, it's true. But *I'm* not here out of guilt."

"Maybe not originally, but it could be keeping you here."

Gil glared at her then walked to the tent.

"What?" She started after him.

Gil whirled around as if he was going to say something, but then didn't. He stood there with his hands clenched at his sides, his jaw sternly set.

Elizabeth clenched her own hands. "Oh, why don't you just huff and puff like the big bad wolf."

Gil blinked. The intensity in his face shifted and he let out a grunt that sounded a lot like, 'fuck you.'

Elizabeth's eyes widened. "Fuck you, too. You need to face some things. You need to look at what you've been hiding from out here and get past it. Get on with living. Bonnie would want that. You know she would."

The look on Gil's face told Elizabeth, in no uncertain terms, that she had just sailed into dangerous waters. He walked over to her so quickly that Elizabeth took two steps back.

"What I'm doing here and why I'm doing it is my business."

"I know it is, I—."

"You've got no right lecturing me about moving on in my life. You've been hiding in that commune for fifteen years. Why don't you move on with *your* life? Get past what your father did and grow up for Christ's sake!"

Elizabeth launched herself at him. She slammed her fists into his chest and punched and kicked him. He got his arms around her and restrained her, but then she kicked him in the leg and he let her go. They backed off, warily eyeing the other.

"This isn't how I wanted it to be." Elizabeth's eyes were welling with tears.

"Life is like that."

Angrily wiping at the tears with her hand, she raised her finger and pointed it at Gil. "You have no idea how cruel you are." She went to the tent and began stuffing her things into her backpack.

Gil crossed his arms. "Go to your parents and find some peace for yourself. Confront your father and tell your mother the truth. You've carried the secret too long."

Elizabeth whirled around. "It's a curse and I never wanted to pass it on to any one else. You're the only one I ever told. The only one!"

Gil was stunned. He figured she had talked to girlfriends at the commune or somebody along the way. He watched Elizabeth stand up and swing her backpack over her shoulder. He stepped toward her.

"You don't have to go. I just – I want you to take care of yourself."

Elizabeth held up her hands and backed away. "I can't stay here anyway. With the news crew and my — your other visitors, this isn't a good place for me to be. You were doing fine before I showed up and you'll do fine after I'm gone." She walked over to the clothesline and took down her towel. She quickly glanced around the camp for any other belongings, and then walked toward her car. Gil followed her.

"That's it? You're leaving for good?"

"You told me it's time for me to move on with my life." She opened the trunk and dumped her backpack in. "See you, later."

19

Darla ducked past the living room window and sprinted down the driveway to the back of her house. Quickly checking to make sure no one was watching, she crouched down and reached behind the shrubbery. Pulling out a broken chunk of concrete from the side of the rear stoop, she shoved the .357 into the hollow space. Replacing the concrete, she looked around again. Satisfied that no one was watching, she walked out into the back yard and sat on a lounge chair. Let them think I've been out here, she thought. If Mrs. Davenport called the police at least my parents won't have to lie. And there was a really good chance, Darla believed, that the woman did call the police. Mrs. Davenport had been scared. Freaky scared. The look in her eyes had been awful. Darla pushed the image of Mrs. Davenport out of her mind and pulled a notebook and pencil from her backpack. She began sketching the neighbor's roofline. The pencil, refusing to obey her command, made tentative, shaky strokes. Darla tried to calm herself but she couldn't stop her hands from trembling. The exhilarating surge of power she'd experienced while holding the gun on Steven Davenport was no where to be found in her encounter with Mrs. Davenport. Instead, all she felt was weak and afraid.

The back door of her house opened. Her father stepped out with a large glass of water. He bent down and poured it into the cat's bowl.

Darla put down her pencil. "Morning."

"Oh, hey. Didn't know you were up."

"It's a beautiful day." Darla forced a smile.

Her father grunted. "I'll know better when I've had my coffee."

He held the glass over the bushes and drained the last few drops of water. "How about I make you some oatmeal?"

"Thanks Dad."

The back door closed. Darla leaned her head back and squeezed her eyes shut. Mrs. Davenport's startled face flashed in her mind. Once again Darla heard that long horrible scream.

• • • • •

Steven came home that night and found Marjorie sitting at the kitchen table reading a paperback book. A half glass of red wine and a plate of cheese and sesame crackers were in front of her.

"Hi," he said, immediately noticing that she didn't look up when he came into the room. "Something smells good." He went to the oven and peeked in.

Marjorie reached for a cracker and broke it in half. "How was your day?" Her voice was matter-of-fact but not unfriendly.

"I had lunch with Marty. Esther is going in for a biopsy on Tuesday."

Marjorie turned to him. "For what?"

"Breast. Regular check-up, the doctor found a lump."

"Oh, no."

Steven poured himself a glass of Pinot Noir from the bottle on the counter. Upon hearing the news about Esther, he had been hopeful that her condition was a factor in Marjorie's early morning break-down. But it was clear from Marjorie's look of total surprise that she hadn't known.

"Marty was pretty shaken up. Other than his gall bladder surgery they've both been pretty healthy."

"I'll call her later."

Steven sipped his wine and tried to get a better read on his wife. They still hadn't discussed what happened at the bench. Marjorie had left that morning while he was showering for work. She seemed distracted, but on the other hand she had made lasagna, one of his favorite dishes. He hadn't heard from the police so he assumed she never called them. He walked to the refrigerator and pulled out a jar of olives.

Marjorie got up from the table. "I dropped off some things to Gil Linnetti. He's an awfully nice man."

Steven forced a smile. "Yes, he is. I enjoyed his company."

"Do you want some?" Marjorie set the plate of cheese and crackers on the counter.

More nice behavior, Steven thought warily. "Thanks." He picked up a cracker.

She went back to the table for her glass of wine. "He said you're welcome any time. He doesn't want you to stay away."

"Well," Steven's mind shifted to spin control, "He may not have said it, but I certainly felt it. It was obvious to me at the time."

"Maybe he was having a bad day."

Marjorie came around the counter. As she walked past him, she rubbed her hand across the small of his back. "The lasagna is almost ready."

"Great." Steven, aware of how she'd touched him, watched her open the cupboard next to the stove and take out two dinner plates. Maybe she's fine, he thought. What happened on the bench didn't seem to be bothering her. It probably had nothing to do with Darla or the accident. Maybe it was hormones or another hot flash. Steven drank his wine. Marjorie got a tomato and some mixed greens out of the refrigerator.

"What kind of dressing do you want on your salad?

"Italian is good."

She smiled and pulled a knife out of the drawer. "These tomatoes are the same kind I got last week."

"From the farmers market?"

"Yes." Marjorie drew the sharp blade through the center of the tomato. The halves fell apart and she began cutting them into wedges.

Steven took another sip of wine as he watched the blade slice through the ripe tomato. It's going to be fine, he assured himself. It is all going to be okay.

During dinner they chatted cordially about Marjorie's busy day. She told him about the woman she met at the farmers market who told her about quinoa and what a fabulously healthy grain it was.

"So I bought some and I'm going to serve it with salmon. Does that sound good?"

"Sure. I'll get a nice bottle of wine."

Later, as they were eating dessert and Marjorie was halfway through her third glass of wine, her profound sense of denial unexpectedly cracked. Lifting a spoonful of chocolate mousse to her mouth she again heard the voice of her long absent daughter.

"No, Dad! No!"

Marjorie dropped the spoon. It clattered off of her coffee cup. Steven shot her a surprised look. Without a word, Marjorie got up and walked around the table. Her face was frozen in an odd smile as she approached him. Hitching up her skirt, she straddled him, her mouth going to his. She kissed him hard and ground her hips into him. His hands went to her ass. She ripped her blouse open and pulled him to her breasts. She reached between his legs, rubbing and squeezing him. He began to get hard. Yes, she thought, fuck me and shut off my brain.

At three-thirty in the morning Marjorie woke up. Steven's arm lay across her stomach. His breathing was quiet and steady. During their lovemaking, her intense passion and wild sense of abandon had happily surprised her husband. And more importantly, it had done exactly what Marjorie needed it to do. But now, in the dark confines of her bedroom, trapped beneath her sleeping husband's arm, there were no further distractions to shut off her brain. The memories of that night began to muscle their way back in.

Rodger Lundquist, one of Steven's clients, was having a birthday party. The weather had been warm and the patio around the Lundquist's pool was decorated in a festive Southwest theme. Trays of frozen margaritas garnished with lime slices and miniature Mexican flags were being passed among the guests. A colorfully costumed Mariachi band played in the corner of the yard. The Lundquist's three young daughters and their son were splashing around in the shallow end of the pool. Sixteen-year-old Danny was launching his sisters into the air. The girls' laughter and utter glee at being human cannon balls had drawn the attention of many of the guests. Steven sipped his margarita, intently watching the children play. Marjorie had seen the same look in his eyes when they were around other groups of children. At first she thought it was a longing to have more kids. During her pregnancy she had developed pre-eclampsia. Having another child, she was told, could be dangerous. But Steven had been kind. "Elizabeth is enough," he had told her. "We're the Three Musketeers." They laughed and she had felt relieved. Perhaps, she theorized, Steven's longing look might have been because he was an only child. Seeing the Lundquist kids carousing together probably reminded him of what he'd never had growing up. On the way home after the party, Steven had told her that the Lundquist's older girl reminded him of Elizabeth. They both had dark hair and were about the same size. "She isn't as pretty though," he said. "Elizabeth is a very pretty girl." Still feeling the margaritas when they got home, Marjorie had playfully stripped for Steven as he got undressed. But her attempt to seduce him failed.

Steven claimed he had work to do. He put on his robe, walked downstairs, poured himself a bourbon and then went into his office and shut the door. Marjorie fell asleep sometime after one o'clock in the morning. When she woke up, the bed beside her was empty. Thinking that Steven had fallen asleep on the couch, she put on her robe to go wake him. At the top of the stairs she heard a sound. Turning to her right, she heard it again: A whimper and then the sound of sheets rustling. It was coming from Elizabeth's room. She heard a deeper sound and the bed creaked. Marjorie walked toward the closed door. As she reached it, she heard Elizabeth say, "No, Dad! No!" Steven's voice came through the door gruff and unintelligible. Sheets rustled, there was a muffled gasp, and then the maple sleigh bed that Marjorie's grandparents had slept in for over sixty years began to creak in a slow, heartbreaking rhythm. Stunned, Marjorie turned away from the door and quickly walked into her bathroom. She took two sleeping pills and in a daze of denial crawled back into bed. She didn't open her eyes until Steven shook her awake the next day to tell her that Elizabeth was gone.

The memory of that morning, making phone calls to Elizabeth's friends and driving around searching for her, no longer felt like a dream. Finally forced to bear witness to the self-deception she had chosen to hide behind, Marjorie lay there in bed no longer able to convince herself that the lie was the truth and the truth was a nightmare best forgotten.

With a knot like a clenched fist in her throat, Marjorie pushed Steven's arm off of her and swung out of bed. He muttered and rolled over as she walked out of the darkened bedroom. In the hallway, cautiously repeating her steps from that night fifteen years earlier, she paused at the top of the stairs. She looked toward Elizabeth's room. This is when I heard it, she reminded herself. She walked over and stood in front of the closed door. The sounds, free to once again be heard, rose up loud and formidable in Marjorie's mind: Elizabeth's pleading, Steven's low muffled groans, the bed's dreadful creaking. Marjorie's eyes filled with tears. The impulse of self-preservation that had induced her numbness and allowed her to turn away fifteen years ago, again worked frantically to subdue her: He is your husband. You worship him. What will you be without him? What can you do to change what has already been done? Elizabeth is strong. She will get over it.

Marjorie willed herself not to succumb to the seductive lure of denial. Instead, she lifted her hand and placed it on the doorknob. The creaking of the bed quickened. Steven liked to speed up and then slow down. He was making love to his daughter the same way he did to her. Bile rose in Marjorie's throat. She turned the knob and pushed the door open. In the faint, gray light of the bedroom she saw them. His tall, lean body was moving on top of Elizabeth. Elizabeth's eyes were wide and angry. Tears ran down her face. The words flew from Marjorie before she was aware that she was speaking. "I'm sorry, Elizabeth. I'm sorry." She said it again, as if hoping her apology would somehow drive the awful images away. But they didn't. The creaking of the bed got louder, the muffled cries more anguished. Marjorie sank to her knees. Clutching at the bedspread she continued her desperate mantra of apology, "I'm sorry, Elizabeth, I'm sorry, I'm sorry Elizabeth, I'm sorry, I'm sorry, I'm sorry."

But the images wouldn't fade. Sobbing uncontrollably and dragging the bedding with her, Marjorie slumped over and curled into the fetal position on the hardwood floor.

• • • • •

Elizabeth watched the couple in the red canoe paddle slowly across North Park Lake. The surface of the water, liquid silver in the late afternoon light, rippled brightly with each paddle stroke. In the front of the canoe, the girl's long, dark hair gently blew back away from her face. The man, tall with short-cropped hair, laughed and let his hand drag in the cool water. Elizabeth wondered what they were talking about. Were they in love? Had they been together a long time? Did she dream about him when she went to sleep at night?

Before walking down to the lake, she had stopped at the pay phone in the parking lot and called the community center at Fair Haven. From Hannah she learned the latest news about her students and the rest of the commune. Lumina had begun spending time with the new boy, Cassidy. His brashness and her shyness seemed to bring out the best in both of them. Trinity and Dylan had gone to visit their uncle in Flagstaff and could not stop talking about their visit to the Grand Canyon. Kiki got twelve stitches in her forehead when she slammed into a ditch riding a four-wheeler at her cousin's farm near Portland. "And Madison," Hannah had said, her voice dropping to a conspiratorial whisper, "I think Shatki and Cassidy's father have become lovers." Hannah giggled into the phone, "I haven't seen Shatki this relaxed in years. She skipped a yoga class last week and we all nearly fell over."

On one level it was enormously comforting to hear about life at Fair Haven. But when Hannah had called her Madison it confirmed to Elizabeth the gulf which had always existed between herself and everyone at the commune. She had hidden her deepest wound from them, playing the part of the free-spirited runaway girl who didn't talk about her past, her parents, or why she was on her own at such a young age. She had folded herself up in the mystery and allowed it to act as a protective shield against all who tried to get to know her. It was both terrifying and liberating to finally acknowledge that she wanted to be seen for who she was. She wasn't Madison anymore, but Elizabeth's dark corners still left her feeling jumpy and uncertain. Still, she wanted out of the bubble of isolation in which she'd held herself prisoner. She wanted to be free of the debilitating anxiety that she would be taken advantage of. Her father had bestowed that gift upon her. It was time to give it back.

Elizabeth got up from the bench. She understood now that her great wall of forgetting, although a helpful coping device, had not allowed her to appropriately deal with what she had gone through. And even though Gil, the only human being on the planet who could see her for who she truly was, had pushed her away, Elizabeth was hopeful that ultimately she would be able to embrace the true reflection of herself that was only now beginning to gaze back at her.

With a wistful glance toward the couple in the canoe, she turned and started up through the pine trees. How easy it would be, she thought, to return the rental car, take the train back to Oregon, and forget about the rest of it. But denial was no longer serving her life. And right now it wasn't about taking the easy path. It was time to face her parents and speak the truth. What would happen after that, she wasn't sure. Maybe her mother would hate her for ruining their happy, well organized life. Maybe her father would deny it and demand that she leave. Or maybe they would hear her out and face the fact that the life they had been living was a forgery. Whatever their reaction was, it didn't matter. Unburdening the family secret she had dutifully carried all these years was the first step in getting beyond where she was currently stuck. The rest was change. And she could handle that, couldn't she?

As she approached her car, a man loading a mountain bike into the back of his silver SUV looked up at her. He was tan and muscular with a salt and pepper goatee. His green eyes lit up and he smiled.

"Beautiful day."

Elizabeth nodded but didn't respond. She pulled her keys out of the pocket of her jeans and unlocked the car. As she was about to get in, she stopped. *He is not my father* she told herself. *He did not force himself on me.* She looked up. The man was leaning against the back of his truck drinking from a bottle of water.

"Hey."

The man lowered his bottle and turned to her. His face was relaxed. He looked to her like he didn't have a care in the world.

"It *is* a beautiful day." She smiled brightly. "Enjoy."

He lifted his water bottle as if toasting her. "You do the same."

And then she was in her car backing up. She gave him a little wave and he shot her a grin. Elizabeth drove away, punched the button for the radio, and rolled down her window. *He is a nice looking man,* she thought. In the rear view mirror she could see him with his leg up on the truck bumper stretching his hamstring. An image of Gil doing the same thing, his long hair hiding his face as he brought his chest down to his knee, flashed in her mind. Elizabeth frowned. *God,* she thought, *will I ever be able to get him out of my head.*

In front of her, the road banked into a long curve.

20

Esther Braverman was on a stepladder watering a pot of yellow begonias when Alma, the Braverman's housekeeper, led Marjorie onto the patio.

"Esther, those are beautiful."

"Hi." Esther lowered the watering can.

"Thanks Alma," Marjorie said as the housekeeper turned to go.

"I'll bring some lemonade," Alma said somberly and walked back into the house.

She knows about the lump, Marjorie thought, noting that Alma's normally boisterous behavior was unusually subdued. Esther set the watering can down next to a wrought-iron chaise lounge.

"Come, sit." Esther gestured to the dark green cushion of the other chaise. She sat as Marjorie walked toward her. She seems fine, Marjorie thought. Not a glimmer of stress on her face. Marjorie, on the other hand, felt nervous. She had decided to tell Esther about the night Elizabeth disappeared. She wanted advice on what she should do. Esther had been a lawyer. She would know the best way to proceed.

Marjorie sat down and leaned back in the chaise. Above them, on the ivy covered beams of the portico, a bird gently cooed. Esther glanced up.

"These doves have been hanging around for a couple weeks now. They make Marty nervous when he sits here reading the paper." She brought her gaze back to Marjorie and winked. "I kinda like it. It's relaxing."

Marjorie smiled. "Esther, you're an amazing woman."

Esther laughed and leaned back on the chaise. "Why? Because I like the sound of doves or because I'm not a hysterical wreck over this lump they found?"

"Both." Marjorie was happy that Esther brought up the lump so she didn't have to.

A long silence fell between them. Esther's eyes were closed and she seemed to be listening to the cooing of the doves. Marjorie saw in the older woman's finely structured face, now softened and lined by the years, a younger woman of great strength and drive. Esther had been a corporate attorney, a college professor, and a mother. In all the years they had known each other, Esther had never slowed down in her philanthropic duties or in her devotion to her children and grandchildren. She was a remarkably gentle balance to her husband's sinewy toughness.

"I had an affair once." Esther opened her eyes and looked at Marjorie. Marjorie's mouth dropped open in surprise. Just then Alma walked out onto the patio carrying a tray with a pitcher of lemonade and a plate of what looked like chocolate-mint Girl Scout cookies. An affair, Marjorie thought, watching Alma pour them each a glass of lemonade. Esther and Marty had been married for 41 years.

"Here you go, ladies." Alma set the pitcher down on the table.

"Thank you," Esther said.

Alma walked back into the house and the doves resumed their cooing.

"He was a tax attorney. We met on a flight from Chicago." Esther picked up one of the cookies, scrutinized it, and then put it on the side of the plate. Marjorie wondered if Esther was waiting for her to ask a question, like, 'Why did you do it?' Or, 'How long did you see him?' But Marjorie was too shocked to speak. She had always looked at Marty and Esther's long and seemingly happy relationship as an example upon which to pattern her own marriage.

"Marty had been working ridiculous hours and he and I hadn't made love in months."

Esther picked up the same cookie and this time took a tiny bite. "I felt ignored. It was foolish of me, and selfish. But it happened."

Marjorie picked up her glass of lemonade and took a drink. Esther raised her eyes from the cookie in her hand and looked out into the flower garden.

"I have been wondering if this lump in my breast is punishment for that indiscretion."

Marjorie reached over and patted her arm as Esther struggled to keep from crying.

"Other than those three weeks in the fall of 1977, I've been a pretty good person. There's no past history of breast cancer in my family. So… I'm having a hard time understanding why this is happening."

"You don't know for sure what it is. The results aren't back yet. It might be nothing."

Esther wiped under her eyes with the pads of her fingers. "I know, but it has to be something. It's a lump that's not supposed to be there."

"It could be benign. It might be a cyst of some kind. You don't know."

"But if I wouldn't have had that affair, if I could have been stronger, maybe this wouldn't be happening to me now."

Marjorie tried to think of something reassuring to say, but her mind was busy contemplating the hell she would be required to suffer for sticking her head in the sand and ignoring the truth about what Steven had done to Elizabeth.

"Listen." Esther gripped Marjorie's hand. "You didn't come over here to see me cry. I'll get myself under control here in a minute." She reached into her pocket, pulled out a tissue and dabbed at her eyes. "I must confess," Esther said, then she laughed. "I guess I just did." She smiled and shook her head. "But what I mean is, since I've known you and Steven, the two of you have been such an inspiration to me. Marty is not an easy man to live with. I love him dearly but he's a lot of work. But when I see how devoted you and that good-looking husband of yours are, and how you stuck together after what happened with Elizabeth, I am encouraged to be more patient with Marty."

Marjorie gazed down at her hands in her lap.

"I'm serious," Esther said, "you both pulled me through some difficult times."

In Marjorie's mind she heard the dreadful creaking of the bed and the low moans. I have my own cancer, she thought. And it's eating me up as we sit here. It's too terrible and ugly to talk about. But if I don't, I'm afraid of what I might do. She watched Esther dab at her eyes with the tissue. To shatter Esther's myth of my marriage and reveal the hideous truth would be cruel. It's not what she needs to hear. Not now.

"Would you like a cookie?" Esther lifted the plate and held it out to her.

"Thank you." And Marjorie politely took one.

• • • • •

Gil struggled to rouse himself from sleep. From somewhere close by, Lindsey called to him again. "Daddy!" Then he heard Drake say, "We miss you."

Dragging himself toward consciousness, Gil's mind filled with streaming images of his children: their cheeks rosy and eyes bright, skimming down the snow-covered ninth fairway in North Park on the same aluminum saucer he'd sledded with as a child, Lindsey in the kitchen on her second birthday with chocolate cake all over her face, Drake doing Kung Fu moves in the back yard and giving fierce high-pitched Bruce Lee yells. Just before opening his eyes, Gil heard Bonnie say, "Honey, I have something to show you."

The inside of his two-man tent was pitch-black. Gil pushed himself up on one elbow. The exhilaration of once again seeing his children faded into a familiar dull ache in the center of his chest. It was just another dream.

Then, from outside the tent, he heard, "Daddy."

Gil threw off his sleeping bag, fumbled to unzip the screen, and crawled out of the tent.

The campsite was dark as he got to his feet. The first direction he looked was across the street at the oak tree.

"Daddy."

Gil's eyes swung back toward the sound of the voice. On the other side of camp he saw a flicker of movement. Instinctively he started toward it. From deep in the rational part of his brain a warning tried to make itself heard. But Gil wasn't listening. He wanted to hold his children. He wanted to kiss his wife. A branch snapped at the edge of the woods. Gil turned.

"Dad."

He spun back toward the tent and saw Drake standing behind the ice chests. Gil couldn't see his face but he could make out the outline of a baseball cap on his head.

"Daddy."

At the sound of Lindsey's voice Gil turned toward the woods. She was peeking out from behind a tree. He could barely make out her hand as she waved. Hi sweetie, Gil thought, stepping toward her. He suddenly felt lighter than he had in months. His children were back.

"Over here, Gil." He turned. Bonnie was standing in front of the tent.

"Mommy has something for you," Drake said.

"She wants to show you," Lindsey called to him.

"Come here, honey," Bonnie said.

The warning he ignored earlier was now shouting in his head. But Gil fought to over-ride it. I see them, he reassured himself. They're talking to me. Remembering the feel of her body and the warmth of her mouth he stepped toward the shadowy figure of his wife. He would hold her once again. He would bury his face in the nape of her neck and breathe in her smell. Drake and Lindsey would laugh and yell for them to stop and to come play with them. It would be like it had been, like it still should be.

Two beams of light shot out of the darkness. They met, illuminating the figure before him. Gil stopped walking. It wasn't Bonnie he was looking at. It was a teenage girl.

"Take a look at this, honey." She pulled up her shirt. Her breasts, large and pale, swayed to and fro. Laugher erupted all around him as flashlights sent swords of light stabbing helter-skelter into the darkness. Gil saw Drake, or the boy who was pretending to be Drake, get up off of his knees and start dancing around, laughing hysterically.

"Titties for Daddy!" The girl who had been Lindsey threw an empty beer can at his feet.

Squinting against the glare of flashlight beams swinging erratically from his face to the girl's breasts to the tops of the trees, Gil watched the teenagers' frenzied antics in stunned surprise. His wife and children…

"What did you do with them!" And then Gil was running. He was no longer a sad, confused victim. He had someone to punish.

The bare-breasted girl had only taken a few steps when he hit her. His forearm in the middle of her back sent her sprawling face first into the dirt. There were shouts and a car started. He turned toward the road. The boy with the baseball cap was halfway down the slope. Gil sprinted after him, righteous in his demand for blood. He tackled the boy, driving him into the ground.

"Get off me!"

Not until you give me what I need, Gil thought, clamping his forearm on the boy's throat. The boy struggled, clawing at Gil's arms. Staring into the teenager's terrified face, Gil waited to feel the pain lift. Nothing happened. Gil pressed harder. The boy's eyes bulged as he frantically thrashed his arms and legs trying to escape. Gil felt nothing inside of himself change. His anger and loss and sadness remained. There was the sound of running footsteps then something smashed into Gil's ribs. The next thing he knew he was laying on his side getting stomped and kicked in the chest and back of his legs.

"You crazy fucker!" A boy kicked Gil in the stomach.

"Asshole!" The girl who'd exposed her breasts swung her leg back and drove her hiking boot into the back of Gil's head.

• • • • •

Elizabeth looked at herself in the mirror. A crease from her pillow ran diagonally across her left cheek looking like a scar mysteriously earned sometime in the night. Her hair was its usual morning rumbled mess, but her eyes — there was something different. She leaned over the sink for a closer look.

"Look at you, all bright-eyed and sassy," she whispered to her reflection. Her image in the mirror smiled. "You're not done yet," she told herself, "but so far, so good."

She had never checked into a motel before. Last night when the clerk saw that she was from Oregon he started chatting her up about his Aunt who had moved there in the 1970s. Although he seemed friendly, Elizabeth quickly said goodnight, went to her room, locked the door, and barricaded it with two chairs and a small round table.

She lay in bed with the lights out for a long time thinking of how far she had come since leaving Fair Haven. Life in the commune was feeling more and more like a thing of the past, but what she was moving toward was still vague and undefined. Alone in the dark, she tried to imagine what would it be like to see her parents again? Would her father apologize? Would he tell her that it had been a horrible mistake, that he was drunk and thought he was in his own bedroom with his wife? But that wasn't true. He knew what he was doing. He had stared into her face the entire time it was happening; that look in his eyes as if he was peering right into her. And her mother, would she be able to sit down and hear the truth of what her husband had done?

Elizabeth rolled onto her side and wrapped her arms around the pillow. She was tired of being custodian of the secret. She didn't want to forgive anyone, but she wanted to get beyond her fears. What was the smart way to go about doing that? Why shouldn't her father suffer for what he had done? Why was it her job to protect her mother? But what if other people found out? Then everyone would know her secret. Everyone would know what her father had done to her.

At that moment, knees drawn up, hugging the pillow to her chest, Elizabeth thought of something she had never consciously allowed herself to face before — what if he had done it to other girls?

21

The next morning Linda McKelvey was dusting the bookshelves in Tom's office when the doorbell rang. Out the window she saw a blue compact car in the driveway.

"I'm coming!"

At the front door, Elizabeth pushed a loose strand of hair away from her face. She heard approaching footsteps on the other side of the door and was struck with a panicky desire to run. You're not ready for this, she thought in a rush. It's too much. Then the door opened and Mrs. McKevey was looking at her.

"Yes."

"Hi, Mrs. McKelvey."

"Hello. Can I help —," Linda stopped talking. She looked closely at Elizabeth. Her eyes widened in surprise. "Oh my God!" She rushed out and threw her arms around Elizabeth. "Oh my God, oh my God. How are you?"

Elizabeth hugged her and started to cry. Linda eased back from her and looked into her face. "I'm so glad to see you."

"Me too."

"Come in. I'll make some ice tea."

• • • • •

Dominic watched the young boy on the floor in the waiting room. A steady stream of odd electronic sounds chirped from his hand-held computer. The slender red-head across the room with sunken cheeks and a furtive look in her eyes had spoken to the boy three times without getting a response. He continued pushing buttons and letting out frustrated grunts and groans. The woman shook her head and went back to flipping through the magazine in her lap.

Dominic glanced at his watch. He had been at the hospital for over two hours. He should have left long ago. The hedge on the Kellogg's side yard needed trimming and Mrs. Palmieri had an oak limb down in her front yard. He leaned forward, resting his head in his hands. The young man's face, pasty white and covered in blood, had been a shock to see. When the headlights revealed his body on the side of the road, Dominic thought it was a pile of rags. Why he stopped he didn't know. He always said prayers for the man and his family, but he didn't stop. This time for some reason he did.

The ambulance attendants said that Gil was concussed and might have internal bleeding. They told Dominic that he might have saved Gil Linnetti's life. Dominic heard their words but he wasn't really listening. Gil's limp, seemingly lifeless body, the blood on his face, and the gravel imbedded in his cheek, had brought back memories of Michael. Although less vivid than they had been years earlier, they still lit up his brain in a firestorm of gore and horror. Fourteen parts, that's what was left of his beautiful boy. Back then he tried to imagine if the fourteen parts were enough to reconstruct Michael into a whole human being. And if not, what was missing? Was it his right hand? Or could it be an ear or a leg? If parts of Michael were missing, who had them? What was being done to them? Were they lying in the jungle for an animal to find? Or had the Viet Cong taken them as victory souvenirs. Dominic had desperately wanted to understand why his only child was blown into so many pieces. He had tried to see in his mind the firefight that ended his son's life. He would visualize the incoming mortars and the return fire from Michael's patrol. In the chaos of that night, two other Americans died. Michael had known them both since boot camp. They had begun and died together.

"Mom." The kid on the floor never took his eyes off the game in his hands. "How much longer? When can we see him?"

The redhead looked up from the magazine. She glanced to Dominic and then to the boy. "Ricky, just be quiet. Play your game. The doctor is going to be out in a little bit."

The boy grunted. After a flurry of button pushing he raised both hands into the air.

"Level six!"

His mother shot him a stern look. "I said quietly."

The boy grinned up at her and in a loud whisper said, "Level six, Mom!" She rolled her eyes and went back to her magazine. Not getting any congratulations from his mother, the boy turned to Dominic and gave him an enthusiastic thumbs-up and mouthed the words *level six*.

A young doctor in a white lab coat came around the corner into the waiting room. His dark hair was rumpled and his eyes glazed with fatigue.

"Mr. Angelo. You should go home. His CAT scan was fine and he's breathing on his own."

Dominic stood up. "I wanted to make sure that…" His voice trailed off. For a long moment nobody said anything. The boy on the floor looked up from his game.

The doctor nodded. "I understand." He checked his watch. "Right." He turned to leave but then stopped and looked back at Dominic. "There are a lot of press people out front. You might want to avoid going that way."

Dominic nodded. The doctor gave him a tight-lipped smile and walked out of the waiting room.

• • • • •

Mr. McKelvey would be home soon and Elizabeth didn't want to block the driveway. She backed her car out and pulled forward along the curb in front of their house. She felt good about what she'd learned in her conversation with Mrs. McKelvey. Sarah and Emily were leading happy productive lives with husbands, and in Emily's case, two children. Unless they had higher, thicker walls of forgetting than she did, it was doubtful that her father had molested them. For that she was grateful.

Mrs. McKelvey had made it clear in their conversation that she was enormously proud of her daughters. She loved them fiercely. Elizabeth was glad to hear that the girls had remained close with their mother. She surprised herself by asking Mrs. McKelvey if her mother ever spoke of her. "Oh, yes," Linda told her. "We always joke around about you girls and all the crazy things you did. Sure she talks about you." On one hand it made Elizabeth feel good that her mother still thought of her, but at the same time, it made her feel guilty.

Linda didn't push for more. She had changed the subject to Emily's boys. When she showed her a picture of them, Elizabeth had burst out laughing. They both looked exactly like Mr. McKelvey.

Out on the street, Elizabeth opened the trunk of her car. She pulled out her backpack and swung it onto her shoulders. She slammed the trunk and started toward the house. She hadn't told Mrs. McKelvey any specifics about the past. She gave her a vague story about being unhappy and wanting her freedom. Linda was kind enough not to ask a lot of questions.

"Come on up," Linda called as Elizabeth walked back inside the house. "I'm putting new batteries in this remote so you can watch TV. I think I have it right."

At the top of the stairs Elizabeth heard the TV click on.

"Yay!" Linda sounded happy.

She followed the sound of the TV down the hall to Sarah's old bedroom. As she approached the door, she heard a reporter on the television say, "…hospitalized this morning after being found beaten and unconscious."

"Oh my gosh." Linda pointed the remote at the screen. "Do you know about this? Your parents—"

Elizabeth cut her off, "I know." She watched the reporter standing in the middle of Gil's campsite. Gil's distraught face filled the screen. More footage of him at the campsite followed. As she watched, Elizabeth felt like she was falling off the edge of something she hadn't realized she was standing on.

"Which hospital?" She swung the pack off of her shoulders, never taking her eyes off the screen. "Which hospital, come on, come on."

"Do you know him?"

The exterior of Passavant Hospital appeared on screen.

Elizabeth turned to Linda. "Where is that?"

"Passavant Hospital. It's off of Babcock Boulevard, by Cumberland."

Elizabeth headed for the stairs.

"Your parents," Linda called after her, "have been helping him."

Elizabeth charged down the stairs.

"They might be at the hospital!"

Elizabeth paused, momentarily considering Linda's words. Then she pulled open the front door and ran for her car.

• • • • •

Darla Seelbach lifted a spoonful of frozen yogurt, closed her eyes and let the cold sweetness slowly melt in her mouth. Brownie chocolate chip was her favorite and she hadn't had it in weeks. Across the round cafe table, Tracy Rockwell was in a similar blissful state.

"This stuff should be illegal it's so friggin' good."

Darla nodded, not wanting to say anything that might interrupt the surge of pleasure she was experiencing. She spooned up more and closed her eyes.

Most of the after church crowd had already drifted out, leaving Dale's Yogurt and Candy Shop nearly empty. Darla enjoyed attending the Catholic service with Tracy. She liked the smell of incense and the kneeling part. It seemed more respectful than sitting in the pews and praying like they did at her Methodist church. She kneeled on the padded fold-down bench, praying for better understanding about what she should do. She didn't want to be a coward. Her parents had always told her that the most important person to be proud of is yourself. She didn't want to look in the mirror in ten years and be disappointed about what she had or hadn't done. She also prayed for Mrs. Davenport. But Darla knew, even as she was doing it, that her prayers for Mrs. Davenport were a blatant negotiation with God: I'm sending positive thoughts and kind wishes to her, so please do what you can to get her horrible scream out of my head. Darla didn't hold out much hope that prayers like hers would be answered.

"Hey, there's that guy." Tracy was looking toward the rear of the shop.

Darla turned. On the TV mounted in the corner, Gil Linnetti's face filled the screen.

Tracey pointed her chocolate covered spoon at the TV. "He's the one whose wife and kids got killed, right?"

"Ssssh!" The volume on the TV was low. Darla heard "hospital" and "severely beaten." Gil's campsite, now surrounded by camera crews, appeared on the screen. Next came a shot of a reporter standing in front of Passavent hospital. The only thing Darla heard her say was, "end of his vigil."

Tracy went back to her yogurt. "How crappy is that? First his family and then this."

Darla's mind raced. Did Davenport do something? Was this his way of sending her a message?

"I have to go." Darla pushed back from the table.

"Why? Jimmy and those guys are coming."

Darla started for the door. She didn't want to start crying in front of Tracy.

"Sorry. I'll try and catch up with you later."

She ran across the parking lot to her car. Once inside Essie, Darla let the tears come. With them came the voice of guilt: *as if killing his family wasn't enough, now you might be responsible for putting him in the hospital. How much damage can one girl do?* Darla cried harder, burying her face in her hands. *If Davenport's wife hadn't scared you, you might have stopped him. You might have kept him from hurting Mr. Linnetti – again!*

"I can't take it anymore!" she shouted.

Through the windshield she saw a man carrying shopping bags. His wife pushed a stroller as they made their way down the lane of parked cars. A girl, one row over, talked on a cell phone while unlocking her car. A Jeep went by with hip-hop music blaring. I want to be normal again, Darla prayed, I want to be like everyone else. The .357 hidden under the back stoop flashed in her mind.

• • • • •

Marjorie swung the Volvo out into traffic and nearly smashed into an on-coming car. Brakes screeched and the other driver's horn blared. Marjorie tossed him a sheepish, apologetic wave. With her heart racing, she accelerated down the road.

Since her talk with Esther Braverman, she had been walking through her life like an actress performing in a play for which she had never re-hearsed. She wasn't sure what she was supposed to do or say or even how to think. The lie that her life had been since the night Elizabeth disap-peared, ground down on her mercilessly, inciting profound self-loathing and despair. Everything was blurring beyond recognition. Behind the lie she willfully clasped to her heart for so many years was a blank void. This colorless, formless future left her dumbstruck in the enormity of its mystery. Who was she? What kind of mother willingly denies the rape of her daughter? And Steven, the man to whom she had devoted her life, her inspiration and guiding light since she was twenty years old, who was he? What kind of man can do what he did and go on with life as if nothing happened?

Marjorie saw, looking back, all the ways in which he steered her into believing that Elizabeth's disappearance was an act of rebellion or the result of drug use. He twisted her and pointed her in the direction he wanted her to go. But ultimately, Marjorie admitted, she had led herself. She simply allowed him to walk her further down the soul-numbing path of denial upon which she had already placed herself.

Looking at his smiling, confident face made her want to punch him as hard as she could. She had slept in Elizabeth's room since hearing her daughter's pleading voice from fifteen years ago. She knew Steven was concerned about her, but she didn't know what to do or say. With so many lies and deceptions was there even any point in discussing it? She couldn't remain married to him after what she knew. Could she? The fact that she even entertained the possibility made her hate herself even more.

Finding Elizabeth was the one thing she could do to make things right. Perhaps Elizabeth had children of her own. Through acts of kindness to her grandchildren she might be able redeem herself in Elizabeth's eyes. She could help provide for her grandchildren in ways that she had been unable to do for Elizabeth.

A minivan traveling in the lane next to Marjorie abruptly swerved in front of her car. She hit the brakes while at the same time reaching for the bouquet of irises sitting on the passenger seat. The van crossed over in front of her and turned into the parking lot of the Giant Eagle. Marjorie repositioned the flowers on the seat. Mr. Linnetti's unfortunate injury had given her a focus and purpose she wished she had every day. Shopping for him had been a welcome distraction. He was a man who would appreciate irises, she'd assured herself. There was something innocent and sweet about him. Blue irises were just the right choice.

• • • • •

"I want to go back to my camp." Gil was propped up in the hospital bed with a bandage on his cheek. He was starting to look better. Elizabeth bent the straw in the water glass and handed it to him. He took a sip.

The police officer who had been there earlier was surprised when Gil refused to give a description of the teenagers. "They were defending themselves," Gil told the officer. "It was a drunken practical joke."

"That's beyond a practical joke." Elizabeth looked to the officer who nodded in agreement.

"It doesn't matter." Gil was calmly resigned. "I started it. They defended themselves. It was my fault."

"It's not your fault they beat you senseless," Elizabeth said after the officer left.

But Gil was resolute. "I reacted with violence. They turned it back on me. It's over." Then he smiled at her. His eyes closed and for a moment the smile remained. Then he let out a long sigh and opened his eyes.

There's something different, Elizabeth thought, something changed in Gil. The bitterness percolating beneath his superficial politeness was gone. He seemed softer, less embattled. She watched him take another sip of water then put the glass down on the table next to his bed. He turned to the window.

Outside, sunlight slanted through the clouds. Gil gazed at the spectacle feeling grateful and content. They had come to him in his unconsciousness — Bonnie, Drake, and Lindsey — all three smiling and happy to see him. Lindsey had jumped into his arms and Drake climbed onto his back. Together they ran and wrestled, and Bonnie kissed him. They held hands, laughing and being silly. He could still feel the sweet pressure of Bonnie's lips. Where they had met, what that place was, he didn't know. But it was real, just beyond where his rational mind permitted him to go. He tried to stay, but Drake waved him away. "Go, Daddy," his beautiful boy said. "Keep doing good things."

Gil turned away from the window. "My memories are like strings to them. They connect me to what exists — what is alive in…" his voice trailed off.

Elizabeth reached for him and rested her hand on his shoulder.

"There is someplace where they are." Gil was intently looking at her.

In his eyes she saw something that she hadn't seen since that horrible day when she stopped him in the woods and begged him to help her. The absolute truth of his soul seemed to be shining through to her.

"They're not lost." Gil was smiling again. "And neither am I. I'm doing the right thing."

Elizabeth nodded and squeezed his shoulder.

"Thank you, Elizabeth, for coming back here to help me. I know it's been hard on you. I've been hard on you. Thank you."

"My pleasure."

His eyes shone up at her. "Please take me back to my camp."

She could almost see the beautiful, daring boy who had rescued her. She knew that who Gil had been to her in the past wasn't going to help in her healing, but still it touched her to catch a glimpse of his sweetness. She leaned down and kissed him on the cheek.

"Okay. I'll take you back to camp."

She walked out of his hospital room feeling as if someone had pulled aside the drapes in a darkened room and flooded her with sunshine.

22

Darla watched two women with Get Well Gil signs and bouquets of flowers walk in the rear door of the hospital. They went to the elevators and pushed the button for the sixth floor. A large contingent of supporters had been filing in since Darla arrived. Upstairs in the sixth floor waiting room, the well-wishers inquired about Gil's status and dropped off gifts. While Darla was up there checking on Davenport's whereabouts, a perky brunette nurse in a blue scrub top came out to speak to those gathered in the waiting area. "Hi everyone. My name is Asa. I'm the head nurse on the floor. Mr. Linnetti regained consciousness on the way to the hospital. All signs indicate that he is doing fine." She grinned. "He's already demanding to leave the hospital." That had gotten a supportive cheer from the crowd.

Darla got up from where she was sitting in the lobby and walked to the glass rear doors of the hospital. She looked out, searching the parking lot for Davenport. In the flood of kindness coming to Gil, she thought, there was no room for Davenport's lies and manipulation. The news crew in the front of the hospital would ensure that Davenport would come to the back entrance, and when he did, she would stop him before he walked inside. Darla went back to the chair and sat down. She put the sweatshirt, with the .357 wrapped inside, on her lap.

Steven Davenport pulled into the rear parking lot of the hospital avoiding the media frenzy out front. He parked the car and reached for the basket of fresh fruit on the seat next to him. He paused, his hand resting on the basket. Damn, he thought, it's always the same. Every time I go to a hospital, Kelly shows up in my mind.

She was blue when he found her, a mottled grayish blue. Slumped over in the corner of her closet, a syringe still dangling from her vein, he thought she was dead. When he felt a pulse in her neck, he ran and called the police. His father was at work, but Steven knew it wouldn't be long before they called him. When his father found out, he would punish Kelly. He would go to her room and in the darkness, Steven would hear it: the grunting, the bed creaking, and then the long silence before his father got up and went back to his bedroom. Every time it happened, more of Kelly disappeared. He had watched her sadness deepen and the distracted look in her eyes harden into hopelessness. But that day, with the needle in her arm, she had looked peaceful. Her mouth wasn't turned down and her expression had softened and relaxed. Even though he knew it was wrong, that he shouldn't feel that way because his sister was blue and maybe going to die, he was glad for her. She looked happier than he had seen her in a long time. Steven had sat in the hospital waiting room for several hours before his father arrived. After talking to the doctors, his father looked strange. His face was tight and his eyes didn't seem to know where to focus. Steven hoped his gaze wouldn't land on him. He tried to make himself invisible in the waiting room. Later, when the doctor came and talked to his father, Steven knew Kelly was dead. The doctor's eyes gave it away. There was weariness beyond fatigue that told Steven his sister was gone. When his father went away with the doctor, Steven walked out the emergency room door. Standing in a freezing wind, he thought about running away. He would hitchhike to some place like Florida or Mexico where it was warm. He'd find a deserted beach where he could swim and live in a thatched-roof shack like Robinson Crusoe. He would live on fish, coconuts, and oranges. Everything else he would need would wash up on the beach. But Steven didn't go. He knew if he tried to get away from his father and got caught, his punishment would be far worse than if he stayed and never tried at all. It was a decision he would regret almost immediately.

On the way home from the hospital his father slammed him against the passenger side door. "You should have known what was going on with her! You should have told me!" He smacked him hard on the side of the head. "It's your fault she's dead!" Steven's last sanctuary of emotional vulnerability was invaded by his father's vicious accusations. Barricaded against two years of brutality, his final remnant of tenderness was routed that night by his father's cruelty. Steven, unwilling to take responsibility for Kelly's death, but too frightened to challenge his father, chose, in a desperate act of self-preservation to cast off the final threads still connecting him to his compassion, empathy and love. He went dead inside. But as in nature, when there is devastation, there is rebirth. Emerging from the fertile plains of Steven's subconscious, came a bottomless void empty of everything but need. This vortex of crippled emotion hungered to feel again. It demanded to be lifted by joy, and rubbed raw by grief. It craved to have bitterness and envy rough it up, and kindness sooth out the sore spots. It wanted to be alive again, not dead. But the connections had been corrupted, the ability to have those experiences lost. But the vortex of need didn't care. It demanded to be satisfied. So Steven went elsewhere for his emotional life, feeding off of others. Tears fascinated him, outbursts of rage, though sometimes confusing, intrigued him. The more complex the emotional situation, the more it captivated him. The girls he had sex with on his trips to Indonesia were a tremendous source of pleasure. Most of them existed in a disturbingly tangled web of conflicting emotions: the need to please, disgust in what they did, fascination with foreigners, the fear of being hurt, pride in their ability to support their families, anger over lost innocence, naïve dreams of a better life, debilitating self-loathing, and the overriding desire to do anything for money. Ellie, the twelve year old who had sold him the mirror frame hanging in the powder room, was a tornado of emotional life. She raged from tears and laughter to pouting insolence and girlish giggles. That was the beauty of children for Steven. All of it was there in their eyes and in their young bodies, passing quickly from feeling to feeling in one extraordinary surge of emotion. It was a pure, rich tapestry from which he could experience everything he was unable to access for himself. But even that treasure trove wasn't enough to satiate him for long. The emptiness inside always demanded more.

Steven opened the door of his car and got out with the basket. Gil would appreciate the fruit. Hospital food left a lot to be desired. He walked toward the door of the hospital, his eyes scanning the rows of cars. Darla's armed warning had been an effective deterrent. But the lure of this new situation was too potent for him to ignore. After suffering the death of his wife and children and then becoming a victim of violence himself, Gil would have an entirely fresh level of emotion to share. Steven needed to look into the man's eyes and see what that felt like.

The elevator doors opened and Elizabeth stepped out into the hospital lobby. Relieved that Gil was going to be okay, she was thinking of a special meal she could make for him back at the campsite. He had said he liked linguini and clams. That wouldn't be too difficult, she reasoned. She glanced toward the glass rear doors hoping the press hadn't made their way there. Seeing that all was clear, she started across the lobby. A teenage girl sitting near the doors suddenly jumped up and ran outside. Elizabeth was trying to remember how to get to the grocery store when she looked through the doors and saw the girl run up to a man in the parking lot. The man was carrying a basket. As the automatic doors slid open, Elizabeth got a clear look at the man's face. Her stomach lurched. She did an immediate about-face and walked back into the lobby.

"Hey, come on, easy," Steven's eyes were focused on the gun barrel poking out from the sweatshirt draped over Darla's arm. "I wanted to bring something nice for your friend, Gil." He held up the basket of fruit.

"I told you to stay away from him. Did you do this? Did you beat him up?"

"What— no. Absolutely not. Why would I hurt him? The poor man has suffered enough."

The voice of guilt rose up in Darla: *End it! Give him what he deserves! It's your responsibility!"*

"How is he doing?" Steven wanted to take control of the conversation. "I hope he's okay."

"Shut up."

"Okay. I'm leaving. But — what did you do to my wife? Did you tell her something?"

"I didn't say anything. I should have told her what you did to me. She deserves to know."

"You have to stop this, Darla. You're acting like a crazy girl. I said I was sorry about what happened between us. I truly am sorry. Can I give you something — a gift that will make it better between us? Money?"

Darla was trembling. She wanted to blast Davenport and his apologies and his money into a bloody pile right there in the parking lot. Instead she motioned with the .357.

"Walk to your car."

"Okay, I'm going." Steven started walking. Darla followed him.

He glanced over his shoulder. "You don't have to — I'm leaving, okay."

Darla didn't say anything.

"What are you going to do shoot me? There are security cameras. They'll hunt you down in five minutes."

Darla remained silent.

"Darla."

Steven heard nothing but footsteps behind him. He suddenly realized that perhaps Darla had crossed a line. Maybe reasoning and shaming were no longer effective methods of controlling her. If that was the case, he would have to take action. It was too bad it had come to this, he thought. But when the opportunity presented itself, he wouldn't hesitate.

Through the glass doors Elizabeth watched her father and the girl walk into the parking lot. Her anger had flared as she observed them talking. It now propelled her boldly out the door. She didn't know what she was going to do, but this girl wasn't going to be another of his victims.

Walking across the parking lot with Darla's gun at his back, Steven Davenport was unexpectedly pre-occupied with a memory of his mother. Sitting in a wingback chair, a vase of fresh daisies on the table next to her, she was knitting a sweater for him. Her hands moved, the needles dipping and turning in a graceful, fluid rhythm as she listened to *La Traviata*. She never raised a hand to wipe away her tears. She continued knitting, letting the wetness fall into her lap, onto his new green sweater. The music filled the house and seemed to Steven to also fill his mother. The moment the turntable needle touched down on any of her beloved records, her eyes would brighten, her face, as if emerging from shadows into the warm glow of a fire would become luminous. She listened to the records only when his father, who considered opera elitist and highbrow, was gone. When Steven was seven years old his father threw the entire collection in the trash. But Kelly, after waiting until her father was asleep, snuck outside and rescued the records from the garbage can. Only five of them had been smashed in their father's rampage. The next day after school, Kelly presented them to their mother. The two women cried together, bonding in a way that Steven knew he would never understand. After that Kelly took charge of the records, hiding them in the back of her closet and bringing them out only when it was safe. After their mother died, Kelly and Steven would play them when they were alone in the house. It was comforting to have those recordings, their mother's secret love surrounding them in the empty house. As Kelly got older she became less interested in opera, but Steven clung to it, cultivating his appreciation and nurturing the link to his mother. When Kelly died, he moved the records from their hiding place in her closet and hid them under the staircase in the basement. They were never played in that house again.

As he approached his car, thoughts of his mother and Kelly and *La Traviata* vanished as he felt the blunt pressure of the gun in his side.

"Unlock it and get in." Darla jabbed the gun into his ribs.

At the top of the hill, Marjorie slowed down. Priding herself on her good luck finding parking places, she turned right, heading for the row of cars closest to the hospital's rear entrance. As she approached, she saw Steven and a young girl talking together. Her initial surprise and displeasure at seeing Steven quickly dissolved as she recognized the girl as the same one who had threatened her in the backyard with the gun. Marjorie watched as Steven, closely followed by the girl, walked to the second row of cars. As Steven opened the door of his BMW, the tightly wrought psychology maintaining Marjorie's outwardly normal behavior snapped. Her hand jammed down on the horn and her foot stabbed the gas pedal to the floor. The Volvo leapt forward, speeding down the row of cars.

Elizabeth turned toward the roar of the engine. The Volvo screeched around the corner at the end of the parking lot and accelerated down the second aisle of cars. Elizabeth looked back in time to see Darla, momentarily distracted by the sound of the Volvo, look up from where she was standing next to the open passenger side door. Suddenly Darla was jerked forward, smashing into the edge of the roof and dropping out of sight between the cars. Stunned for a moment, Elizabeth was about to run to help her when she heard a gunshot. Partially drowned out by the Volvo screeching to a stop with its horn still blaring, the sharp report of the gun sent a jolt of adrenaline through Elizabeth. She ducked behind a car.

"Steven!" Marjorie jumped out of the Volvo.

He got out of the BMW. "Hi honey."

Elizabeth, still crouching behind cars, ran to the row closer to her father's BMW. Where was the girl, she thought? What had he done?

One aisle over, crouching behind a red SUV, Darla peered in the direction of Steven's BMW. There was a roaring in her ears and her hands were shaking. She glanced across the aisle for an escape route. She saw

Elizabeth also hiding behind a car. Their eyes met. *Don't move*, Elizabeth mouthed to Darla, gesturing with her hands for the girl to stay where she was. Darla glanced toward the BMW then back to Elizabeth. She nodded her head. Elizabeth quickly walked to her car and backed out of the parking place. As she drove to the next aisle she could see her parents still talking beside the Volvo. She stopped where Darla was hiding and opened the passenger side door. Darla shot from her hiding place like a spooked rabbit. She ducked down on the floor, her entire body trembling.

"Go!"

"Are you hurt?"

"Just drive!"

Elizabeth drove slowly down the lane of cars. One aisle over, her father turned to watch as she drove past. Elizabeth turned right and pulled out of the hospital lot.

"You can get up."

Darla looked at Elizabeth, unsure if she should trust her. "Is he following us?"

"No. It's okay."

Darla sat up in the seat. "Turn left up here."

"I heard a gunshot. Are you okay?"

"I have no idea what you're talking about.".

"Did he try to do something to you? Did he touch you?"

It was subtle but Elizabeth saw it. The flinch: the psychological and physical contracting inward to hide her secret. Darla turned slightly toward her and then twisted away. She began to quietly sob before collapsing into uncontrollable gasps.

Turning left at the next street, Elizabeth pulled over in front of a one-story red brick house. A gray cat was sunning itself on the front stoop. Darla buried her face in her hands and with shoulders heaving continued to cry.

Elizabeth's mind shifted back fifteen years earlier when she waiting in the woods for Gil. At times she wasn't consciously aware of exactly what she was crying about, but still it poured out of her. Everything had changed. Her father had become a violent stranger. She was no longer an innocent girl. And her mother hadn't protected her when she needed it most. She felt isolated and alone with nothing between her and the brutality in the world. Huddled against a massive old log lying next to the running path, she had grieved until her stomach cramped and her eyes burned. Then Gil came down the trail.

Elizabeth reached out and gently rubbed Darla's trembling shoulders. Darla clenched then relaxed, allowing herself to be comforted.

"I don't know what happened," Elizabeth said gently. "But I want you to know I'm here to help."

Darla's shoulders stiffened. She raised her head. Her eyes were puffy and red.

Elizabeth reached into the back seat for her purse. "I have a tissue." She pulled it out and handed the pack to Darla. Just then Darla's cell phone rang.

"Thanks." Darla took the tissues from Elizabeth. She reached into her bag for the phone. Glancing at the illuminated readout she saw Steven Davenport's number.

"It's him!" Darla dropped the phone as if it had given her an electric shock. For a tense moment she and Elizabeth stared at each other until the phone stopped ringing. Then, as if a spell had been broken, they both moved. Darla opened one of the tissues and blew her nose and Elizabeth relaxed back into her seat.

"My name is Elizabeth."

Darla looked at her but didn't say anything, still trying to determine if she could trust her.

"It's okay. I'm on your side."

"I'm Darla."

"Glad to meet you, Darla."

"Thanks for helping me."

"I'm glad I was there. So what happened?"

"You asked if he touched me. Why would you say that?"

The look in Darla's eyes made Elizabeth think of a child lost in a crowd looking for a familiar face. Elizabeth took a breath and slowly let it out. She knew Darla's future. She had lived the years of self-doubt, shame, and romantic dysfunction. If there was any way she could help Darla avoid even one small step of that disheartening journey, she wanted to do it. She needed to do it.

"When I was a little younger than you," Elizabeth struggled to keep her voice steady, "Steven Davenport raped me."

Darla's mouth opened in surprise. "What happened? Did he get in trouble? Did he go to jail?"

Elizabeth averted her eyes. The gray cat was still sunning itself on the porch.

"No. I never reported it."

"What?"

Elizabeth took another breath. "It would have been —"

Darla's hand shot out smacking Elizabeth sharply on the side of the face.

"You let him go?" Darla began pummeling her with both fists.

Elizabeth raised her arms to protect herself. For a moment she fought to shield herself from the attack, but then the guilt of her long silence greedily surrendered to Darla's punishment and she let her arms drop. Two vicious slaps to her face put a buzzing sound in her head. Another caught her on the side of the neck. She opened her eyes as Darla reared back to hit her again. I deserve this, Elizabeth thought, staring straight into Darla's rage. It has been a long time coming. Darla swung her hand and the blow slammed Elizabeth's head back against the window. She tasted blood in her mouth.

"I'm sorry, Darla. I'm sorry."

"Fuck you." Darla hit her again. "He just tried to kill me!" Then, as abruptly as her attack began it suddenly ended. Bursting into tears, Darla hung her head and sobbed.

Elizabeth, her face and neck blotchy red and stinging, helplessly looked on. It was as if she was watching herself fifteen years earlier. On the long drive to Oregon with Gil she had cried hysterically. It came in waves, crushing her down then hurling her back to catch her breath, only to once again be cruelly smashed with grief. She saw in Darla that same teetering-on-the-edge frailty. She leaned over and wrapped her arms around the girl's shoulders.

"Shhhh." Elizabeth gently rocked Darla back and forth. "I'll help you." She held her tighter, as if the strength of her embrace might some-how return to Darla what had been lost to both of them.

• • • • •

Marjorie had never made it into the hospital to visit Gil. Steven's rambling denial of being with the girl she had seen in the back yard so infuriated her that after talking to him she got back in her car and drove away.

In his matter-of-fact, why-can't-you-understand-this tone of voice that made her feel both stupid and insanely violent, he'd told her that there had been several people walking behind him when he went to his car. There was a young lady who was parked near him. Maybe that was the girl Marjorie had seen. When she told him that the same girl threatened her with a pistol in their back yard, he'd laughed it off and said it was probably one of the neighborhood kids playing around with a toy gun. He told her not to worry, and then scolded her for not telling him earlier about the gun incident.

Marjorie looked at herself in the mirror of the downstairs bathroom. He'd lied about the girl just as he'd lied about Elizabeth. Her fingers tightened on the edge of the marble counter top as she stared into her own eyes: *He slithered into your life like a snake seeking shade from the heat of the day. And for all these years, out of your own foolish need, you sheltered him, made love to him, learned about opera, bought his fresh fucking flowers and did his cooking. You played by his rules. You didn't question him about work or travel or anything. And what did you get in return for your trust?*

Marjorie turned away, unable to go on with her self-interrogation. It disgusted her to admit what she had allowed to happen with her life. Then from somewhere deeper came a resounding command — *Finish it!* Reluctantly she again found her eyes in the mirror.

The woman staring back at her looked frightened and lost. And then there it was — the truth she had been unwilling to face: *was a comfortable lifestyle, a positive image in the community, a lying husband, and a vanished daughter all you want from life?* She stared at herself, weighing the truth of what she'd finally acknowledged. Tears welled in her eyes and she bent over the sink. She found herself staring at the bottom edge of the hand-painted mirror frame. Her chest immediately tightened and she recoiled from the childish finger painting and splashes of bright color. It was suddenly clear to her why she'd always hated the frame. Some poor little Indonesian girl that he had taken advantage of probably painted it. In her mind she saw Steven humped over the girl's petite body, touching her, kissing her, telling her that she was pretty and sweet and offering to buy her dresses and video games. Marjorie reached out and with an anguished cry ripped the mirror off the wall.

· · · · ·

Steven picked his cell phone off the front seat then put it down. If he called again it might frighten Darla into doing something foolish. Or, he wondered, was she already telling her story to the police? He wasn't sure how she was able to disappear so quickly from the parking lot. The woman in the blue compact he'd seen may have somehow helped her escape.

He turned left and headed back toward Babcock Boulevard. If he drove by the police station and her car was there, at least he would know what was coming. He considered the risk he'd taken going for the pistol. He'd grabbed her arm and yanked her forward, smacking her into the roof of the car and ripping the gun from her hand. For a moment it was tangled in the sweatshirt but he got it free, bringing it level with her head. In the split second it took him to pull the trigger, she had jerked sideways. The gun went off, smashing his eardrums, and sending a bullet into the car next to his. But the bottom line was — he had missed. Steven reached under the seat. The forged steel and walnut grip of Darla's gun was reassuring. At least he had that.

23

Lemon juice lightened the surface of Elizabeth's cup of tea. Across the table at Eat'n Park, Darla dipped a French fry into a small dish of barbeque sauce. Reluctant at first, Darla had to be coaxed into telling her story of meeting Steven Davenport. It sickened Elizabeth to hear about her father's promises of a trip to New York, visits to the opera, and the spooky way he'd stared at Darla during dinner. It fueled her with an even greater desire to see him punished. He was a predator and he needed to be stopped.

"He said he wanted to show me the stars." Darla dragged another French fry through the barbeque sauce. "That's why he pulled over on that dark stretch of Hargrove Avenue." She looked at Elizabeth. "I know, I know, I'm stupid. I made a lot of mistakes."

"It's okay. You did the best you could."

"No, I didn't." Darla's gaze pinned Elizabeth to her chair. "My best is so much better than that."

"What he did wasn't your fault."

"No. But the rest was."

Elizabeth was about to ask what she meant when Darla pointed a finger at her. "What about you? How did it—you know—what happened when he got you?"

Got me, Elizabeth thought, what a compassionate way of putting it. She pushed her fork to the edge of her plate. "Tell me the rest of your story first."

Darla's eyes narrowed. "Oh, it's okay for me to talk about it, but not you. Ooooh, big secret you got raped."

The sound of her words in the half empty diner jarred Elizabeth. It was the first time the words had been said to her. She didn't try to hide her irritation.

"You haven't exactly gone running to the police. Have you?"

"That's right, I haven't. But it wasn't 'cause of that."

Elizabeth leaned back in her chair and crossed her arms. "Why then?"

"I'm not telling you. You aren't saying shit to me."

They stared at each other, painful secrets hovering in the air between them. Finally Elizabeth leaned forward.

"So this happened the night of the accident?"

Darla nodded.

"Well, Gil Linnetti is an old friend of mine. That's why I was at the hospital. If you have any information regarding who crashed into his family please let me know."

Darla just stared at her.

"What's the rest of it?"

They continued staring, sizing each other up. Then Darla pointed her fork at Elizabeth. "You're Mr. Linnetti's friend?"

"Yes. I met him when I was a little younger than you."

Darla considered this. "If I tell you, you can't say anything to anyone."

"Of course not."

"If you do, I'll – well, you won't like it. I'll make sure everyone knows what Davenport did to you. I'll tell the TV and newspapers."

"Why would you do that? Why would you be so mean?"

"Because," Darla lowered her gaze. "I did something bad, and I don't want anyone to find out."

"I would never say anything. I'm not like that."

"Are you sure? It's the worst thing you can imagine."

"It can't be worse than what happened to us."

"Yes, it can."

Elizabeth searched Darla's face for a clue to her secret. It suddenly occurred to her that maybe she didn't want to know. Perhaps Darla's journey had been something quite different and possibly more horrible than her own.

"I want you to know," Elizabeth said choosing to ignore her fears, "that I'm not sure how I can help you, but I'll do everything I can. So, yes, I promise not to tell anyone. You have my word."

Darla chewed on her lower lip then leaned forward. "Good. Okay. So… Davenport raped me, and when he – anyway, I got away from him. I jumped into his truck. I was scared and freaked out, you know, and I just blasted out of there. I floored it." She took a breath struggling against her feelings. "I got my seatbelt on but I couldn't find the headlights. She – Mr. Linnetti's wife pulled out in front of me."

Elizabeth's hand went over her mouth. "Oh God."

Darla gripped the edge of the table and forced herself to go on.

"I didn't know what to do. Davenport was running down the road yelling at me. I didn't want him to get me again, so I took off into the woods." Darla wiped the tears coming down both cheeks. "It was wrong to leave them like that, I know. But – I saw them – his wife and kids – they…" She squeezed her eyes shut as the smashed bodies of Gil's family flashed through her mind.

Elizabeth pushed back her chair and stood up. She was light-headed and stood swaying as if she'd had too much to drink.

"This has got to stop. Enough."

"I tried to end it today. But he got my gun. He shot at me."

Elizabeth stared at her, mouth agape. Rape and attempted murder, *who* was her father, *what* was he?

The cash register at the end of the counter chimed and the drawer slid open. Elizabeth dropped back into her chair. "We have to go to the police."

"They'll send me to prison. My parents – they aren't – I won't put them through that. They shouldn't have to suffer for —"

"It wasn't your fault."

"I was driving the car with the lights off!"

"You were trying to get away from—"

"It doesn't matter. I called a lawyer's office in Philadelphia – pretended I was writing a paper for school — changed the details, but that's what they said. I would get put in jail."

Elizabeth cradled her head in her hands. "I have to stop him. I should have done something years ago."

"Yeah, why didn't you?"

"Because he's my father."

• • • • •

Steven Davenport walked into his house and immediately knew something was wrong. Jagged pieces of mirror littered the floor outside the powder room. He pulled Darla's revolver out of his jacket pocket.

"Marjorie."

There was no answer.

Not seeing Darla's car at the police station, Steven now considered the possibility that she had forced her way into his house. Inching forward, he eased up next to the powder room door. At his feet he glimpsed a reflection of himself in a large piece of mirror and was momentarily startled. He stepped around the doorframe and pointed the gun into the powder room. The mirror was ripped from the wall. Pieces of it were in the sink and on the floor. The frame was gone.

"Honey."

The house was quiet.

Catching a whiff of smoke, he moved down the hall toward the kitchen. A yellow dish towel was lying on the counter but everything else was in order. The smell was stronger now. With the gun ready in his hand, he quietly moved through the kitchen into the living room. Around the corner of the sofa he could see the fireplace. Something was smoldering. Steven cautiously moved forward, eyes scanning the living room. It was empty. Squatting in front of the fireplace, he peered at the charred remains of the mirror frame he'd brought back from Indonesia.

· · · · ·

From her suite at the Hilton, Marjorie gazed across Point State Park at the confluence of the Allegheny and Monongahela rivers. The fountain at the tip of the park was ablaze in lights. A paddlewheel ship cruised past with its upper and lower decks teeming with partygoers. Marjorie lifted her glass of chardonnay and took a drink.

It hadn't been as difficult as she'd imagined: packing her clothes, final looks around the house, loading her things into the car, and then pulling out of the driveway. It was all done with a certain calm detachment. She hadn't cried or hesitated. Smashing the mirror and burning the frame seemed to have liberated her.

She walked across the hotel room to the nightstand and picked up a framed photograph. Taken when Elizabeth was nine, it showed her standing at the bottom of a hill next to her bicycle. Marjorie couldn't remember where the street was or who had photographed her, but the look on Elizabeth's face was priceless. Flushed and wide-eyed from having just sped down the hill, she was on the verge of laughing when the picture was taken. All that light in her eyes, the thrill of adventure beaming from her young face, this was her brave young girl. She was a daughter capable of making heart-wrenching decisions and doing what she had to do to protect her life.

I *will* find you, Elizabeth, Marjorie silently declared to the youthful image of her daughter, and I will not stop until I do. She put the photograph back on the nightstand and sat down on the edge of the bed.

Outside it began to rain.

· · · · ·

The rhythmic push pull of windshield wipers and the rattling down pour on the roof of the car could not drown out the piercing silence that had settled between Elizabeth and Darla. Pinned down by their guilt, they grimly stared at the road ahead of them.

Elizabeth's desire to see her father punished for what he did to her had unfortunately become even more complicated. To have him arrested would expose Darla to manslaughter charges. For Elizabeth that wasn't an acceptable option. Darla had already suffered enough.

As she pulled to a stop at a light on McKnight Road, the sound of rain on the roof grew louder. A black SUV pulled next to them with techno music thumping from inside.

"I'm telling you." Darla's voice was just audible above the hammering rain. "He's crazy. The look in his eyes – it was – you didn't see it." She shot a quick glance at Elizabeth. "He didn't care. He pulled that trigger like I was nothing."

Elizabeth stared at the red traffic light hanging above the intersection. Through the falling deluge a pink halo misted around it. How had she and her mother lived for all those years with him, Elizabeth wondered, and not known how sick he was?

The light changed and the black SUV sped off. As Elizabeth pulled through the intersection, Darla turned to face her.

"If we go to the police, I end up getting arrested and my parents go through hell."

"We might be able to negotiate something with the district attorney."

"Yeah and if not, I'm screwed."

Elizabeth shook her head. "There's got to be a way."

"It's up to us."

The tone of her voice made Elizabeth glance over.

"I don't want to give him the chance to attack some other girl." Darla's voice was low and deliberate. "I know he's your father, but he doesn't deserve to live."

Having executed him countless times in her mind on the ride to Oregon, this wasn't a new concept to Elizabeth. But hearing someone else actually say the words made it feel frighteningly real.

"I want his sick ass dead," Darla went on. "I don't want to have to worry about him coming after me or what he might do to someone else."

Elizabeth thought of all the years she wanted to be free of what happened to her. But to have a life without the smell of him, the sickening feel of his hands on her body, and the pressure of him between her legs was a miracle she knew could never happen. To be certain that he was dead and could never hurt her or anyone else might be as much peace as she could hope for, but at what price?

"The police will find us," she said. "There's too much evidence: the cell phone calls, the episode with my mother in the back yard, the hospital, emails. You'll go to prison for the rest of your life."

Darla's eyes flared angrily. "No! We just have to be smart."

"You're a fighter Darla and that's wonderful. I admire you. You're stronger than I was at your age, but fight for something that will move your life forward. Don't destroy it over him. He's not worth it."

Darla made a dismissive sound in the back of her throat. "Yeah, well maybe Mr. Linnetti will feel differently than you." She began working at her split ends. "At least you and me are alive. His whole family is dead because of your father."

Elizabeth yanked the steering wheel hard to the right. The car veered dangerously off the road, sliding through the mud before coming to a stop. She grabbed Darla by the arm and pinned her against the door.

"Gil has been through enough! Don't you dare tell him!"

Darla pushed Elizabeth. "Get off of me!"

Elizabeth didn't let go. "He's had to —" she hesitated and then went on. "I don't want him to have to face —"

"The truth! If either of you had done the right thing fifteen years ago, his family would be alive today — and I would still be a virgin!"

They stared defiantly at each other, and then Elizabeth sighed and released her grip on Darla.

"Sometimes," Elizabeth said, her voice betraying her fatigue, "the right thing is a moving target."

Darla glared at her then went back to her split ends. Elizabeth checked her side mirror and pulled back on to the road.

The fight still not out of her voice, Darla said, "He deserves to know. You would want to know."

Elizabeth clicked on her high beams as she entered a dark stretch of road. "What if you tell Gil and he decides to call the police?"

Darla let go of her hair. "I don't think so. From what you say, he cares about you. And me, I'm sixteen and I got raped. He's not going to want to cause us any more problems. So I don't think he'll turn me in. He'll want to go after your father."

Elizabeth stared into the headlight beams carving through the darkness. It would be horrifying to tell Gil that his heroic act of kindness fifteen years earlier had contributed to his family's death. He'd wanted to report it to the police back then and she begged him not to. How could she expect him to even look at her again after learning the truth? But Darla was right, he deserved to know.

"Okay. We'll tell Gil."

Darla raised her eyebrows. "And if he agrees with me will you try and stop us?"

Elizabeth thought for a moment. The hatred of her father rose up, righteous and unyielding. He had shattered her physically and emotionally; backing her so far into herself it was only now that she was beginning to emerge. How many others he had touched with his sly brutality she didn't know, but she was certain that there were more. For years they had suffered: furtive glances, the debilitating confusion at a man's touch, and years of esteem shattering nightmares. What about them? Didn't they have a say in this? If she couldn't do it for herself, she could make a stand for their loss.

"No," Elizabeth heard herself say. "I won't stop you."

Darla nodded. "Good."

"Tomorrow we'll go see Gil."

• • • • •

Light from the hallway spilled into the darkened room illuminating a portion of Steven's face. He was sitting behind his desk with Darla's .357 in his hand. He'd discovered that Marjorie's suitcase and carry-on were missing, along with clothes, several pairs of shoes, and her makeup and toiletries. She hadn't left him a note or a message. When he called her cell phone she didn't pick up.

Outside a furious clap of thunder boomed. Steven raised the gun. Pointing it across the room at the bookcase, he brought his finger to rest on the trigger. Marjorie had never left him before. Her loyalty and devotion was a constant he had always depended on. Like a luxurious velvet cloak flung over a mirror, Marjorie's unfaltering devotion had provided him shelter from the horrible truth of his own reflection. With her gone and the veil lifted, he was now unable to avoid seeing himself. The confusing disconnect between who he believed himself to be and what his actions showed him to be, left Steven feeling as if he were suddenly adrift. With no way of controlling himself, he floated higher and higher, fearing all the while that at any moment he was going to begin a terrible fall.

24

"Hey!" Darla hit the brakes as a green Jeep veered in front of her car. She flipped the driver the finger. "Idiot."

Could this girl, Elizabeth thought, watching Darla out of the corner of her eye, actually follow through with what she had threatened last night? Killing was not an easy thing. In her own fantasies of punishing her father she had shot, stabbed, and run him over with a car. But fantasizing and actually doing the deed were two different things.

Turning into the entrance of the hospital, Darla felt more optimistic than she had in a long time. Killing Steven Davenport, a dark, bitter fantasy harbored since he'd attacked her, was emerging into a real possibility. During her drive that morning from Everton she'd sung to the radio while considering how to eliminate Davenport from the world of the living. Her father was a fan of *Forensic Files*, a TV show about murder investigations. She'd watched it with him countless times. Hair, fibers, tire tracks, dirt samples, all of it would have to be considered. It would be complicated, but she could work it out. Davenport had to be stopped. She wondered how Gil would react to the idea. Was revenge as bright in his heart as it was in hers?

She hadn't mentioned anything to Elizabeth about her previous encounter with Gil. Having witnessed her attempted suicide, Gil would better grasp the full extent of her suffering. It would probably make him more sympathetic, Darla thought, and more willing to go along with her plan.

Elizabeth put her hand on the door handle to get out of the car. "If he's having a bad day we aren't going to discuss it, okay?"

Darla nodded. "And if the dude in the other bed is around, don't say a word. We'll take Mr. Linnetti down the hall or something. No one can know about this."

In Gil's hospital room they were surprised to see that he was out of bed and dressed.

"Not another day." Gil was tying the laces of his boots. "I hate hospitals."

Elizabeth stepped toward him. "But —"

"I'm fine. The hot shower did more for me than anything else. Man, that felt good."

"What did your doctor say?"

"He told me not to exert myself, and to watch out for dizziness and headaches." Gil grinned. "Staying in here is what'll give me a headache."

Elizabeth smiled. Not only was she glad to see him up and around and in good health, she was pleased that he was exhibiting a more out-going attitude.

Darla stepped forward from where she had remained by the door. "I'm glad that you're feeling better."

"Thanks."

"Gil, this is Darla."

"Hi." Gil stood up. "Can you guys give me a ride back to my camp?"

Darla grinned nervously. "Sure. Happy to help out."

Gil's eyes narrowed. He glanced quickly from Darla to Elizabeth then back to Darla.

"You're…the one I saw…" His voice trailed off. Darla nodded, but didn't speak.

"You two know each other?" Elizabeth turned to Darla for an explanation.

Before either of them could respond, Asa, a young nurse pushing a wheelchair entered the room.

"Mr. Linnetti, your chariot has arrived."

Gil was still looking curiously at Darla. "I can walk."

Asa gestured for him to sit in the wheelchair. "Hospital rules."

Elizabeth instinctively reached for his arm. He allowed her to take it, but his eyes remained on Darla.

Asa pushed the chair closer to Gil and set the break. "Your sister called again. She wants to make sure you aren't sneaking out of here against doctor's orders."

Gil pressed his lips together and shook his head. "I should have never called her. I knew it would freak her out."

"She was very sweet. She's looking out for you."

Gil stepped over to the wheelchair and sat down. He looked from Darla to Elizabeth and then to Asa. "Just get me outta here."

Asa clicked off the brake. "Hi Ho Silver." And she wheeled him toward the door.

•••••

Sunlight poured in the hotel window. The rain the night before had scrubbed the sky clean. Today, Marjorie thought, looking out at the cloudless blue expanse, I am beginning a new life. Today I will be a better woman and a better mother.

The hotel telephone rang. Without thinking, she picked it up. "Hello."

"You sound cheery this morning." It was Steven. Marjorie's legs went rubbery and she sank onto the edge of the bed.

"I checked with the credit card company," he said. "They were very helpful."

Marjorie lifted her gaze to the abyss of sky outside her window. For an educated woman, using a credit card to check into the hotel had not been especially bright.

"Well, when can I expect you home?"

"Steven —"

"Or would you rather I came and got you."

"No don't. I won't be here."

Silence. She could hear him breathing. When he finally spoke, his tone had changed. It was his lover's voice, tender and intimate.

"Come home, sweetheart?"

It was Steven at his manipulative best. She wanted to reach through the phone line and claw his eyes. She took a breath, willing herself not to confront him about what he'd done to Elizabeth. To use that to slap him down right now would only give him the opportunity to fabricate a lie. Keep him guessing, she told herself, that way he was less of a threat.

"If it's about that girl," he said casually, "I don't know what else to tell you. She isn't anyone I know. I mean, if you think you saw her in the back yard and again at the hospital maybe she's some kind of stalker or something."

"Goodbye Steven." Marjorie hung up the telephone.

Fifteen minutes later she was packed, checked out, and on her way across town.

• • • • •

Dominic heard what sounded like a door slam inside the Davenport's house. He looked up from weeding the flowerbed just off the patio. Another crash, this one louder, came from the other side of the house. He squatted down and continued working. He knew that what happened in the homes of his clients was none of his business. Their ex-wives, lovers, feuding relatives, and addicted children were not his concern. He was only there to make their yards look beautiful, and he followed this rule implicitly over the years. One of the rare moments when he violated his rule was the morning after Elizabeth Davenport disappeared. "My little girl is gone," Mrs. Davenport had said as he walked by her lugging PVC pipe for their sprinkling system. She dabbed a tissue under eyes swollen from crying. Dominic hadn't known what happened or why, but the grief in her face was undeniable. He had reached out and touched her arm in a gesture of support. When he turned away he saw Mr. Davenport, a distant look in his eyes, watching them through the French doors. At the time, Dominic formulated several opinions, none of which were complimentary of Steven Davenport. The man was like a brightly colored balloon, Dominic thought, dancing on the wind, attracting the attention of admirers, but inside there was nothing of substance. Dominic had never said anything to anyone, not even Irene, but he always believed that Davenport had something to do with Elizabeth leaving home.

Dominic looked up from the flowerbed. In the kitchen Steven Davenport was turning away from one of the cabinets. Walking over to the table just inside the French doors, he paused and looked down at something in his hand. It took a moment for Dominic to realize what he was holding — a revolver. Davenport slipped the gun into the pocket of his jacket. Dominic busied himself with the weeds in the flowerbed but his mind was focused on the gun. What was Davenport doing with it? In over 20 years of coming to their house he had never seen Davenport with a gun or heard him talk about guns. Why now, Dominic wondered? Then he remembered the young woman in the blue car.

• • • • •

"I'm glad you're doing all right now." Gil was looking over at Darla.

She glanced at him next to her in the front passenger seat. "Yeah, that was a — I was having a bad day."

Gil turned to Elizabeth in the back seat. "So how do you two know each other?"

"I was going to ask you the same thing."

Gil looked at Darla. "She brought flowers to where the accident happened."

"Then I tried to shoot myself." Darla let out a nervous laugh. "But I missed."

"It wasn't funny at the time."

"I didn't really miss. Your daughter – I don't know, she – I saw her real quick in my head — it scared me and I jumped. It made me miss."

"My daughter?"

"When I closed my eyes, bam, there she was. Scared the crap out of me."

"How did you know it was my daughter?"

"From watching the news. After the…"

Gil nodded thoughtfully. "Sometimes I see her too."

"I'm glad she did that. I didn't really want to die."

Elizabeth was stunned. First, she couldn't believe that Darla tried to commit suicide in front of Gil, and second she was shocked that Darla had chosen not to tell her.

"Why were you so upset that day?" Gil watched Darla's eyes shift from the road to the rear view mirror.

"I'm gonna' pull in here." Darla caught Elizabeth's eye in the rear-view mirror and gave her a nod.

This is it, Elizabeth thought. In the parking lot of Dunkin' Donuts Gil was going to hear the truth. Darla maneuvered past a beer truck and drove around the back. As she parked in the last space at the rear of the lot, Gil turned to her.

"So why were you going to shoot yourself?"

"I'll get you a cup of tea. I'll be right back." Darla hopped out of the car.

Elizabeth watched her walk across the lot. Unsure of how to begin the discussion with Gil she shifted awkwardly in her seat.

"Is she really okay?" Gil was watching Darla.

"I think so."

Hearing the uncertainty in her voice, Gil turned to Elizabeth.

"Don't worry," Elizabeth said, "She's not going to do herself any harm."

"I hope not." He thought for a moment. "Lindsey helped her. That's nice."

"It's pretty amazing."

"How do you know her?"

"I met her at the hospital when I came to visit you."

"She was at the hospital?"

"Yeah."

"Why?"

"She wanted to make sure you were okay."

"But why? Who is she?"

Elizabeth didn't want to tell him. He had already been through so much.

"And why did she try to kill herself?" Gil was looking at her. "She's – just a kid. What can be so terrible?"

"Wait for her to come back." Elizabeth felt relieved and cowardly at her avoidance.

Gil sat quietly in the front seat. After a moment he cleared his throat. "This is something bad, isn't it?"

Elizabeth desperately wanted to lie. She wanted to reassure him that Darla was just a confused, young girl, and that she was getting better, and with their support she would go on and have an adventurous and fruitful life. But that wasn't the whole truth. And this was the day that Gil was going to finally hear all of the truth.

"Yes." Elizabeth kept her voice as steady as she could. "It's bad."

Gil sighed.

"I'm sorry."

Gil turned and looked across the parking lot. "She's so young." Darla was coming back carrying two cups.

"Yes."

Darla walked up and handed Gil his cup of tea through the open window.

"Thanks."

"Careful it's hotter than all get out." She walked around to the driver's door. Gil didn't look at her when she got in the car.

Darla glanced at Elizabeth. "So, are we ready to do this?"

Elizabeth nodded. Just then a pickup truck squealed through the parking lot. Darla turned and looked out the window. In the split second that she turned away, Gil opened his door and got out of the car. He walked quickly toward the Dunkin' Donuts carrying his cup of tea.

"What the hell." Darla watched him walk away.

"Gil!" Elizabeth opened the door and got out of the car. "Come back."

He stopped with his back to her. "It's so good. The smell of the…" His voice trailed off.

"Gil." Elizabeth took a step toward him.

The comforting aroma of fresh donuts reminded Gil of when his father used to stop at the little bakery on Perry Highway on the way home after church. He would slip Gil some money, and with Jackie at his side, the two of them would buy donuts for the family. Jackie went for the ones with chocolate icing and Gil always picked glazed. His mother got powdered sugar and his father had plain.

"We need to tell you something." Elizabeth took another few steps toward him.

He didn't respond. He breathed in the sugary smell, feeling slightly dizzy. His father never asked for the change back, Gil remembered. He would wink at him and say, "You can buy the donuts next Sunday." But his father always ended up giving him more money.

The driver of a brown Ford blew his horn and steered angrily around Gil. "Get outta' the way!"

Gil turned around looked into Elizabeth's anxious eyes. Inside the car, Darla's somber expression was even less of an invitation. He didn't want to go back. He could live the rest of his life without hearing any more bad news.

"Come on, Gil. I need to talk to you. It's something I should have told you a long time ago."

Gil didn't move. A dull ache had started at the back of his head.

"Will you come back and listen?"

He shot a wistful glance back at the donut shop then let out a sigh. "Okay."

Elizabeth wanted to reach out and hug him as he walked past her. He had been in such good spirits when they left the hospital. Now, he was back to being distant and sullen. She didn't want to be the bearer of bad news. She wanted to be a force of goodness in his life. But this had to be done. No matter how hard it was. She opened the car door and climbed into the back seat.

"Go ahead," Darla said immediately, her eyes shifting from Gil to Elizabeth. "You start."

Elizabeth didn't hesitate. She knew that if she did she may never get the terrible words out of her mouth. "You know when you helped me all those years ago." She leaned forward over the front seat. "I didn't want you to know who my parents were. I didn't want them to find out about me."

Gil nodded.

"And you kept my secret. You were a man of your word. I appreciated it at the time, but now I know that it was wrong. I should have told you."

A glimmer of alarm flashed in Gil's eyes.

"My father —" Elizabeth paused, fighting back her emotions. She didn't want to break down. She wanted to remain as clear and direct as possible. She steadied herself and looked into Gil's eyes. "My father raped Darla too."

Gil's mouth slowly fell open. He looked at Darla who somberly nodded.

Elizabeth went on. "But that's not all. He attacked Darla the night your family was killed. She managed to get away from him and —" Elizabeth stopped. As much as she wanted to prevent it, her eyes were flooding with tears. She pressed on. "Darla jumped in his car – and as she was getting away she crashed into your wife and children."

Gil blinked, looking from Elizabeth to Darla.

"It was me." Darla began to cry. "I was the one driving."

Gil looked confused. "But —"

"I'm so sorry." Darla was now sobbing.

"But it was Steve Davenport's car that hit —"

"Yes." Elizabeth reached for Gil's shoulder. "He's my father."

The look on Gil's face darkened. "No. That's not right. You told me your last name was Sandin."

Elizabeth gently squeezed his shoulder. "I'm sorry I wasn't honest with you. That was before I knew what he'd done to Darla."

"Steve is the one who attacked you?"

"Yes."

Darla wiped at her eyes. "And me too."

Gil looked as if all the air had been sucked out of him. His mind struggled to process this new horrible information in some kind of reasonable manner, but like sand in a combustion engine, it brought him to a grinding standstill.

"We wanted you to know the truth," Darla said. "You've lost a lot because of him."

Gil didn't respond. He was staring blankly at something in the space between himself and Darla.

Elizabeth stepped in. "If we call the police, Darla will be arrested for — at least manslaughter. But if we don't, my father will be free to hurt someone else."

"I want to kill him." Darla watched to see how this landed on Gil.

Gil squinted at Darla. "This – *girl* killed my family?"

"I was trying to get away from—"

"Maybe I ought to kill you."

"Gil!" Elizabeth grabbed his arm and shook him.

Darla's eyes widened. She covered her face with her hands and began sobbing again.

Gil watched her, his face an intractable mask.

"It was an accident." Elizabeth shook him again. "The bastard raped her."

Darla muttered, "I'm sorry."

"Sorry?" Gil smacked the dashboard with his hand. "What am I supposed to do with sorry?" You killed my family, how does sorry help me? How does sorry fuckin' do anything for me?" He hit the dashboard again as a sob ripped from his throat. He threw his cup of tea out the window and in an anguished rush he began pounding on the dashboard with both hands.

Elizabeth stared at him, stunned and frightened at his violent emotional outburst. Every cry he let loose, every jarring blow he delivered rattled her to her fragile center. She had contributed this pain to his life. It was her choice that left him vulnerable to this suffering. But even as she felt wretched for her part in his agony, she couldn't help admiring his willingness and ability to express his grief so fully. It reminded her of what else may be lurking behind her self-imposed desire to keep it together and not allow herself to fall apart.

Darla clung to the steering wheel, tears streaming down her face. Elizabeth reached over the seat to comfort her, but Darla pulled her shoulder away.

Gil stopped punching and leaned his head on the dashboard. Edgy silence settled in the car. Elizabeth tried desperately to find something she could say to fill the emptiness, something that would keep him from drifting further away from them. But before she could think of anything Gil spoke.

"Why didn't you turn on the headlights? Bonnie would have seen you." He raised his eyes. The detached coldness from a moment ago had been replaced by a deep penetrating sadness.

Darla let out an anguished gasp. "I—I ask myself that every day. I was scared — I fumbled around — I couldn't figure out how to turn them on."

"But the lights, if…" He didn't finish. The "if" hung in the air between them like a bell tolling for a ship lost in the fog.

"It's my fault." Elizabeth tried to comfort Darla, but she pushed her away. "It started with me. I didn't report him."

"It's *his* fault," Darla blurted. "He needs to have his balls chopped off."

Gil turned and looked out the windshield. "The two of you…"

"If we go to the police," Darla said, "we have no proof of what he did to us. It would be our word against his. And Davenport will tell them the truth about me and the accident."

Gil grunted. "Going to jail is a cheap price to pay for what you did."

"Stop it, Gil," Elizabeth said. "She's suffered enough. We all have. My father is the perpetrator here, not Darla."

Gil looked at the overflowing dumpster in the corner of the parking lot. Three birds picking at scraps of food flitted in the jumble of cardboard boxes and trash. Steven's fatherly arm around his shoulders flashed in Gil's mind. He thought of the talks they'd had and the Tupperware containers of Cheerios, cake, and lasagna, and the bottles of spring water Steven had faithfully delivered to the campsite. Had he been acting out of guilt for what he'd done? Or was it some kind of sick, depraved game he was playing? A man who rapes his own daughter would be capable of anything. And what else had he done in the years between attacking Elizabeth and the most recent incident with Darla? Gil squeezed his eyes shut, reluctant to consider any more lives traumatized by Davenport's depravity.

His instinct had been to call the police. When he found Elizabeth on the trail, that's what he'd wanted to do. But instead he honored her wish for secrecy. After leaving her at the commune he had plenty of time to think about the ramifications of what he'd done. During the long drive back home from Oregon, he'd come to the conclusion that he was proud of the risk he'd taken to help her. He knew Kona and Jasmine would make sure she was well taken care of. She would get a new start in a progressive community of caring, thoughtful people. That had to be a better option, he had concluded, than what she faced with her parents or in a foster home. And he liked the fact that no one would ever know. It would be the secret benchmark of his capabilities. He had used that experience many times in his life for motivation in overcoming obstacles. But now, sadly, all these years later, he discovers that he had been wrong. His teenage act of service and bravery, rather than granting freedom and opportunity had instead brought greater suffering. His family was dead because of the secret he had held.

The recurring dream flashed in Gil's mind, and once again he saw himself artfully slicing up the driver who killed his family. The scene elicited in him a dark, seductive power. To have the control, focused rage, and supreme satisfaction of reducing his enemy to a gibbering bloody mass. He looked across the front seat at Darla. She was the monster he had been hunting. She was his family's killer. The steel blade he'd held countless times in his dreams was intended for her. But as he studied Darla's tear-streaked face, the thought of slipping the knife between her ribs gave him no satisfaction. She was a child, and she had been running from her own fiend.

It's in each of us, he thought, shifting his gaze out the window — the bloody smear of revenge. The face of the boy he'd chased down and tackled at the campsite appeared in his mind. Clamping his forearm on the teenager's throat, he'd wanted to punish him. He wanted to make that boy suffer for tricking him into believing he could have his family back. With revenge at hand, he had waited for the feeling of relief that he ached for. But nothing happened. His agony hadn't lifted. So he'd pressed harder, hoping that by inflicting more pain he would be granted his release. The boy's eyes had bulged, his fingers frantically clawed at Gil's arm. But Gil felt no different. The weight of his loss remained.

"He needs to be punished!" Darla smacked the steering wheel, piercing the silence in the car.

Elizabeth nodded. "I agree."

They both looked at Gil. But Gil didn't respond. He was staring out the window.

This time it was more intense than he'd ever felt before. Bonnie and the kids, their potent presence was making him feel giddy and at the same time on edge. And then he unexpectedly went calm, washed through with a deeply serene and utterly peaceful acceptance. This was what he had been waiting for at his campsite. These complex, terrible circumstances were why he had been continuing to live through the rain and mud and solitude at Hargrove Avenue. This was the cause beyond his own personal tragedy that he had been looking for. "Go Daddy," Drake had said, "Keep doing good things." Yes, Gil thought, keep doing good things.

Suddenly he felt ashamed. His reaction to Darla had been cruel. Telling her he wanted to kill her was not doing good things. This lovely young girl, Gil thought, glancing over at Darla, wants to kill Steven Davenport. She wants revenge for her violation and suffering. But revenge is not a good thing. It will only lead to more suffering.

"Hel-looo!" Darla was waving her hand at Gil.

He moved then, slowly nodding his head. When he turned to them, the look in his eyes was different. The sadness had been replaced by something brighter.

"Maybe," Gil said, his voice strangely calm, "the reason I've stayed at my campsite so long was so this whole thing could be brought out into the open." His eyes squinted as he worked the thought over in his mind. "Maybe we're being asked to do something more difficult than commit a murder."

Darla frowned. "Like what?"

"Forgive."

25

Marty Braverman re-crossed his legs and looked up from the stack of papers in his hand.

"Steven, this surgical group, do they have any idea of what they're getting into? Their investment record shows that they haven't been willing to exercise a great deal of patience. Three times they've sued to pull their funding from deals when things slowed down or went long. I'm not sure I want to do business with people that quick to hit the panic button. We don't want to get screwed."

Marty's voice came to Steven as a muffled jumble of sounds underscoring the sharp-toned litany already trumpeting in his mind: *Bring Marjorie home. Locate Darla to find out what she's going to do.*

Steven was uncertain how to accomplish these things, but the loaded revolver inside the desk inches from his hand made him feel that somehow it was possible. He leaned forward on his elbows pretending to study the proposal on his desk. He had always worked things out. This time wouldn't be any different.

"… and she laughed like I haven't heard in years," Marty was saying. "It's been quite a time. The little things, Steven, it's always the little things that keep you close."

Steven looked up. He had no idea what Marty was talking about but the man was smiling so Steven also smiled.

"We've been looking at old pictures," Marty continued. "Telling stories about way back when. Funny stuff about the kids and when we were first going steady." He paused and looked down at his hands. "Doctors are encouraging but…" He shrugged and kept his eyes lowered.

It's Esther, Steven realized. He's talking about Esther. Steven shifted a sober expression onto his face. "She'll get through this."

"I hope so. I'll tell you, the last few days certainly have been a revelation. I married a remarkable woman. Always knew it, but…" Marty's voice trailed off as his eyes sought privacy in the paperwork.

Steven thought of Marjorie. She had brought much into his life. He'd never before experienced the level of kindness and comfort she so graciously offered him. After they had been dating for several months, he remembered thinking that he may never meet another woman like her. He considered what it would mean to be married. He knew that his interest in young girls might be a problem. But with Marjorie he could have a life. He would move in the social circles that would make a difference in his business. There would be no stopping him if he had access to the right people. So he'd asked her to marry him. He never doubted the wisdom of that decision. Marjorie's thoughtfulness and attention to detail had helped him realize his dream. Her kind efforts to bring him in contact with investors, and the example she set maintaining friendships, paved the way for him to open his own business. She was a marvel at a cocktail party and together they had reaped the benefits.

When they got married the idea of having children was not completely clear in his mind. He'd never told Marjorie that he didn't want them, but it wasn't a subject he frequently raised. "Children," his mother-in-law advised him, "have a way of opening your heart and showing you who you really are." He had seen the change in his friends upon the birth of their children. Men with no obvious capacity for gentleness or nurturing suddenly were changing diapers and twisting their faces into comical masks and speaking in baby talk without regard for what anyone thought. One colleague had burst into tears telling the story of his son's first base hit in a T-ball game. He began to consider that the birth of a child might also create a change in him. Perhaps the profound experience of bringing new life into the world would shatter the mute numbness that had possessed him since the day Kelly died. He might finally awaken from his long emotional slumber. So when Marjorie decided that she wanted to get pregnant, he had agreed.

During her pregnancy he attended to Marjorie's every need. He made sure the house was stocked with the oranges, melon, and apples that she craved. He ordered a case of organic almond butter from a health food store. As far as he knew Marjorie had never eaten almond butter in her life, but suddenly she had to have it. She would spread gobs of it on slices of apple and eat it with a look of absolute ecstasy.

Over the course of Marjorie's pregnancy he had allowed himself to fantasize about holding his newborn child and weeping for joy like he had seen parents do on television and in the movies. He and Marjorie decided not to find out the sex of the baby. His daydreams about his child flipped back and forth between sports scenarios and ballet classes. Even as he played out the fantasies over and over he knew in the back of his mind that none of it might come true. For him to visualize deeply feeling the joys of fatherhood was an entirely different reality than actually being able and willing to do it.

On the day Elizabeth was born his hopes were high. Marjorie's desire to give birth naturally without drugs made the morning rich in heightened emotion. From Marjorie's ferocious intensity coping with the pain, the nurses' concerned attentiveness, and the young doctor's wry attempts at levity, so much was going on in the birthing room that he had felt more alive than at any time since before his sister's death. As he watched Elizabeth's head crown and her shoulders slide into the doctor's waiting hands, he eagerly anticipated the surge of feelings he had dreamt of for nine months. When the doctor held Elizabeth up for Marjorie to see, he still had hope. His wife, her eyes infused with a light he had never seen before, wept joyfully. But he felt nothing; only the same titillating yearning that had plagued him for years. With an actor's happy smile he graciously accepted the congratulations of the doctor and nurses. He kissed Marjorie and stroked her hair. And when Elizabeth was presented to him he obediently held her, keenly aware that her tiny, warm presence had not been the key to his release after all.

"…oh they had a very nice chat," Marty was saying. "Esther is so fond of your Marjorie. She's been a good friend." Marty wagged his finger at Steven. "And you. You make it hard on a gruff old crank like me. I have to hear about it all the time. Steven does this, Steven and Marjorie do that," he let out a burst of air that was almost a laugh. "If you weren't such a good business partner, I'd have to get clear of you."

Steven, thankful that Marjorie hadn't said anything to Esther — at least nothing that was passed on to Marty — offered a curt smile. "I'm not all that great."

"Sure, sure." Marty grinned and waved a hand at him. "Tell that to my wife."

• • • • •

Marjorie lit her first cigarette since high school. She inhaled deeply and immediately regretted it. Violently coughing, she dropped the cigarette and crushed it into the asphalt with the bottom of her sandal. A surge of littering-guilt immediately struck and she bent down and picked up the cigarette. She walked over to the trash can near the entrance of the market and threw away the butt and the entire pack she'd just bought. Well, that didn't work, she thought, and started back to her car.

Her visit to the bank had left her anxious. Removing Steven's name from her accounts was the first practical step in separating their lives. It brought up a cyclone of feelings, the strongest being a liberating and at the same time over-whelming sense of absolute autonomy. Steven had managed her finances for nearly all of her adult life. The act of denying him access to the money she had once been more than willing to share with him, brought home all too profoundly the truth of where they now stood.

Marjorie got into her car. Her next stop was Benjamin Korth's office. He had the reputation for being the best divorce attorney in town When she called earlier in the day to make an appointment she was told that he was unavailable. But when she gave her name to Korth's assistant, there was an immediate change in the woman's tone. Marjorie was then put on hold. When the line clicked back on it was Ben Korth. He politely informed Marjorie that he would be happy to meet with her later that afternoon. A lawyer's nose for money, Marjorie thought, happy that her social standing and Steven's financial reputation would serve to get her away from her husband sooner rather than later. Once the paper work was filed, Marjorie decided, she would devote all of her time to finding Elizabeth.

Marjorie considered what would happen once she found her daughter. Would she tell her the truth? Would she admit that during the past fifteen years she had lived in a fog of denial? She tried to see herself through Elizabeth's eyes. What would be the impact of that confession? Would it ruin their chance for a meaningful reconciliation? If Marjorie chose not to admit it, how would Elizabeth ever know? Maybe that was the safer way to go, Marjorie reasoned. Why put what will most certainly be an awkward situation on even more tenuous ground? Elizabeth hadn't come to her after Steven's attack. The only reason for that, Marjorie concluded, was that Elizabeth had wanted to protect her from the truth about Steven. The thought of her young daughter coming to that difficult decision brought tears to Marjorie's eyes. She thought of Elizabeth's journey and wondered what she must have gone through. Had she lived on the street? Had someone else abused her? Were drugs and violence a part of her sweet child's life? And if that was the case, had she wanted her mother to come for her? What if for all these years, Elizabeth had been secreting hoping and waiting for her mother to rescue her? But she tried, Marjorie reminded herself. The private investigator had searched everywhere. Marjorie turned on the radio to drive the painful thoughts out of her head. Screeching electric guitar filled the car. She would find Elizabeth, she told herself, and then everything would be fine.

· · · · ·

Elizabeth walked past the framed photographs on the wall not wanting to look but unable to turn away. In them she saw Gil's progression from boy to man: the darkening of his hair, the thickening of his body, his pretty wife, their adorable children, family vacations at the beach, a cabin in the forest, and many birthday parties. There was laughter on their faces and tenderness in their eyes. It was the rest of his life. Everything he became after rescuing her. The gaps, long a mystery, were being filled in.

"Sit down, Darla." Gil gestured toward the family room. "Make yourself comfortable. I'm going to open up the place."

Gil's house was nothing like Elizabeth imagined it would be. Her youthful long-haired image of him seemed to contrast with the formal, conservative décor. Compared to her funky A-frame, Gil's house seemed exceptionally grown up.

"Put some water on." Gil was heading for the stairs. "I'll be right down. We'll have tea."

He paused at the foot of the stairs. Looking up toward the second floor he seemed to brace himself. Elizabeth's heart went out to him. Seeing those empty bedrooms would be terrible. She thought of walking over and taking his arm so he wouldn't have to face the absence of his family alone. But touching him or showing him affection was probably not a smart thing to do. Not in the house he shared with his family. It might make him feel uncomfortable. Instead she walked into the kitchen and filled the kettle.

The house, conservative as it was, was nicely furnished, Elizabeth admitted. Gil's wife had excellent taste and a good eye. The family photographs were a nice touch, and the way the TV area and the kitchen flowed together made sense. Of course there were things she would have done differently, like the color of the drapes – Elizabeth stopped herself. This isn't about comparing myself to her, she reminded herself. She turned on the gas burner and set the kettle to boil.

Elizabeth looked out over the tile counter separating the kitchen from the family room. Other than needing a little dusting, the person Gil's father hired to keep an eye on the place had done a good job. The house was reasonably clean, the lawn was cut, the bushes trimmed, and all the utilities were on. For a moment she allowed the long held fantasy of being Gil's wife to flash through her mind: the spacious home, the safe neighborhood, walks together in the evening, strollers, and the sweet faces of cooing babies.

"This sucks. We have to stop your father not let him off the hook."

Darla's harsh whisper succeeded in pulling Elizabeth out of her cozy domestic fantasy. "Remember Darla, Gil is doing you a favor."

"Letting your father go isn't doing any favors for the next girl he gets."

"We aren't letting him go."

"What would you call it?"

"Gil brought us here for a reason. Let's listen to what he has to say."

Darla glared at her then flopped into a leather recliner and began plucking her split ends.

Upstairs, Gil thumped his hand on the window frame in Drake's room. He tried again to open it but it wouldn't budge. It had been a problem since the day they bought the house. Having considerably more patience with mechanical things than he did, Bonnie was the one who always managed to get it open. Gil pressed his hand to the glass fondly remembering his son's good-natured kidding. "Mom is stronger than you. See how fast she got it open."

It would be difficult, Gil thought, but he knew the moment that he walked through the front door that he would have to sell the house. There were too many memories, too much love. It would be an anchor holding him in place. But as hard as it was for him to be back in the house, he knew his decision to return home was right. His vigil had served its purpose. The bigger truth had been revealed. He took his hand from the window and walked down the hall to the master bedroom.

After months of sleeping in the tent, the maple four-poster bed he and Bonnie found at a yard sale in Lancaster looked huge to him. Bonnie was so excited when they finally got it set up that she'd bounced on it like a little girl.

Gil walked to the window and opened it. Across the street his neighbor, Cindy Garrity, was standing on her front stoop looking at Gil's house. She's probably wondering who's car is in the driveway, Gil thought. He made a mental note to call her and then he walked to the closet to change his clothes.

In the kitchen Elizabeth removed the whistling tea kettle from the burner. She had found mugs and a box of tea bags.

"What's he doin' up there?" Darla was still plucking away at her hair.

"You should stop doing that. It makes it worse."

Darla made a face like she smelled something unpleasant and continued her grooming.

It was easy to understand how Darla felt, Elizabeth thought. The idea of forgiving her father made Elizabeth feel like a bank teller who, after being robbed, stops the thief on his way out to give him a drawer of money that he'd overlooked.

Gil came down the stairs in fresh jeans and a white golf shirt. "Feels good to wear something different."

"Tea is served." Elizabeth began pouring hot water into the mugs.

The doorbell rang.

"It's probably my neighbor." Gil walked toward the front door. "She's been watching the house for me. I'm sure she's wondering what's going on."

Darla got out of the chair. "I don't even like tea." She walked over and picked up one of the cups.

They heard the front door open. There was a shout. Gil yelled, "Hey!" Darla looked down the hallway toward the door. "Oh shit." Elizabeth came around the counter. A crowd of reporters was outside the door.

"Mr. Linnetti! Just a few minutes of your time!" Celia Davis stepped forward with a microphone. "Gil, why has your vigil ended? What brought you back home?"

Gil instinctively stepped back, trying to keep his distance from the unruly press. This gave the reporters a clear look into the house.

"That's the woman! She's in there!"

Gil immediately stepped forward blocking the doorway. The cameramen scrambled to reposition for a clear shot. Gil pulled the door shut behind him.

"Who is she?" Celia Davis leaned toward him sensing a scoop. "Is she the reason you've come home?"

Gil knew that unless he fed something to the jostling horde of reporters and cameramen, they would close in and tear his life apart. He held up his hands. "Okay, there's no need for pushing and shouting."

The crowd quieted as he stepped forward. Three microphones were thrust toward his face.

"Thank you for all of your prayers and concern. The time has come for me to pick up what's left of my life and move on." He looked down for a moment trying to gather his thoughts and then continued. "The grief that kept me at the campsite on Hargrove Avenue was—" Gil paused, searching for the right words, "lifted after my recent altercation. My isolation, honorable as it may have been, was turning me into someone I didn't want to be. It was time for me to stop agonizing about what happened and start putting one foot in front of the other and move toward the possibilities that lay ahead of me. That's what Bonnie and the kids would want."

There was a murmur from the knot of people. Gil heard someone say, "What about the woman?"

"A friend of mine has been kind enough to come and help me. She isn't a mystery woman or my new girlfriend or the reason I've left the campsite. She is someone I knew growing up and her friendship means a lot to me. But I know that when she leaves and returns to her home, I'll be on my own. Living with the loss of my family isn't going to be easy. I have a long way to go. But with friends and family by my side, I will do the best I can. I ask you all now to please respect our privacy and give us the time we need to get over this tragedy. Thank you."

He nodded to Celia Davis who gave him a supportive smile. Gil opened the front door and walked back into the house.

26

Gil sat down on one of the stools at the kitchen counter. There was a long moment of silence.

Darla gave him a thumbs-up. "You did good."

Elizabeth nodded. "Yeah, I think they'll leave you alone now."

Gil slowly shook his head. "I don't know. They're a sneaky bunch." He went to a cupboard and pulled out a bottle of aspirin. He shook two into the palm of his hand.

Elizabeth slid a mug of tea in front of him. "Are you okay?"

Gil nodded, then popped the aspirin into his mouth and washed them down with the tea. Outside they could hear the news vans pulling away.

"All right." Gil lowered his mug to the counter. "Now, your father. I want us to sit down with him and talk this thing out."

Darla groaned. "That's messed up. What if he tries to kill us? He has my gun."

"Everything you've ever wanted to say to him, we can make it happen."

"And you think he's going to go along with that." Darla shook her head. "I'm telling you this guy is crazy. We should definitely be armed."

Gil made the time-out signal with his hands. "Darla, this isn't about what we can do to him — it's about what we can do for ourselves." He looked away, his eyes focusing on something Darla and Elizabeth couldn't see. "This is the reason I stayed at Hargrove Avenue. I know it. It's meant to be."

The brilliant gleam in his eyes momentarily inspired Elizabeth to agree with him. But then she caught herself. How did he know for sure? Zealously believing that there was some sort of plan at work might simply be Gil's justification for ending his vigil. Or perhaps his head injury was worse than the doctors believed. And what about *my* pain, she thought, will doing what he wants help rid of that? But as much as Elizabeth wanted her father to suffer for what he had done, under Gil's steady beam of faith she felt her need for revenge gently melting away.

"Good," Gil said, seeing the look of acceptance come into her face.

"And then what?" Darla slumped back in the leather recliner. "We have this big to-do. We talk to him, tell him how he messed up our lives and who knows, maybe he even tells us why it happened. Then what? Do we just let him go on living his life? Gil, do you really think talking about this is going to change how he is? No way!"

"I believe that truth begets truth."

"Oh, come on!" Darla sprang out of the chair. "That's BS! He attacks girls!" She quickly looked to Elizabeth for support.

"She's right." Elizabeth got up from her stool and put her arm around Darla's shoulders. "From what I've read, sex offenders aren't easily rehabilitated. We're not psychiatrists."

Gil leaned forward putting both hands on the counter. "I know that. All I can tell you is that it feels right to me — the three of us confronting him – it's what's we're supposed to do. After that we'll see what happens."

Darla pulled away from Elizabeth. "What feels right to me is seeing him dead."

Gil shrugged. "Do you want to go to jail?"

Darla glared at him.

"What if we took Darla to the district attorney?" Elizabeth walked over to the stool and sat down. "Try to get her immunity for the accident. In exchange we would both testify against my father for what he did to us. And if you came in and insisted that they don't press charges against her it might work."

"The problem with that," Gil said, "is once you tell them the truth they have all the power. They might say, yeah sorry, and charge Darla anyway. Do you want to risk that?"

Elizabeth looked to Darla.

"I don't want to go to jail." Darla looked dejected. "And I don't want my parents to suffer because of what I did. But forgiving him? How can I do that?"

A ponderous silence settled over them as they considered their options.

"I'm not a murderer," Gil said quietly. "And I don't think you are either."

Elizabeth caught Darla's eye. "We would no longer be victims. We would be, you know, taking steps, trying to heal."

Darla desperately wanted to lift the walls that had closed in on her since Davenport attacked her. She wanted to be free of the nagging voice of guilt and shame. Erasing Steven Davenport from her life seemed to be the clearest way of getting out of that box. But even if she didn't want to admit it, she knew Elizabeth and Gil were right. If she killed Davenport, the police would find her and she would go to prison. And although a part of her was nearly willing to pay that price, she didn't want her family to suffer. Their lives would be ruined. They would forever be the family of the teenage murderer. She imagined kids at school pretending to point guns at her sister and calling her terrible names. She saw the judgmental looks her parents would be forced to endure from people in the grocery store and at church. No, she wasn't willing to put them through that.

She looked at Gil and then at Elizabeth. "Shit…"

Gil nodded. "Okay then."

• • • • •

Steven Davenport saw it that night on the news. Gil Linnetti was standing at his front door facing the cameras. Steven immediately noticed the difference in Gil. The forlorn sadness that had darkened his features was gone. His face was animated. He looked considerably happier. He's found something, Steven thought, the weight has been lifted. Steven looked away from the television and picked up his glass of vodka. He had been drinking three vodkas a night since Marjorie left. All will be well the warm haze of alcohol informed him — If Darla hasn't gone to the police by now, she's not going to go. Marjorie is upset, but in a couple days she will come to her senses, return home, and this whole mess will be over. Everything is working out the way it's supposed to. Steven drained the glass and looked back to the television.

A neighbor was telling reporters how happy she was that Gil was back in his house. An image of Gil's house appeared on the screen. The yard was empty. All the other reporters were gone. Celia Davis' voice came up over the image.

"This may be the end of Gil Linnetti's strange, heart-warming odyssey on Hargrove Avenue, but it is not the end of the mystery. Who killed Gil Linnetti's wife and two small children? Who is responsible for leaving this home empty of a family's joy and laughter?"

The camera slowly panned the length of the house to where Celia Davis was standing in the road. With great solemnity she concluded, "This is Celia Davis reporting for Channel 2 News."

Steven blinked as a Dodge truck commercial suddenly blared from the television. He grabbed the remote and pressed the mute button. For a moment he stared at the screen. There was something… He closed his eyes, forcing himself to replay the newscast in his mind. Muted, as if she was speaking from under a blanket, the reporter mentioned Gil's wife and children. The camera started its slow pan from the house to Celia Davis. Steven froze the image in his mind. There! Over the reporter's shoulder, on the other side of the street, was a car. The faded silver paint, dented rear quarter panel, and rusted trunk confirmed his suspicions. It was Darla's Ford. His eyes snapped open.

She told him, Steven realized. That's why Gil left Hargrove Avenue. He knows the truth.

• • • • •

Marjorie parked her car and glanced anxiously up the dark street. She knew it was unlikely that Steven would see her, but still she was nervous, she didn't want to get into a confrontation. She was starting to feel strong on her own. Giving him the opportunity to try and manipulate her would be dangerous. Marjorie got out of the car and walked toward the house. If Linda hadn't sounded so strange on the telephone she never would have risked coming back into their neighborhood. "Please come over," Linda insisted, "I need to talk to you right away." One of the most grounded people she knew, for Linda to be that on edge meant something was terribly wrong. Not her grandsons, Marjorie thought, please, not that.

As Marjorie walked down the front walk toward the McKelvey's house, movement in the upstairs window caught her eye. When she looked up no one was there. A flash of fear prickled the back of Marjorie's neck. What if Steven is in the house, she thought. What if he tricked Linda or maybe even forced her into calling? But what about Tom, Marjorie remembered, trying to calm herself. She'd heard his voice in the background when Linda called. Tom was a big guy. He wouldn't let Linda get pushed around. No, she thought reaching for the doorbell, this isn't about Steven.

Elizabeth's hand froze on the upstairs banister when the doorbell chimed. Linda and Tom McKelvey had offered to be there with her, but Elizabeth told them she could handle it. So they went to a movie. Now, with her mother at the front door, Elizabeth wished the McKelvey's had stayed.

When Elizabeth told Gil that she wanted to inform her mother about their plans, Gil had said, "I think that's fair. She should know." Then he added, "Do you want me to be there with you?" The tenderness in his eyes made her want to touch him, to hold his hand. But she didn't. "Thanks," she said firmly, "I'll be all right." Her mind had whirled with questions — would Marjorie be happy to see her? Would she believe the story of the rape? And if she already knew what happened that night, would she be angry that her secret was no longer buried out of sight? Either way, Elizabeth had concluded, the confrontation would be difficult.

As she started down the stairs, Elizabeth reminded herself not to initiate an embrace. She wanted to wait and see what Marjorie did. It would demonstrate, Elizabeth reasoned, if her mother knew what her father had done. At the foot of the stairs she glanced at herself in the hallway mirror. The young girl her mother had last seen was gone. She was a woman now. Elizabeth took in a long, calming breath. She heard her mother's voice from sixteen years earlier — "Get your hair out of that pretty face." Elizabeth pulled her hair back, checked herself one more time, and then opened the door.

Marjorie was momentarily surprised. Not expecting to see an unfamiliar face at the McKelvey's, she opened her mouth to ask for Linda but then suddenly stopped. Her mouth hung open, her eyes slowly widening in stunned recognition of who was standing in front of her.

"Elizabeth."

Elizabeth didn't move or say a word. She was waiting to see what her mother would do.

My God, Marjorie thought staring at her daughter, she's even prettier than I'd dreamed. Marjorie's next thought was: I will never let her out of my sight. No one will ever hurt her again.

"Come in." Elizabeth stepped aside. Marjorie walked past her resisting the nearly over whelming urge to grab her and give her a hug. Maybe she hates me, Marjorie thought, I don't want to upset her. She walked into the McKelvey's kitchen, a room she had been in countless times before but which now felt strangely foreign. She stood next to the counter, her hand moving nervously from her purse to the base of her throat then back to the purse.

Elizabeth took all of this in as she crossed the room to her mother. I will give her one more chance, she thought, stopping in front of Marjorie. She looked into her mother's eyes. Reach for me, Elizabeth willed her. Throw your arms around me and tell me how happy you are to see me. Marjorie didn't move. This isn't a woman who has finally found her long lost daughter Elizabeth thought bitterly, this is a woman who is guilty. She knows what he did to me. The wrenching impact of Elizabeth's disappointment surprised her. She had been holding out more hope than she realized. Struggling not to cry, she managed to restrain all but one lone tear. It trailed down her cheek stopping at the edge of her jaw.

Marjorie watched it course down her daughter's face. A tear, she thought. Perhaps she doesn't hate me after all. She reached out and with great tenderness wiped the tear away. Elizabeth, feeling her mother's touch for the first time in fifteen years, was unable to stop herself. "Mom," she whispered. Marjorie drew her into her arms. Holding tightly to each other they wept. Finally Elizabeth lifted her head from where she'd buried it in Marjorie's shoulder. She looked at her mother's once perfectly made up face now in shambles. "Wow, we're a mess."

Marjorie gripped her tightly. "But we can get better."

Elizabeth nodded, but there was uncertainty in her eyes. She led Marjorie to the table.

They both sat down. Elizabeth exhaled a long breath and looked at her mother.

"Did you know that Dad raped me?"

Marjorie flinched, the words striking hard. The temptation to deny it was strong, but instead she willed herself to return her daughter's gaze. This will be the hardest thing I have ever done, Marjorie thought. To say a simple one word response that will either bring us together or blow us apart for good. She studied Elizabeth's face wanting to memorize every inch of it. There was a great possibility that her daughter would get up and walk out the door and she might never see her again. Marjorie wanted to at least have a picture saved in her mind.

"Yes, I knew. But it wasn't until the other day that I actually remembered it." She looked away, her eyes focusing in the space between the table and the back door. "I heard sounds that night…through your bedroom door. It was — too horrible for me to — I went into some kind of shock, I think." She looked back at Elizabeth with shame and regret in her eyes. "So I convinced myself that it didn't happen — that I hadn't heard anything. I blanked it out." She put her head in her hands. "I know it sounds awful. I'm so sorry."

As hard as it was to hear, Elizabeth was relieved that Marjorie had not consciously been ignoring her for all those years. Similar to what she had done with her great wall of forgetting, her mother had also chosen denial to cope with the ugly truth.

"I did have a private investigator searching for you," Marjorie said.

"Really."

"Your father and I tried to find you."

Elizabeth looked at her mother, surprised. "Why would my father want to find me?"

"What do you mean —" Then Marjorie stopped herself. "Oh."

Those three years of searching had been full of disappointment and frustration. There was the letter from Chicago that temporarily lifted her spirits, only to be crushed once again when the investigator was unable to find Elizabeth. Marjorie searched her memory for the investigator's name. Steven had handled it. Every few weeks Steven would tell her where the investigator had searched and any tips he'd discovered. In fact, she never once saw a written report or an invoice for services rendered. Steven, she thought with growing dismay, had managed everything.

Marjorie hung her head. "Oh, my God."

"He didn't want to find me, Mom."

Marjorie burst into tears. What a stupid cow, she silently chided herself.

"I know how devoted you are to him," Elizabeth said.

Marjorie's head immediately came up. "Not any more. I left him. I'm filing for divorce."

Without thinking Elizabeth asked, "Why? What happened?"

"Because, I finally remembered what he did to you."

"What made you all of a sudden remember?"

"There was a girl in our yard, she had a gun, and I—I was so frightened – I guess it pulled the memories to the surface. I felt— It was —"

Elizabeth took her mother's hand in both of hers. "That was Darla, Mom."

"You know her?"

"Yes. He raped Darla too."

Marjorie's mouth fell open. "Oh God, is she all right?"

"No, Mom. She's angry. Just like me."

Marjorie looked down. "If only I had said something back then."

"Yes, me too."

Neither of them spoke for a moment, the cost of their silence a painful bond.

Elizabeth squeezed Marjorie's hand. "Unfortunately there's more."

Marjorie's face drained of color as Elizabeth proceeded to tell her about Steven's involvement in the accident that killed Gil's wife and children.

"But Steven said it was a car-jacker. He told me—he told the police. He said—" She stopped, too stunned to go on.

"Also, that day at the hospital when you drove up and were talking with him in the parking lot," Elizabeth paused making sure her mother was listening. "He had just grabbed a gun from Darla and shot at her. He tried to kill her."

Marjorie's look of horror deepened. "He shot at—"

"Yeah, and he still has the gun."

Marjorie put her head in her hands. "God, what have I done?"

The words were out before Elizabeth could stop them. "That's who you chose over me Mom, a lying bastard who rapes girls and tries to kill them."

Marjorie cringed. "Yes. You're right. I've been a terrible mother." Then, with a maternal intensity unexpressed in far too long, she added, "But I promise I will never abandon you again."

Elizabeth, feeling a mixture of sorrow and elation for what she'd just said to her mother, slid the ceramic cowboy pepper-shaker back and forth on the table.

"I didn't call the police because I knew what it would do to you. I thought you'd be lost without him."

Marjorie stood up and came around behind Elizabeth and wrapped her arms around her daughter's shoulders. "I'm stronger than that now."

Elizabeth closed her eyes and surrendered into her mother's embrace. Marjorie began gently rocking her back and forth. "Have you gone to the police?"

"No."

"Why not?"

"We don't want to get Darla in trouble for the accident. It's Gil's idea. He wants us to talk with – my father. He thinks it will be good for all of us."

"But what does he think Steven will do? If he had been willing to take responsibility for his actions he would have done it long ago."

"I know, but what else can we do. We want to protect Darla."

Marjorie continued rocking Elizabeth tenderly back and forth. "Do you think you can all go through with it?"

Elizabeth's voice was soft and dreamy. "It's Darla who worries me. I think she still wants revenge."

Marjorie held her tighter. "Yes, I understand how she feels."

27

At the intersection of Hargrove and Gorham an early morning breeze sifted through the branches of the oak, softly rustling its leaves. Gil leaned forward and rested his hand on the scarred trunk.

"I have come to say goodbye to this place. It has served me well." He pressed his hand harder against the tree trunk as if he was seeking to tap the power it possessed.

"Bonnie, I think this is why you inspired me to stay here. Give me strength in what I'm about to do. Tell Drake that Daddy is trying to do good things." He paused, scuffing his boot in the dirt. "I'm so sorry for what happened, Bon. I kept a secret that maybe I shouldn't have. I'm going to try and make it right. I love you all."

Across the street, Elizabeth watched Gil. They had come to the campsite at first light hoping to avoid any reporters. It had worked. They were the only ones there. She finished folding the tent, and as she was stuffing it into a nylon sack, Gil came up from the road.

"This shouldn't take too long." He picked up one of the coolers and started down to his Land Rover. Earlier, when Elizabeth told Gil about the conversation with her mother, he was pleased. Gil believed that even though Marjorie hadn't told Steven why she'd left the house, her departure would have a strong impact on him. And if Steven was rattled and vulnerable it might increase their chances of getting him to be honest.

They were loading the final garbage bag into the back of Elizabeth's car when Dominic Angelo's pickup truck pulled off the road just ahead of them.

"This is the guy I told you about," Elizabeth said to Gil. "He's the one who found you."

Dominic limped at first, his legs stiff from sitting, but then his gait loosened as he approached them.

"I know it's you." Dominic was grinning. "I remember the blue car. Don't try and hide."

Elizabeth smiled sheepishly. "Sorry about the other day. I was —"

"It's okay," Dominic stopped in front of her, a broad smile lighting his face. "I'm just pleased as pie to see you. And you too." He looked at Gil. "Glad you're up and around."

"Thanks for helping me." Gil extended his hand. "I was – doctors said I was lucky."

Dominic shook his hand. "Didn't like seeing you that way."

"Must have been bad," Elizabeth said.

"It was." Dominic's face momentarily darkened. Then he pursed his lips together and dropped his hands to his sides. "No use trying to sneak up on it. I need to tell you something."

"Okay." Elizabeth couldn't help noticing his discomfort.

"I don't know for sure why you left home, and I don't know why you're back, but I've been around your family for a long time and I've never seen your father with a gun. The other day he had a pistol in his hand. Looked like a big one." Dominic stuck his hands in the pockets of his worn khakis. "Maybe it has nothing to do with you being back, but I thought you should know."

Elizabeth and Gil exchanged a look.

"Thanks." She reached out and gave Dominic's arm a light squeeze.

"Sure."

"Hey, remember the ribbons. Our secret game?"

"Yeah, you bet." Happy to let her change the subject, Dominic smiled warmly. He glanced at Gil and then back to Elizabeth. "She was the nicest little girl. Oh, we had some fun back then."

"Yes, we did."

"I'm glad you're okay. I really am. You be careful."

"Thank you." Elizabeth patted his arm. Tentatively she asked, "And your wife, is she well?"

He shook his head. "Lost her. Eight years ago."

"I'm sorry."

Gil bowed his head. "Sorry for your loss."

"She was a good one. I wasn't so great but she was."

"How about Michael?" Elizabeth was surprised she remembered his name. "And his kids. A couple of them, right?"

Dominic's face brightened. She was a light, he thought, a sweet light that hadn't changed in all the years she'd been away.

"Oh Michael and the family are doing fine." Dominic happily fell back into his old lie. "Busy, you know. He called the other day. Was putting in a light fixture, some new fancy thing in his kitchen, he nearly got electrocuted. Had to call me to help him out."

Gil laughed. "He's lucky to have you for advice."

"You bet he is." Dominic was suddenly feeling more energized than he had in months. "And he raised some good kids, too. They really spoil their Pop Pop."

"As they should," Elizabeth said.

Dominic glanced away. The thought of grandchildren choked him up. "So you pulled up stakes?" He gestured to where Gil's camp had been.

Gil nodded. "Time to get on with things."

"Yep." With his emotions better under control Dominic turned back to them. "You take care. Both of you."

"Nice to meet you, Dominic." Gil patted him on the shoulder.

"Same here." Dominic gave Elizabeth a tender look. "Thanks for asking about Michael. Means a lot."

• • • • •

Marjorie drove by the house a second time trying to gather her courage. The BMW was in the driveway so she knew he was home. All the goodwill and confidence gained in her talk with Elizabeth disappeared at the thought of once again facing Steven. Even though he had lived a lie and made their marriage nothing but a false front propping up his depravity, Marjorie feared she might still be emotionally vulnerable to his coercion.

Fully aware that continuing to drive up and down the road would get the neighbors talking, Marjorie willed herself to turn around and go back. This time she would do it, she told herself. She would pull into the driveway, go in through the garage, and that would be it. It was what had to be done — for Elizabeth.

• • • • •

Steven hadn't slept much. The thought of Gil Linnetti knowing the truth about Darla and the accident had propelled his mind into a complex damage control analysis. He'd considered liquidating as many resources as he could and going on the run. All night he'd wrestled with what to do, but in the morning none of it made any sense. If he fled to South America or Indonesia, and Gil didn't turn him into the police, then he would have destroyed his business and his marriage for nothing. And if they did turn him in and he fled, he would undoubtedly be caught. But if, instead, he quietly waited, minding his own business and acting as if nothing was amiss, perhaps it would all go away. Or he could negotiate a deal with Gil and Darla. They had to know that if they turned him in, Darla would be arrested for her involvement in the accident. And knowing Gil, it wasn't a stretch to believe that instead of going to the police he would choose to protect Darla. In fact, Steven decided, it was almost better if Darla told Gil what happened. Gil might act as a moderating force and rein her in. That would be helpful in an immediate sense, but ultimately Steven concluded, Gil would take some type of hostile action. His loss was too great. He would be unable to let it go.

As he watched the steam come off the surface of his coffee, Steven began considering the ways in which Gil might retaliate against him. And more specifically, what he could do to protect himself. In mid-thought he abruptly pushed back his chair from the kitchen table and stood up. He listened. The garage door was opening.

· · · · ·

The barrel of the .22 pistol jabbed into Darla's stomach. She shifted in the back seat of Gil's Land Rover, inconspicuously moving the gun to a more comfortable position. The bulky sweatshirt she was wearing, although too warm, perfectly concealed the weapon. It wasn't a match for the .357 Davenport had taken from her, but if something happened the .22 could get the job done.

"Take a left at the stop sign." Elizabeth pointed at the intersection just ahead.

Darla silently watched the manicured lawns go past. She was happy with her decision to come armed and ready to the meeting with Davenport. Her father had left the .22 in the basement after cleaning it. He called it his varmint gun. With a nine bullet clip she knew she would have three more shots than Davenport if he came after them with the

.357. She secretly hoped he would try something. It would be the excuse she needed to blow him away.

Elizabeth felt like she was going to vomit. No longer able to hide behind her protective wall, the thought of being in the same room with her father, let alone speaking to him, left her queasy with disgust. She feared that even hearing his voice might spin her into an emotional state that would prohibit her from doing what needed to be done. She wanted to be strong. She wanted to heal. She wanted to be a whole woman.

Only a few times before in Gil's life had he experienced the absolute certainty he now felt. The first was when he made the decision to drive Elizabeth to Oregon, another was when he asked Bonnie to marry him, and the third was when he and Bonnie decided to have a family. Then, like now, he knew with all his being that he was doing the right thing. He felt supremely confident that he was where he was supposed to be, doing what he was meant to do. Something good would come from this meeting, something important. And that faith, that absolute conviction in the action he was about to take, made him feel unstoppable.

• • • • •

At the sight of Marjorie coming up the basement stairs Steven's face broke into a wide smile. Right when he needed her most she had come back to him.

"Hi baby." Steven reached for her as she climbed the top step.

Marjorie grinned as she slid past his intended embrace. "Good morning. What are you still doing in your pajamas?" She was fighting to remain calm. She needed to keep him as passive as she could.

"Moving slow this morning," Steven said, still smiling. "It's good to see you."

Marjorie turned and faced him. A nearly overwhelming impulse to charge at him and shove him down the basement stairs forced her to acknowledge that perhaps her fear of falling victim to his manipulative charms was no longer valid. Disgust and rage was all she felt.

"Are you okay?" Steven stepped toward her.

"I'm fine." Marjorie pushed out what she hoped sounded like a genuine laugh. "Sorry about the mirror. I know you liked it."

"It's all right. Just a mirror. It's you I've been worried about."

"I know, I went a little nuts." She smiled hoping to put him at ease. "Why don't you go take your shower and I'll make breakfast. We'll talk."

Steven's smile broadened. "I'm really happy to see you." He started for the stairs.

Okay, Marjorie thought as she went into the kitchen, I'm handling this better than I thought I would.

"What did the girl in the back yard say to you?"

Marjorie turned. Steven was smiling but his eyes were deadly serious. "Is that why you left?"

Marjorie's body went dead still. Her throat tightened. "I – it's —" Her mind scrambled and then quickly found the spin she needed. "It wasn't that she said anything. It was who she reminded me of."

For a moment Steven didn't move. Marjorie feared that he had seen through her performance. Then Steven slowly nodded. "Right — of course." The tension in his face disappeared. "I should have realized – I'm sorry."

"I'm sorry too."

"I love you." His lover's voice purred. "I'm glad you're back."

"Go get showered." Marjorie turned to hide her revulsion. "I'm starving."

She heard him go up the stairs. When the water in the shower went on, she immediately ran to the study. Certain the gun would be in his desk, Marjorie quietly eased the four drawers open one at a time. It wasn't there. She searched his briefcase. Not finding it, she went upstairs to the master bedroom. Determined to get the pistol away from him before Elizabeth and the others arrived, Marjorie slipped into the walk-in closet. A quick search through his things didn't turn up the gun. She began to panic. She had left her daughter in harm's way once before and refused to do it again. She looked under the bed and behind the pillows. Inside the bathroom, the shower stopped. Marjorie ran out of the bedroom and down the stairs.

The morning sun was gleaming off the upstairs windows when Gil pulled over in front of the Davenport's house. He shut off the car. "Let's go."

Elizabeth craned her neck looking out the window. "Is that my mother's car?"

Gil turned and looked at the white Volvo in the driveway. "I thought you told her to stay away."

"I did."

Darla slid to the edge of the seat. "What's going on?"

"Why would she come here?" Elizabeth turned to Gil.

"You tell me."

Darla leaned forward toward Elizabeth. "Would she tell him what we're gonna' do?"

"Of course not!"

"Screw it." Gil opened his door. "Come on."

"I'm not going in there if she warned him!" Darla smacked the headrest with her hand.

"My mother wouldn't do that."

"Fine. Whatever." Darla adjusted the .22 under her sweatshirt and got out of the car.

They crossed the lawn to the front door. Glances shot between the three of them. Gil nodded to Elizabeth who reached out and rang the doorbell. The night she ran away was the ending of one part of her life and the beginning of another. In the tense moment before the door opened, Elizabeth realized that she was once again at the threshold of beginnings and endings.

The front door swung partially open. Marjorie, looking distraught, peered at them around the edge of the door. "I'm sorry. I was trying to find the gun before you got here. I don't know where he put it." She gestured them in. "He's upstairs getting dressed."

Steven heard the doorbell and looked out the bathroom window. A white Land Rover was parked in front of the house. Buoyed by Marjorie's return home, Steven didn't dwell on it. But as he was running a brush through his wet hair he suddenly stopped and listened. He didn't hear anyone talking downstairs. He went to the bedroom window and looked into the back yard. The patio was empty. If she's in the house with a visitor, Steven wondered, why can't I hear them talking? He stood at the top of the stairs and listened…nothing. No one was saying anything. Darla, he thought. He quickly finished getting dressed. Reaching behind the headboard of the bed, he pulled out the .357. Draping his suit coat over the pistol, as he had seen Darla do in the hospital parking lot with her sweatshirt, he walked out of the bedroom and started down the stairs. He wasn't going to be surprised by her again.

Darla heard him coming down the stairs. Her pulse jumped, and from a dark corner of her mind the voice of guilt, quiet since her confession to Elizabeth and Gil, shouted in her head — *Kill him! Kill him now!* Squatting down behind the couch, pretending to look at framed photographs on the end table, her hand slipped under her sweatshirt.

Elizabeth's hands moved nervously in her lap. Her stomach, fluttery before entering the house, now mercilessly churned. She glanced at Gil next to her on the couch. He was serene, a beatific smile slightly parting his lips. What was he thinking, she wondered?

Marjorie listened to Steven's footsteps descend the stairs. He would blame her, she knew that for certain. But no matter what he did or said, nothing was more important than giving Elizabeth and the others a chance to face him.

Steven walked into the room.

His expression changed. It wasn't dramatic, Marjorie thought, but there was a definite shift. His eyes moved from Gil to Darla and then to her. She could see his confusion about who Elizabeth was.

"Say hello to your daughter." Marjorie gestured to Elizabeth. "She's come a long way to see you."

Davenport shifted his gaze. His surprise was obvious.

"Hello." Elizabeth forced herself to look him in the eyes. Her palms were sweating but her voice was strong and resolute. Here I am, she thought. You didn't destroy me.

Steven briefly held her gaze then looked away. It's over, he thought. Everyone knows everything.

"We want to talk with you." Gil gestured to the armchair next to the couch. "Come, sit down."

Davenport even didn't move.

Darla watched him carefully. She didn't like the way his coat was draped over his arm.

Her hand closed around the grip of the .22. If he swings even an inch in our direction, she told herself, I'm gonna do it.

Thoughts of his clients' reactions pinged like rifle shots through Steven's mind. Marty Braverman would not only cease doing business with him, he would go out of his way to make sure no one else did. Not in Pittsburgh or anywhere. No one would trust him. He had raped his own daughter. Life as he had known it was over. Next stop a jail cell. And what happened to men like him in prison? The weight of the revolver in his hand reminded him of other options.

"Steven," Marjorie said sharply. "Sit down."

Darla could see that he was conflicted about what to do. She inched the .22 out from under her sweatshirt and eased the safety off.

Gil stood up. "Steve, we know this is uncomfortable. But it's time to get it all out in the open."

Steven turned slightly toward Gil. Darla saw the muzzle of the .357 under his jacket.

"He's got the gun!" She leapt up from behind the couch. In the panicked second it took to level the .22 at Davenport, she watched his eyes shift from Gil to her. He looked surprised to see the gun in her hand.

"Put it down! Put it down! Put it down!" Darla was pointing the .22 at the center of his chest. Davenport didn't move. Absolutely still, his finger resting on the trigger, he stared at the gun in Darla's hand. His first thought was of Kelly. Would he see her if Darla pulled the trigger before he did? It would be nice to talk to her. He felt a flush of warmth across his back. Then he thought about seeing his father again.

Kill him! Kill him! The voice of guilt railed at Darla. She forced herself not to listen. She had to protect the others from Davenport and her father's gun.

Gil calmly eased up off of the couch.

"Steve, please put the gun down. Help us understand why all of this happened." Gil stepped toward him. "We can do this together."

Davenport's eyes shifted from Darla to Gil. Davenport eyed him blankly.

"Give me the gun." Gil took another step closer. "Let's talk."

Darla, her hand trembling, shifted her position to maintain a clear line of fire.

Gil held up his hands, palms forward, in a gesture of submission. "Elizabeth has lived a long time with questions only you can answer."

Out of the corner of his eye Steven saw his daughter staring at him. This must look silly, he thought. He closed his eyes.

Moments of clarity following periods of stressful analysis had been a hallmark of Steven's investment career. Trying to broker the right players into the right deal for the right money at the right time was always a highly complicated proposition. But with time and effort, near perfect solutions reveal themselves. Or sometimes they happen in an instant. With his finger still gently resting on the trigger, Steven was suddenly aware that his muddled confusion was lifting. In its place came a surge of clarity: If they're going to have me arrested, they wouldn't confront me like this. No, Steven thought, they have no intention of turning me over to the police. They're protecting Darla. I still have a chance. I can make this work.

He handed the gun to Gil.

28

"Darla give me your gun." Gil was removing bullets from the cylinder of the .357.

Darla was still staring at Davenport. "You're lucky. I almost shot you."

"I'm glad you didn't."

"I'm not."

"The gun, Darla." Gil held out his hand.

"I don't trust him."

"Darla."

"You're lucky." She glared at Davenport, then handed the .22 to Gil.

Gil ejected the clip from the .22 and put it in his pocket with the other bullets. He placed the gun next to the .357 on the coffee table.

Darla looked at the .22. There was still one in the chamber.

"Sit down." Gil gestured Steven toward the chair.

Steven walked over to the armchair. He carefully draped his jacket over the back and sat down. For a moment the only sound in the room was bacon sizzling in the skillet. Steven shot a quick glance at Elizabeth. He could see some of Marjorie's features in her face and a little of his own mother. That pleased him to think that his mother was alive in Elizabeth. Yes, he thought, that's a good thing.

Elizabeth felt his eyes on her but refused to look at him. Instead, she visualized Sky in one of his vibrant tie-dyed T-shirts standing in a sun-brightened meadow. Give me the power to do this, she asked the vision. Help me face this monster.

"We all know what you did, Steve." Gil's voice brought Elizabeth's focus back into the room. "The rapes, your involvement in the death of my family, all of it." He paused, letting his words sink in. Davenport didn't react.

Don't even try and deny it, Darla thought watching him, or I'll rip your fucking face off.

"All of us have suffered at your hands," Gil went on, his voice rising and then remaining steady. "I want you to answer our questions and talk with us about what happened and why it happened." Gil let that settle on Davenport. "Can you do that?"

Davenport looked at Marjorie. "You better check the bacon."

She snapped at him. "Answer the question!"

Davenport nodded. "Yes. I'll talk with you." He shot a look at Elizabeth. It was surreal to see her all grown up. Where had his little girl gone?

"It'll be best if you can open your heart and let the truth out," Gil said. "We all need that—you most of all."

Gil reached over and touched Elizabeth on the leg.

"Go ahead."

Elizabeth struggled to pull in a breath. There didn't seem to be enough oxygen in the room. She tried, but could not bring herself to look at her father. It would've been easier if Darla had just shot him, she thought. It would be over and none of this agonizing discussion would have to happen. Elizabeth remembered her students at Fair Haven and the unwavering encouragement she provided to them to always stand for themselves. She remembered Lumina struggling to make eye contact with the class. Time to walk my talk, Elizabeth realized. Pushing back against the crippling static of anxiety, she rallied her courage and silently declared to Steven — I'm not afraid of you. You're a sick, twisted man and you *will* give me the answers I need.

She forced herself to face him. He was staring at his hands in his lap. Relieved that he wasn't looking at her, Elizabeth's courage kicked up another notch.

"For the last fifteen years I have tried not to think of you. I worked hard to block out everything about you. I lived a good life. I helped other people. But no matter how I tried to isolate myself, you were never far away. She paused, struggling to keep her emotions under control. "Why? Why did you rape me?"

Steven's mind ticked through options until he found what he thought would serve him best. "I have a problem."

"And that problem is what, exactly?" Elizabeth gestured to the others. "Please, tell us."

"You both know."

"Tell us."

"Answer her!" Marjorie demanded from the kitchen.

Steven fought the urge to glare at his wife. Now is not the time, he told himself. I have to be smart.

"I have a weakness. For young girls. I'm not proud of it. I've tried to stop but —" He shook his head, looking forlorn. "Elizabeth, what I did was the worst violation a man can make. I have no excuse. If I hadn't been drinking I might have been able to control myself, but that wasn't what happened. I'm sorry. With all my heart I'm sorry for what I did to you."

"Oh God," Marjorie muttered.

Davenport looked over at his wife. "I know this is hard for you to hear, honey. But it's got nothing to do with how I feel about you. I love you and always have. It's — something – else that's a part of me. It's not easy to explain."

After years of denial and restraint Marjorie looked as if she was going to come over the kitchen counter at him. "You're a liar and a rapist! How's that for an explanation!"

Stunned by her ferocity, Davenport knew he had to do something or the situation might escalate further out of control. "But honey," he insisted in his best seductive voice, "You're the love of my life."

Marjorie glared holes through him. "Doesn't work anymore, Steven."

Seeing that he wasn't going to get any understanding from her, Davenport turned to Gil.

"What happened to your wife and children is a tragedy," he said. "And I share that responsibility with Darla."

"What?" Darla jumped up. "If you hadn't attacked me —"

"You were driving with the lights off."

"Stop it!" Elizabeth pointed a finger at her father. "Don't you dare try and lay the blame on anyone else."

Steven lowered his head submissively and nodded. "I'm sorry."

"How long have you been molesting girls?" Elizabeth articulated each word as a clear indictment of his actions.

Steven had to restrain himself from shooting her a nasty look. Who does she think she is, he thought, talking to me like that? Then with practiced ease, he allowed his voice to go soft.

"It has been a lifelong struggle."

"Your whole life?" Darla couldn't believe it. "Since you were a kid?"

Steven nodded. Flashes of countless grope and grabs done as a teenager flashed strobe-like through his mind.

"Why? What made you like that?"

Steven looked out the window.

"Darla asked you a question," Elizabeth said.

"You don't care why. This is about making me suffer."

Darla gave a bitter laugh. "Unless I pin down your arms, jam my hand over your mouth and nose so you can't breathe, and shove a broomstick up your ass, there's nothin' I can do that'll come close to how you made *me* suffer."

Steven stared back at her. And if I had been a second quicker pulling the trigger in the hospital parking lot, he thought, I wouldn't be listening to your mouth flap right now. Instead of saying that, he willed himself to look dejectedly down at the floor.

"Answer Darla's question," Elizabeth said.

Steven looked from Darla to Gil and then Elizabeth. He had read the faces of a lot of gamblers in his investment career. He learned to sense which aspect of the deal mattered the most to any prospective investor and then to leverage it to his own advantage. He could tell by the collective intensity of their interest that this was what they had come for. He considered Darla's question: What made you like that? He had never discussed his childhood with anyone. It wasn't a pleasant journey. But, Steven thought, if I tell them that twisted tale and it earns me some sympathy and possibly helps me out of this messed up situation, then maybe it's a good idea. He leaned back in his chair, weighing his options. He waited a minute longer allowing their anticipation to grow. I'll tell them, he decided, but I'm getting everything I can for it.

"I will tell you on one condition. None of what we discuss here ever leaves this room. And you can't go to the police." He looked at each of them to make his point.

"Or you'll do what?" Elizabeth was unshaken by his power play.

"You'll go to jail. It's not just me and Darla in the hot seat here. Elizabeth, you'll be charged for obstruction of justice for protecting Darla from prosecution."

"Obstruction of justice versus multiple rape charges, hummm, you're the big loser there."

"For all I know you have a tape recorder running somewhere."

"They don't," Marjorie said. "Tell them what they want to know."

Steven had no other cards to play. "Okay, but it's not a cheery tale."

With a casual, steady pace Steven told them the story of his brutal upbringing. He explained his mother's love of opera and took them step-by-step through her long horrible death from stomach cancer. He chronicled his sister's suffering at the hands of his father and his own beatings and years of abuse. When he got to the part where he found Kelly overdosed in the bedroom closet, Marjorie began to sob.

"How do we know," Elizabeth said, "that these aren't more of your lies?"

Steven shrugged. "Your mother has seen the scars. She knows what my body has been through."

Marjorie nodded. "He told me it was from sports – and a car accident. But it never seemed right."

"No, I'm sure it didn't." Feeling a warm prickling sensation, Steven reached up and rubbed the back of his neck. "After Kelly was gone, I was the only one around for him to beat on. My life became a weekly survival test. I tried to convince myself to report him to the police or someone, but I knew if something happened and I was sent back to him, he would make it even worse. So I never said anything to anyone."

Marjorie folded the tissue she had used. "Did you ever get away from him?"

Steven paused. He hadn't thought about it in decades and didn't want to discuss it now.

"Long story."

"That's why we're here," Gil said.

Steven shook his head.

"Since I've known you," Marjorie said, "I thought you were adopted. That's what you told me and I believed you. For once in your life tell the whole truth."

"Or we can call the police," Elizabeth said, "Would you like that?"

Steven had not spoken of that night since it happened. It was the deeply buried secret inside the labyrinth of all his other secrets.

"He got drunk one night. Fell asleep with a cigarette burning. Gutted the house. I barely got out in time. He didn't."

"So that was my grandfather." Elizabeth was staring into her cup of coffee.

Gil watched Steven carefully. He had seen something in the man's eyes that didn't feel quite right. Was it a flicker of pride?

"Did the police investigate?"

Steven's piercing blue eyes narrowed at Gil. "He was a drunk and everyone knew it. They didn't need to investigate."

Gil casually reached for his cup of tea, but kept his eyes on Steven. "Lucky for you."

Another fluttering sensation swept through Steven. He stood up. Marjorie and the others looked up at him waiting for his response. He didn't say anything. He simply picked up his coffee cup and carried it to the sink. As the warm water ran over his hands he remembered the night of the fire. With his hands and feet feeling like blocks of ice, he had taken control of his life with a single wooden match.

Elizabeth watched him at the sink. A mystery to her before, her father was now even more of an enigma. Like a bomb ticking away for years under their roof, he had finally exploded. But if he had turned in his father, or later admitted to his own violent past, or if he had sought help, her rape may never have happened. So much wouldn't have happened.

"I don't get it." Darla picked at her hair. "The reason you attack girls is because your father attacked your sister, what was her name – Kelly?"

Steven whirled around. "Don't talk about my sister!" His fist slammed down on the counter. "It's not your place! You don't know!" A glass tumbled, rolled, and shattered on the floor. A startling high definition memory exploded in his mind. His father was charging across their kitchen, swinging his belt and knocking dishes off the table. "Christ!" Steven leaned on the counter for support. Images and sounds rushed up from the past: his mother's face in her coffin, groans in Kelly's bedroom, belts, fists, mop handles, broken teeth, blood in his mouth, blood in his eyes, Kelly blue in the closet, sad eyes, tired eyes, dead peaceful eyes, bring her back, your fault, your fault, your fault, lighting the match, the pungent roasted smell of his father's burned body.

Steven's grip on the counter was slipping as the horrible torrent of images swept through him: hands, fingers touching, probing, naked girls crying, frightened eyes, shameful eyes, Elizabeth's breasts, reaching to comfort, to find feeling, to be in control, Darla's face, muzzle of the gun, the children's bloody bodies, wreckage, flames. His own words echoing in his head as if from down a long darkened hallway: this is the pain, this is the heat, this is the loss. This is the pain, this is the heat, this is the loss. This is the pain, this is the heat, this is the loss.

29

"Over thirty years, *thirty years*, and he never told me?" Marjorie reached up and pulled coffee mugs out of the cabinet next to the sink.

"How creepy was that?" Darla was sitting on the couch.

Elizabeth shut the fridge. "He's so full of shit. He makes me sick."

"He suffered abuse for years," Marjorie said. "That kind of constant trauma affects the way a person feels and thinks."

"Yes, mother, but he did nothing to try and get help."

"He wasn't able to. He couldn't see what he'd become."

"He looked me right in the eyes" Elizabeth said, "and jammed his hand over my mouth. Believe me he knew what he was doing."

"Honey —"

"What I don't get is how *you* couldn't see him? I mean, you had to have some idea that the man wasn't normal?"

Marjorie stared hollow-eyed back at her daughter. Yes, how could she have not better seen the darkness in him? She'd witnessed odd behavior, but how could she have known the full depth and meaning of it? He was so good at deceiving her. She was never able to find her way through the house of mirrors he'd built.

"You're right, honey. You're right. I wish I could have protected us both from him."

"What about protecting other girls," Darla said. "We can't let him go wandering around free. He'll do it again." She shot Elizabeth a look. "Unless we stop him."

Marjorie picked up the pot of coffee. "Do you want coffee?"

"Thanks." Darla got up and walked around the counter.

Marjorie poured her a cup. "Cream?"

"Yes, thank you."

Marjorie opened the refrigerator and pulled out a quart of Half & Half.

"We have to do something," Darla said.

Marjorie filled a small ceramic pitcher. "What do you mean? Have him arrested?"

"No."

"Let's see where Gil is going with this." Elizabeth shot Darla a look that said *not now.*

"What are they doing?" Marjorie handed the pitcher of cream to Darla.

Elizabeth glanced out the French doors to the patio. "I don't know. They're just standing there."

"Are they talking."

"Doesn't look like it."

"That's strange."

Darla poured cream in her coffee. "I hope Gil knows what he's doing."

Outside a warm breeze skipped across the yard. Gil watched a cardinal hop to a higher branch in a maple tree. Steven's family revelations had taken Gil by surprise. In this first meeting Gil had hoped to force a crack in Steven's tightly controlled façade. He never expected anything this dramatic so soon. Steven's disclosure of his grim, damaged childhood was a vindication to Gil. His quest for a higher cause was indeed coming to fruition. With this kind of potent beginning, it felt truly possible that they might be able to pick up the tattered shreds of their lives and begin the process of weaving each other back into some semblance of wholeness. It wasn't going to be easy or painless, Gil knew, but he could see that it was achievable.

One bullet in the chamber — He flashed to the .22 on the coffee table. He could still avenge the death of his family and put an end to Steven's reign of brutality. That option was still there for him. Gil lifted his eyes to the pale blue sky. I am better than that, he told the vengeful voice beckoning in his head. Justice isn't about a body count.

Steven took in a long breath. "Thanks. I really needed some air."

"That was some powerful stuff you brought up."

"Yeah."

Gil watched as the cardinal ruffled its feathers.

"I'm sorry about all of it," Steven said. "I really am."

"So am I."

"I've caused a lot of pain, I know."

"You need help beyond what we're doing here. This is about giving us a chance to heal."

"Yeah, absolutely, I want to change. I do. I don't want to live like that anymore."

Gil nodded but didn't say anything.

"I think what you're doing to protect Darla is commendable. You're a good man, Gil."

"I'm trying." Gil turned away from the yard. "Come back inside and tell them what you just told me."

Darla and Elizabeth were sitting at the table and Marjorie was on the couch absently flipping through a magazine. All three women immediately looked at Steven when he walked in from the patio. He held up his hands.

"Talking about everything that's happened, everything I've done. I'm willing to do what's necessary. I want to help you… and myself."

"And what happened to you as a kid isn't an excuse." Darla was parroting Elizabeth's earlier argument. "You could've gotten help."

"And I should have. But I wasn't capable, not then."

"Why not? You knew what you were doing was wrong."

Steven shifted from one foot to the other. "Knowing and being able to do something about it are two different things." He walked to the armchair and sat down. Gil moved to the couch.

Elizabeth followed Davenport with her eyes. "You liked it. That's why you didn't stop."

Steven shook his head. "It's —" He paused searching for the right words. "Like a motor inside of me, propelling me in a direction I don't always have control over."

Elizabeth pushed her chair back from the table. "What if I had gone to the police after what you did to me? You would have gone to prison. Didn't you think of that? Didn't you consider what you were doing to Mom?"

Steven leaned his head on his hand. "It's not like —" he stopped, struggling to clarify his thoughts. "If I was capable of that kind of rational thought I would have greater control. When this compulsion takes over all those other concerns go out the window." He lowered his gaze to the floor. "I don't want to hurt anyone anymore."

"Good," Gil said.

Steven raised his head. "After what I've done I think it's remarkable that you'll even be in the same room with me."

"It's not easy," Elizabeth said.

Steven nodded and lowered his eyes.

Darla shifted in the chair, curling both legs under her. "Okay, so this – whatever you called it – engine inside of you pushes you to molest girls, but what made you shoot at me? What's your excuse for that?"

Steven shrugged. "Self-preservation. I thought you were going to take me somewhere and kill me."

"I was. Or I thought so anyway. Don't know if I could have really done it."

"You seemed pretty determined to me."

"I wanted you to stay away from Gil. You were lying to him and that was wrong."

"What you did was very brave."

"Don't try and be nice to me." She plucked a paper napkin from a holder on the table and blew her nose.

"It was wrong to deceive Gil, and after you warned me I should've stayed away from the hospital."

"Why didn't you?" Gil leaned forward and put his elbows on his knees.

Steven's gaze drifted up to the ceiling and then back down to Gil. "I could say that I wanted to make sure you were all right, but that's not the whole truth."

"What's the truth?"

"I'm not sure you'll understand."

"Just say it."

Steven got up and walked to the French doors. In the back yard a raven hopped off the edge of the patio to the lawn. He watched it probe its beak in the grass.

"Something happened when Kelly died." He lifted his hand to a glass pane in the door. It felt cool on the warm palm of his hand. "Something got shut off inside of me."

Darla looked at Elizabeth. Gil sat forward on the couch.

"I went to the hospital to see Gil because I thought —" he stopped. Leaning his forehead against the glass he felt the urge to smash his hands through the panes and slash his veins open. It would be over then, he thought, all of it. The impulse passed and he lifted his head. "This is difficult."

"So is sitting in the same room with the man who raped me," Elizabeth said.

"Yeah," Darla said. "Just fuckin' say it."

Steven walked back to the chair and sat down. He crossed his legs and folded his hands in his lap. "I wanted to see Gil so I could experience what he was going through – the emotional turmoil. That's as close to having feelings as I get."

"Huh?" Darla looked at Elizabeth.

Elizabeth scratched her head. "So you're like a vampire feeding off other people's pain and suffering?"

Steven lowered his gaze to his hands.

"God," Marjorie muttered.

Gil stood up and walked over to where Steven sat in the chair. "What about now, Steve? What are you feeling now?"

Steven's mouth slowly opened and his eyes blinked. "When I – the thing that happened in the kitchen – talking about my father and sister and all of it – something let go. It's…"

He raised his hands and let them drop into his lap.

"Good." Gil gave him a reassuring smile. "That's why we're doing this."

"I don't care what you're feeling," Elizabeth said. "This isn't about you. It's about us getting clarity."

"Fine," Steven said. "Come on, Darla you first. What can I do to help you?"

Elizabeth glared at him. Had he done that on purpose, choosing Darla to go first? Was he still fucking with her?

Darla squirmed uncomfortably in the chair. "It's hard. So much, ya know. Okay. So first — I still see them. It's gotten a little better, but —" she looked down at the table. "If the headlights were on she wouldn't have pulled out."

Gil let out a long breath. Marjorie covered her face with her hands. Elizabeth looked out the French doors.

Darla ran her fingers through her hair. "I don't want to see their bodies anymore"

"It was my fault, not yours," Steven said.

Elizabeth turned her attention back to the table.

"I know this might be a weird thing to ask." Darla scanned their faces. "Just tell me what you guys think. If God knows that I was scared and was trying to get away, does that mean I won't go to hell because of what I did to Gil's family?"

"Oh, Darla." Marjorie walked over and put her arm around Darla's shoulders.

"Seriously," Darla said. "I want to know."

Marjorie hugged her. "You aren't going to hell. It was a horrible accident."

"But some of it was my fault."

"No it wasn't," Steven said.

"I agreed to meet you."

"You shouldn't have done that," Marjorie said, "but it wasn't —"

"Darla, I want you to understand this. What happened — all of it was my fault. I manipulated you, I took advantage. You're an innocent victim."

"But does God see it that way?" She looked around the table. "Does anybody know?"

Elizabeth slapped her palm on the table. "Stop with the God questions! My father brutalized you! It wasn't your fault!"

Gil put his hand on Elizabeth's arm. "It's okay. She can talk about whatever —"

Elizabeth snatched her arm away from Gil. "If God doesn't understand that she was trying to get away from him, who cares what he thinks!"

Darla threw her arms up. "I do! I don't want to go to hell!"

"The only person going to hell is him!" Elizabeth pointed at Steven. Glances shot around the table as the room went quiet. For a moment no one said anything. Steven pushed back his chair and stepped away from the table.

"Come on, Darla. You can hit me."

Darla didn't hesitate. She stood up and faced him. Steven moved to the center of the room.

Marjorie started to protest. "I don't think —"

"It's okay." Steven waved Darla toward him.

She walked over in front of him. Her fists were clenched and her eyes already brimming with tears. "You can't hit me back."

Gil stood up. "He won't."

She raised her hands and widened her stance. "Why did you do it? I was trying to – I just wanted to be older."

"I'm sorry. I was —" Darla threw a punch and hit him in the stomach. "Oooph,"

"Fucker." Darla punched him again, this time harder. Steven took it without backing up. Darla swung again hitting him in the chest. Gaining confidence, she stepped closer and began pummeling him with both hands.

"Get him!" Elizabeth was on her feet.

Steven tucked in his elbows and held up his arms to protect his face. A low guttural sound was coming from Darla as she hammered him. Steven grunted, gritting his teeth against the pain.

Gil raised his hands. "Okay. That's enough."

"Let her go!" Marjorie grabbed Gil's arm.

Sobbing and throwing punches as hard as she could, Darla slammed his arms trying to hit him in the face. "Ughhhhh!!" She screamed in frustration and drove her knee into his crotch. Steven dropped to the floor.

Darla stood over him, her mascara-streaked face was held high. "Don't you touch another girl, or I'll fuckin' kill you."

Steven groaned. Elizabeth got up from the table, put her arm around Darla, and led her into the bathroom. Marjorie and Gil watched as Steven slowly got to his feet.

"When do I get my turn?" Marjorie looked pleased.

Steven put a hand to his ribs. "Give me a minute."

"Forget it. I *would* kill you."

Steven gingerly sat at the table. Marjorie studied him.

"All those years together… nothing but lies."

"I love you, honey. I do."

"That's pitiful."

They shared an intense look as Darla and Elizabeth walked back into the room. Darla had washed away the smeared makeup and tears. The enraged gleam in her eyes, though somewhat dimmed, was still there. Elizabeth too had a fiery look.

"So mother, how do you feel about being married to – How did you put it, a fucking liar and a rapist?"

A hard look came onto Marjorie's face.

Elizabeth sat down. "Come on, your turn to share."

Darla picked up her coffee cup and as she walked toward the counter for a refill, she shot Steven the finger behind his back.

Marjorie, holding her gaze on Elizabeth said, "All right." She leaned back in her chair. "I feel like the last thirty-five years have been a lie. The life I was living, the man I was married to – none of it was real. I've been sleepwalking through a nightmare."

"You could have done something about it," Elizabeth said.

Called out in front of the others, Marjorie's face flushed with shame. "To think that fifteen years ago I could have stopped him. It makes me – I let you down, and Darla too, and myself."

"Elizabeth," Steven said, "I can't tell you how to feel, but —"

"Mother was talking."

Steven continued anyway. "Don't blame your mother. I did it. I'm the cause of what you're feeling. She — It's not her fault."

"You both piss me off. It was all about you. You wanted to have sex with me, so you did. Mother didn't want to deal with it, so she denied that it happened. What about me? What about your child, the person you're supposed to nurture and protect?" Her eyes sloshed with tears. "Jesus, you deserve each other."

Gil reached over and put his hand on her back. Darla pulled a tissue from the box and handed it to her.

"This is difficult for all of us." Gil looked at Marjorie and Steven. "But if we keep at it, we'll get better."

"Oh, God." Elizabeth blew her nose.

Marjorie sat forward in her chair. "You're right, honey. We failed you."

"I wish I could erase it from your life," Steven said. "I'll do anything you want. Do you want to hit me?"

Elizabeth wiped her eyes with the Kleenex. "This sucks," she said. She balled up the tissue and threw it across the kitchen. It bounced off the cabinet next the oven and dropped out of sight behind the counter.

"We can't change what happened," Marjorie said, "but we can make a difference in how you live the rest of your life."

"This isn't ever going to go away." Elizabeth punched her thigh. "We can talk and cry and go over all this stuff, but I'm never going to get him or what he did out of my head!"

Steven reached for her.

"Leave her alone!" Marjorie rose to her feet. She came around the table to Elizabeth. "It's all right. I hate him for what he did to you. And to Darla, and me."

"He didn't rape *you*."

Marjorie squatted down next to her. "You're right, he didn't." She stroked Elizabeth's hair.

Elizabeth turned to her. "I don't want to talk it out and let my feelings get yanked around and then have nothing change. I need to get past this."

"And you will."

"When? I'm tired of being pissed off and sad and screwed up."

"It takes time."

"We'll be okay." Darla gave her a teary-eyed grin.

Gil patted her back. "Trust what we're doing."

"Why don't *you* trust it!" Elizabeth turned to him. "You act like you're some kind of Zen master wielding your secret powers." She clenched her fists and shook them at Gil. "What do you feel? He's responsible for your family getting killed? How can you just sit there and not say anything?"

Gil felt his face get warm. "I'm trying to give us all a chance."

"Fine." Elizabeth leaned back in her chair. "Now it's your turn."

Darla nodded in support of Elizabeth. "Yeah, we're all in this together."

Marjorie said, "Go ahead, Gil."

He shifted in the chair. It was one thing to encourage the others, but for him to voice his pain was something else. The inside of his mouth had turned to sand. Just say it, he told himself. He brought his eyes up and locked them on Steven's face.

"You manipulated me. You preyed on my vulnerability and my trust." He pointed at Darla. "And I'm forced to help a second young woman deal with what you did to her. How is it okay to force yourself on an innocent girl? Huh? How would you like to get raped?" Gil gripped the arm of his chair as his voice got louder. "You're a predator and I'm done cleaning up after you." Something inside of Gil broke open and he could no longer control his words or his emotions. "If I had just put down the newspaper and driven them! I might have been able to get out of the way. Maybe I would have seen it coming." He sobbed and gulped, trying to find a way through his minefield of grief. After a moment, he wiped his face with his hands and leaned his elbows on the table. Staring blankly ahead, he didn't say anything for a long time. Then he spoke, his voice steady and firm. "But I am also capable of mercy and forgiveness." He closed his eyes and bowed his head.

Steven watched, a reverent expression softening his face. Then he too closed his eyes and bowed his head. "Dear heavenly father."

Gil looked up. Elizabeth, Darla, and Marjorie all stared at Steven.

"I alone am responsible for the accident that took the lives of Gil's family. Dear Father, bring Gil the kindness and support he needs to return to a productive, rewarding life. And help him understand that he's not at fault. I'm to blame for what happened to his family. I take full responsibility." Steven paused, his eyes still closed. "And Darla – she's an innocent victim. Please help her see that it wasn't her fault. I am the one you must hold responsible."

Across the table Darla gulped back a sob.

"God, I ask you to give my daughter the healing she needs. There is nothing I want more than to see her happy and fulfilled. I'm very sorry for what I've done to her, and to my wife, and Darla. I take responsibility for their pain and suffering and I ask you to heal the pain I've brought to them." He paused and then added, "Thank you God. Amen."

Steven opened his eyes to see Gil struggling with his emotions. Darla and Elizabeth were quietly sobbing. Marjorie was the only one looking at him. The look of gratitude on her face told him that he had done exactly the right thing.

Steven leaned back in his chair. Good, he thought, maybe that will shut them up for a while.

30

At the sound of Elizabeth's old bicycle lock being wrapped around the door knobs, Steven sadly shook his head. Held captive in his bedroom by a lock and cable that he had bought for the person imprisoning him, it was laughable. Only he wasn't laughing. Through the door he heard the snap of the lock. He waited a moment and then gently tried to pull them open. There was give but not much. He looked at the hinges. A smile flicked across his face. The genius crew downstairs didn't notice, he thought. The hinges were on the inside. All he had to do was pop the pins out and he could take the door down. Escaping wouldn't help his situation, but it certainly was good to know that if he had to, it wouldn't be a problem.

Steven walked over and lay down on the bed. He squashed the pillow into an acceptable form behind his head and looked up at the ceiling fan. He ran his fingers along the tender left side of his ribs. Darla had landed a good one there. He rolled onto his right side. As he was well aware from doing business at the highest level, when faced with staunch opposition it's vital to have a contingency plan. So, he reasoned, what is my best strategy? In negotiations it's often wise to demonstrate a willingness to concede a point in order to ensure that the deal gets done. The opposition appreciates your flexibility and commitment to the transaction. In this case, Steven thought, the geniuses downstairs have demanded change. So if he wanted to succeed in this transaction that's what he'd have to give them. He must surrender who he's been and become a new man — a domesticated predator. What the hell does that even look like? Steven got up and walked to the bathroom. His reflection in the mirror showed red-rimmed eyes with dark circles under them. He splashed cool water in his face and reached for a towel. After briskly rubbing his face, he once again looked in the mirror. Whatever it looks like, he silently told himself, you will be that guy. You have successfully avoided incarceration your entire life. You can do this. You will do it.

Downstairs, Elizabeth waved goodbye to Gil and Darla as they pulled away in Gil's Land Rover. She shut the front door. As she turned and walked toward the kitchen the fact was not lost on her that, for the first time in fifteen years, she was alone in the house with both of her parents.

"Well, that was awful." Marjorie took another swipe at the edge of the sink with her dish towel then dropped it on the counter. "But it certainly went better than I thought it would. How are you doing?"

"I feel like crap." Elizabeth plopped onto the couch.

Marjorie walked over to her. "Thank you for agreeing to stay with me tonight."

Elizabeth shrugged.

Marjorie sat down next to her. "I'll check out of the hotel tomorrow and move into the spare bedroom."

Elizabeth picked at a loose thread in the sleeve of her shirt. "I'm going to get my stuff from the McKelvey's."

"Really?"

"I want to keep an eye on him myself – I think." Elizabeth rubbed her face with her hands. "This is crazy what we're doing. It's crazy."

"Yes, it is. But like Gil said, we want you and Darla to have the time to sort through stuff with him."

Elizabeth stared at the fireplace. "He's a sick man. I mean really."

"I'm proud of you for taking care of yourself all these years. You're a remarkable woman."

"Yeah, right."

"You had the courage to make your life better."

Elizabeth leaned her head back on the couch. "I'm sorry I never called you. That wasn't very nice."

Marjorie waved the thought away with a brush of her hand. "You did what you had to do."

"It was hard, Mom. Away from everyone I knew. It was scary."

Marjorie stroked her hair. "I don't know how you did it. You were just a girl."

"I owe a lot to Gil for helping me."

"Yes. He got you somewhere safe."

"If only…" Elizabeth didn't finish her thought.

"Tomorrow we'll make another step in the right direction."

Elizabeth stared into space searching for a glimpse of a future that neither of them was capable of seeing clearly. "Will it ever be enough?"

"You won't know unless you try." Marjorie patted her on the leg. "Are you going to be okay in your old room? I can stay in there if you want."

Elizabeth thought for a moment. "I think I can face it."

"Do you want me to come with you?"

Elizabeth appreciated the protective tone in her mother's voice. "Thanks. I want to do it on my own."

"Of course you do."

Marjorie kissed Elizabeth on the cheek and got up off the couch. "I'm going to bed so I can think straight in the morning. Turn off the lights when you come up."

"I will."

Elizabeth watched her mother head for the stairs. The thought of going into her old bedroom was daunting. She hadn't been in there since the night her father raped her. She stood up and walked to the cabinet next to the fire place. She opened it. The photo albums were still there. She pulled one out and began turning pages: grade school class photos, their vacations to Washington D.C. and the Virgin Islands, her six-year-old face beaming at a birthday party at the zoo. It was fascinating to see her carefree young self in snapshots with her parents. Absent for so long from any family or childhood references, Elizabeth had not only forgotten what she looked like as a child, she had forgotten that she and her parents had once been happy. The memory of her parents' physical beauty had also faded. With her father's chiseled jaw and deep blue eyes, and her mother's trim, athletic figure and perfect hair, they looked to Elizabeth like movie stars. She turned the pages of the photo album, smiling at some shots and getting teary-eyed at others. Intrigued as she was by the family pictures and the memories they inspired, what kept her flipping through the albums wasn't a sense of nostalgia. It was fear. Walking back into her bedroom was a reunion she was willing to put off for as long as possible.

• • • • •

Gil's house, a repository of all the memories of his family's life, was now like a confusing foreign library with volume upon volume of texts that Gil was unable to fully enjoy. From all around him, stories of their lives buffeted his mind from the past to the present and back into the past: the wall next to the refrigerator where every six months they marked the kids' heights, the windows by the kitchen table that were perpetually covered in Lindsey and Drake's art work, Drake's secret hiding place behind the living room couch, and Bonnie's unending and often hilarious battle with ants around the kitchen sink. In the upstairs hallway his children's laughter whirled around him in the darkness. Wandering into Drake's room, his heart ached at the sight of the neatly made bed and the floor completely absent of toys. Most of Drake's things had been boxed up and given away. Gil's mother thought it would be best. Gil agreed at the time, but now he sadly wondered what little boy was playing with Drake's remote control race car or his first baseman's mitt or the telescope his parent's had given Drake for Christmas. Gil sat down on the bed. Digging his fingers into the center of the comforter he squeezed tightly as if doing so might somehow reconnect him with his dead son. After a moment Gil slumped over onto his side, pulled his knees up, and closed his eyes. At the campsite it had been one thing, but here with family reminders everywhere, the power of the past was nearly unbearable. Dwelling in the memories, Gil reminded himself, only reinforced his loneliness. He roused himself out of Drake's bed and went down the hallway. Robotically going through the process of getting undressed and brushing his teeth, he crawled into the four poster bed and stretched out. Feeling the empty gulf of Bonnie's side of the bed, Gil tried to lift his spirits by talking to her.

"It seems like I'm making a difference, Bonnie — this thing with Steven Davenport. It's a tricky situation and I hope that I'm —" The bone-weary look in Elizabeth's eyes when they had said goodnight flashed in his mind. "I want to do right by these women. I do. Please Bonnie, be with me. Don't let me mess up. You too Drake and Lindsey, I need all of your help. I love you guys."

It was a long time before he was finally able to fall asleep.

• • • • •

That night Darla smuggled her father's guns back into the house. It had been a long day and she was glad to be home and happy to be unburdened of the responsibility of the handguns. Trudging up the basement stairs, she couldn't deny the primal satisfaction she experienced punching Steven Davenport. It had knocked something loose inside of her. A kind of tautness had finally uncoiled and she was feeling lighter than she had in months. But what about Davenport, she wondered? Sure, they were locking him up in the house, but how long would that last? The four of them would continue to talk and maybe what Davenport did and said might be good for them, but what then? They would still have to turn him over to the police at some point. They couldn't let him back out on the street. And if he was taken into custody, Davenport would make sure that she would go to jail too. Unless, Darla thought as she reached the top of the stairs, I decided to —

"Hi, sweetpea." Her father grinned.

"Hey, Dad."

Her mother walked into the room. "There she is. How was your day?"

Darla shut the basement door. "Volunteering is really rewarding."

"Well, good for you," her father said. "Helping others is a fine thing."

Her mother went to the sink. "Honey, I'm so proud of you. Working with the elderly is a very generous thing to do with your time."

Darla looked at her trusting parents. They couldn't see her lie. They didn't know where she had been or what she had gone through. All they knew was that they loved her and wanted the best for her. It was her own stupid need for more that had put her into the orbit of Steven Davenport. Now everything was different and messed up and she was lying to her parents. And what if she had to go to prison? What then? How would her parents be able to live normal lives after that? They wouldn't. It would be impossible.

Darla was suddenly gasping and sobbing. She ran to her mother and hugged her. Joanne Seelbach, bewildered by her daughter's emotional outburst held her tightly and looked to her husband for answers. Jim got up from the Lazy Boy recliner where he was reading the newspaper. Uncertain what to do, he shifted his weight from one leg to the other and rubbed the palms of his hands together. After a few minutes Darla stopped crying. Her mother leaned to her ear.

"What was that all about?"

Darla pulled her face away from her mother's shoulder and wiped her eyes with the tips of her fingers. "Wow."

"Yeah, wow." Jim crossed his arms. "What's going on, sweetpea?"

Darla pushed her hair away from her face and looked at her mother. "I love you both so much, I can't even tell you." She turned to her father. "I just really love you guys. I'm so lucky." More tears began to fall but this time it was Joanne Seelbach.

"Oh Mom, I'm sorry." Darla hugged her mother.

Her father stepped to them and awkwardly put his arms around them both. Footsteps thudded on the carpeted stairs as Darla's sister, Teresa came down from her bedroom.

"What's everybody doing?" She walked into the room and saw them hugging. "Oh brother." She turned around and walked out.

• • • • •

Upon opening her bedroom door, Elizabeth was relieved to discover that she wasn't immediately overwhelmed with dreadful memories. Her mother had taken down all of her personal things and the room now resembled just another spare bedroom. Elizabeth was relieved that it didn't look the same as it had the night her father attacked her. It would have made it even more difficult to be there.

As she undressed she felt a kind of jaunty pride in holding up so well at the scene of her demoralizing violation. But the minute she climbed into bed and heard the creak of the antique slats, the past rushed up, squelching her positive thoughts and feelings. But this time the memory was not as vivid. The energy felt to her less immediate, as if a buffer of space had been inserted between her and what had happened. She lay on the bed staring up at the ceiling as the rush of dread and loathing flowed through her. One day, what happened in this room will become an undefined blur, she thought, a surreal dream that no longer makes her heart race and her palms go sweaty.

Living in denial behind her great wall of forgetting had succeeded in allowing the memory to remain strong. Feeding on her silence, those awful memories had strangled her ability to experience the full range of her emotions. She wanted more joy, more trust, more belief in herself. So although it was an inheritance she would rather not have been granted, she understood her father's inability to feel. But no matter how much she could empathize or how honest he came across or how different he seemed from the remote, controlling father she grew up with, she still didn't trust him. Before falling asleep, she braced a chair in front of her locked bedroom door.

31

"Don't look away when I'm talking to you." Elizabeth glared at her father across the kitchen table. "You're here to listen to what we have to say and answer our questions."

Elizabeth's confidence had grown. The initial confrontation with Steven had stripped away a layer of fear. Also, facing her bedroom and its shroud of memories had lifted her spirit. Her old sense of daring was galloping back into her life. "Unraveling our knots is what gives us the length and strength to reach our highest expression," Sky once told her. Under the forest canopy harvesting a bed of chanterelle mushrooms, she had nodded, never for a moment believing him, but as always, appreciating the kind tenor of his voice. Now, all these years later, she understood what he was getting at. It was the lightness. The sensation that her breath was flowing with greater ease in and out of a body no longer encumbered by shame and secrecy. With no way for her anger to cultivate power in the face of these new uplifting feelings, it was beginning to loosen and diminish, absorbed into the circle of the group's collective damage.

As commanded, Steven brought his gaze back to Elizabeth. It was all he could do to keep from walking out of the room. Hearing the hours upon hours of their suffering and trauma was like listening to the whine of a dentist's drill. But he could see no reasonable escape from the crosshairs of their attacks. He had to allow them to batter him, like Ali doing his rope-a-dope against George Foreman, until they had exhausted themselves. Only then would he be able to make the situation work to his advantage.

"I built this wall and shut myself off from you and Mom and everything that had happened earlier in my life." Elizabeth folded a leg under her. "I couldn't bring myself to think about what you did. That was my survival technique — to pretend that before I arrived at the commune I hadn't existed. I had no life. And when I finally did allow myself to remember what you did to me…I threw up."

Darla leaned forward on the table. "So that crap you just told us about bringing something positive to the lives of the girls you rape, that's a lie. You brought nothing to me. You wrecked my childhood. All that stuff is in your head. It's not real."

Elizabeth nodded. "That's you making it okay to continue doing what you do."

Steven looked from Elizabeth to Darla. He knew he shouldn't do it but he was tired of getting hammered by them.

"I know you're right, I do. But why haven't any of them turned me in. It must be because they got something out of it, right?"

"Are you —" Marjorie started to say.

"They're scared to death!" Elizabeth was up out of her chair and yelling. "That's why they didn't do anything!"

"Okay, okay," Steven said, secretly pleased to get a jab in. He forced himself to look compliant. "I know I'm screwed up. I know that. But I'm making progress."

"This isn't about you," Darla said, repeating Elizabeth's comment from the day before.

Gil watched Steven's eyes, hooded with shame, shift down to the table. He felt a compassionate impulse to reassure Steven that he was doing well and that one day he might be able to live a fully honest and loving life. But Gil caught himself. As much as he wished to believe that his efforts on behalf of the others were also benefiting Steven, he knew that it was a long shot. Steven was a highly duplicitous man capable of anything. Last night when they locked him into his bedroom his lack of resistance surprised Gil. Steven had simply done as he was told with no complaints. Was the man only acting contrite or was he actually trying to heal and take responsibility for his actions? Gil wasn't sure. Steven had tricked him once. Gil had no intention of allowing it to happen again.

Gil offered up a silent prayer of support to Bonnie and immediately felt comforted. Last night it had been especially difficult sleeping in his bed. Even though the sheets had long been washed and changed, he imagined he could still smell Bonnie. Her bath lotion, in the blue and green bottle and smelling like the ocean, had once again lit up his senses. It was Bonnie, his beautiful, loving wife, Bonnie. But when he opened his eyes the bed was empty.

Gil looked across the table at Steven. "I miss my wife." He said it without blame or anger. Stated simply as fact, it hung in the air, a signpost for the journey they had all chosen to take. No one spoke. Steven didn't know where he should look so he stared at the table.

"I miss my virginity," Darla said.

Elizabeth shifted in her chair. "I miss my childhood."

Without hesitating Marjorie said, "I miss my certainty."

They looked at each other around the table. Their eyes settled on Steven.

He had no idea what to say. Sharing his thoughts about feelings that he was unable to experience was not something he was in the habit of doing.

"I miss feeling." He said it without thinking. But the minute the words were out of his mouth he knew that it was the most honest thing he had said in years. It surprised him. The others could see it on his face.

"Well done," Gil said.

"Hey, I'm trying here. It's all I can do."

"We appreciate that."

The women around the table nodded. Inspired by their affirmation, Steven's confidence ticked up a notch. "Good. So what can I do today to make progress for you guys?"

"First of all," Marjorie said, "What would it take for you to go into therapy? With a professional?"

Steven leaned back in his chair. "I'm up for whatever I need to do to make this right. For you guys and for myself."

"Really?"

Steven looked Marjorie in the eyes. "Absolutely. Honey, I'm committed to the healing process."

"Don't call me honey."

Steven shrugged.

"Therapy," Gil said, "is a definite course of action. But first let's move forward with what we're doing here."

Darla caught Gil's eye and half-raised her hand. "I have a question?"

"Go ahead."

She turned to Steven. "You said that you're up for doing whatever you can to make this right for us."

Steven nodded. "Yes. And I mean it."

Darla wasn't sure if Gil and Elizabeth would like it, but she was going to say it anyway. "This is what you can do to help me. Turn yourself in to the police and take responsibility for what you did to us, but don't tell the cops it was me driving the car."

Steven didn't know how he should respond. In the silence he heard Marjorie mutter, "From the mouths of babes…"

Before he could speak, Darla turned to the others. "Isn't that what we're doing here? Aren't we taking responsibility for our actions? I messed up — bad. I did. And I know it. But why should I have to go to jail for trying to save myself from him?"

"No one said you're going to jail," Elizabeth said.

"None of us want that," Marjorie said.

"But what happens when we're done punching him and getting him to tell us why he raped us?" Darla shot a look to Gil. "I get what you're doing. I do. But as good as this might be for us, where can it lead?"

"Healing is a process. We have to move forward one step at a time."

"Easy for you to say. You aren't facing the possibility of going to jail."

"No, I'm facing the rest of my life without my wife and children."

Darla's mouth hung open and her face flushed. "I'm sorry. I'm an idiot."

Marjorie reached over and put her hand on Darla's arm. "You're afraid, Darla. We all are. And that's okay."

"This is new ground for everybody," Gil said.

Darla looked over at Steven who was gazing down at his hands on the table. "What about it, Mr. Davenport? Why don't you step up and do the right thing?"

"I wish I could." Steven continued looking at his hands. "Do you know what happens to guys like me in prison, Darla? They don't last long. That terrifies me."

"You should have thought of that before you did what you did," Marjorie said.

Steven raised his eyes to his wife. Didn't she see that he was trying to elicit sympathy? Couldn't she see that? He turned back to Darla. "And so, the only thing keeping you guys from sending me to a grisly death in prison, is the fact that if I go, so do you. I'm sorry I can't be a bigger man and say I'll let you off the hook for what you did to Gil's family, but I guess I'm not that noble — at least not when it comes to saving my own life."

Darla studied his face for a moment. "So that's your answer?"

Steven nodded. "I'm sorry."

Darla tapped her fingers on the table as her anger and frustration thumped against the inside of her head. "Cause that leaves me with a couple options."

"What do you mean?" Elizabeth said.

"Darla…" Gil was afraid of what she was about to say.

"I can send you to prison and suffer whatever my fate is, or I can shoot you myself and roll the dice on whether I get caught or not." She glared at him. "How's that for saving your life fuckhead?"

Steven lurched across the table at Darla, but before he got to her she snatched up her glass of water and threw it in his face.

"Steven! Sit down!" Marjorie shouted.

Steven sputtered and wiped water from his face.

Darla, pumped with adrenaline, rose up out of her chair. "Were you gonna hit me? Is that what you were trying to do?"

Elizabeth put her arm protectively around Darla's shoulders. "Don't ever raise a hand to her. Or anyone else — you hear me?"

"You pathetic creep." Darla glared across the table at Davenport — not with the defensiveness of a sixteen year old victim, but with the knowing swagger of being the better player. She had shut down Davenport's little game of poor-poor me and they all had seen it.

"Steven, it looks like you're starting to have some feelings." Marjorie smirked. "That's what happens when you get pushed into a corner."

"Like you pushed all of us." Elizabeth walked back to her chair.

Steven ducked his head and looked sheepish. He'd been foolish. Now he would have to act quickly in order to win them back. "I'm sorry. It's hard — the way you talk to me – it's disrespectful."

"How do you think your cellmate Butch is going to talk to you?" Darla grinned.

Elizabeth couldn't stifle her laugh. Even Marjorie chuckled.

Steven lowered his head submissively and stared at the table. He would find a way. He would do whatever was necessary to get out from under their control and away from this needless humiliation.

32

Digging up weeds in the flower bed of the Davenport's Zen garden, Dominic was surprised to find himself thinking of Reggie. A black and brown Doberman with a nasty disposition and an uncanny ability to escape from his yard, Reggie had run amuck in the Davenport's neighborhood for years. He had snarled and barked his way into a bad reputation before finally disappearing one chilly fall evening. The O'Dell family, Reggie's owners, put signs around the neighborhood and ads in the newspaper, but Reggie was never found. Two years later the O'Dells moved to Milwaukee. Three years after that, Dominic was planting a bed of petunias in a neighbor's flowerbed and uncovered the skeletal remains of a dog. On a corroded brass tag hooked to a steel choke collar was the name, Reggie. The Harringtons, in whose flowerbed Dominic found what was left of Reggie, never learned of his discovery. After that Dominic looked at mild-mannered Beth and Jim Harrington in a new light. Killing a neighbor's dog, no matter how mean, and burying it in a flowerbed was something he never could have imagined them doing. People can really surprise you, he had thought at the time.

Strange, Dominic thought as he pulled a large black plastic bag from his rear pocket, that dead dog coming into my head. He began dumping branches and weeds into the bag. After edging the beds he would cut the grass and that would be it for the day. He reached down for the edger and heard someone walk up behind him.

"Looking good."

Dominic turned to see Elizabeth Davenport. She was holding a glass of lemonade.

"Figured you might be thirsty." She held out the glass.

"Thanks." Dominic took it from her hand.

"This is awesome – you did a great job." Elizabeth looked around the garden.

"Your mother designed it. I try to keep it lookin' nice."

She sat on the bench and crossed her legs. "Yeah. It's peaceful."

Dominic took another drink of lemonade. "Your mother put it in after you went away."

Elizabeth gazed across the garden. "She told me about that."

Dominic put the glass on the ground next to the birdbath, picked up the edger and went back to work. Occasionally he would glance over at Elizabeth who was gazing up at the trees. He knew she was back living there because two days earlier when he came to work he had found white ribbons tied to the Rhododendron bushes beneath her window. When he looked up, there she was smiling and waving to him. She had come out with a cup of coffee and talked with him while he worked around the yard. Oregon is where she had gone, she told him, living on a commune with a bunch of people who didn't work regular jobs and went into the mountains and picked mushrooms. Sounded kind of strange to him, but he was happy that she was back with her family. They talked a little about Michael and how life had been since Irene's passing. It wasn't anything he normally talked about, but with Elizabeth it had always been easy.

"So how is it being home?" Dominic wiped sweat from his forehead with a blue bandanna.

"Good. It's different, you know. Everything is… different."

"You were gone a long time."

"Yes, I was." Elizabeth stood up. "But I'm happy to be back." She walked past him toward the house. "See you later," she called cheerfully over her shoulder. Dominic watched her go. He didn't believe her show of happiness. He had seen the tears in her eyes.

• • • • •

Darla and Jimmy Vita stood on the edge of the cliff over looking the greenish blue water of Alice's Point.

"Let's do another one." Darla looked thirty feet down at the surface of the water.

"Tracy, do a jump with us," Jimmy called over his shoulder.

Tracy, glistening in tanning oil, raised her head from her beach towel. "You guys are like a couple of fish."

"Come on!" Darla flung droplets of water in Tracy's direction.

Tracy pushed her sunglasses up on her head. "My bathing suit practically went up my butt last time."

"Then why don't you dive." Jimmy widened his eyes at her.

Tracy took off her sunglasses. "Did those other guys leave yet?"

Darla glanced toward the other end of the quarry. A wooden platform fifteen feet higher jutted out from the cliff. A guy with long, flowing brown hair and a protruding gut sat on the end of the diving platform swinging his legs and drinking a can of beer. Four other people, at least one of them a woman, sat around smoking and talking.

"Nah," Darla said. "They're still over there."

"That one guy is friends with my brother," Tracy said. "I don't want my Dad to find out I was here. He thinks it's dangerous."

"Come on Rockwell," Jimmy said, "don't be a girly girl."

"Jimmy, leave her alone."

Tracy dropped her sunglasses on the towel. "Okay dick grabber, let's do this."

"All right!" Jimmy and Darla backed away from the edge of the cliff. Darla got between Tracy and Jimmy and put her arms around their shoulders.

"I love you guys!"

Tracy laughed and gave her a squeeze around the waist. Jimmy pumped his fist.

"Okay," Darla said. "One, two, three." And they ran toward the edge of the cliff.

Jimmy yelled, Tracy screamed, and as the force of their running leap propelled them away from the cliff, Darla began to laugh. She fell toward the welcoming embrace of cool water, laughing in the knowledge that Davenport no longer had power over her. With no gun and no one restraining him, she had stood up to him. The water in his face, his stunned look, it had empowered her. She was better than she was on the night of his attack. She was smarter and tougher, and that felt awesome. Whatever ended up happening, she was determined to enjoy this new intoxicating freedom. And to top it off, there was a cute guy who just started working with her at the ice cream counter.

The three teenagers hit the water and plunged below the surface. Darla opened her eyes. Sunlight shot down through the silent green. She saw Tracy swimming for the surface. Jimmy was on his way up too. Darla hesitated, wanting to enjoy for as long as possible the play of light in the water and the extraordinary feeling of weightlessness.

• • • • •

The produce section of the Giant Eagle was crowded. Elizabeth wheeled the grocery cart through a gauntlet of children, shopping carts, and store employees. Marjorie walked next to her, her eyes sweeping the displays. `

"I'm thinking of making a fruit salad," Marjorie said. "How's that sound?"

"Fine by me."

They stopped in front of the grapes. Marjorie examined several bunches.

"Here we go." She carefully began filling a plastic bag. "Peaches would be good too." She looked across the aisle. "There they are."

Elizabeth watched her mother move to the display of peaches. It was strange to be grocery shopping with her again. As a girl she loved to come along and help. Her mother allowed her to pull the items off the shelves and put them in the cart. It made her feel grown up. The grocery list was the best part of the process. Checking off the items as they went through the store was an important job, her mother had told her.

"Do you like artichokes?" Marjorie was putting the sack of peaches in the cart.

An awkward aspect of getting to know each other again, Elizabeth thought — learning what we like to eat.

"Love 'em,"

"Good. Me too."

Elizabeth picked up a pear and smelled it. "I got an email this morning from Lumina, the girl I told you about in Oregon."

"Yes, I remember. You're very fond of her."

"She's got a boyfriend, Cassidy, her first. She's so cute about it. Anyway, she's on her way across country with Cassidy and his father. They're heading to up-state New York to visit Cassidy's grandparents. Lumina wanted to know if they could stop here for a quick visit as they're passing through."

"Of course."

"But what about…"

"Oh."

"I really want to see her. But I don't like the idea of him being anyway near her."

"We can manage that."

"But do you think it's a good idea?"

Marjorie gave Elizabeth a reassuring pat on the arm. "Tell her to come. It will be good for you to see her."

"I miss her tons. Elizabeth's emotions surged. "She's the daughter I'll never have."

"What do you mean? You've got plenty of time for children."

"But who will want me?"

"Oh honey." Marjorie put her arms around Elizabeth.

"I see his face, Mom – sometimes when I'm with a man. It's so screwed up."

"We're working through that. It'll get better. I know it will."

Elizabeth tried to control her emotions but she wasn't successful.

"You're beautiful and strong. You're going to have a wonderful man in your life one day who will cherish you."

"Is everything okay?"

Marjorie turned to see a man standing next to them. It took her a moment to realize that it was her handsome admirer from the pool. She barely recognized him in the gray sport coat and black slacks. She had never seen him dressed in anything more than a bathing suit.

"I'm sorry to intrude," he said stiffly. "May I be of assistance?"

Marjorie quickly glanced at Elizabeth. "Thank you. But we're fine."

Elizabeth snorted a tearful laugh.

He pulled out a handkerchief and handed it to Elizabeth.

"Thank you." She wiped her eyes and nose.

"I'm Edward Peet." He offered a quick half smile to Marjorie. "We know each other from the gym."

"Thank you, Mr. Peet, for wanting to help."

"Would you like to sit down somewhere?" Edward gently put his hand on Elizabeth's arm.

"Don't touch her!" Marjorie snatched his hand away.

Stunned, Edward could only stare at her.

Marjorie grabbed his handkerchief from Elizabeth and thrust it at him. "Thank you."

With Elizabeth in tow, she hastily began pushing the grocery cart down the aisle.

• • • • •

That morning Gil had wakened dreaming of making love to Elizabeth. No, he'd commanded himself, not in the bed Bonnie and I shared. Guilt sucker-punched, he'd rolled over and tried to shove the erotic images to a distant corner of his mind. It hadn't worked. The kiss at the campsite rushed back at him. Elizabeth's body was lean and strong in his arms. There was an intensity about her that was different than Bonnie, an athletic aggressiveness. A fantasy of undressing Elizabeth had unfolded in his mind — his hands caressing her hips and back, her lips – he'd abruptly stopped the fantasy. A sick, shameful feeling, like a hard cold stone in his belly, made him feel as if he'd just made love to Elizabeth right in front of Bonnie.

"I don't think it's the best time," his father was saying over the phone.

The morning breeze coming through the screen door felt clean and refreshing on Gil's face. He watched a boy on a green bicycle ride past the house. Gil turned from the front door and his morning memory of Elizabeth, and switched the cell phone to his other hand.

"I don't care if the market is soft right now, Dad. Renting the house isn't an option. I don't want to have to come back here and deal with – all of this." Gil walked down the hallway to the kitchen. "It's not that I *want* to make less money, I just don't care right now. I have other priorities." Gil opened the refrigerator and pulled out a carton of orange juice. He grabbed a glass out of the cupboard and filled it from the carton. He pulled an oatmeal cookie out of a cardboard box sitting on the counter and took a bite. "You don't have to come up, Dad. That's not why I'm telling you. You guys have been encouraging me to get on with things and I'm sayin' that's what I'm doin'. I've been working with a support group and I'm feeling – okay. Not sure when I'm going back to work but —" Gil listened to his father on the other end of the line, his eyes softening. "Thanks Dad. You've been incredibly fair. I'm grateful." He took a drink of the orange juice. "Hey, tell Mom I got her care package and the cookies are killer. I'm eating one right now." He popped the rest of the cookie into his mouth. "So, no worries, Dad. I'm gonna' sell this place and I'll get what I can and that'll be fine." He took the glass of OJ and walked out of the kitchen back into the den. "I will. I love you guys. Talk to you soon." He hung up the phone.

Selling the family home was another break in his bond with Bonnie and the kids. But the past was the past, he stoically reminded himself. The only way to freedom was moving forward. He sat down on the couch and willed himself to breathe in the fresh, unfettered air of the future.

33

Steven leaned his forehead against the window. Shadows stretching across the back yard marked the decline of the setting sun. In the sky, pink hues were just beginning to streak the blue expanse. An image of the the Pacific Ocean flew into his mind. Yes, he thought, Santa Monica, the warm spring evening when he had stood alone on the beach watching the sun dip into the chilly waters of the Pacific. Marjorie had not come with him on that business trip. After the awesome colors of that sunset had faded, he'd walked over to the Third Street Promenade. Lots of lovely girls were out shopping and going to the movies. In Starbucks he met Shelly. She was his all-time favorite. There had been little crying and no scratching. She was docile and polite. She even thanked him for not hitting her. What was Shelly doing now, he wondered? She must be in her mid-thirties, probably with her own family. Did she remember me, Steven wondered?

From downstairs came the not so quiet music of The Beatles — The Abbey Road album. Since Marjorie's return to the house, she no longer catered to his preference for opera. She and Elizabeth played whatever they wanted at whatever volume they chose. He missed the fresh flowers and doting care Marjorie had lavished on him. Sleeping alone in their king size bed was the hardest adjustment of all. He missed the comfort of her body next to his. His home, once a place of nurture and relaxation was now a prison offering only loneliness and humiliation. They wouldn't even allow him go to work. Unable to meet the surgeons for further meetings, he had managed to close them in the Arkansas shopping mall deal only because he invoked Marty Braverman's name. Marty's clout in the investment world was a tool Steven was rarely permitted to use. But in this case, because Marty believed him to be at home enjoying

Elizabeth's return, Steven was permitted to disclose Marty's participation. The hope was that it would inspire confidence in the deal. It had worked. Two hours after letting them know about Marty's involvement the surgeons were onboard. But Steven's ability to function in this controlled manner couldn't go on forever. He needed to be free. An idea had come to him the night before while watching television. It was smart and made sense on a lot of levels.

"Gil's here." Marjorie was calling to him from the other side of the bedroom doors. "We can start now."

In as cheerful a voice as he could muster, he said, "Okay!" He walked to the bedroom doors. Great, he thought, back to the incessant droning of their misery. He would find a way tonight to present his idea. It could work, he told himself, and if it did — freedom.

"There was a place like that near Butler," Gil was saying to Darla when Steven walked into the kitchen. "We used to swim there all the time when I was growing up."

"Tracy's brother told us that twenty-five years ago some guy got drunk and accidentally drove off the cliff." Darla scrunched up her face. "Supposedly the car's still on the bottom of the quarry and his skeleton is behind the wheel."

"Lovely." Elizabeth put out a plate of cheese and crackers.

"Nasty, huh?" Darla flashed her a grin. "Dead guy on the bottom."

Marjorie came around the kitchen counter with a teapot. "Is the water clean enough for swimming?"

"I guess so."

Marjorie poured Gil a cup of tea. "You be careful. Places like that are dangerous."

Steven sat at the table. Elizabeth scooted her chair in next to Darla. Marjorie put the teapot on a hand-painted tile coaster in the center of the table then she sat down. She turned to Steven in the chair next to her.

"We stopped by and saw Esther today."

"How is she? Marty told me that the hair loss thing wasn't going to bother her as much as he thought it would."

"She found a wig that she loves. Likes it more than her real hair." Marjorie shook her head and smiled. "Esther said Marty's been sweet as can be, waiting on her hand and foot."

"He's a good man." Steven reached for the teapot. He gestured to Marjorie but she declined. He poured himself a cup.

"Elizabeth why don't you start things," Gil said. "You've talked about a lot of stuff but you haven't shared your feelings about your parent's marriage."

Elizabeth looked surprised. Across the table, Marjorie gave her an encouraging smile.

"Honey, just be honest."

"And if anyone knows how to be honest," Steven said, trying to lay on the charm, "It's you. When you were, I don't know, seven years old I think, I came home one night and you looked up at me and said, 'Where did you get that tie?' And then you scrunched up your face and stuck out your tongue." He looked at Marjorie. "Remember that."

"I remember."

"Busted by the fashion police," Darla said.

"It *was* an ugly tie as I recall," Marjorie said.

"Probably a Christmas present from your grandmother," Steven said to Elizabeth.

Marjorie frowned. "I doubt it."

"Seriously, their marriage?" Elizabeth was looking at Gil. "What marriage? There was no honesty, no devotion. It was a hiding place. Somewhere he could crawl back to after…"

Steven's jovial expression was gone. "I love your mother."

"You don't have feelings," Elizabeth said. "You told us that yourself."

Steven pointed at Marjorie. "I love this woman. I have adored her for my entire adult life. I don't want to go another day without her by my side but you're driving us apart."

"I'm not doing anything. You caused it."

"Yes, I did. And I'm suffering because of what I've done. But now I'm feeling things and remembering stuff I've never dealt with before. I'm becoming another person."

"You're so full of shit."

"No, I'm not. Do you know what I was thinking when I got up this morning? I want to establish a women's shelter — some kind of educational, therapeutic, center for women who've been abused. And I want you to run it, Elizabeth. You all can have positions there. Wouldn't that be amazing? To turn this negativity into something positive for others

— right, Gil? I mean, isn't that a better use of our skills and experience than the four of us isolating here and beating up on each other?"

Steven looked around the table. Their faces said it all. He had hit a home run. He considered launching into more details but decided not to push. Aggression was rarely the right tack when attempting to move people in a new direction. Let them find the way, he reminded himself. They'll put themselves on the path. He raised his cup of tea, took a sip, and waited.

"That's an inspired suggestion." Gil thoughtfully nodded his head.

"I agree," Marjorie said. "What better way to transform this tragedy."

"I like the idea of helping other girls," Darla said. "That would be perfect."

Elizabeth eyed her father warily. "And what do you get out of this?"

Steven shrugged. "I put together the funding, find the real estate, and make the legal arrangements – I get the satisfaction of creating something positive for women."

"Can you do all that over the telephone?"

"What do you mean?"

"From your bedroom. Will you be able to accomplish it from upstairs in your bedroom?"

Steven stifled an urge to give her smartass comment some pushback. This was a moment to choose his words carefully.

"Selling this kind of idea – it requires a lot of meetings with potential investors, city and state officials, the whole nine yards. Building trust and instilling confidence is not an over-the-telephone process. You have to be able to look someone in the eye."

"Oh, so you want to do this women's project so you can be free to abuse more women."

"No. I want to contribute to the community."

He's good, Elizabeth thought. He came up with a deal that would be a substantial win for a lot of people. It was a project that Gil and Darla and her mother would all be proud to be a part of. Yes, the city would have a wonderful new facility to potentially help hundreds of women, she would have a satisfying career, but her father would be free to continue to live his twisted, evil life. *That* wasn't up for negotiation.

Gil stood up. "I like how you're thinking Steven. Wanting to help others is exactly the path you should be on." Gil paced across the room.

"But your freedom isn't part of that process. We can't allow you to interact with people. Not now. This is too tenuous a process. We need you to be focused on *this* work, with all of us. What happens after that – we'll discuss it when we get there."

Maybe Gil had a plan after all, Elizabeth thought. Something he's been keeping to him self.

"That's fine, Gil." Steven did his best to mask his disappointment. "You're the boss. I wanted you guys to be aware of how I'm thinking these days."

"Good." Gil walked back to the table. "Now let's get back to what we were discussing."

Steven reached for his cup of tea. His hand trembled slightly as he brought the cup to his lips. What's this, he wondered, feeling the tremor intensify. It took him a moment, but then he realized what it was. He was angry – deeply, vengefully angry.

· · · · ·

Crickets droned in the dark. Something in the shrubbery bordering the back yard moved. Wearing white boxer shorts, a sleeveless T-shirt, and carrying a hand saw, Dominic Angelo walked into the yard.

"I think this is a good one." With the saw he pointed at a twelve-foot blue spruce. "A little thin in the one spot but I'll turn that toward the wall." He got down on his hands and knees and crawled under the branches of the spruce.

In the next yard over a dog growled and barked. Dominic shifted his position to get the blade of the saw onto the trunk of the tree. The dog barked again, this time louder. Dominic blinked. He and Irene hadn't brought a dog to the Christmas tree farm. The dog barked again.

"Irene?" Dominc peeked out between the branches.

The dog continued barking.

"Irene…"

"Rufus!"

Dominic immediately recognized the voice. It was Baron, his burly neighbor down the street. What was…? Dominic looked down at the saw in his hand. A fuzzy clarity began to reveal itself in Dominic's mind. It wasn't time to cut down a Christmas tree. It was the middle of the night and he was halfway down the block from his house. Dominic shook his head trying to clear away his confusion. It had seemed so real

— Christmas time with Irene and Michael. She was wearing the burgundy colored scarf Michael had given her for Mother's day. She had kidded him about the jaunty angle of his hat.

Dominic hung his head. Then, disoriented and ashamed, he crawled out from under the tree. Praying no one would see him, he scuttled low to the ground in a defeated, lurching shuffle, quietly making his way home past his neighbors' swing sets, barbeque grills, and garden gnomes.

• • • • •

The sun was coming up as Elizabeth sat down to meditate. Shards of light arced through the gray morning clouds. In the tree above her a finch called in rapid-fire chirps. She glanced up trying to see it through the foliage. Hidden somewhere in the leafy branches, its sound was insistent and demanding. Unable to locate the bird, Elizabeth closed her eyes and let her mind begin to quiet. Sky had taught her that the goal in meditating was to allow your mind the freedom to be still. No worrying or planning or analyzing — simply being moment to moment with each and every breath. She felt her body settle back against the trunk of the tree. She took a deep breath and slowly let it out. Her shoulders relaxed and she felt her back press against the tree.

Her feelings for Gil had developed into a strong, quiet caring. Coming through experience and shared struggle, it made her girlish fantasies about him feel hollow and foolish. Their trust and friendship wasn't based on romance or sex but on mutual respect and a desire to help each other through their grief and loss. He had demonstrated, in his willingness to protect Darla and help the rest of them, what Sky had been teaching all along. Forgiveness was indeed a path to growth and freedom.

Above her in the tree, the bird started again with its frenzied call. Elizabeth opened her eyes. Streaks of blue had spread across the sky. Morning has broken, she thought, remembering one of Sky's favorite songs. She wondered what he would advise her to do. Should she go back to Fair Haven and continue teaching, or stay in Pittsburgh and forge a life near her mother. A decision needed to be made soon. Shatki would have to find a replacement for the coming school year.

"Oh, sorry."

Elizabeth turned to see Dominic standing there holding a long-handled shovel.

"Oh, hey, Dominic. Private time with mother nature."

"I'll leave you to it."

"No, it's all right." She waved him over.

He frowned then pressed his lips into a terse thin line. He swung the shovel onto his shoulder.

She noticed his mood. "Everything okay?"

Dominic ignored her question. "Whatever happened before you left, you were smart to take care of yourself."

"It's really complicated. I hope I'm doing the right thing being here."

"If you're helping yourself, that's what counts."

Eager to change the subject Elizabeth asked, "What's up with you today? "Not feeling well?"

Dominic considered telling her that it was the Pirates loss the night before that put him in a bad mood. But that wouldn't help relieve his anxiety. Maybe telling her what was happening to him would settle him down.

"I had a —" Dominic stopped himself. He looked down at the ground and then up to Elizabeth. "I think I'm getting that old codger disease."

"What do you mean?"

He looked off through the trees. "Last night I thought I was with Irene and Michael getting a Christmas tree."

"Was it just a dream?" Elizabeth wanted to sound encouraging.

Dominic, still looking off, shook his head. "I was halfway down the block in my neighbor's back yard. Had a saw in my hand."

"Oh Dominic, I'm sorry. Has it happened before?"

He didn't say anything.

"It's okay."

Dominic shrugged. "Irene – She visits me and we talk sometimes. Been going on for a few years. This other stuff – forgetting how to get to clients' houses – that's only been the last year or so."

"Have you told Michael?"

Dominic shook his head. "Didn't want to bother him."

"What does your doctor say?"

"Haven't been. Don't like 'em much."

"You should go. Maybe a doctor could help figure out what's going on."

"Probably tell me to move into a home somewhere. End up not being able to remember what day it is or what I had for lunch." Dominic grunted and shook his head.

Trying to sound casual Elizabeth said, "Do you have nice talks with Irene?"

This seemed to perk him up. He turned back to her, the beginning of a smile appearing at the corners of his mouth. "She's kinda' bossy, like she knows everything."

Elizabeth laughed.

"Tells me it's one of the privileges of being dead." He shook his head. "She's something."

"What do you talk about?"

Dominic hesitated, and then quietly said, "Michael. We talk about him a lot."

"She's keeping an eye on those grandchildren I'm sure."

Dominic didn't say anything, but he couldn't stop the tears that came into his eyes. Elizabeth got to her feet.

"I know you miss her, I'm sorry."

Dominic wiped his eyes. "One of the things that caused problems with me and Irene – I wouldn't talk about Michael."

"What do you mean?" Elizabeth stepped toward him. "You talk about him all the time."

Dominic dropped his head and shuffled his feet. "No, I don't. Not the truth." He glanced back toward the house. "I better get to work."

Elizabeth reached out and held his arm. "Dominic, if I've learned anything, it's that talking helps."

He lowered the shovel from his shoulder and leaned on it. For a long moment he didn't speak. "He doesn't have children."

For a moment Elizabeth was uncertain what he meant. They had spent hours talking about Michael's kids. Dominic couldn't mean him. But the anguished look on the old man's face told her that she was wrong.

"He doesn't have children or a wife. He doesn't call me for advice or send pictures. We don't talk about the Pirates or Steelers games or how it is to be a father. Michael died in Vietnam. Blown up by a mortar."

Elizabeth didn't know what to say.

Dominic gripped the handle of the spade. "I'm sorry I lied to you."

"It's, no it's okay."

His face was masked in sadness. "I wasn't a good husband after Michael was killed. Irene deserved better."

"I'm sure you did the best you could."

Dominic shrugged and looked off into the trees. Elizabeth squeezed his arm. He sighed. "I didn't want to let go of him – not all the way. Irene tried to get me to accept it, but I couldn't."

"I'm sorry."

"It was fun pretending with you — what his life might have been. It made me feel close to him."

"I liked it too. You talked to me like I was a grown up."

Dominic turned back to her. "You're still the sweet person you were back then."

"A few more bumps and scrapes."

He nodded. "Life'll do that."

34

Darla watched Chad spread sunscreen across his smooth, tan chest. Beads of water hung in his sandy blond hair. She was pretty sure that he liked her. Whenever he came to work he always said something nice — "Cool shirt. I like that necklace. Pigtails, classic!" He had even said something to Jimmy Vita, who of course told her about it. "He asked me if you have a boyfriend. When I said no, he was surprised. He thinks you're hot."

It had happened casually. They were at the ice cream counter talking about how warm it was outside and she brought up Alice's Point, and jumping off of the cliffs. Chad said they should go together sometime and she said that would be fun and he said how about Friday and she said yeah that's good.

Darla looked at his lips wondering what it would be like to kiss him. Early on when Steven Davenport was being nice to her, his kiss made her feel like she was falling through the air with so many sensations shooting through her that she almost couldn't breathe. She knew Chad would be different. He wasn't a grown man. She wanted it to be sweet and gentle — just a kiss, nothing else.

"Do you want some?" Chad held up the bottle of sunscreen.

"Thanks." Darla reached for it.

"I'll do it for you." Chad crawled across the blanket to her.

Darla tensed. He moved behind her and sat down, stretching his legs out on either side of her. She looked down at the fine blond hair on his right leg. A scar zigzagged below his knee. Behind her she heard him rubbing the lotion between his hands.

"I like your freckles." She felt his warm fingertips trace across the base of her neck. Excited that he had touched her that way, but anxious because she couldn't see his face and was unable to see what his eyes were telling her, she fought the urge to spin around. *Everything is fine,* she told herself, *he's not a rapist.* Chad's hands moved gently across her shoulders spreading the lotion. He pushed up the back strap of her bikini top as he continued applying the lotion then he slid it down and moved to her lower back.

"You probably get really tan."

"Sometimes," Darla managed to say. "But I don't like baking myself."

"Okay." Chad got up from behind her. "You're done."

He moved to his side of the blanket and sat down.

"Thanks." Darla's nervousness was beginning to subside.

"This was a good call." Chad grinned cheerfully. "I like this place." He stretched out on the blanket. Darla let her eyes travel down the length of his body. His muscular, flat stomach rose and fell as he breathed. She liked the way he looked next to her, peaceful and relaxed. *But what if he knew what happened to her? What would he think then? Would he still want to kiss her? Would he blame her? Maybe he already knows. Maybe it's something that men can sense about women.* She tried to calm the fears racing through her mind. *He is a boy and I am a girl,* she reassured herself. *We'll work it out together.* She nudged him with her foot.

"Hey."

Chad turned to her. The look on his face was gentle and kind. He didn't stare at her like Mr. Davenport. He didn't have that predator look in his eyes. *He's a nice boy,* Darla told herself. *I can trust him.*

"I'm going to get a little sun, do a few more jumps, and then I want to kiss you."

Chad blushed and looked shy for a second then grinned. "Like I said, I like this place." He reached over and held her hand. She waited to see if he would let go. He didn't.

Darla laid back into the warm embrace of the sun, closed her eyes, and let all of her fears run free.

• • • • •

"They'll be here sometime late this afternoon." Marjorie glanced around the master bedroom. "It'd be nice if you tidy up in here."

Morning sun splashed across the floor in front of where Steven was sitting on the edge of the bed. "Are you really going to let them see how you lock me up in here?"

"No. I'll lock the door after they've gone to sleep."

"Honey, this is ridiculous. I'm not going to hurt anyone. I'm looking forward to meeting Elizabeth's friends. Please don't do this to me."

"When we get back from the grocery store I'll let you out." Marjorie walked out of the bedroom and closed the doors. "And Steven," she said as she wrapped and locked the cable around the door knobs, "be on your best behavior in front of Elizabeth's friends. It's the least you can do for her."

Her footsteps faded as she went down the stairs.

My best behavior, Steven thought bitterly, what am I, a leaky Cocker Spaniel who might ruin the carpet? He strode across the bedroom and looked out the window. Outside in the back yard, sunlight lit up bright in the trees. He heard the garage door go up and Marjorie's car back out. He listened as the car went up the driveway to the street. This is bullshit, he thought, I'm not a dog that needs caging up. He turned to the locked bedroom doors. His eyes slid over to the hinges. Knock the pins out, he thought, and the sunshine will be mine.

• • • • •

"It was funny I thought." Elizabeth was looking out the window of the car as the houses in the neighborhood went by. "Sarah and Emily created a story about me. 'The legend of Elizabeth,' that's what Sarah called it."

"They needed to solve the mystery of what happened to you."

"If they only knew the truth."

"What did you tell them?"

Elizabeth leaned her head back remembering the previous night's telephone conversation set up by Linda McKelvey. Elizabeth had never done a conference call before.

"I told them that I was rebelling — that I wanted to live another kind of life. They asked me tons of questions about what it was like at Fair Haven."

"I bet they did."

"They were a little disappointed though. They always thought that an older boy had swept me off my feet and we ran away together. They were both sure of it. Once in Florida during spring break, Emily called Sarah to report that she had seen me with a older guy with long hair and two earrings."

Marjorie smiled sadly. "I wish that was the reason you left."

Elizabeth turned and looked out the window, but didn't say anything.

"So they're all vegetarians?"

"I'm not sure about Cassidy and his father, but Lumina is."

"We'll make something tasty for everyone."

"Yep, a nice friendly dinner — you, me, my friends, and my father the pedophile."

Marjorie flinched. She wasn't sure if her daughter had considered it fully, but if in the end they did turn Steven over to the police, and his case went public, Elizabeth would face an awful public stigma. Marjorie gripped the steering wheel. Protecting Elizabeth from that gruesome circus would be her primary focus. It was a job she would like to avoid, but that wouldn't be possible. Prison was where Steven belonged. Unfortunately, getting him there would cost all of them a terrible price.

· · · · ·

The crowd at the counter was four deep when Steven Davenport walked into McDonalds. He slapped the sports section he was carrying against his thigh and made his way over to the line. Kids jostled and talked boisterously. One boy with a blue Mohawk was bobbing his head to music blaring in his ear buds. Steven lifted his eyes to the menu overhead.

"She doesn't even like him. She told me."

"That's not what I heard."

Steven turned to his right. In the line next to him were two teenage girls. They leaned toward each other whispering. Their faces were intensely focused, their hands gesturing spontaneously. Steven smiled. Freedom, he thought, is a glorious thing. To drive my own car, to go to McDonalds, it's as it should be. I'm no longer their cowering puppy. I'll continue to meet with them and listen to them whine about how I destroyed their lives, but I'm no longer their prisoner. That stupid game is old and tired and over.

"Can I help you?"

Steven turned away from the girls. An acne challenged boy behind the counter was looking at him.

"Milkshake, please. Chocolate."

"Anything else?"

"That's it." Steven handed him the money. The girls next to him had stopped talking and were now giggling.

"Your change, sir."

Steven turned back to him. "Thanks."

The kid stepped away and returned with Steven's milkshake. Steven gave him a nod and walked over and sat down at a table near the door. He raised his milkshake and took a long satisfying pull on the straw. He turned his head back toward the newspaper, but his eyes weren't on the headline story of the Pirates slug fest rout of the Reds. It was the girls in line he was watching.

$$\bullet\ \bullet\ \bullet\ \bullet\ \bullet$$

Dominic stood by his back door with the warm sun on his face. He looked down at the photograph of Michael in his hand. They had been on a vacation in Canada when the picture was taken. Eleven year old Michael was leaning on a paddle next to a wooden canoe. His eyes were wide and full of mischief. Dominic remembered the two large-mouth bass Michael caught on the lake. Michael had teased him as they ate the fish for dinner because Dominic hadn't caught anything. The memory of that fine sunny day and his son's successful fishing adventure was crystal clear in Dominic's mind. What wasn't clear to Dominic was how to drive to the grocery store. Last night he had idled in his truck at a stop sign for ten minutes uncertain if he was supposed to turn right or left. He nearly broke down and cried. Instead, he turned around and drove home. He had been shopping at that grocery store for 42 years.

Dominic glanced down at the grinning image of his son. How many days or months would it be, he wondered, before he no longer remembered the boy in the photograph? And when would the woman next to him in the wedding picture become a stranger?

He closed his eyes and tried to see a vision of himself content and living in the future. But there was nothing. No son or wife or truck or flowers to plant or shrubs to trim. No sun on his face in the morning, no donuts, and no Juicy Fruit. The only thing he could see in his future was the institutional reek of an elders' facility, and a screeching, wobbled-headed crowd of other half-brained old people patiently awaiting death to finally release them from their worn-out bodies.

$$\bullet\ \bullet\ \bullet\ \bullet\ \bullet$$

She sat down two tables away. The mini skirt and rose tinted granny glasses caught his attention. She crossed her bare legs and leaned her elbow on the table, pressing a cell phone to her ear. She was probably fifteen or sixteen, Steven guessed, with long dark hair and lightly tanned skin.

"I don't care," she said angrily into the phone. "You should have told me." Her voice suddenly got louder. "It's not *my* fault! Why would you say that? Scott? Scott?"

She stared at the phone for a moment then slapped it down on the table. Glaring at it, willing it to ring again, she waited. When it didn't ring, her lower lip pouted and she struggled not to cry. She took off her sunglasses and leaned her head on her hand. That gesture of utter dejection brought Steven forward in his seat.

• • • • •

Gil was standing in the middle of the aisle carefully looking over the bottles of red wine.

"It's always tricky, isn't it?"

He turned to see a woman smiling at him. She was petite with big brown eyes and straight dark hair. She gestured to all the bottles on the shelves.

Gil nodded. "Yeah, it is."

"I like reds, but the girlfriend I'm having over for dinner is into white."

"I'm looking for a Pinot Noir."

"Oh, my favorite. I know a couple excellent ones if you want a recommendation."

"Oregon is supposed to make some good stuff."

"See, you know what you're doing." The woman flashed him another friendly smile and took a step closer. "Are you going to a party?"

"No, I just want to — have it at the house." Gil suddenly felt awkward and shy.

"Oh, that's nice." Her eyes moved to the bottles of wine on the shelves. She seemed to be contemplating something. "It would be fun to have dinner together sometime."

Surprised and unable to formulate a response, Gil could only stare back at her.

"But *you* have to bring the Pinot." She offered another smile and extended her hand. "My name's Jill."

He reacted instinctively and took her hand. "Gil."

She laughed. "Gil and Jill, how crazy is that."

"Nice to meet you."

"Yeah, same here. Hey, shopping for wine and — there you go."

Gil knew that he should come up with some witty chitchat to move their conversation forward, but what he really wanted to do was run outside for a breath of fresh air. It felt as if something massive had begun pressing down on his chest. He swallowed and tried to breathe the pressure away but it didn't let up. Jill was looking at him, waiting for him to take the next step.

"Wow." Gil cleared his throat trying to feel better. "This is cool meeting you like this. You're really pretty and you seem like a nice person — someone I would be happy to spend time with."

Jill's eyes registered his growing discomfort. She took a half step back. Gil pressed on. He wanted the pressure to go away.

"It's not you. I'm – it's kinda soon for me. My wife and kids died in a… I love Pinot Noir. One day I would like to drink a glass with you, but…" His words trailed off and he stood before her feeling foolish and ill-equipped. "Sorry…"

Jill smiled through pressed lips. "It's okay. I'm very sorry for your loss."

"I'm trying to, you know, get though the next —"

"It's okay."

"Maybe in a few more months I'll be…" Again words escaped him. Gil shrugged.

Jill laid her hand supportively on his arm. "Take care of yourself. Really." She turned and walked down the aisle. As Gil watched her go he felt the pressure begin to lift from his chest. It was bitter sweet relief. When, he wondered, would his life ever again be simple and effortless.

• • • • •

The charcoal gray Volkswagen Beetle turned left into the driveway of a house in Braden's Woods. Set back off the road behind a screen of spruce and oak trees, it was a rambling one story with black shutters and a double front door. As he drove past, Steven thought he saw the blue flash of a swimming pool in the back yard. He turned up the volume on the CD player. *Fedeli,* Beethoven's only opera was playing. The light-hearted, soaring melody of its first theme was one of Steven's favorite pieces of music.

In the rear view mirror he watched the girl get out of the freshly washed Volkswagen. He knew he shouldn't be following her, but like a recovering alcoholic who sniffs his friend's glass of scotch, he was convinced that a whiff of his past behavior wouldn't hurt him. He had followed her from McDonalds to the car wash. Standing in one of the bays hosing off the Volkswagen, the sun had haloed a stunning rainbow of colors around her. He told her the change machine was jammed. Then he offered her a twenty-dollar bill if she would give him the quarters he needed to wash his car.

"Okay, sure." She started digging through her purse. "You must really need to get it clean."

"Yeah, my daughter's wedding is tonight."

The girl had looked up at him over the top of her pink-lensed granny glasses. "Oh, awesome. That's really great."

"Big day." Steven flashed his most charming smile. "My wife was supposed to take it to the car wash but she wasn't able to get away during work. It's tough to get things done with both of us working. I'm sure your parents have the same problem."

The girl handed him a bunch of quarters and a balled up gum wrapper. "I know I have more." She went back to searching in her purse. "Yeah, my parents are always working."

"And you're stuck taking care of your brothers and sisters, right?"

"No. My brother is away at college. Hey!" She pulled out four more quarters. "I found 'em."

"Perfect." Steven handed her the twenty. "You saved my life."

"Thanks." She happily folded the bill in half and slipped it into her purse. "I hope your daughter's wedding is really beautiful and everything."

Steven had blazed her with another smile. As he turned away he felt that old familiar spark flicker. Now, watching her walk away from the VW toward the house, he felt it again. This time it was more intense.

35

Marjorie pressed the garage door opener clipped to the visor over her head. As the door rolled open and she pulled the car into the garage, she backtracked over the grocery list to see if they had forgotten anything.

"We got the celery, right?"

"Yeah, Mom."

"How about the—"

"Shit!"

"What?"

"That fucker. I knew it!" Elizabeth was staring at the empty space where Steven's car had been.

"Oh, no." Marjorie jammed the car into park.

"Should we call the police?"

Marjorie's mind was spinning. Where would he go? Was he gone for good? Maybe he went to the office. "I'll call him on his cell first." She got out of the car. Calling the police would open the gates to the media circus that she desperately wanted to avoid.

"Do you think he's trying to get away?" Elizabeth slammed the car door.

"I don't know, but—"

"We told him!"

Marjorie had her cell phone out. "Damn! I don't get reception down here." She dropped the phone into her purse and headed for the basement door.

"Mom, Lumina's going to be here in —"

"Call Gil and let him know what happened."

• • • • •

Steven heard his cell phone ringing but didn't answer it. The girl's arm was up behind her back. Straining against his hand, her teeth desperately gnawed as she tried to bite him. He tightened his grip, pulling her back tight against him.

"There's nothing you can do. I'm going to make love to you."

She screamed into the palm of his hand.

"Shhhh. You'll feel good."

Her struggle intensified. He had experienced it before. The final burst of fear. Gripping her tightly, he felt the familiar surge of power in his body. She must feel it, he thought, she has to know it'll be good for her.

• • • • •

After getting Elizabeth's call, Gil went by Steven Davenport's office to look for him. He wasn't there. Gil came down in the elevator with a cold knot of dread tightening in his stomach. He tried to reconnect to the certainty that had steered him onto their collective healing path. His resolute faith in that choice anxiously flicked along the craggy surface of the contracting knot looking for a way to infiltrate and transform it. Perhaps this was another of Steven's power games; he would be back, grinning confidently, just in time for dinner with Elizabeth's friends from Oregon. Or maybe Steven was simply showing them that he was no longer their prisoner. That was probably it. He was attempting to reclaim his power and autonomy. But he definitely wasn't out hurting anyone, that wasn't possible.

By the time Gil got to his car, he wasn't sure what he believed. The only thing he could remain focused on was finding Davenport. The rest – that would be determined later.

• • • • •

"I'm sure he's stuck on a conference call." Marjorie shifted the telephone to her other ear. "I know, I know, he's a working machine. Okay. Hugs to Esther. She tells me you're the best husband in the world." Marjorie glanced over at Elizabeth who was standing at the kitchen counter chopping carrots for the salad. "You're blessed to have each other. Thanks Marty. Bye, bye." She hung up the telephone.

"So where is he, Mom? Why hasn't he called you back?"

"I don't know."

"Should I be calling Darla and warning her?"

Marjorie let out a sigh. "That's – yeah, you should do that."

Elizabeth reached for the telephone. As she started to dial, Marjorie's cell phone vibrated on the counter.

"It's him!" Marjorie pressed the button. "Steven where the hell are you?"

• • • • •

Cassidy's father called from the turnpike exit and Marjorie gave him directions to the house. Twenty minutes later, their white Chevy Blazer, splashed and swirled with 2800 miles of road grime, pulled in the driveway.

"Hey!" Elizabeth waved from the front door.

All three occupants tumbled out of the car in a tie-dyed, blue-jeaned burst of energy.

Lumina and Elizabeth met in the middle of the front yard in a running hug that nearly knocked them both over. Cassidy and his father began pulling their backpacks out of the rear of the Chevy.

"It's so good to see you!" Elizabeth hugged Lumina. She whispered in her ear, "How's it going with Cassidy?"

Lumina leaned away from her and grinned.

"Good for you guys."

"Thanks, *Elizabeth*. It's so weird to call you that."

"Yeah. I'm still gettin' used to it."

Marjorie watched from the front door. The long hair and unruly dress gave her a clearer understanding of the culture Elizabeth had lived in for the last fifteen years. My daughter the hippie, she thought.

"Mom, come meet everyone!" Elizabeth waved her over.

Marjorie walked out into the yard. As she came closer, she saw how pretty Lumina was. Her first thought was that she had made a mistake encouraging Elizabeth to invite her friends to come to the house. But the joyful look on Elizabeth's face was undeniable. Seeing Lumina made her happy. For that Marjorie was grateful. When Steven got home, Marjorie assured herself, she would watch him like a hawk.

• • • • •

Steven took a clean sweatshirt out of his locker and pulled it over his head. The sauna was a trick he'd discovered years ago. The hot, dry heat helped release the adrenaline and endorphins and shift his body back to normal. It was part of his ritual after being with a girl.

He slipped his loafers on and ran his fingers through his damp hair. He'd told Marjorie that he was sweating on the treadmill when she called him and that it wasn't until he was in the locker room getting ready to go into the sauna that he'd seen her message. She was furious with him for leaving the house, but she knew that working out was his way of relieving stress. Angry as she was, it sounded as if she'd believed him.

Steven had considered the consequences of never returning to the house. He'd clicked through the steps he would have to take to liquidate his accounts. He'd considered various ways to get out of the country undetected. If he disappeared would Elizabeth and Darla go to the police and tell them what he'd done. Perhaps his absence would be satisfaction enough. They would go on with their lives and he could start over someplace far away. Ideally, he'd decided, in a country with no extradition with the United States.

But instead of leaving everything behind, he had called Marjorie back and explained to her that he'd left the house to go to the gym. The thought of leaving his successful business and allowing his reputation to be shredded in the press was intolerable to Steven. He had worked too hard and found too much pleasure in the game. He could find a way out of this mess. He might have to go to extreme measures, but he would make it happen. There was no other choice.

"Ready to go home?"

Steven's jaws clenched at the sound of the voice behind him. Then, with a grifter's practiced ease, he said, "Oh hey, I didn't know you were a member here." Without turning around he gave a tug on the sleeve of his sweatshirt to make sure the fresh bandage on his wrist was covered.

"I'm not." Gil stepped around to face him. "You broke the rules."

"And Marjorie sent her watch dog."

"We wanted to make sure this wasn't another of your lies."

"Well, here I am, post workout and sauna."

"So you say."

Steven picked up his gym bag. "I'm hungry."

"I'll escort you home."

"Just don't yank too hard on the choke collar, it chafes my skin." Steven grinned and walked out of the locker room.

• • • • •

The tofu artichoke casserole was heated up, the baked chicken was nearly done, and a chocolate cake iced and ready to go. Marjorie stirred the baked beans and took a sip of lemonade. Outside came the sound of laughter and playful taunts. Marjorie went to the window.

Cassidy and his father, Jeremy, had put up a badminton net that hadn't seen the light of day in over fifteen years. On the side of the net closest to the house, Cassidy swung his racket at the shuttlecock launching it over the net. Lumina lunged, returning it to Elizabeth who barely got her racket on it and just tipped it over the net for the point. Jeremy and Lumina booed and shook their rackets. Elizabeth danced in a circle. Cassidy gave her a high five.

Marjorie smiled. Having that exuberant energy around the house was inspiring. She imagined the raucous clamor of grandchildren, a fantasy that for so many years she had been denied. Marjorie was certain that with Elizabeth's years of teaching she would make a wonderful mother. Her patience and willingness to give would serve her well in raising children.

Marjorie checked the baked potatoes in the oven then glanced at the clock. It was ten after six. She'd already made way too many concessions in her life for Steven. She wasn't waiting for him. She walked to the French doors and opened them.

"Dinner is ready."

Marjorie and the others had just started eating when Steven finally arrived.

"I know, I know," he called to them as he came up the basement stairs, "I'm late. Sorry." He walked into kitchen smiling broadly. "Had to get my workout and sauna." Steven's eyes panned around the table. Elizabeth looked like she was ready to pounce on him and tear out his throat. Marjorie's eyes glittered with icy indifference. He kept his gaze moving when he saw Lumina. He knew they would be watching for his reaction.

"I'm Steven Davenport." He extended his hand to Jeremy.

"Jeremy, and this is my son, Cassidy."

Cassidy tipped his chin up at Steven. "Nice to meet you."

"Welcome to our home."

"Lumina, this is my father." Elizabeth didn't look at him.

The girl gave him a warm smile. "Hi."

"Great meeting you. Elizabeth told us all about you."

Lumina blushed four shades of pink and shot Elizabeth a look.

"All good." Steven laughed and walked to the kitchen sink to wash his hands.

She doesn't know, he thought as he turned on the water. He glanced back at Cassidy and his father. Elizabeth never told them.

"I hope you had a nice day." Marjorie's voice was cheery but her eyes maintained their icy gleam.

"Yeah." Elizabeth added her chilly gaze to the assault. "You should have told us you were going out."

"I needed a workout. I've been feeling kinda caged up."

Elizabeth found no humor in his comment. She gritted her teeth and immediately turned away. Steven didn't care. He was having fun.

Seeing Elizabeth's reaction, Marjorie quickly sought to maintain control. "Steven, there's chicken in the oven."

"Thanks, honey."

He finished rinsing his hands in the sink. One scratch, he thought eyeing the edge of the bandage poking out from where he'd pushed up his sleeve. Marcy clawed the top of his right wrist. The girl was a fighter. She didn't stop struggling until he'd pinched her nose shut and cut off her air. After that she was perfectly docile and cooperative. "It's not my first time or anything." He'd heard that same flat, unemotional tone from other girls after they'd stopped fighting. "It doesn't matter. Just be nice. Don't hurt me. I promise I won't tell anyone." When he didn't respond she added, "My name's Marcy. What's yours?" Other girls had done the same thing, asking his name. They wanted to make it feel less impersonal. They wanted to pretend that it was something other than what it was.

"I'm Dan. But you can call me Danny."

"Okay." She immediately seemed more at ease.

Davenport remembered her emotional phone conversation at McDonalds. "You had sex with Scott didn't you?

Marcy looked startled. "What? Did he tell you that?"

Davenport didn't say anything.

"Is that why you're doing this? Cause he told you I let him?"

"He doesn't treat you like he should."

She had dropped her head and started quietly crying. "It was just a couple times. He was telling me all sorts of nice things and —" She paused then let out a sigh. "I can't believe he told you."

Davenport put his mouth next to her ear and slipped into his lover's voice. "Now you can get back at him. I won't tell anyone if you don't." She had given him an anxious, frightened look. But he didn't care anymore. He was done playing games.

Steven grabbed the dish towel and dried his hands. Tomorrow, he thought, I'll go into the back yard and clear some brush. That would be a good excuse for the scratch. He tugged down the cuff of his sleeve and joined the others at the dinner table.

After eating dinner they played charades. It was fun and reminded Steven what his life was like before Elizabeth ran away — all the kid's games, the talking, laughter, and exuberant energy bouncing off the walls.

"*Heaven Can Wait*," Jeremy shouted.

Lumina was stretching her arms over her head and pointing toward the ceiling.

"Before her time," Elizabeth quipped, enjoying Lumina's freedom in front of the group.

"*Angels in the Outfield*?" Cassidy asked tentatively.

Lumina shook her head no, but gestured with her hands that he was on the right track.

Steven caught Elizabeth's eye and gave her a smile. She quickly turned back to Lumina. I'll win her back, Steven thought. It's just going to take some time. But we can all have this again. I can make it happen.

"*City of Angels*," Jeremy called out.

Lumina pumped her fist. "Yes!"

• • • • •

"This is such a cool house," Lumina whispered in the dark. "And your parents seem awesome." In the silence that followed, Elizabeth could hear the question that Lumina wasn't asking — Why did you leave?

On the other side of the bed Lumina squirmed and turned over. A thrasher since she was a little girl, every morning her bed looked like it had been hit by a tornado.

"Am I going to have to get out the restraints?" Elizabeth playfully poked her in the back.

Lumina giggled. "Sorry."

Through the open window came a whoop from the back yard followed by muffled laughter.

"Those two are crazy." Lumina rolled over again. "They're playing their stupid star game."

Jeremy and Cassidy had bedded down in the back yard in their sleeping bags. Marjorie initially bristled at their desire to sleep outside. "I have a perfectly good guest room for you." A look from Elizabeth and she'd quickly relented. She found a plastic drop cloth in the basement to keep them off the damp ground.

"You get one point for shooting stars that you see going left to right," Lumina explained, "and two points for ones going right to left."

Another muffled cry went up from the yard.

"Dorks." Lumina laughed again. "They're never going to want to get up in the morning."

"Why do you get more points for the stars going right to left?"

"Because it's easier to spot the ones going left to right because that's the way we're trained to read."

"Huh?"

"Yeah, I think it's dumb too."

They listened to the murmur of the star game. After a few minutes Lumina said, "Do you think you'll come back and teach?"

"I'm not sure yet."

"Don't let us keep you from doing what you need to do. All of us, we'll be fine."

"I know. But I'll miss you."

There was a long silence. Elizabeth could feel Lumina's eyes on her.

"Life doesn't always wait until you're ready." Lumina gently poked her in the side. "You know."

Elizabeth couldn't help but smile. "You get two points for that one. That was definitely a right to left shooting star."

"Love you." Lumina snuggled into her pillow. "I'll try not to kick you."

"Promises, promises."

• • • • •

Gil lay in bed unable to sleep. Thinking that a cup of chamomile tea might help, he threw off the covers and headed downstairs to the kitchen.

As he stood at the sink running water into the kettle, he thought of Bonnie. "Just put it in the microwave," she used to tell him, "It's faster." But he liked it the old fashioned way. The sound of the kettle rumbling and the whistle going off was as much a part of enjoying a cup of tea as drinking it. He put the kettle on the stove and turned on the gas burner.

How, he wondered, was all of this going to work out? The group had seemed to be making progress and then suddenly Steven went missing and there was panic. It had instantly reminded him of the danger of what they were doing. Was it the right thing? Was he feeling anxious because he knew on some deep level that he was wrong, that he had made a mistake? Or was he simply standing at the edge of that gaping abyss called faith, and the only way to move forward was to have the courage to step out into the void?

Alone in his kitchen, Gil patiently waited for the water to boil.

36

They left the next morning just after eight o'clock. Cassidy had defeated his father fifteen to nine, staying up until two o'clock in the morning playing the star game. They were groggy but with several cups of coffee, some good-natured kidding from Lumina, and half a dozen cinnamon rolls, they'd bundled up their sleeping bags and loaded everything into the Blazer. With handshakes and tearful embraces, everyone had said good luck and goodbye.

Steven could still feel her in his arms. Lumina had turned to say goodbye and suddenly embraced him. He reacted without thinking, happy to wrap his arms around her. Realizing what he had done, he quickly made sure the hug was of appropriate duration. As they separated he was careful not to show any overt reaction. But he had felt it. She was a lovely girl.

At the end of the driveway, Elizabeth was raising her hand and waving one last time. The Blazer rounded the bend and was gone. Elizabeth slowly lowered her arm. She stood there for a moment then walked back toward the house. Marjorie was waiting on the front stoop.

"That was hard," Elizabeth said, "saying goodbye."

"What a delightful girl. You two have a special bond. I can see it."

"I hope she couldn't tell what was going on. Last night… that was awkward."

"I think it was fine."

"Where is he? I want to talk to him about yesterday."

"He said something about clearing brush out back."

"When did he start working in the yard?" Elizabeth followed her mother into the house. "Dominic does all that for you guys."

"That's what I said, but he wants to do it himself."

"He's avoiding talking to us about leaving yesterday."

"You're probably right." Marjorie peered out the window. "I want to make sure he's out there." She caught a glimpse of movement through the trees. "Okay." She turned back to Elizabeth. "I don't know what Gil is planning, but Steven belongs in prison. There's no question in my mind. I don't like the price we'll all have to pay in order to make that happen, but I don't see any other way. I was sick yesterday agonizing over where he had gone and what he might have done. This counseling we're doing – it's not going to fix him. It can't."

"I don't want Darla to get in trouble. But I agree."

"And sweetie," Marjorie came around the counter to her. "What I'm most afraid of is what you'll face. It's awful what the media —"

"I haven't wanted to think about that." Elizabeth leaned into her mother.

"I'm sure there are ways to try and keep your identity a secret."

"But does that ever really work?"

Marjorie held her in her arms. "I'll talk to a lawyer and see what I can find out. Okay?"

Elizabeth nodded.

Outside on the patio they heard footsteps. They turned toward the French doors as Steven walked in.

"I'm done with that mess." He plucked a leaf off the front of his work shirt.

Elizabeth crossed her arms. "What did you do yesterday?"

"Went to the gym." Steven headed for the stairs. "I'm gonna' jump in the shower."

"Get back here!"

"I will speak to you after I shower." Steven had his authoritative tone back in his voice.

When he came down twenty minutes later Marjorie and Elizabeth were sitting at the table finishing their coffee.

"My faithful watch dogs." Steven went to the counter and poured a cup for himself.

Marjorie bristled. "Maybe you should stop being a smart-ass and be grateful that we haven't thrown you in jail."

"Yes, I am grateful. I'm no longer your bitch, but I'm grateful." He casually took a sip of coffee enjoying his new attitude. "There'll be no more locking me up in my own house. No more limitations on what I can do."

Elizabeth stood up. "You're a sick man. We can't pretend that we don't know that."

Steven lowered his cup to the kitchen counter. "I'm busting my ass to help you, okay. I'm doing everything you ask of me. I've told you things I haven't talked about with anyone – ever! What do you think I'm going to do? I don't want to go to prison."

"Mom." Elizabeth's voice was sharpened to a cutting edge. "It's gonna be great when you're finally divorced from this psycho."

"Elizabeth." Steven's voice was eerily calm. "I'm happy that you've come back to us. You've been exceptionally kind to me in light of what happened. I'm grateful for that. But by no means assume that you have control over what your mother and I do about our marriage. It's between us." He paused, letting his words sink in. "Is that clear?"

"What happened to your wrist?" Elizabeth was staring at the fresh bandage poking out below the cuff of his shirt.

Steven gave it a casual glance. "I just did it out in the yard. It's nothing." He picked up his cup of coffee and started out of the room. "I'll be in my office reading the paper and harming no one."

Elizabeth watched him walk away but her mind was ticking back – something…? Wrong, something was wrong. What was it? What? A low-grade nausea began swirling in her belly. She gritted her teeth so that she could focus and try and remember. What happened? What did — all at once it was there. In her mind she saw Steven saying goodbye to Lumina, Lumina surprising him with a hug, Steven happily embracing her, the sleeve of his shirt sliding up, and the bandage on his wrist poking out below the cuff of his shirt.

· · · · ·

His breathing was ragged and desperate. He tried to relax and let his body go but all he felt was an over-whelming desire to stop. Christ, Gil thought, this used to be so effortless. The trail curved ahead of him. He let out his stride hoping that more speed might push him past the pain. His arms pumped at his sides. Sweat flowed down his back. Above him sunlight flashed through the trees. I can do this, Gil thought, cheering himself on, overweight or not I can still run. The rhythmic patter of his feet on the trail was familiar and comforting. The burning in his lungs was not. He eased back as he started down the hill toward Jones Creek.

Elizabeth had been encouraging him to get back into running. She told him it would help him deal with his stress. As he reached the bottom of the hill and pounded over the wooden bridge, Gil wondered what she would think of his running now — probably laugh.

Over his shoulder he heard footsteps.

"On your left."

In a blur of motion a teenage boy ran past. Gil watched the kid cruise effortlessly up the hill. Damn, he thought. I used to be able to do that.

Thirty minutes later he was back at his car chugging from a bottle of water and trying to stretch his rubbery legs. When he checked his cell phone there was a message from Elizabeth. Her voice was tense. He called her immediately. She picked up on the first ring.

"He did something, I know it. Gil there's was no reason for him to lie."

"What are you talking about?"

She quickly told him about Davenport's explanation for his injured wrist. "But if he did it out in the yard, why was the bandage already on his wrist when he hugged Lumina?"

"I—I don't know."

"There's only one reason he'd lie about it."

"But — he seems like he's really, you know, into what we're doing."

"He's fooled a lot of people for a long time."

"Did you tell your mother?"

"No. I didn't want to freak her out."

Across the baseball field, Gil saw the teenager who passed him on the trail. Watching the runner's smooth stride, Gil fought a sinking feeling.

Elizabeth groaned. "If he hurt another girl I don't know how I'll live with myself."

"I made the decision not to turn him in. It wasn't you." Gil got into his car.

"But I went along with it."

"It's been good for us. Darla too."

"I know but – if he did it again…"

"It might be nothing."

"I went online and checked the papers for any recent reports of rapes. I even called three hospitals to see if any girls had been brought in. I didn't find anything."

"Well — that's good."

"But why would he lie?"

"I don't know. We'll ask him tonight. The meeting's at seven, right?"

37

Micaela had just stolen into camp and announced that Don Jose's mother was dying. Steven listened spellbound as the girl called out to God to protect her. The music softened, reflecting her devotion to Don Jose. The solo, touching in its tenderness, had made *Carmen* one of his mother's favorite operas.

Steven leaned his head back on his desk chair and thought over the day's events. Lumina was a sweet girl. He could see why Elizabeth was so fond of her. It had been fun having young people in the house again. In time, he thought, maybe there would be grandchildren to visit. Yes, he thought, that would be nice.

Steven's thoughts were swept back into the music. The Toreador chorus had just returned. Beautiful, Steven thought, just extraordinary. A moment later the lush chorus died in a wash of distorted echoes.

• • • • •

Darla was the first to arrive that night for their meeting. Bubbling over with news about Chad, she immediately pulled Elizabeth aside.

"The sweetest guy! We went to the quarry and I kissed him. I told him I was going to do it and then I did." She grabbed Elizabeth's arm and fake swooned. "He's a great kisser!"

Elizabeth, trying to hide her distraction about her father, gave Darla a hug. "I'm so happy for you." She held Darla out at arm's length and looked her in the eyes. "Nothing else happened, right?"

"Shut up! No! Just some really fine kissing." She puckered her lips.

Elizabeth smiled. To see Darla this happy meant the world to her. "Good for you," she said. "I want to meet him. Chad, the master smoocher."

"Hi, Darla," Marjorie said coming down the stairs.

"Hey, Mrs. Davenport. Something smells good."

"Vegetarian lasagna. How have you been?"

"Good."

"Very good." Elizabeth gave her a pinch on the side.

Darla immediately shot Elizabeth a wide-eyed little sister to big sister look that said, *don't you dare tell her*.

Elizabeth laughed, pulled Darla into a hug, and whispered, "Don't freak out tonight. Promise me you'll keep it together."

"What? What's going on?"

The doorbell chimed.

"I'll get it." Elizabeth looked at Darla, waiting for a response. Darla, suddenly feeling far less happy than when she'd arrived, reluctantly nodded.

Elizabeth walked to the door and opened it. It was Gil. She stepped forward and without saying a word embraced him. "I'm scared."

Gil hugged her. "It's going to be okay, no matter what happens."

Ten minutes later, with a huge pan of lasagna and a brimming bowl of Caesar salad on the table, they sat down to eat.

"I would like to say a prayer." The downward plunge of forks immediately halted. Gil looked around the table. "If nobody minds?"

Marjorie glanced at him, uncertain what he was up to.

Steven clasped his hands together. "Please, go ahead."

Everyone bowed their heads.

"Dear God." Gil concentrated on keeping his voice steady. "If we have failed you, please forgive us. Our intention in these gatherings was to prevent anyone else from getting hurt. If we mistakenly allowed that to happen, please help us to make amends. Give us the strength and clarity to do what must be done." He paused hoping to feel a level of certainty or guidance, some indication that he was doing the right thing. He felt nothing. There was only the beckoning abyss that he had felt before. Step forward it seemed to call to him. You will not plunge into nothingness. Trust and you will find your way to the other side. Unsure of what else to say, Gil simply added, "And thank you for this delicious meal, amen."

Gil raised his head. Across the table Marjorie was giving him a questioning look.

"What was that about?" She looked from Gil to Elizabeth. She could see that something was on their minds. "What's going on?" She turned to Steven.

"I was wondering the same thing. Is everything all right, Gil?"

Elizabeth leaned forward in her seat. "Mother, where did he tell us he hurt his wrist?"

Marjorie hesitated, unsure of what was going on. "This morning clearing brush in the back yard."

"Whose wrist?" Darla was trying to figure out what was happening.

Elizabeth nodded. "And that was after Lumina and those guys drove away, right?"

"Yes."

Elizabeth turned to her father. "I saw you say goodbye to Lumina."

Steven raised his hands defensively. "I didn't do anything wrong?"

"No you didn't. But your sleeve pulled up when you hugged her. The bandage was already there — before you went in the back yard."

Steven stared at her for a second, and then he began to laugh. He hit the table with the palm of his hand, his laughter loud and obnoxious. "Wow! You're really suspicious. The mystery bandage!" He laughed again.

It took all of Elizabeth's restraint to keep from hurling her plate in his face.

Steven leaned back in his chair, his smile radiating confidence and power. "I was working in the yard before you got up. Cassidy and his father were still snoozing in their sleeping bags." Steven casually lifted a forkful of lasagna then paused. "After they left, I went back out to finish what I'd started."

Elizabeth, remembering that her father was already in the kitchen when she came downstairs that morning, flushed with embarrassment. In that moment of vulnerability she realized that in the back of her mind she had been holding back. Since the day they began their meetings, she hadn't truly wanted her father to change. She needed him to remain a monster. What he had done to her would somehow become less horrible if he was rehabilitated.

Marjorie lips were slightly parted and her face was still as a mask as she looked at her husband. In her mind, she watched herself move through the house that morning. Having not slept well because of her concerns for Lumina, she was already up for an hour before Steven came down the stairs. He had smiled to her, poured himself a cup of coffee, and sat down at the kitchen table where she was reading the news on her iPad.

He's lying again. She watched him take another bit of lasagna. I unlocked his door and later, when he came downstairs, he sat with me at the kitchen table until Cassidy and Jeremy came in from the back yard. He never left my sight. And he never went out into the yard. She watched Steven calmly spread a thick layer of butter on a piece of baguette. He believes that I won't say anything – again. He believes I'm a woman who will protect a man who rapes girls.

"Did he do something?" Anxiety had stretched Darla's voice thin.

Marjorie, without saying a word, suddenly shot out her hand and pinned Steven's arm to the table. With her other hand she ripped the bandage off his wrist.

Steven yelped and pulled his arm away.

"Let me see it!" Marjorie tried to grab his arm. Steven held it away from her. Marjorie jumped out of her seat and smacked him hard in the face. Steven rocked back in his chair. Like a wild animal going in for the kill, Marjorie launched herself at him. Both of them crashed over onto the floor.

"Get off of me!" Steven shoved her away.

"What did you do? I sat at the kitchen table with him all morning. He never went out in the yard."

The look in Steven's eyes told Marjorie that he never expected her to out him. Then he blinked and the vulnerability was gone.

"You went upstairs for a while honey," Steven said getting to his feet. "Don't you remember? That's when I went out back." He turned to Gil. "She's getting forgetful."

Marjorie took Gil's hand and stood up. "I never went upstairs. Let me see your wrist."

"I got a scratch on my arm in the back yard. That's it, end of story."

"Call the police." Darla was hanging on to her chair as if it was a life raft. "I don't care anymore what happens."

Elizabeth grabbed the telephone.

Steven let out a snort of laughter. "Please, this is ridiculous. Come on, come on, let's sit down and finish this lovely meal." He moved toward the table.

"Did you molest another girl?" Elizabeth held up the phone as a threat. "Is that where the scratch came from?"

"No. Of course not." Steven sat down at the table. "I did it in the yard. Whether your mother wants to remember it or not, that's how it happened."

He ate a bite of lasagna. "Honey, this is great."

Gil struggled to maintain his calm. "We want to know the truth."

"I just told you."

"Screw it," Darla said, "just call the police."

Steven's expression darkened. "If you call the police and tell them I raped some girl or that I raped you or Darla, I'll deny it." His eyes swept over the three of them calculating the impact of his words. This was a negotiation he couldn't afford to lose. "During the trial, all of your personal lives will be exposed to public scrutiny. Darla, do you want some defense attorney asking if you enjoyed kissing me? We both know that you did, but do you really want that revealed in front of your parents and everyone watching Court TV? Or how you were the one who pushed to meet me in person: 'Lets have dinner. Please meet me for dinner.' I have the emails. And did you ever tell me how old you were? Did you? No. You wanted to be a grown up. You didn't want me to know you were underage. My attorney will make it obvious to the jury that you were young, obsessed and when you didn't get what you wanted, you cried rape." He swung his gaze over to his wife. "And Marjorie, how will you feel when it comes out that you condoned what happened between Elizabeth and me?"

"I never —" Marjorie started to say, but Steven kept talking.

"For fifteen years you knew and did nothing about it," he said. "You didn't go to the police. You stayed with me and we lived our lives happily ever after. What jury would believe that a mother could do that? And if they do buy it for some ridiculous reason, what will that do for your fine blue blood family reputation? Forget about your society crowd. They'll shun you faster than you can say cotillion."

"That's enough." Gil stepped toward him.

"And you, Gil." Steven got a vicious gleam in his eye. "Playing God. You could have handed me over to the police. I caused the death of your family. You suspected me of raping two young girls. And instead of doing something about it you chose to bring us together and *talk* about it." Steven shook his head. "Boy, oh boy, who's going to think *that* was a good idea?"

"I did it to help everyone!"

"No. You needed to do something that would validate the loss of your family." Steven changed his voice in an impersonation of Gil. "If I can just heal them — if I can turn Steven Davenport into a productive member of society then the horrible death of my family will have meaning." Switching back to his normal voice he said, "But instead, while you people were trying to redeem yourselves, another innocent girl got raped, so you say. Well, shame on you. I'm guessing the public isn't going to like you very much. The media's poster boy for grief and loss will suddenly be thought of as a self-serving, deluded accomplice to rape."

"We did it to protect Darla." Elizabeth was coming to Gil's defense.

"You did it out of guilt. You didn't have the guts to stop me years ago and now you have to live with yourselves knowing that others have suffered so you could be safe." He could see by their stunned expressions that he had them back on their heels. And now the clincher — "With the team of lawyers I can afford, they might even convince the jury that you three had a predilection for the criminal mind and chose to hang out with me so that you could have the thrill of experiencing my depraved secret life. Maybe you encouraged me to do the last rape. Maybe you even helped me pick her out."

Elizabeth put down the telephone.

38

For a moment Gil couldn't respond. A black rage was trumpeting him to violence. He took a breath. "You act like an animal. God will treat you like an animal."

Steven gave a bitter laugh. "*He* turned me into an animal. How else do you want me to behave?"

"You did this yourself," Elizabeth said. "Don't blame anyone else."

"Ah, my loving daughter."

Her hands clenched into fists, Elizabeth glared defiantly at him. "You know what? I'm not afraid to take responsibility for what I've done. So you go ahead and lie in court, we'll see who wins." She picked up the telephone.

Steven's mind quickly snapped through the options left to him. If he was going to stop her, he had to make a bold move.

"If you call the police, you'll never find the girl."

The room instantly went still.

"Another victim will needlessly suffer in silence." He looked at each of their startled faces. "I think you guys are already carrying enough guilt. You don't want that too, do you?"

Marjorie moaned. "You did it? You attacked another girl?"

"You call the police you'll never find out."

"No, No!" Darla put her head down on her arms.

"Guess what?" Defiance radiated bright and hot from Elizabeth. "She'll come forward when she sees your face plastered all over the newspapers. We won't have any problem finding her." She raised the phone to dial 911.

Steven launched himself out of his chair. Elizabeth jerked back in surprise but not quick enough. He smacked the phone from her hand

and with his arm clamped around her waist pressed the tines of his fork against her carotid artery.

"Everyone, stop talking – don't move – I'll end this right now if you don't do as I say."

Stunned by his sudden move, they stared blankly back at him.

"Put your cell phones on the table. Now!"

Gil tried to keep his voice calm. "This isn't going to do —"

"Let her go," Marjorie pleaded.

"I better see cells phones."

"Mine is in my purse upstairs," Marjorie said.

Through clenched teeth Elizabeth said, "I wish Darla had shot you when she had the chance."

Steven pulled her back tightly against him. "Gil, where's your phone?"

Gil dug it out of his pocket and put it on the table. Darla did the same.

With Elizabeth shuffling in front of him, Steven walked to the base unit of the portable phone in the kitchen and yanked it from the wall. It clattered to the floor.

"Okay," he said. "Go over and sit down, all three of you, on the couch."

With a quick forceful motion Elizabeth drove her elbow back into Steven's midsection. He gasped and dropped the fork. Fighting to hold on to her, he saw Gil coming across the room. Steven clamped his arm around Elizabeth's throat.

"Stay back!" he shouted at Gil. Elizabeth, unable to breath, stopped struggling. Steven yanked open a drawer and pulled out a six inch knife. He put it to Elizabeth's throat.

"Sit down!" He dragged Elizabeth across the kitchen. He opened a drawer under the microwave. "This is not what I wanted to happen, people!" He tossed a roll of shipping tape to Gil.

"Tape their hands behind their backs — ankles together too. No fuckin' around."

Marjorie stared at the blade pressed to Elizabeth's neck. The size of a steak knife but with a thicker blade, she used it to cut up vegetables for stir fry and fruit for smoothies. She once nicked her finger with it prying apart frozen hamburger patties. It was a good knife, and it was very sharp. Now it was at her daughter's throat.

"Let Elizabeth go." Marjorie was pleading from the couch. "Steven don't hurt her."

"And tape their mouths shut. Need a little quiet around here."

Elizabeth weakly lifted her head. She saw Gil move toward her mother. Curled on the couch, Darla looked like a feral animal ready to strike.

"Sit down." Davenport moved Elizabeth to the table. She sat down facing the others with Steven behind her holding the knife to her throat.

"Would you really kill me?"

"I'm not going to prison."

Gil hesitated before taping Marjorie's ankles together. Once everyone is tied up, he thought, Davenport can do anything he wants. He can kill all of us.

"Steve. I'm not going to tie them up."

"Yes, you are."

"No. I'm not going make it easy for you to kill us."

"I have no desire to kill anyone."

"I can't trust you."

"I don't care."

"It's better for one person to get hurt than for all three of us to be killed."

"How sweet. He's willing to sacrifice you, Elizabeth. And I thought you two had a thing going."

Gil felt his face get warm. Without taking his eyes off Steven, he took two quick steps back to the fireplace and picked up the steel poker.

"No one is going to get sacrificed."

Steven slowly shook his head. "Is this really what Bonnie and the kids would want?" He grabbed Elizabeth by the hair. She grimaced but didn't cry out. He pressed the blade to her throat. "I can't believe little Lindsey would want you to be responsible for Elizabeth getting her throat cut."

"No!" Marjorie cried.

Manipulating him by using his family tragedy no longer worked. Invoking Lindsey's name only fueled Gil's sense of purpose. "Darla," he said. "Go to the French doors."

Darla slowly stood up.

Davenport pressed the blade to Elizabeth's throat. She gasped as a trickle of blood ran down her neck.

Gil held up his hands to Davenport. "If Darla runs out and goes to the neighbor's house, this is over. So if you draw one more drop of blood, Darla will run and I will break every bone in your body."

Davenport saw in Gil's eyes something he'd never seen before. Gone was the sadness and confusion of his days at the campsite. Also absent was the sympathy and compassion seen during their healing talks. What he saw now was darker and far more dangerous.

"Ah ha! The beast awakens."

Gil raised the poker and took a step forward. Davenport shook his head.

"Darla if you don't sit down, when I leave, and I will get out of here, I'm going stop and have a visit with that baby sister of yours."

"You sick fuck!" Elizabeth struggled against him.

Steven tightened his grip on her. "So what's it gonna be Darla? Time to be all grown up."

Gil looked at her. "I will not let him leave the house. I promise."

Darla was ashen. "He knows where I live."

Steven shook his head. "Asking a sixteen year old girl to put her family's safety on the line? That's not very nice, Gil. Would God like that?"

"Don't worry about me," Elizabeth said. "Do what Gil says."

Darla closed her eyes, took a breath, and then opened them. She looked at Elizabeth then turned to Gil. Slowly she walked to the French doors. Her fingers lightly touched the handle. She turned and looked back at Gil.

Steven's precarious hold on the situation was slipping away. His mind raced for a solution to get back in control. He needed time. He had to formulate a plan. He pulled the blade an inch away from Elizabeth's neck.

"Darla, don't. I just want time. That's all. I need to look at my options. But if you don't do as I'm asking, some of you will get hurt."

Darla glanced at Gil, her eyes pleading for him to tell her what to do.

"Ask her to sit down." Steven was looking at Gil. "You keep the poker, and I'll have Elizabeth over here, that way we're even. But please, nobody run or do anything stupid, okay?"

For a brief, tense moment Gil considered Steven's words. Then he shifted his eyes to Darla.

39

Gil turned away from where Darla and Marjorie were dozing on the couch. At the table next to Davenport, Elizabeth slouched in a chair with her hands and feet taped. Gil watched Steven at work on his laptop. For most of the night, Steven had been busy searching the internet and occasionally jotting things in a spiral notebook. The non-stop opera playing on the stereo, pleasantly distracting at the beginning of the night had become annoying. With plenty of tension and drama already in the room, Gil didn't need to hear more of it played out in Italian and German.

Gil eyed the knife inches from Davenport's right hand. Several times throughout the night he thought about jumping him, but even with Steven distracted by the computer it would only take a second for him to get his hand on the knife. Elizabeth was too close to risk it.

"Okay," Steven said cheerfully to the computer screen. He quickly typed something then stopped. "That'll work." With a satisfied expression on his face he leaned back in the chair. "I think I've got it figured out." He stood up, stretching his arms over his head. Gil eased forward in the chair, contemplating a quick move while Steven's hands were away from the knife. As if reading his mind, Steven lowered his arms.

"A couple more hours." Davenport picked up the knife. "After the banks open."

"So you're going on the run?"

Steven sat back down at the table. "No. I'm relocating." He glanced at the notebook next to his laptop. He had discovered that although the United States has an extradition treaty with Cuba from the 1920s, it was not honored. Cuba rarely turned over any U.S. fugitives. He could fly to Mexico City and get a direct flight to Havana. Liquidating his accounts would provide him with enough money for cash incentives to officials and enable him to live simply but comfortably for the rest of his life. It wasn't what he wanted to do, but his options had run out. He put the knife down and began double-checking the account numbers to ensure that the transfer would go through without delay.

Elizabeth caught Gil's eye. She quickly glanced over at the knife then back at Gil. She did it again, then slowly nodded her head. Any trace of mercy generated for her father during their healing sessions had been transformed into ruthless determination by the knife he'd held to her throat. She wasn't going to let him get away. She pressed her feet to the floor and shifted in her seat.

"Sit still." Davenport glanced over at Gil and the others then went back to his accounts.

Gil could see that Elizabeth had repositioned herself to the side of the chair closest to Davenport. She had also moved her feet to a different angle. He didn't know what she was going to do, but he intended to protect her any way he could. Gil got his feet set and tightened his grip on the poker.

"Huh." Davenport leaned back with his hands clasped behind his head. "I think it's going to —"

Elizabeth lunged forward, throwing herself onto the table and covering the knife with her body. Gil charged across the room. Davenport frantically groped for the knife underneath Elizabeth. Unable to get his hand on it, he grabbed her by the hair and reached for her throat. Gil swung the poker hitting him just above the elbow. The blow drove Davenport backwards against the kitchen counter. Gil came around the table after him and Davenport bolted for the French doors. Gil chased him, swinging the poker head high.

• • • • •

Dominic balled up the Juicy Fruit wrapper and dropped it in the ashtray. The morning talk jock on the radio was gabbing about the president's plan to save social security. "Call in and give me your thoughts," the jock said.

"No thanks." Dominic pushed a dusty cassette tape into the player. Jerry Jeff Walker's voice filled the cab.

Dominic parked in front of the Davenport's house behind the Land Rover and Ford Escort. After several frustrating minutes staring into the bed of the pickup trying to remember what he was supposed to do, it finally came to him — cut the grass and trim the side hedge. Irritated, he yanked the tailgate open.

Lately, everything seemed to be getting heavier. His tools felt like they had been filled with lead. As he approached the Davenport's back patio, he shifted the hedge trimmer to his left hand, instantly feeling relief in his right shoulder. He abruptly stopped walking. It wasn't the weight of the hedge trimmer that made him stop, he'd heard something. Turning toward the house, he heard it again. It sounded like someone crying. Remembering what happened before when he'd gotten confused about hearing the young girl crying in the back yard, Dominic waited. Then he heard it again. He hesitantly walked over to the patio stairs.

Through the French doors he saw Elizabeth on her knees. She was next to someone lying on the floor. Suddenly she reared back and slammed her fist into the person's chest. "Tell me!" Both of her hands were red. It looked like blood.

The leaden feeling in Dominic's arms suddenly intensified. He bent down easing his tools to the ground. Dread, like a suffocating layer of sticky molasses, spread over him. He moved up the stairs to the patio before it could render him immobile. Elizabeth raised her head. There was blood crusted on her shoulder from a cut on her neck. She raised her bloody hands in front of her face and slumped away from the body on the floor. Dominic stepped closer.

It was Steven Davenport. At least that's who Dominic thought it was. The man's face was a bloody mash. One of his arms jutted out at an unnatural angle.

Dominic's legs sagged. He reached for the doorframe. Thoughts of Michael's gory death flew through his mind. For a moment he was dazed and uncertain what to do. Then, seeing Elizabeth's anguished expression, he forced himself to walk into the house.

Marjorie looked up from where she was sitting on the couch. A smear of blood ran down her cheek and across the front of her shirt. Eyes dazed and unfocused, she seemed to look right through him. Darla, sitting cross-legged on the floor in front of the couch, didn't have any blood on her hands but her legs and feet were splattered with it. She was holding a fireplace poker that looked to be matted with hair and blood. In the armchair across the room, Gil lifted his head from his bloody hands. The torment in his eyes made Dominic turn away. Hearing wheezing breaths coming from Davenport, Dominic squatted down next to Elizabeth.

"He's not dead."

Steven's eyes flickered open. "Help me," he sputtered through bloody, smashed lips.

Elizabeth came forward on her knees. "Tell me!" When Davenport didn't respond, she reared back to hit him again. Dominic grabbed her arm. She looked surprised that he stopped her. "He raped another girl," she explained. "He needs to tell me her name. We have to help her."

Dominic gently lowered her arm. "What happened?"

Elizabeth gazed blankly at him as images of Gil rushing after her father shuttered through her mind — *Aïda* playing on the stereo, the poker flashing through the air, Steven fighting back, the frightening look on Gil's face as he savagely punched Steven over and over again, and the frenzy of all of them kicking and stomping Steven to a bloody mess.

"He raped me and Darla and then we all tried to talk – so we could —" Elizabeth's voice broke and she let out a sob. "But then he raped another girl. It had to stop."

Dominic shot a glance at Darla and then down at Steven's battered face. The coffee and donuts in Dominic's stomach churned.

"He can't stay here. He needs to go to the hospital."

"Let him die." It was Marjorie from up on the couch.

"Not until he tells us her name or where she lives." Elizabeth leaned over, inches from her father's shattered face. "Tell me and you can live."

Dominic grabbed her by the shoulders. "Elizabeth. I understand what happened but the police might not." He struggled to his feet, a plan formulating in his mind.

"Mrs. Davenport — I'm going to take him to the hospital and you three are going to clean up the house. I mean really clean it. Get rid of all the blood. Make sure everything looks normal. Throw all your bloody clothes away. Get them out of the house."

Gil leaned forward in the chair. "It's my fault. I couldn't stop."

"Doesn't matter." Dominic hitched up his sagging trousers. "I'm going to take care of it." He looked around the room, his mind still struggling to make sense of what he was going to do. "I'll make up a story. I'm an old man, they'll believe me. We were in the woods — looking for rocks for the garden. He took a fall." He looked to see if they were listening. "Come on, come on. Get moving."

Marjorie and Darla stood up. Marjorie went to the kitchen and started gathering cleaning supplies.

Dominic looked over at Gil. "I'm going to pull my truck down the driveway – we'll take him out through the garage."

"Yeah." Gil blinked his eyes as if he had just woken up. "I'll help you."

• • • • •

The wind through the open window of the truck was warm against the side of Dominic's face. He let his hand hang outside bracing against the force of it. It wasn't so hard to imagine, he thought, what it would be like to fly. His hand dipped and climbed, moving with the pressure of the streaming air. Before she died Irene had six weeks of flying dreams. Every morning she'd tell him stories of zooming around in her flannel nightgown.

Dominic looked over at Davenport sitting next to him. His breathing was steady and he seemed comfortable. "How are you doing?"

His smashed lips parted. The jagged stumps of his shattered teeth were pink with blood.

Davenport muttered, "We almost to the hospital?"

"Yeah."

"Thanks."

Dominic checked his rear view mirror. Traffic was light. There were a couple cars but they were a good distance behind him. He looked back at Davenport and saw that he was trying to wipe his mouth with the sleeve of his shirt. It was such a feeble gesture that Dominic almost felt sorry for him. Dominic shifted his gaze to the left and down the steep drop off to the Ohio River.

Before Michael was born he and Irene had traveled with Mitch and Gayle Herman down the river to Cincinnati on an old sternwheeler. Oh, that was fine adventure, Dominic remembered: the four of them on the top deck passing Mitch's silver flask of brandy, the sky full of stars, the wide Ohio sliding them along. Irene, his bride for only a year, had loved the fall colors dappling the hills.

Dominic reached into the glove compartment and dug out a cassette tape. Patsy Cline, she was Irene's favorite. He slid it into the player and turned up the volume. He glanced over at Davenport.

"I've always liked country music. How about you?"

"Not so much."

Davenport tried to breathe more deeply but he couldn't. Something was preventing him from expanding his chest. Ribs, he thought. They busted my ribs. I'm okay, he assured himself. I've taken beatings before. I'll get through this.

"Hey," Dominic said, "do you remember Reggie?"

"Who?"

"The big Doberman who used to be in your neighborhood. Got loose all the time, scared the kids."

Steven thought for a moment not saying anything.

"This was a long time ago. When Elizabeth was little."

Steven finally nodded. "Bit the mailman."

"Bit a lot of people. Well, Reggie disappeared one day and never came home. People thought he got stolen or hit by a car and went off to die. But I know what happened to him."

Steven looked at Dominic, curious about the story.

"He was buried in the Harrington's flowerbed." Dominic chewed his lower lip. "I never told anyone that before."

"In a flowerbed?" A bubble of blood had formed in the corner of Davenport's mouth.

"Yep, that nice quiet couple with the chubby blond daughter, they killed Reggie and buried him in their back yard. Isn't that something?"

"The Harringtons killed that dog?"

Dominic nodded, his eyes focused on the road ahead. "Reggie was bad. He'd been causing trouble for a long time."

Steven's eyes registered surprise as if seeing something for the first time. "Hey. This isn't the way to the hospital."

Dominic jerked the steering wheel to the right. Tires screeched as the pickup careened into the other lane. Turning back hard to the left, he stomped the gas pedal to the floor.

40

Elizabeth tightened her grip on the living room chair and slowly raised her eyes to Officer Mills.

"Going 65 or 70 miles an hour," Mills said, "with no guardrail along that section of highway, there wasn't anything to stop them. Launched off that bluff and… I'm very sorry for your loss."

A tall, barrel-chested man with a kind, compassionate air, Elizabeth wondered if he was frequently assigned to break the news to the families of victims. Ninety feet, he had said. The truck fell ninety feet and crashed and burned on the deserted site of an old J & L steel mill. Helped along by cans of oil and gas in the bed of the truck, both bodies were badly burned.

Mills slid the police report back into a manila folder. "Had Mr. Davenport ever gone with Mr. Angelo before?"

"Occasionally," Marjorie said, reaching over and holding Elizabeth's hand.

"They talked about getting some bigger rocks for the garden," Elizabeth said. "Maybe Dad wanted to help him pick them out."

Mills eyes shifted off Elizabeth to the pen in his hand. He clicked it once and slipped it into his shirt pocket.

"A motorist traveling behind the pickup said that everything was normal until the driver lost control and swerved off the road."

"Oh, God." Marjorie held her face in her hand.

Elizabeth bowed her head.

Mills pursed his lips and nodded. "Probably a heart attack."

· · · · ·

Through the French doors Elizabeth watched thirty of her father's friends and clients drinking, smoking cigars, and reminiscing about deals he'd negotiated and profits he'd earned for them. She turned away from the patio and looked toward the kitchen. With Esther Braverman hovering at her side, Marjorie was pulling plastic wrap off a fruit platter.

"He was such a dear." Esther gave a slight tug to the back of her new wig. "Such a sweet man."

She's holding up well, Elizabeth thought, watching her mother pull a fork out of the drawer. The memorial service at Simon's funeral home had been mercifully short. Uncle Pete gave a brief eulogy. Her cousin Tim read a Wendell Berry poem, and her aunt Ellen told the story of when she first met Steven. "He called me Helen the entire night," she had said with a tearful smile, "until the end of the evening when he realized his mistake. He apologized and, in that charming way of his, explained that my beauty reminded him of Helen of Troy." She laughed, dabbing a crumpled blue tissue to the corner of her eye. "That was Steven."

Elizabeth took a sip of Pinot Noir. Please let this day end, she thought.

"To a happier future," Linda McKelvey whispered as she wrapped Elizabeth in a hug from behind. Elizabeth turned and embraced both Linda and Tom.

"Thanks for everything."

"Let us know what we can do for you." Linda gave her another squeeze.

You can get me out of here, Elizabeth thought, as she watched them walk toward the front door.

"He was like a brother to me." It was Marty Braverman. Elizabeth turned to him.

"He felt the same about you, Uncle Marty."

"You come home after all these years and then this happens. It stinks."

"We had some time at least. I'm glad I came back when I did."

"A real standup guy." Marty struggled against his emotions. "What a waste." He shook his head and walked over to Esther.

Elizabeth turned back to the guests on the patio. What was it like, she wondered, those final moments — the shriek of tires, the heart-stopping second of going airborne, the murky waters of the Ohio River stretching before him, and then the long drop? What had gone through his mind in those final awful seconds of free fall? Had he begged for forgiveness? Had he called out the name of the last girl, the one he'd refused to give up? Or was he defiant and damning them all until the end?

It doesn't matter, she thought. He's gone and I'm grateful he won't hurt anyone else.

• • • • •

"That was soooo fun!" Darla said, stepping out of the elevator. "It's the fastest thing I've ever been on. Oh my God, look!" She ran across the 86th floor observation deck and took in the view. The setting sun cast New York City in a soft golden light.

The Empire State Building had been Elizabeth's idea. Marjorie gave them the flight and tickets for the Metropolitan Opera but this view was what Elizabeth wanted to show Darla.

"And the World Trade Center was down there." Elizabeth pointed downtown.

"Okay." Darla looked in that direction.

"We'll take a cab tomorrow and see the memorial."

Darla reached over and held Elizabeth's hand. Although it had been Darla's first time on a plane, she had held Elizabeth's hand and succeeded in keeping her calm the entire flight to New York.

"*The Magic Flute* was awesome and all," Darla said, her emotions bubbling up, "it was an amazing production, but that elevator ride and then this," she spread her arms wide trying to encompass the view, "this is the best thing ever!"

They looked out at the city for several minutes without saying anything. Around them visitors laughed and posed for photos from different vantage points. Darla wiped a tear from her face.

"I'll never forget what Dominic did for us."

Elizabeth squeezed her hand. "I know."

• • • • •

Gil slid the paint-soaked roller into a plastic bag. He turned and examined the pastel blue walls of the dining area.

"Looks super." Marjorie wrapped another serving dish in newspaper. "Thanks."

She had been very specific — make sure nothing remains from what happened that night. He meticulously cleaned and painted the walls, and sanded and resealed the hardwood floors. Marjorie would now be able to move into her new condo on Mount Washington knowing that any evidence of the past was truly behind her.

"Mom." Elizabeth was calling her from the living room. "What do you want to do with these old photo albums?"

Marjorie paused. Everything in their life had been a lie. Even her memories were tainted.

"Keep what you want. I'll go through the rest."

"I don't want any pictures of him." Elizabeth walked into the room.

"Then cut him out and let it just be me and you."

"Okay, good."

Marjorie carefully laid the serving dish in a cardboard box. "This one's full. Where's the tape?"

"Right here." Elizabeth tossed Marjorie a roll of packing tape. It bounced on the counter and landed on the floor.

"Nice!"

Elizabeth shot Gil a grin. He had really stepped in and helped them — condo shopping for Marjorie's new place, painting, fixing the floors. Although it still seemed strange to her that they hadn't kissed again, it was probably for the best. Neither one of them was ready. Time would heal, and then who knows?

"Still no word?" Marjorie was looking at Elizabeth.

"Nothing."

"It's a blessing."

"I wanted to find her."

"We all did, but…"

There had been one photograph of Steven that ran in the newspaper after his death. Elizabeth was certain that his other victims would see it and come forward with their stories. It would be difficult, but she wanted to be there for them in any way she could, especially the last girl. But not a single victim had filed a report.

"I understand their reluctance." Marjorie finished taping the box closed. "What would they gain by going public now that he's dead?"

Elizabeth sighed. "Maybe she'll come in to the women's center when you get it going."

"I can't think of a better use of his money than contributing to her healing."

Gil pressed the lid closed on the paint can. "You're doing a great thing for the city."

"I'm doing a great thing for women."

· · · · ·

The afternoon before Elizabeth was to leave for Oregon she invited Gil and Darla over. With Marjorie and a pitcher of iced tea, they gathered together on the back patio.

"I love your new haircut." Marjorie gave Darla a hug. "It's adorable."

"Thanks. I got tired of picking my split ends so I chopped it off. Chad likes it too."

"Chad likes it too," Elizabeth teased.

"Shut up."

Elizabeth draped her arm around Darla's shoulders.

Gil caught Darla's eye. "So, how have you been doing?"

"Okay. Some bad dreams."

Out in the yard a blue jay squawked. Elizabeth pulled her closer.

It's there Gil thought, unspoken but right behind their eyes — they're still struggling to assimilate what we did. It didn't add up in neat rows or columns. It was sideways and cross-angled — a gray multiplicity of shadows one over the other in a puzzling blur.

"I wish we'd found the last girl," Elizabeth said quietly.

Darla nodded.

"Dominic was a brave man." Marjorie sipped her drink.

"To Dominic." Darla raised her glass.

"Yes." Elizabeth lifted her drink. "And to the last girl."

Marjorie joined them. "The last girl."

Gil nodded and they all drank.

Out in the yard, a breeze whispered through the tree tops.

It's not enough, Gil thought. Celebrating Dominic and extending hope to the last girl, it's not enough. What about when Darla stomped on Steven's arm and broke it? Was the ecstatic look on her face normal? And when Marjorie heard Steven's whimpering moans, was the victorious light in her eyes shameful and wrong? Was Elizabeth an evil person for grinning as the sweet metallic scent of her father's blood overpowered her memories of his aftershave? What about the heady sense of redemption he felt while punching Steven's face into a bloody pulp? What about that? What did that make him?

Gil lowered his eyes from the trees and looked at Marjorie, Darla, and Elizabeth. Had he done the right thing? Had he led them in the right direction? Would all of them get through this and be okay? He needed to know. He wanted the comforting embrace of absolute certainty. He wanted to be good. But he didn't feel any of that. It felt like he was falling — somewhere between shadows and light.

ACKNOWLEDGEMENTS

I am grateful to Laurel Derry for her legal expertise, Jan Barber for medical advice, Eric Treibatch for his insights on commercial real estate, Nancy Shanks Mark Fudoli, Betsy Rapoport, Marc Clopton, Bill Dow, Rebecca Shemwell, Beau L'Amour, Lawson Strickland, Andre Dubus III, Claudia Whitman, and Sara Quay for their editorial feedback and enduring support.

ABOUT THE AUTHOR

Charles Van Eman is also the author of the novel, *On The Way To Pomona*. He has worked as an actor, director, screenwriter, teacher, and researcher. He currently lives north of Boston.

Visit his website – charlesvaneman.com

27756251R00170

Made in the USA
Lexington, KY
22 November 2013